HUMAN HUNGER

HUMAN HUNGER

Ondragon Book 1

ANETTE STROHMEYER

Translation from German edited by Sarah Rimmington

Cover design by James Iacobelli

ISBN: 978-1-0394-5663-1

Published in 2024 by Podium Publishing
www.podiumentertainment.com
Podium

HUMAN HUNGER

PROLOGUE

1835, a few miles south of Lake Kabetogama,
"Rough waters," on the border with Canada
under British rule

Alan Parker reined in his horse and signaled to his two companions, Lacroix and Two-Elk. The old trapper listened to the snowy forest. A few paces ahead of him was the clearing where the Walcotts farmed their land. The family's log cabin was exactly halfway between their hunting grounds and the Fort Frances trading post. Each time they passed here, they would stop at the Walcotts' home or spend the night in the barn.

It was already getting dark and the view was clouding over. The log cabin was a squat black block that had seemingly fallen out of nowhere into the snow-covered landscape. Lights flickered invitingly from the windows, smoke was rising from the chimney. Everything looked as it always did.

But something was wrong.

Parker frowned and tried to identify what it was. A crow let out a raucous call in the distance. One of the horses snorted.

And then he had it.

"No dog!" said Two-Elk behind him at the same moment.

Parker nodded and pulled his shotgun from its holster on the saddle. The Walcotts' dog, a crude mix of breeds, usually barked when anyone approached the farm. Today, however, it was eerily quiet.

It could well be the Walcotts no longer have a dog, Parker thought, but he wanted to be sure. He cocked the hammer of his shotgun.

Here in the woods, far from any civilization, you had to be prepared for anything.

He spurred his horse and it entered the clearing at a walk. Still nothing moved. In the house everything continued quiet. Parker's uneasiness grew. He raised the shotgun. Two-Elk and Lacroix left the pack horses with the furs and swung out behind him.

"Walcott?" called Parker.

Two crows flew up from the roof ridge into the lightless sky, but Parker kept his eyes on the locked wooden door.

"John? Eleanor?" he called again.

Still no answer.

The falling night bathed the log cabin and adjacent barn in blue shadows. Parker noticed it was beginning to snow. The flakes floated silently through the glimmer of light outside the windows.

He signaled to Two-Elk and slid out of the saddle. Shotgun at the ready, he approached the door, in front of which a jumble of tracks could be seen. Parker studied them, then leaned against the outside wall of the house. He furrowed his brows. Among the human shoe prints was a trail he couldn't place. As if someone had walked barefoot through the snow.

Someone without toes.

Parker followed the trail with his eyes. It came like a blue ribbon, straight out of the forest. Sweat broke out under his leather clothes and he pushed his hat back onto his neck. He couldn't say why, but the strange trail triggered a dark fear in him. Involuntarily, his fingers clutched tighter around the barrel of the shotgun.

Something had gone to that house.

Something from the woods.

It was probably still inside. In which case it had certainly heard them coming.

Parker felt his companions growing impatient. He nodded to them, took a deep breath, and threw his shoulder against the door. It flew open with a loud bang, hitting the inside wall. Quickly, Parker jumped back into the cover of the outside wall. He saw Two-Elk and Lacroix taking aim at the bright opening from the back of their horses. Light cut through the darkness and illuminated the trampled snow around the doorstep. An acrid, sweet smell filtered out, bringing back terrible memories for Parker. He hardly dared breathe. How often had horrific things happened in remote log cabins?

Now move your skinny ass, old man!

Determinedly, Parker turned into the doorway and peered over the shotgun, aiming into the interior of the log cabin. The picture that met his eyes was worse than anything he had seen before.

Parker swallowed. Then a shot rang out.

CHAPTER 1

2009, northern Minnesota,
St. Louis County, State Forest Road

The engine of the Ford Shelby Mustang gave a rich roar as he pressed down on the gas pedal. Satisfied, Paul Eckbert Ondragon saw a cloud of dust rising from the gravel road behind him. He looked ahead again, expertly dodged a pothole, and steered the car back to the middle of the road that wound through the seemingly endless Minnesota woods. Three-quarters of an hour ago, he had turned off 53 onto the narrow Forest Route, and no one had come his way since. Not even a logging truck. It was pretty remote here, up near the Canadian border. Nothing but forest. Forest and lakes.

Ondragon wondered what kind of people lived in these widely scattered settlements. God-fearing and hard-working American citizens? His lips twisted into a contemptuous grin. More likely hillbillies!

He swerved around another pothole. Hot rubber slid over dark basalt gravel, and the weed-covered shoulder came dangerously close. Ondragon countersteered and got the Mustang's lurching rear end under control again. His cowboy boot remained unflinchingly on the gas pedal. Chewing on his gum, he popped a bubble and turned the music up louder. "Hotel California" by the Eagles. The melody boomed through the open window into the dense forest, echoing back across the valley from the tall conifers.

After a couple of miles, the road made a bend and the shore of a lake came into view. The sunlight refracted off the surface of the water as if it were crumpled aluminum foil.

It must be here somewhere, Ondragon thought, keeping his eyes peeled. The directions were on the passenger seat. Abruptly, his foot switched from the gas to the brake, and the car came to a skidding halt. The Mustang protested with a gush of exhaust fumes that spilled forward.

Popping another gum bubble, Ondragon put the car in reverse. He backed up a hundred yards and stopped in front of a sign.

CEDAR CREEK LODGE, 8 MILES it said in red letters that looked like dried blood. But where was the turnoff? Ondragon glanced in the rearview mirror. Not a soul to be seen. Only the rest of the dust cloud, which was gradually dissipating. He turned off the music and instantly found himself in a completely different world. Birds chirped and insects hummed. Somewhere a brook rippled.

Nothing else.

No car noise, no high-rises, no neon signs, no Starbucks. It was a world as far removed from the universe in which he lived as an alien planet. The only difference was that instead of little green men, this was inhabited by deer and raccoons.

"Almost the same thing," Ondragon said to himself, and hit the gas again. "I'm sure the turnoff will come."

He was right. After three hundred yards, he turned the Mustang into a road that was in even worse condition than the previous one. Ondragon cursed and navigated the dapper classic car—which stood out in this area even more than his dark gray suit—around the potholes. It would be an eternity before he reached the lodge.

"I should have taken the shuttle service after all." He longed for a cold Budweiser, but instead fished a lukewarm bottle of water from the back seat and drank it down in three large gulps.

"No comparison!" he groaned, still thirsty. He was about to throw the bottle out the window, but stopped mid-motion. This bottle came from another world. It was a UFO. It had no place here.

Suddenly, something crossed the path—something big, gray. Startled, Ondragon slammed on the brakes, making himself swallow his gum. When the Mustang finally came to a standstill, Ondragon turned and looked back at the road.

There was nothing, only swirling dust. Frowning, he looked

ahead. He had definitely seen something. And it had been much too big to simply disappear. Where had it gone?

A crackling sound reached his ears, and Ondragon turned his head, carefully scanning the undergrowth to his left. Over there, among the shrubs and the silvery trunks of the aspens, something was moving. Or was it just the wind brushing through the branches and making the shadows dance? Ondragon clicked his tongue. In any case, it was gone now.

"Fucking forest!"

He stepped on the gas pedal. It was probably just a stupid moose; there were hundreds of them running around here. Man, this was going to be fun! He let out a loud sigh. He hoped he would soon reach his destination, otherwise he would change his mind.

Half an hour later, he finally reached the parking lot in front of the lodge. He parked the Mustang next to four off-roaders, a dusty pickup truck labeled CEDAR CREEK LODGE, and a red Prius. Damn eco-crates! They always made him feel bad.

With a disapproving look at the Toyota, Ondragon pulled the key out of the ignition and got out. It was already toward evening and the parking lot was bathed in purple shadows. The forest exhaled a cool darkness. Only on the roofs of the buildings and the tops of the conifers was the reddish-golden light of the setting sun still glowing. Ondragon opened the trunk and took out two large travel bags, his eyes falling on the elongated metal suitcase. He would leave it in the car for the time being. Maybe he wouldn't need it at all. He slammed the trunk lid shut and jumped in fright. A young guy was standing next to the Mustang, whistling through his teeth. He had a three-day beard and a slight squint.

"Wow, a '67 Shelby GT500 Fastback! You don't see a sweet number like that around here very often. How much does she do?"

"Over a hundred eighty miles an hour!"

Another whistle. "May I?"

Ondragon nodded, and Squinter ran his hands reverently over the matte black surface. Custom-made in LA, as was the interior. Ondragon knew the guys from West Coast Customs personally.

The fellow walked once around the car, his lips stretched into a wide grin. "That's one hot lady. Really!"

"Thank you."

Squinter came back to him. "You must be Mr. *On Draegen*. May I take your bags?"

"It's Ondragon!" Ondragon hated it when people mispronounced his name. "On-dra-gon. Emphasis on the first syllable. It's not an American name."

"Really? It's cool anyway." Squinter straightened his red baseball cap with the washed-out Chicago Bulls logo. His choice of basketball team showed taste at least.

"And who are you?" asked Ondragon.

"Oh, 'scuse me. I'm Peter Parker. I'm the bellboy here."

"Are you kidding me?" Ondragon was beginning to get impatient. What kind of lodge was this, that could afford such strange employees? Maybe he should reconsider his plan to invest his money here.

"Uh, why?" Squinter sheepishly pushed up the sleeves of his plaid shirt. Now he looked like he was trying to compete with lumberjack giant Paul Bunyan.

"Ever heard of Spider-Man?" Ondragon tapped his forehead with a finger.

His interlocutor's gaze remained blank. Only a few seconds later did it click. "Oh, you mean the guy who turns into Spider-Man. Yeah, his name's the same as mine!" He gave a half-witted grin.

"I can't believe it. I guess your parents were comic book fans?"

"I don't know. It was my great-grandfather's name. Was there Spider-Man back then?" Peter Parker scratched his head under his baseball cap. "Never mind. Just call me Pete. I prefer that anyway. Now, may I carry your bags up to reception?"

Ondragon hesitated, but then nodded.

Grinning, Pete picked up the two bags. "Please follow me, Mr. *On Draegen*."

Ondragon rolled his eyes and followed on the heels of the eccentric factotum. *Let's see what other strange creatures are hanging around here*, he thought.

The main building of the lodge was situated a little above the parking lot on a well-trimmed lawn that looked as incongruous here in the wilderness as a hunter in a silk kimono. The large log complex consisted of a three-story central structure with a hexagonal floor plan and a roof that was covered with wooden shingles and looked like the apex of a crystal. From this central "tower," two lower residential wings forked backward. Behind them was open space.

Cedar Creek Lodge was not as luxurious as the famous Cirque Lodge in Utah, but it was not besieged by paparazzi either. For most of the photographers, the facility was simply too deep in the woods. The more remote the location, the more protected you were from the gossip-hungry world. Ondragon looked up at the entrance. His stay here would cost him a lot of money, but it was also his last chance, and he hoped it would be worth it. After all, Dr. Arthur, the director of the clinic, had an excellent reputation.

He leaped up the top step to the entrance and strode through the door, which Pete was gallantly holding open for him. Ondragon took a close look around the small reception area. In the dim light, a leather sofa stood in front of a fireplace, above which hung a huge pair of elk antlers. On a ramshackle table made from twisted roots, several glossy magazines waited for relaxed hands to flip through them, and on the wooden floor was a thick, green, patterned rug that was presumably meant to complement the lawn outside. The Pendleton wool blankets on the sofa and the electric lanterns on wrought iron hooks completed the impression of a cozy hunting lodge in the mountains. Just what Ondragon had hoped for. A cozy ambiance with a touch of wilderness. He turned to the reception counter, next to which another glass door was set, protecting the rest of the building from unauthorized access. A young blonde woman who looked like she had stepped out of an advertising brochure appeared behind it and smiled at him.

"Welcome to Cedar Creek Lodge, Mr. Ondragon. I'm Sheila."

At least she had pronounced his name correctly. She had probably been thoroughly briefed about his foibles. Things were looking up with the staff! Ondragon smiled back benignly.

"If you'd like to sign here, please." She tapped a form with a green-painted fingernail that matched the carpet. "Then I can give you your room key. You'll also need to give me your car keys."

Ondragon paused in the middle of signing. "My car keys?"

A professional smile appeared on Sheila's face, and he saw that she had an artificial diamond on one of her canines.

"It's part of the program, Mr. Ondragon. You're supposed to be fully committed to it."

". . . and not run off in the middle or anything?"

"That's right," Sheila said. "We have some difficult cases here and . . ."

". . . I'm one of them?"

Sheila looked at him. "Dr. Arthur will be the judge of that."

Ondragon bit his tongue. He wasn't used to anyone telling him what to do. And he was going to have to get his act together if he was going to get through this. "I understand it," he said. "But keep those keys safe. If there's so much as a hint of a scratch on my baby, I'll hold you responsible!"

"Your car keys go in our safe." Sheila motioned with her pretty chin toward the office behind the counter. "I assure you, no one will go near your car."

Ondragon cast a sidelong glance at Pete, who was wearing a lop-sided grin.

"All right. Here you go." He was about to slide the keys across the counter but then thought again and removed the fob. As he did so, he caught Sheila's amused look. "My talisman," he said apologetically, and quickly put the thing back in his pocket. He knew that a pink enamel heart with a bear on it didn't do much for his image, but the damn thing had once saved his life, after all!

Sheila nodded and took custody of the Mustang's keys. "Did you have a good trip?"

"Depends on how you look at it. Bad roads and animals jumping out in front of the car. But otherwise, very picturesque."

"Yes, the forests here are swarming with wild animals. Moose, deer, bears, and so on. But don't worry, they're not dangerous."

"Do I look like I'm scared?"

Sheila threw an inscrutable glance at his fancy suit before looking back at his face. "There's one more thing: Dr. Arthur places great importance on a peaceful atmosphere in the lodge. He wants his guests to be able to relax without any restrictions. So you also need to hand over your cell phone, if you have one with you."

Ondragon raised his eyebrows in surprise. Secretly, he had suspected the institution would have a rule like this. With a contrite expression, he reached into the inside pocket of his jacket, pulled out a Blackberry, and slid it across the counter.

Sheila looked at him steadfastly. "The other one too, please!"

Crap! Ondragon fished the iPhone out of his pocket. "And I'm not even allowed to look at it once the whole time?"

"That's right." Sheila's eyes revealed clear satisfaction, although she was trying to remain serious. Reluctantly, Ondragon conceded defeat, placing the cell phone in her hand. Green fingernails closed around it like the leaf blades of a carnivorous plant.

"Thank you, Mr. Ondragon! Do you have a computer with you? A netbook or anything like that? Because the internet is off-limits too."

"No, I don't have one. I only use my smartphone when I'm on the road."

"Good, then Pete will show you to your room now. Dr. Arthur will see you tomorrow morning at ten o'clock in his office on the second floor. You are already registered with him. Dinner is at seven in the Lakeview Salon at the rear of the building. If you have any questions, ask me or Pete. Have a pleasant stay."

Ondragon bit back the comment on the tip of his tongue and instead gave Sheila a chummy wink. "All right, see you later." He turned to the bellboy and followed him with a spring in his step through the second glass door, brushing his fingers unobtrusively over the third cell phone in his pants pocket.

In the tower, they climbed the stairs to the third floor. While Pete struggled ahead with the two heavy bags, Ondragon followed, scrutinizing him. The boy looked about twenty-five and was built like a scarecrow. His worn-out jeans flapped around his legs as if the latter were made of pliable bamboo. Ondragon wondered if he had other duties than carrying the guests' luggage.

"Where are you from, if you don't mind me asking?" inquired Pete, turning to face him as he walked.

"LA."

"Ah, that's where many of our guests come from. *California— home of fruits and nuts!*" Pete cackled. He sounded like a quacking duck. Ondragon couldn't get the image of Daffy Duck and Elmer Fudd out of his head.

Arriving on the next floor, Pete turned left and shuffled in his worn hunting boots down a long, carpeted hallway broken up by tasteful seating. Here too the walls consisted of tree trunks piled horizontally on top of one another, interspersed at regular intervals with burgundy doors. A few pictures hung here and there. In passing, Ondragon looked at an expensively framed oil painting that showed Indigenous peoples disguised as wolves, creeping up on a group of red-coated cavalrymen in the snow. Another depicted a lonely log cabin.

Suddenly, one of the doors opened, and a peroxide-blond man in a lame designer sweatsuit stepped out into the hallway.

"Hey, Mr. Shamgood, how's it going?" Pete greeted him as he passed.

"Good, thanks." The man turned his head toward Ondragon. "Ah, and it seems my day is about to get even better!" He raised his eyebrows suggestively, looking Ondragon up and down.

"Well, then . . ." Pete shuffled on, and as Ondragon passed the guest, he could clearly sense Mr. Shamgood watching him with interest. He even thought he heard a faint whistle. Annoyed, he gritted his teeth.

"Well, Mr. *On Draegen,* here we are. This is your room, number six." Pete opened the door, entered, and placed the bags on a large wooden chest at the foot of the bed. Ondragon's eyes immediately fell on the balcony and the magnificent view.

"Wow!" he said, opening the balcony door and walking outside.

"Not bad, huh? That's Moose Lake." Pete came up beside him and pointed to the clear mountain lake, out of which rose rounded, rocky, pine-covered islands. The shores were lined with reeds and mighty conifers.

"The lake is shaped like a cucumber," Pete went on, "and it's almost three miles long. Sometimes actual elk come to feed here. Mostly at dusk. Plus, it's great fishing. If you need fishing gear, Cedar Creek Lodge has everything an angler's heart could desire. Ask me or Frank—he's the gardener."

Ondragon hated fishing. Complete waste of time when you could buy the fish in the supermarket next door or even better, ready to eat in a restaurant.

"And over there, that's Mount Witiko." Pete jerked his thumb toward a bizarre rock formation.

"Witiko," repeated Ondragon, looking at the almost black peak, split in two, rising from the impenetrable green of the forest from between the flatter hilltops. *Possibly volcanic in origin*, he thought.

"It's a name, from the Ojibwe. And the mountain is one of their sacred places. They hold rituals and stuff there. If you're interested, the library has all kinds of maps and books about the woods and the Indians."

An unexpected tingling sensation ran down Ondragon's spine. Library! If you only knew, boy.

Pete noticed nothing and just babbled on. "The history of this area is Dr. Arthur's hobby. It's not my thing, but I sometimes look at the creepy pictures in the books. Especially the ones of the mountain monster." The bellboy chuckled and adjusted his baseball cap—seemed to be a habit of his. "Well, I'd better be getting back downstairs, Sheila's waiting for me. I wish you the best of luck, Mr. *On Draegen*."

Pete went over to the door.

"Oh yeah, before I forget." He turned again. "On the nightstand are the *Golden Rules*. Dr. Arthur wants every guest to read them and, of course, obey them." Pete grinned and disappeared.

Ondragon stood for a while on the balcony, looking at Mount Witiko reflected darkly in the smooth surface of the lake. Then he went back inside, took off his jacket with the red satin lining, and looked around the room that was to be his place of residence for the next few weeks. The wide bed was made of debarked logs, as were the table and two chairs. In the corner by the picture window were a heavy leather armchair and a round side table of dark walnut that had an electric lantern on it. In the other corner next to the door loomed a veritable colossus of a cabinet: antique stain and hand-forged hinges. Ondragon turned the large key in the lock and opened it. Several storage compartments, a clothes rail, and a safe with a key-pad. No television! Ondragon pursed his lips. He didn't know what he thought of it all yet. He closed the cabinet and turned around. Above the bed hung a light blue tapestry in the style of the West Coast Indigenous peoples, with a white raven on it. It was carrying the moon in its beak. Everything looked rustic but classy and encouraged you to feel at home.

How many other "guests" were staying here, besides him and the obviously gay Mr. Shamgood? Ondragon decided to ask Sheila. He wanted to know who he was living with here, after all, while having his private problem dealt with.

He took a critical look at the bathroom. It was spacious and tiled in light blue and brown. An impressive enamel clawfoot bathtub crouched under the window like a white beast. Ondragon noticed the thick, soft piles of fresh towels and began to look forward to a hot shower after dinner. He went back to the room and sat down on the bed. His gaze fell on the mirror hanging opposite him.

His face looked tanned and vital, and his green eyes shone combatively from under the broad, dark brows, whose effect when he raised them, he was well aware of. But he also saw clearly the tired pallor behind the California complexion, and the dark circles under his eyes. The worry lines on his forehead deepened as his appraising gaze lingered on his nose. Most women found it attractive, but it was far too pointy for him. It made him look like some kind of smart-alec bird. But the nose gave him a more determined and energetic look, which he needed in his job, so he had come to terms with it. His gaze slid downward. His shoulders and arms under his fitted, eggplant-colored shirt were muscular from all the workouts he indulged in to help him relax. Krav Maga and kendo. But also sometimes a game of street ball on the Boardwalk in Venice—the toughest basketball court in the world.

All in all, he looked like a likeable guy in his early forties, a successful management consultant with hardly any quirks. Quite normal, in fact. But what few people knew about, and what he always tried to carefully conceal, was his obsession with analytical mind games. The *centrifuge*, he called it, and there was nothing he could do about it once it got going. No matter what he looked at, he had to instantly break it down into its molecular parts, had to see the true structure behind it, the secret driving forces. Machines, people, politicians . . . problems. It was an addiction, a dark power that was difficult to control. *But that was not why he had come here.*

"No, Paul Eckbert, we're here to be honest with each other. And if I'm honest, you look like shit, my dear. You're in desperate need of a vacation. A vacation from yourself." He bared his teeth and stuck out his tongue. "Son of a bitch!"

He felt the smuggled iPhone vibrate in his pocket. The display showed the number of his assistant.

"Yeah, Charlize, what's up?"

"Oh, you've got a signal!"

"I'm surprised too in this wasteland."

"Chief, I'll make this quick; we've got a request in from Japan." Although her voice had been shot into space and back, he could hear the deep, sensual tones quite clearly. An almost melancholy longing came over him.

"Yakuza?" he asked.

"No."

"Then let Dietmar have it."

"He's in Dubai right now and he's unavailable. Sheikh Al-Mazoum is demanding his full attention."

"Oh, Charlize, then think of something. I certainly can't handle it. You know . . ." In fact, his assistant was the only one who knew the reason for his stay at Cedar Creek Lodge. And Ondragon still wondered if it had been wise to let her in on it. Charlize had integrity, no question, and she'd rather chop off a finger than spill company secrets. But what did she think of him? If she had thought his quirk was just a fad before, she must now think he was completely gaga.

"It's okay, Chief, I'll take care of it; my Japanese is much better than yours anyway."

Ondragon smiled. Charlize Tanaka had been a real stroke of luck. The thirty-two-year-old Brazilian of Japanese descent had been assisting him for five years and it was hard to imagine the company without her. She was a top-notch researcher and was ideally suited to spicy special assignments that only a woman could handle. She was a femme fatale in the most fatal sense. And Ondragon had to constantly remind himself of his own number one rule in her presence: no sex with employees.

"What's it like out there in the wasteland, Chief?"

"So far . . . wasteland-like. Keep me posted, Charlize. Sayonara!"

"Sayonara, Boss."

Ondragon put the cell phone in the nightstand drawer and ran his hand through his short black hair. It was a paradox. He made his living by solving other people's problems—extremely difficult matters that often required unusual measures—and he had never been squeamish about it. His unsparing, direct manner had earned him a name in the worlds on both sides of the law, even in the early years of his work. He always found a solution that satisfied his customers. Always! Yes, that was his passion, his magic. Solving problems. Ondragon let out a dry laugh.

"It's just my own problem I can't get a handle on!" With a sarcastic grin, he extended a hand to his reflection. "Ondragon Consulting. I solve your problems quickly, reliably, and cleanly, but don't ask about my own." He sighed, took off his holster with the SIG Sauer, and put it in the drawer with his smartphone. Fortunately, Sheila hadn't asked him for a gun. He would have been extremely reluctant to give it up. A man like him didn't only have friends, after all.

His eyes fell on a stack of loose papers lying on the nightstand, held together by a band. On the top sheet was written: *Golden Rules.* Obviously, a special copy, just for him. He glanced at his wristwatch. Twenty minutes until dinner. Enough time to familiarize himself with the house rules. He removed the band, set the cover sheet aside, and began to read.

CHAPTER 2

*1835, Kabetogama,
Walcott farm*

It must have been the goddamn Injuns, Lieutenant!"

"Don't talk such nonsense, Hancock. And stop cussing."

"But who else could have done it? Just look at this disgusting mess. Jesus, Mary, and Joseph! Even the children . . ."

"I can see that too, Hancock." With a scowl, Lieutenant Stafford trudged through the snow in front of the Walcotts' log cabin while his bearish sergeant surveyed the scene inside. Both held a cloth to their noses as the sickening stench from the cabin was now polluting the entire area.

Alan Parker and his two companions waited a little to one side, by their horses. They had led the soldiers here from nearby Fort Frances in a breathless two-day ride. By now, fresh snow had fallen. Several handbreadths deep, it covered the clearing and the roof of the log cabin and bent the branches of the white pines downward. Of course, there was also nothing left to see of the tracks.

The cold, wet air cut into the trappers' lungs, and they pulled their fur collars tighter around their necks. Their breath rose in little white clouds. It was the end of March and it would be a while before spring came.

Another sound of disgust came from the house. The lieutenant shook his head and walked over to the three trappers. He wore the saber and the golden officer's badge openly for all to see over his meticulously buttoned gray wool greatcoat. He had a serious look on his face, which was pale under his black officer's hat. The colonel at

Fort Frances had assigned him to investigate the case and if necessary take the first steps toward solving the murders. *The lieutenant gives the impression of being a very conscientious man*, thought Parker, *although his bearing seems a little too arrogant for the wilderness.*

"Well, Mr. Parker?" Even his accent was exaggeratedly aristocratic. "Why don't you tell me again what happened and what you saw? Maybe now that we're on the scene, something else will occur to you." He pulled out his little notebook again and licked the tip of the pencil. His tongue was already black.

"As I told you before, Lieutenant, we were on our way from our hunting grounds to the trading station and were going to rest here as usual. The Walcotts are . . . um, were, good friends, so it was all the more shocking to us to find them so horribly mauled." A salty lump formed in Parker's throat and he gave a cough. He was a hardbitten kind of guy, having lived in the woods since he was twelve, but what had happened to the Walcotts had scared the hell out of him. He tried to swallow the lump along with the bad memories, but he couldn't. The images of the events rose before his mind's eye again. He saw himself going over to the hut and pushing open the door. Saw himself kneel down and aim his shotgun inside. Saw himself facing the worst nightmare he had ever seen.

The shaggy shadow had filled the entire doorway, like a gigantic, hairy locust, its folded legs ready to leap. Parker had gone to shoot at the bony body, but the creature had been faster. Before he could pull the trigger, the matted fur and a foul stench had enveloped him and settled suffocatingly on his face. A sharp stab had torn through his shoulder, then the force of the impact had knocked him to the ground. Struggling to breathe and unable to move, Parker had lain there. The creature had stared down at him motionless. Its eyes had been glowing red points.

Parker shook himself at the memory. Today, in the cold light of day, the sentiment seemed foolish, but in that breathless moment he had been ready to die.

Then a shot had been fired.

The beast, whatever it was, had let go of him with a hissing sound and fled into the forest with huge unnatural leaps. Parker had lain there and continued to stare into the night sky, dazed, the cool snow-flakes falling on his face.

"And what do you think it was, this . . . thing?" asked Stafford, cutting into Parker's thoughts. The lieutenant's nose was red from the cold and little ice crystals hung in his blond whiskers. "A wolf or a bear?"

"Nothing like that." The old trapper wiped his tired eyes with his glove. "It didn't look like anything I've ever seen."

"Maybe it was a werewolf," Sergeant Hancock suggested. "Some of the settlers in the area claim there's one here." He grinned, but the lieutenant didn't bat an eye. It was plain to see he didn't care much for that kind of humbug.

For a while, no one said anything.

"Not werewolf," Two-Elk finally said into the silence. "Werewolf is spirit of the whites. But this is spirit of Ojibwe, brothers of the Council of Three Fires. Wendigo—powerful spirit, evil spirit. Always hungry! Always eating!"

"Why of course, the Wendigo," exclaimed the lieutenant with a sarcastic laugh, tapping his forehead with his pencil. "I'd forgotten all about him. Another one of those mythical characters. Let's see who else it might have been. A Sasquatch, an ogre, the cruel Harpies, or vampires. Yes, it was the vampires." Stafford exhaled irritably. "Wendigo, werewolf, they're all figments of the imagination! There are no such creatures. They're just horror stories."

"I wouldn't be so sure about that, Lieutenant," said Parker. "There are places in these woods that no man has ever gone. Mysterious places. The Indians know about them and know the creatures that dwell in those places. They—"

"That's what I said. It was those goddamn savages!" the sergeant blurted again, earning a scowl from Two-Elk. But the Englishman ignored the stocky Chippewa warrior and continued talking, unabashed. "It's obvious; you only have to look inside the hut. Granted, it takes a real man to look closely at it, but who except those damned redskins is capable of such gruesome carnage? They're animals on two legs. Red beasts! We must punish them for this before they do any more damage!"

"Now, hold your horses, Sergeant. We're here to investigate the matter, not jump to conclusions."

But Hancock was not to be deterred and went on railing against the people. And as Alan Parker listened to him, he couldn't stop another sliver of memory from drilling deep into his mind. The inside of the cabin! Blaring and indelible, it had burned itself into the tortured convolutions of his brain.

When he had recovered from the attack of the sinister creature and Two-Elk had helped him to his feet, he and his companions had hurried into the log cabin. The stench that had hit them had been horrible, animalistic somehow; a mixture of freshly ripped-out entrails, wildcat urine, and decay. Bloody lumps of flesh and organs had littered the entire living space. Silvery intestines had hung from the ceiling beams like gruesome garlands. Bones had been torn from shiny bluish joints and skin from muscles. And someone had mutilated the torsos beyond recognition and stacked them neatly in one corner of the house. From another angle, the scalped skulls of the family of four had stared plaintively at the trappers. But that had not been the worst of it. The horrifying thing had not only slaughtered the Walcotts like cattle, it had also begun to eat the corpses. Bite marks had been clearly visible in the soft tissue of the torn limbs. As if a pack of dogs had feasted on them.

Lacroix had vomited in the snow outside, while Two-Elk had continued to stand by Parker, staring at the carnage and muttering unintelligible incantations to himself. The Chippewa had quickly taken something from a small pouch and stuck it to the doorframe with spit. Then they had locked the log cabin's door tight and hurried away from this sullied place. Their ride to the fort had been like a headlong flight, hunted by the horrible sight of the slaughtered family and the knowledge that something incomprehensibly evil was lurking out there in the forest. Something that had come straight up from the putrid depths of hell.

"I've got it!" exclaimed Sergeant Hancock, still not finished with his diatribe against the people. "It was an Injun in a bearskin. The stinking scum dressed up." He turned to Parker. "You say yourself it had fur and moved funny."

The old trapper looked from the hulking sergeant to his two companions and then to the lieutenant, whose watery blue eyes were regarding him expectantly.

"If it was a human in disguise," Parker said with a shrug, "it was a damn big one. At least ten feet tall! Much bigger than the withers of a moose."

The lieutenant shook his head. "No one is as tall as that."

Damn right! And no human leaves bite marks like that, Parker thought. He grabbed his shoulder and a cold shiver gripped him. No, he knew better. All he had to do was look at the wound. The only problem was that the lieutenant wouldn't believe him.

"I shot the son of a bitch," Lacroix spoke up. Discomfort and exhaustion were written all over the French Canadian's weathered face. And Parker knew that his loyal friend would surely have preferred to be sitting in a warm dive bar at the trading post, watching buxom girls dance, than to be returning to this godforsaken place.

"And I hit it!" Lacroix ran his hand proudly over his pitch-black mustache. "*Certainement!* I am sure of it. But it didn't trouble it much, and it didn't bleed. With three jumps it disappeared over there into the woods. If you ask me, it looked like a huge wolf, all skin and bone, on long legs like stilts." Parker saw the lieutenant's skeptical look. He knew exactly what the fine English toff thought of them. But they hadn't drunk too much gin, nor were they concocting a story to get their heads out of the noose. On the contrary, they had been stone-cold sober. Unfortunately!

"*Alors,* however . . ." Lacroix raised his shoulders. "It was already dark, and I couldn't see the thing that clearly. In any case, it left strange footprints." Now he crouched down and traced the toeless track that had also caught Parker's eye and awakened that inexplicable fear in him. The lieutenant wrote carefully in his notebook.

"Well, if you ask me, Lieutenant, those three gin drinkers there had one too many and—"

"Hold your tongue, Hancock!" With a disapproving look, the lieutenant flipped his book closed. A deep crease appeared between his brows. He turned to Parker. "Like the colonel and the governor, who happens to be at Fort Frances at the moment, I am very much in favor of a reasonable and complete investigation of this unsavory incident. That means I am considering all possibilities without reservation. Unfortunately, my enlightened mind and my Christian upbringing prohibit me from believing in nonsense such as werewolves or the Wendigo. These are fairy tales, the simpleminded chatter of even more simpleminded people who have gone too deep into the godless swamp of these woods. But what else can you expect than Sodom and Gomorrah? Anyone who carouses with dirty Indian whores and brings stinking bastards into the world instead of marrying good, God-fearing British women, and who instead of doing honest work allows himself to be seduced by the lust for gold and grubs around in the dirt up to his elbows, should not be surprised when God comes to punish him. What a squalid country!"

Now Parker's jaw dropped. "Are you saying the Walcotts were not God-fearing people? This family worked hard, scratching their hands raw in this cursed earth every day to wring from it the little they needed to survive. But they never doubted God. The Walcotts were honest and upright people. Simple, yes, but that doesn't mean they deserved to be torn apart and eaten alive, and then have you cast slurs on them afterward! What's more, you, my dear Lieutenant, have not the faintest idea of what it means to live in these woods you call squalid. The rich snobs in your distant homeland have us to thank for the fact that they don't have to make their fancy hats and collars out of rat skins!"

"Alan, *calme-toi*." Lacroix took him by the arm.

"But I don't want to calm down. People like our lieutenant here come into the wilderness and think the damn silver spoons in their mouths have given them some kind of wisdom. Yet they can't tell a bear from a beaver. They don't even believe the evidence of their eyes! If I or any of my friends say that what caused this hideous massacre was neither man nor beast, you can take our word for it. Because I grew up here and I will be buried here while you go back to your fine, civilized England. I don't give a shit about you and your self-righteous godliness!" Parker spat out. He turned to his friends. "Come on, I can't stand this gentleman's presence any longer. Good luck with your investigation, Lieutenant. Now, if we may, we'd like to pay our last respects to the Walcott family and bury them." Parker walked past the irritated-looking officer. Lacroix and Two-Elk followed him.

"Do you think that was smart, calling the lieutenant names like that?" the French Canadian asked once they were out of earshot.

Sullenly, Parker grabbed a hoe that was leaning against the barn wall. "Smart or not, this guy just won't listen. We've said all there is to say. It's up to him now to make any damn sense of it. I just want to get out of this neighborhood as fast as possible." *Before what's out there comes back for us.* Parker didn't say it, fearing that would bring disaster. He took a few steps toward the forest and began hoeing, first moving aside the snow, then the frozen earth. Silently, his friends helped him.

As he worked, Parker grew warm and felt the burning pain in his shoulder. He gave a slight groan. Two-Elk and Lacroix looked up in concern.

"It's all right. The wound just got a little infected. Nothing bad," Parker lied, forcing himself to smile. In reality, he felt the nameless fear reaching for him from the edge of the forest. An icy cold breeze passed over his face, and he tried not to look at the dark underbrush. Parker couldn't remember ever being afraid of the forest. He pressed his fist against his shoulder. The creature's bite pulsed with every heartbeat, blazing cold in his flesh as if a sharp icicle had bored into it. Parker caught Two-Elk's gaze and read in his black eyes what he was thinking. His people had known the legend since the beginning of time. And he too knew the terrible and powerful being whose path they had crossed.

Wendigo.

Fear ate through Parker's body like newly hatched maggots, spreading coldly, whispering through his veins.

CHAPTER 3

2009, northern Minnesota, St. Louis County,
Moose Lake, Cedar Creek Lodge

Click.

Ondragon looked up from his notepad and over to the large picture window of his room and clicked his pen. It was 7:20 in the morning. Outside, the weather was almost celestially beautiful. The sun was dispersing the mist on the lake and making the dewdrops glisten on the branches of the trees.

Click.

Ten minutes until breakfast. His *centrifuge* was already running at full speed. What he had gathered about this place so far in the run-up to his trip was not yet enough to fully satisfy him. Ondragon looked down at the notepad.

Click.

Cedar Creek Lodge, in the middle of the lonely woods of northern Minnesota, just an hour's drive from the Canadian border, was a state-of-the-art treatment center, but it also offered its guests both the comfort of a luxury hotel and the reliable medical care of a private hospital. It differed from the other top places, however, in that it did not accept patients with addictions. "Minor cases" were for other facilities to take care of. That was fine with Ondragon. Normal crazies were enough for him; he didn't need to be surrounded by junkies.

The spacious Cedar Creek Lodge compound could accommodate up to twenty patients in tastefully furnished rooms, and of course took special requests into account. An award-winning chef provided for culinary well-being and a real headwaiter brought the ambience of an exclusive restaurant. There was nothing like good food, after all. On the first floor of the west wing, discerning guests would find a lounge and a spa complex with Jacuzzi, sauna, and fitness room, and the east wing housed the dining room and kitchen. Alongside the medical program, guests could go hiking, picnicking, canoeing, or fishing, play archery or tennis in the idyllic natural surroundings, and jog along the wonderfully soft forest trails; there was even bear-watching and a guided trek on horseback. The lodge had five horses and a riding instructor. Stays should be as enjoyable as possible in every way and be remembered fondly.

At least there will be no lack of peace here, Ondragon thought, retracting the pen cartridge.

Click.

The head of the clinic was Dr. Arthur, past fifty, British born, and a recognized specialist in all manifestations of phobias and anxiety states.

Click.

Dr. Arthur had the idea for a special clinic out in the unspoiled natural world, far away from all the distracting influences of civilization back during his studies at University College London. After his two dissertations in psychology and medicine, for which he graduated *summa cum laude* in record time, he was offered a postdoctoral position at the Mayo Clinic medical school in Rochester, Minnesota, one of the most renowned medical research institutions in the United States. There, as the youngest up-and-coming talent in psychology, he began his detailed work on patients with social phobias, for which he received the Award for Research from the American Psychiatric Association in 1995.

Click.

A stellar career. The man either had no private life or a brain the size of a planet. In any case, Dr. Arthur found willing investors to support his clinic project. And once Cedar Creek Lodge opened for business in the summer of 2000, it recouped its construction costs within two years, which of course more than satisfied its private backers. In no time at all, the "CC Lodge," as it was called by those in the know, became a veritable magnet for film stars and starlets, business moguls, and prominent politicians. A hotspot for psychosis-ridden millionaires.

Click.

The therapy was not cheap, but its success validated Dr. Arthur's unusual approach, with the relapse rate for patients seeking treatment at the remote clinic being much lower than at similar facilities. The lodge was fully booked all year round, and had a long waiting list.

Click.

So much for the lodge itself. Now for the staff. Ondragon had tried to subject them to a thorough investigation as well. Unfortunately, he had quickly hit stony ground. The hard rock of the analog and digital databases had yielded only a little information about the two other psychotherapists employed by Dr. Arthur at the CC Lodge. Both, of course, had excellent reputations. Dr. Pollux was an authority on depression and death wish, and Dr. Zeo an expert on personality disorders. Both assistants, and the nursing staff, lived year-round in small log cabins located in the woods behind the main building, while the director of the clinic resided in the "tower."

Ondragon put pen to notepad and added in meticulous handwriting: *Dr. Pollux, Reto, 49, Swiss citizen, and Dr. Zeo, Lucy-Ang, 46, American of Chinese descent.* He wrote in German, the language of his father.

Click.

All that was missing now was more detailed information about the remaining employees and the current "inmates." But Ondragon doubted he could get this information legally. He had stupidly messed things up with Sheila on the very first day. She wouldn't even tell him the name of Frank the gardener's dog.

Click.

So he had to resort to other means. Breaking into the lodge reception office without leaving any traces was one of the easier exercises. He would probably even be able to crack the safe where the car keys were. He grinned.

Click.

So if he felt like it, there was nothing to stop him from taking a trip to the nearest town, even if the *Golden Rules* of the lodge expressly forbade it. But Ondragon had never taken much notice of prohibitions.

Click, click.

The town of Orr was forty miles away—about an hour away in an off-road vehicle, probably more like two in a Mustang. The self-proclaimed fishing and outdoor paradise on Pelican Lake was actually a small, run-down logging backwater with 250 residents. Only in summer did a few hiking and canoeing fanatics stray there. Besides plenty of unspoiled nature, there were two vacation lodges, two general stores, a Spur gas station, an auto repair shop, a railroad crossing, and an elementary school. Wow!

Click.

Ondragon flipped the notepad closed, a mini ring binder with flexible plastic covers. Once it had served its purpose, he would burn it. He always did that. He rose from his rumpled bed and tucked the notepad into the pocket of his gray suit pants. He wore a tailored, rose-colored shirt with no tie and plain, brown leather shoes. His cowboy boots stayed in the closet; they went with the Mustang. Besides, he wanted to give the audience at this establishment another good look-over before deciding on a more casual outfit.

He went to the closet, took out the matching jacket, and threw it over his shoulder. At the same time, he went through his usual routine, checking that the safe in which he had deposited all his personal belongings and his gun was securely locked. After all, the maid was only supposed to see what he was pretending to be: a businessman. He didn't need to hide the fact that he had money; that was obvious anyway. If your income was below a million dollars a year, you didn't even try to book into the CC Lodge.

Ondragon took one last look in the mirror, brushed his hair back from his forehead, and left his room. He turned the key twice in the lock and dropped it into his trouser pocket, where it joined his talisman, jingling.

Breakfast was served in the dining room on the first floor. Like any good hotel, you could choose from the buffet or inform the waiter of the dish you desired, which would then be freshly prepared in the kitchen. In order for the lodge to be able to meet all of its guests' wishes, it asked for their preferences in advance, so that no one had to go without during their stay, no matter how unusual their wish might be. This pleased Ondragon, who had often stayed in upscale hotels and greatly appreciated the benefits of outstanding service. Even at dinner the previous day, he had been impressed by the professionalism of the dining room staff. Quite the opposite of the table manners of some of the guests. Once again, it had become apparent that people with money and status symbols were not automatically well brought up. Though Ondragon had had a good upbringing rather forced upon him, he was grateful to his father, with whom he otherwise cultivated a very ambivalent relationship, for at least insisting on impeccable behavior at all times. Even if often in a damn painful way. The old bastard had loved his cane!

Ondragon turned to the smartly dressed headwaiter, who greeted him with a friendly smile and escorted him to his table. It was the same table as the night before, which stood in a pleasant corner next to two large ornamental plants, and offered the perfect view over the whole dining room, including the guests. This had been his express wish and he suspected that the table had been moved to this position especially for him.

"Good morning, Mr. Ondragon. What would you like to drink?"

Pleased with the man's correct pronunciation, Ondragon replied, "Good morning, Carlos. A triple espresso with cane sugar, nice and hot, please. A freshly squeezed orange juice to go with it."

The headwaiter nodded. "How shall I have your porridge prepared?"

"Unsweetened with plenty of milk and a dollop of cream, the good Swedish way." Ondragon smiled as the waiter moved away to pass on his order. He had been born in Sweden and raised on the inevitable *Havregröt*. The stuff didn't look very appetizing, but it was reliably filling. Besides, Ondragon didn't much like stuffing his belly at an early hour; it paralyzed the gray matter and made him put on weight. He liked to eat well, but controlling your food intake was always paramount.

The espresso and orange juice arrived and Ondragon added a heaping spoonful of brown cane sugar to the steaming black liquid. Before taking the first sip, he breathed in the seductive aroma.

Espresso: coffee in its most concentrated form. It was his secret fuel. Without coffee, he was a very unbalanced person. Bad coffee was a disaster. First and foremost, American coffee. Horrible! The espresso shots at Starbucks were the only coffee that could be drunk without sending you blind on the spot.

"Your porridge, sir." The waiter placed the bowl of gray porridge on the table in front of him. Ondragon pulled out the spoon. He tasted and nodded to the waiter in satisfaction. Porridge and espresso were to his taste. With a discreet bow, the headwaiter withdrew.

Eating his breakfast, Ondragon inconspicuously observed the other guests. It was half past seven and not all the patients had sat down to breakfast yet. Ondragon had chosen this time deliberately because it would allow him to take a quiet look at the early risers and then scrutinize the other guests as they gradually joined them. His hand felt for the notepad. He would meticulously note which characters were here, and perhaps even find out why. In return, he would reveal nothing of himself. It was always like that, and it was better that way.

He routinely scanned the tables, each of which had no more than three people seated. Most of the patients, however, took their breakfast alone, and he knew a few of them from the previous evening. Ondragon counted nine of the total of twenty guests. Some, with varying degrees of gusto, were devouring their food, which ranged from delicately toasted bread garnished with lettuce leaves to hamburgers dripping with fat. The others were sipping tea or coffee from cups and leafing through magazines and newspapers. No one was reading a book. Ondragon's hand tightened involuntarily around the notepad. He thought of his appointment with Dr. Arthur at ten. Could the man fix his problem? Could he free him from his weakness?

Unconsciously, Ondragon concentrated on the guests and applied his well-rehearsed knowledge of human nature. In order not to attract attention, he made mental notes for the time being. Later, he would write them down on the notepad and check them against the data he would get tonight—without the permission of the prickly Sheila.

He began his observation at one of the two shared tables directly in front of the large window, which provided a magnificent view of the lake. Sitting at it were three flat-chested teenagers in avant-garde getups, with joyless faces. They were poking affectedly at their scrambled eggs, mashing them rather than eating them. Models, Ondragon guessed. At the next table sat a grossly overweight, overly made-up lady in her early sixties, together with an even older gentleman with a bald head and a gold lapel pin. Presumably an aging movie diva and a Republican politician. The two milieus were known to have a penchant for each other.

At the single table closest to the headwaiter's reception desk sat a Latino guy with a shiny Elvis quiff. He was wearing tight jeans and a black Ed Hardy shirt with torn sleeves, and was around thirty years old, Ondragon estimated. Probably some kind of artist from the music industry. One table away, in a gray shirt and an orange cashmere tank top, a man perched like a fishhook; scrawny limbs and a featureless face with rimless glasses. His thinning dark brown hair was combed sternly to one side. He actually looked like the classic law student, but his age gave the lie to that stereotype. He was around forty and wore a heavy signet ring on his left hand. Ondragon assigned him to the most superfluous and useless of all professions: real estate agent.

At the third table, a few steps away from the real estate agent, a young man was also eating porridge. Ondragon raised his eyebrows. This guy was the epitome of an overprivileged kid. Blond, slightly wavy hair that fell modishly into his face, gray eyes framed by striking blond eyelashes, and a pale complexion. He wore a mint-green polo shirt with the collar turned up, along with fashionable white jeans and canvas shoes with rubber soles. A pair of Ray-Bans sat on his head like a beauty queen's coronet. A preppy straight out of a fashion catalog. Ondragon had pretty much grown up with Waspy gear like this, from school uniforms to Barbour jackets, which was probably why he despised the style so much. At Harvard, it had been especially hard to resist. His deviation from the unofficial dress code back then wasn't the first time that had marked him as an outsider. Ondragon pursed his lips. That little boy over there had certainly been drilled into conformity. Mr. Ray-Ban was probably the son of a rich industrialist or a board member of a big company, but he was definitely European—you could tell by the porridge and the brand of his jeans.

Ondragon turned to the fourth table. There, a likeable-looking guy was leafing through an *In Touch* with a relaxed expression. Ondragon grinned. If a man who had passed puberty was looking at this magazine, it could only mean that he was either a paparazzo and wanted to see what scandals had escaped his lens, or that he was a victim of the photographer mob. In fact, Ondragon did recognize the man's face. His name was Charlie Bloom and he was a popular actor on a sitcom series. He obviously had quite different problems than his alleged alcoholism!

The fifth table was occupied by a scowling, long-haired anarchist type. He had his back to the picture window. On his sleeveless black T-shirt was a double axe, which had just split a diabolically snarling skull, above which was written *hatchet* in bloody letters. The word was also visible in several places on his arms, which were covered in tattoos. He wore dark sunglasses and looked like a creature of darkness that had been brutally dragged into the light of day. He was munching on his burger with grim determination, stabbing at it as if he were Freddy Krueger himself. Ondragon didn't know much about the metal scene, but he guessed the guy belonged to a band, probably called "Hatchet." He would use his smartphone to research the band on the internet later, assuming there was a connection here.

He drank the last mouthful of his espresso before turning his attention to the attractive woman at the sixth table. She was reading a newspaper and her head was slightly tilted, causing her black hair to fall in smooth cascades over one half of her face. Nonetheless, Ondragon could make out her exotic features: high cheekbones, dark almond-shaped eyes, and delicately curved lips. Asian, perhaps?

Exactly his type.

He guessed she was in her early thirties. She seemed oddly out of place, possibly due to her pleasantly unaffected appearance, and wore only a plain, dark green V-neck sweater and black pants, along with a silver chain and pendant. Ondragon liked understatement. Nothing about her had the air of showiness or an excess of dollars. In that, she was markedly different from everyone else there, including himself.

The woman felt his eyes resting on her and looked up.

Ondragon held her gaze for a while and nodded politely. If he had looked away immediately, it would have been too suspicious. The woman nodded back, but did not smile and turned back to her newspaper. It rustled softly.

Ondragon suddenly sensed he was being stared at. He pretended to devote himself entirely to his orange juice, glancing casually over the rim of the glass. Disgruntled, he noticed that the headwaiter had seated Mr. Shamgood at the table directly next to him. The guy, whose face was shaved as smooth as a baby's, turned to him quite unabashed and inspected him through unnaturally blue contact lenses. His salon-tanned skin contrasted grotesquely with his peroxide-blond hair. Mr. Shamgood was still wearing his lame sweatsuit, which he probably thought was the bee's knees. For Ondragon's taste, however, the shimmering fabric fit a little too snugly, accentuating the man's apparently well-endowed private parts, which was almost certainly deliberate. A cloud of penetrating aftershave wafted into his nose, smothering all the smells of breakfast.

"Good morning, Mr. Ondragon! Right?"

"Mr. Shamgood," Ondragon greeted back coolly, turning back to his porridge.

"Manager?"

Ondragon felt the man's gaze crawling over his clothes.

"Sort of. Management consultant." That was the role he slipped into when subjected to intrusive questions. He even kept a couple fake business cards on him for really tough cases.

Shamgood waved a hand in delight. "Ah, a fellow stress-sufferer. I know all about that. You see, I'm a fashion designer; I'm sure you'll have heard of the Tommy Shamgood label. Right?"

He certainly had; this confirmed Ondragon's suspicions about Mr. Shamgood from the day before. The self-made designer's fashion label had been very successful over the last ten years, and it was said Shamgood had sold his shares for a billion dollars. *He* could definitely afford this place. Ondragon wondered what kind of synaptic misconnection had brought him here.

"I rarely wear name-brand gear," he said indifferently, finishing his last spoonful of porridge. "I get a lot of things tailored." With a wave to the waiter, he ordered himself another triple espresso, hoping the aroma of the coffee would drown out the designer's intrusive perfumed aura.

"I see. And where are you from?"

Ondragon rolled his eyes inwardly. The guy wouldn't let up.

"LA."

"Really, and I thought you were from Sweden. Your accent gives you away." Shamgood winked at him suggestively.

The guy had a good ear, you had to give him that. Ondragon had deliberately spoken to the fashionista with a slight Swedish accent; he loved to confuse people.

"My mother is Swedish," he answered simply. That was true, but it belied the fact that he, like his father, actually had German citizenship.

"Ah, the Swedes! A very permissive people. Right? Are you equally permissive?" Ondragon lowered his spoon, piqued, while Shamgood raised his eyebrows over his fake blue eyes.

"I don't know what you mean by that. I think I'm like any other normal person."

"*Normal!*" Mr. Shamgood gave an impulsive snigger. "That's good! That's really good!" He took a deep breath and fanned a hand in front of his face as if he were too hot. "Hah, *normal!* How that sounds. As if it could be literally true. But we both know it's not, right?" He winked at Ondragon. "Let's face it, if we were normal, you and I wouldn't be here. But the very idea of being normal is exceedingly appealing. May I ask what little ailment brings you here?"

"You may not!" Ondragon had enough of this forced conversation. He turned away and tried to ignore the offended grumbling from the fashion designer. To his great relief, five other guests had meanwhile taken their seats for breakfast. Unfortunately, the interesting woman with the newspaper had disappeared. Ondragon cursed himself inwardly for allowing himself to be distracted by

Mr. Shamgood. But he would surely meet the enigmatic lady again soon. The confiscation of car keys meant no one could leave, and tonight at the latest he would know her name and where she came from.

Ondragon left the restaurant shortly after nine and made a short tour of the first floor of the west wing. He had seen all but one patient at breakfast and completed his list of people. Only "number twenty" apparently did not eat in the mornings or took breakfast in his room. He would check that too as soon as he could match the room numbers to the people. With a little mental effort, which he had painstakingly honed over the years, he managed to stop the *centrifuge*. For the time being.

Take it easy, Paul. This is just a fun way of passing the time, he reminded himself. *No real problem to solve. After all, I'm not here to work.* He glanced at his wristwatch. Twelve minutes until his appointment with Dr. Arthur.

Ondragon turned around in the entrance of the spa area and walked cautiously down the corridor, which branched off left to the dining room and the terrace, reaching the heart of the lodge: reception.

Sheila had her back to him. She was searching through an index card box, her green-painted fingernails clicking softly over the cards. Ondragon took the opportunity to glance through the open office door. He could see closed filing cabinets and a desk with a bluish computer screen glowing on it.

He cleared his throat loudly, and Sheila wheeled around.

"Oh, good morning, Mr. Ondragon. Is there anything I can do for you?" She looked a little breathless with shock, but her smile seemed genuine today. The fake diamond on her canine tooth sparkled in the light of the halogen spotlights hanging over the counter. Something about her appealed to Ondragon.

"Maybe I just wanted to see if my car was still there."

"Well?" Sheila tilted her head jauntily. She seemed in a better mood than yesterday.

"Hold on." He raised a hand solemnly, walked backward to the entrance, opened one of the glass doors, and peered down into the parking lot. There it stood in all its glory. His Mustang!

"All's well. Still here." Ondragon exhaled, feigning relief, and went back to the reception counter. "Now I'd be keen to know if the keys are still in their place."

"Of course!"

"Could I see? I'm a little persnickety."

"All right, if you must. Come on." Sheila turned and disappeared into the office. He followed her into the tiny room. The safe was set into the back wall and was standing open. It was a small model made by Sentry Inc. There were also no surveillance cameras in the room.

"So, here they are." Sheila took the car keys from a small box and dangled them in front of Ondragon. "Happy?"

He nodded and gave her his "nice colleague" smile. Sheila put the keys back and closed the vault door, but did not reset the combination lock. Ondragon saw the last digit of the four-digit combination. It was a seven.

They left the claustrophobic room, and Sheila looked visibly relieved when the counter was between them once more.

"I wouldn't be able to take a look at your card index, by any chance, would I?" ventured Ondragon. "I'd be awfully interested to know who else is here . . ."

"That information is strictly confidential!" Sheila placed a protective hand on the box and glared at him. So that was where the guest information was.

"No worries, I thought so. Sorry. My mistake." He walked toward the glass door but abruptly turned around. "Oh, I almost forgot. I had another little request."

"Yes?" Sheila now sounded suspicious and her posture was visibly tense.

"Who do I speak to if I want a different breakfast table?"

"Aren't you happy with it?" The brows above her girlishly made-up eyes drew together irritably. Ondragon sensed that her mood had changed definitively. His gaze fell briefly on her fingernails. She was obviously never going to give him the green light.

"No, no, the table is perfect, it's just my neighbor. I don't want to name names, but I'd like a little more privacy at dinner. I'm sure you understand."

"Of course, Mr. Ondragon. I'll pass your request on to the dining room manager." She glanced at the small clock on the counter. "It's three minutes to ten. Almost time for your appointment."

Well, that wasn't very nice. She was drawing a clear line between herself and him, an inmate at the facility. This line said: *My head doesn't need rewiring, but yours does.*

Ondragon pursed his lips. Little minx!

"And who do I complain to if I'm unhappy with the staff?"

"Me!"

Of course.

Sheila jutted her chin forward. "Your appointment!"

Capitulating, Ondragon raised both hands. "On my way. See you soon!"

Irritation churning in his stomach, he climbed the stairs to the second floor of the tower, where the offices and consulting rooms were located. He stopped in front of a door with a polished brass sign.

"Jonathan A. Arthur, PhD, MD," he read, trying to ignore the rising sense of panic in his chest. He straightened his shoulders and knocked. Hearing a friendly "Come in," he opened the door and found himself face-to-face with the man on whom he had pinned all his hopes.

Dr. Arthur rose from his comfortable swivel chair behind a massive desk and stepped with his hand outstretched toward Ondragon, who—out of habit—took a quick look around the room. No crowded bookshelves, no dusty stacks of paper, no overflowing reference library. Instead, he saw locked antique, French-polished cabinets, an archaic-looking fireplace, and an old filing cabinet on which stood a plaster sculpture of Diana, Roman goddess of the hunt, with a bow and arrow. Oil paintings hung on the walls, and the large window at the back looked out onto the lake. Ondragon smelled polish and waxed pine and relaxed a little. He walked over the hand-knotted Persian rug toward Dr. Arthur and shook his hand. The man was over a head shorter than he was, but his handshake was firm.

"Welcome, Mr. Ondragon. It's a pleasure to meet you. Please take a seat." Dr. Arthur pointed to a sterile-looking stainless steel chair that did not at all match the rest of the décor.

"I know the chair is a little unsightly. You might say it's the ugly duckling amongst my furniture," he explained in a cut-glass British accent. "But you know, I also treat a lot of people with a phobia of germs and infections. These individuals don't like to sit on upholstery or similar surfaces, and prefer more neutral objects. They would also never shake my hand like you did, Mr. Ondragon."

Ondragon looked involuntarily at his palm.

"But that's not your problem, as I know." Dr. Arthur smiled mildly.

Ondragon nodded and sat down on the chair in front of the oak desk, on which a classic green library lamp was burning. He felt a slight prickle on the back of his neck.

"I trust everything is to your satisfaction so far?" Dr. Arthur sat down as well. It was not only the man's genial manner that surprised Ondragon, his appearance was startling too. He had expected an ossified, old-school, Freudian-style psychiatrist in a bow tie and steel-rimmed glasses. Instead, the doctor of both psychotherapy and medicine wore his gray curly hair tied back in a casual ponytail, and had a fashionable musketeer beard. Although he was wearing the obligatory white coat and underneath it a jacket and tie in true English style, a single glance into his light brown, almost yellow eyes revealed that Dr. Arthur was anything but normal.

"Thank you, I feel very at home. The lodge really is very comfortable," replied Ondragon, keeping his annoyance with Sheila, Mr. Shamgood, and the outrageous *Golden Rules* to himself for the time being.

"I'm glad to hear that. Well, this first conversation is just to get the two of us acquainted with each other. I set great store by a relaxed atmosphere, as you can easily see from this building. So I would also like to keep the formalities to a minimum and call you Paul, if you don't mind."

"All right, as long as I get to call you Dr. Arthur?"

The clinic director nodded in agreement and continued, "At Cedar Creek Lodge, our aim is to eliminate all the negative influences of everyday life; that is part of the therapy. For me as a therapist, the person behind the ritualized behaviors is interesting. You, Paul, are a warrior, a modern-day knight of innovation. You're good at what you do, there's no question about that, but what we need is your raw, unprotected inner self, if you know what I mean. First you need to shed your everyday armor and become Adam again, unspoiled and pure, and then we can access the real you and free you from your fears. This is the basis of my method. I will make you free again, remove your fears, while completely renouncing what I see as the brutal method of exposure therapy. I promise you, the object of your fears will not come near you until you want it to. Not even the word will pass my lips unless that is your express wish. I will use hypnosis, the only proven tool. It helps with deeply submerged memories. Do you agree with this approach?"

Ondragon nodded.

"Good, then let's not dwell on trivialities for too long. I have already gone through and provisionally evaluated the information on your origin, childhood, and youth. The result is interesting, as you have a truly extraordinary curriculum vitae. And I must confess that I am curious to know more about you. But it is only in the course of therapy that it will become clear whether I'm right about the causes of your phobia." Dr. Arthur reached for a silver ballpoint pen. "Before I explain the planned therapy, will you allow me to ask you one question about your phobia?"

Ondragon nodded again.

"Please answer as spontaneously as you can." Dr. Arthur paused. "Paul, what color is your fear?"

Ondragon stumbled. He had not expected this. He had to think.

The yellow eyes looked at him expectantly.

"Well." He began to sweat. "I . . . I think it's something like, well, honestly . . . I have no idea." Helplessly, he shrugged his shoulders. He was uncomfortably hot and could feel sweat on his forehead. Embarrassed, he looked out the window. It wasn't going to be much fun if such a ridiculously abstract question could drive him into a corner. What would it feel like when he was really baring his soul? Was he even ready for that? He looked at his hands, and suddenly the color came into his mind. Why of all things . . . ?

He shook his head. "You know what," he said with amusement, "it's green!"

"What shade?"

Ondragon had resolved not to be more astonished than necessary, and this time he answered without hesitation, "Dark green, like pine needles." *Just like the green of the enigmatic woman's sweater.*

"Pine-needle green, hmm. How odd. Thank you, Paul." Dr. Arthur made a note, then looked up and grinned wryly. He looked like the living incarnation of Buffalo Bill. "You can rest easy, Paul. This is not a psychological test or anything like it. The methods I use are based entirely on my own studies. I have developed an independent system of evaluation that is different from any known way of working. My 'secret recipe,' so to speak, and, if I may say so in all humility, one of the reasons Cedar Creek Lodge is so successful. But now to your course of therapy." Dr. Arthur took a printed sheet from the top shelf and slid it over to Ondragon. "This afternoon, you will see Dr. Zeo. She will do an initial screening for any dissociative personality disorders. This is essential to our procedure, because we must first rule out any split personalities you might resort to. Once we have the results, all subsequent sessions will be conducted under my supervision."

Ondragon read the schedule and saw that he had no more than two hours scheduled per day. That seemed a little thin and he asked why.

"The therapy intensifies step by step. But the first week is for acclimatization. Relax, Paul, enjoy the peace and quiet. You will need strength for the battle with your anxiety."

Ondragon folded the plan twice, tucked it into the inside pocket of his jacket, and looked into the bizarrely colored eyes of his interlocutor. "May I ask you something too, Dr. Arthur?"

"Of course, go ahead." The gray-haired psychotherapist clasped his hands together on top of the desk.

Ondragon leaned forward and grabbed his armrests. "Who invented those stupid *Golden Rules*?"

CHAPTER 4

1835, Kabetogama,
fur trappers' lonely log cabin,
50 miles from Fort Frances

Smoke rose from the log cabin chimney and mixed with the haze of the dull winter day. The pale March sun had not yet been able to penetrate the dense mass of cloud. It was very quiet in the deep snow-covered forest around the clearing. Only two sets of footprints led away from the hut, one to the woodpile and the other to the privy. Otherwise, the gray snow cover lay untouched like waterlogged wool. Now and then the icy north wind hissed over the tops of the spruces, freeing them from the crushing weight of snow. The white lumps made dull thumps as they landed on the ground. It was thawing. Soon another Arctic night would descend upon the deserted land-scape, bringing with it the mysterious calls of the endless wilderness. Everything seemed peaceful. But suddenly the door of the log cabin was torn open and a man came rushing out. Groaning, he dragged himself a few steps into the clearing. He was wearing only pants and a shirt, his face sunken and feverishly red. Halfway to the privy, he paused his lurching stagger, bent over, and pressed both hands to his taut abdominal wall. There was a choppy retching as Parker vomited. Steaming, the lunch he had eaten two hours ago splattered into the gluey snow. He struggled to catch his breath as the cramps shook him.

Only when there was nothing but corrosive bile left in his stom-ach did Parker straighten up and look at his two friends, who had followed him out.

"Again," he groaned apologetically, wiping his beard with a handful of snow.

Two-Elk nodded and put his coat around Parker's quivering shoulders.

"That's not to say I didn't enjoy it," Parker added jokingly. But it didn't work. The old trapper saw the scowls of his friends grow even grimmer. He felt infinitely exhausted as Lacroix led him back to the log cabin by the arm, like he was an old man. Behind him, Two-Elk buried the vomit in the snow and urinated over the spot to keep the wolves away.

Inside, Parker sank into a chair before the fireplace. The smell of the raw animal hides and tanned pelts hanging from the ceiling beams and stacked in bales throughout the cabin soothed him. Lacroix exchanged the coat around Parker's shoulders for two wool blankets and swaddled his friend in them so tightly that only his shaggy head peeked out the top of the bundle. The French Canadian poured cold tea from a battered enamel teapot into Parker's cup and held it to his brittle lips.

"Drink, Alan. You have to have something in your stomach."

Parker swallowed the bitter liquid without protest. They had tried hot tea before, but it had ignited a veritable hellfire inside him and only exacerbated the strange fever that had spread through his body from the wound. Just like the food, he had thrown it up again.

"The beast has poisoned you." Lacroix raised a hand and waved it around Parker's nose. When he was angry, his French accent intensified. "*Tabernac!* This is not just gangrene!"

Parker was too weak to answer.

"If it doesn't improve in the next few days, we're going to have to get help."

"Where from? The quacks at Fort Frances?" Parker croaked.

"*Mais non.*" Lacroix jerked his chin toward the Chippewa man. "From his people."

Parker looked at Two-Elk, who was silently stoking the fire in the grate.

"They know what medicine to use for the . . ." Lacroix did not speak further. "*Putain de merde!* Why did we have to show up at the Walcotts' on that day, of all days, and run into that damned beast!"

"It's no use crying over spilled milk." Parker could barely breathe under the thick layer of wool. His feet ached as if they had swollen into tree trunks.

It had been a week since they had been interrogated by that smug lieutenant and buried the remains of the Walcotts. Stafford had been visibly reluctant to let them go; to him, the investigation into the murders was far from closed. Parker had sensed he did not trust them. But, after all, the Englishman knew where to find them, and so they had returned that same day to the log cabin on their hunting grounds. They were not people who liked much hurly-burly, and the people of Fort Frances would literally have mobbed them if they had heard the story. They craved any news, no matter how insignificant, and unsolved murders were a welcome change. Parker and his friends, however, shunned the noise of people; they loved the quiet of the forest.

However, the silence outside no longer seemed quite so reassuring. It seemed increasingly threatening. Although there was nothing to indicate the presence of anything other than the familiar inhabitants of the forest.

The sinister creature remained invisible; a mere memory, a shadow that lived only in Parker's restless dreams.

"I'm way too hot," he whined. Beads of sweat stood out on his forehead. "Please at least let me take off the blankets." He began to try to peel himself out of his cocoon, but Two-Elk stepped toward him and stopped him.

"No! We can only stop it if you keep the heat inside you."

"But I'm dying of heat!"

"Your body fights the fever. It is good." The Chippewa man held out a piece of the dried deer meat to him. Parker's mouth watered, his stomach gurgled longingly. He had to eat something. Despite the danger of disgorging this piece of food as well, he took it between his teeth and chewed. He had expected the usual wildly spicy taste of the air-dried delicacy, so he was all the more surprised to find that it tasted like moldy moss. Dry and brittle, it crunched between his teeth. Perhaps the dried meat was rotten. He looked more closely at the next piece, but it seemed fine. He forced himself to swallow it.

Two-Elk fed him until he had had enough.

"That'll do. Thank you, my friend. I think I'll keep it down." That's what he'd thought at dinner. They'd see.

The unfamiliar sensation of a full stomach made Parker sleepy, and a little later he nodded off gratefully in his chair. As dusk fell, silence descended on the cabin. Only the crackling of logs in the fire could be heard. Lacroix sipped a freshly brewed coffee, as black as the night outside the door, and watched the Chippewa man deftly repairing one of his snowshoes.

Both started up from their rest when suddenly a violent gust of wind banged against the hut. All the shutters shook. Startled, the fur trappers looked at the door. Howling, the wind hissed around the outer walls as if it wanted to tear the dwelling down. Then, abruptly, it stopped.

Parker blinked out of his blankets with red eyes and looked questioningly at his two friends. They had not seen a storm coming.

A muffled neighing sounded from the adjacent stable. The horses were also restless. One of them would have to see to the animals if the storm did indeed get up.

All at once they heard a dull thud above them, and they looked up at the sooty woodwork. Dust trickled into their eyes.

"There's something on the roof," Lacroix whispered.

Two-Elk reached for his knife as a long, drawn-out groan drifted in to them from the icy night.

CHAPTER 5

2009, Moose Lake,
Cedar Creek Lodge

Dr. Arthur's lecture on the *Golden Rules* was still echoing in Ondragon's ears as he went back to his room and did exactly the opposite of what the psychotherapist had advised. He got his iPhone out of the safe and logged on to the internet. There was even a connection.

You must learn to separate the important from the trivial, Paul. Use the internet and the telephone as little as possible. Let go. Trust your employees; you'll see, your business will get by without you. And don't resist the Golden Rules, *they are there for your own good.*

Pah!

Ondragon pushed Dr. Arthur's well-meaning words to the back of his mind and checked his email. He found nothing special, just confirmation from Charlize that she had contacted the Japanese, and a message from his best sales representative, Dietmar, informing him of progress in the Middle East, with the solution to a *Standard*-category problem. At Ondragon Consulting, they divided problems into four categories: *No Problem, Standard, Sherlock,* and *Magnum.* The first category they didn't deal with at all, forwarding them immediately to local detective agencies or similar contractors; the last category was reserved exclusively for him, the boss.

Ondragon turned off the cell phone, pulled out his notepad, and carefully recorded his observations from breakfast. Sussing out the structure of the CC Lodge required only *Standard* problem skills.

Once he had noted everything down, he took off his jacket, lay down on the bed, and went through everything again in his head. In the process, contrary to his usual habit, his eyes drooped closed.

Strange, thought the final part of his brain that was awake, *something about this place makes me sleepy. Is the relaxing atmosphere of the lodge already taking effect? But I've downed six espressos!*

When Ondragon awoke, he checked the time. Twelve thirty. Lunch was already underway downstairs. Groaning, he sat up. If he ate anything now, he'd be half asleep all day. So he decided to switch to sports. He didn't like hanging around, and this way he could at least get out and explore the area around the lodge.

He put on his long sweatpants, a T-shirt, and a gray hoodie. He would have liked to do some kendo, but this extravagant hobby had no place here. Ondragon locked his cell phone in the safe, and put the talisman in his pocket and a piece of gum in his mouth. He picked up the key and left the room. The hallway was empty. On the stairs he met the death metal musician.

"Hey, man, you all right?" Hatchet greeted him casually, brushing a black strand of hair out of his face with a tattooed hand. He already looked a bit fitter than he had that morning, although he was still wearing his sunglasses.

"Of course," Ondragon replied, blowing and popping a gum bubble.

"Well, have fun, man! I'm going back to bed for now."

"Sweet dreams."

"Sure thing, see you around." Hatchet shuffled away, the chains on his pants clinking softly.

Grinning, Ondragon reached the first floor and walked into the entrance hall. Sheila was on the phone, and he nodded gallantly to her. You could never give up.

Outside the lodge, the heat was sweltering; the entrance was languishing in the blazing midday sun. Ondragon cast a longing glance at the Mustang, but then followed the path leading around the lodge on the right, at a relaxed pace. The main building and outbuildings were surrounded by bushes and tall conifers that were casting patches of cool shade onto the trimmed lawn behind the lodge. Deck chairs and umbrellas lined the terrace, and some of the guests, scantily clad, were lying cultivating their skin cancers. All that was missing to make the illusion complete was a pool. No one would suspect that this facility bore more of a resemblance to an insane asylum than to a harmless hotel.

Ondragon passed the large wooden building where the employees lived. It was located around two hundred yards from the lodge and looked out over the lake, whose surface was as smooth as glass, like the gateway to another world. Not a breath of air stirred, and Ondragon could already feel the sweat running down his back. High up in the branches of the trees, birds were chirping.

I'll just go as far as the boathouse, then I'll take off a layer, he thought, and walked on down the path that meandered picturesquely along the lakeshore.

When he reached the boathouse, he was barely out of breath. His frequent exercise was paying off. Ondragon took off his sweater and knotted it around his hips. He glanced back across the water to the lodge.

"Nice view, isn't it?"

Unwillingly, he wheeled around, annoyed at his lack of alertness. Were his senses already suffering from the quiet atmosphere so much praised by the doctor? He resolved not to be lulled by it, and looked at the guy in overalls, who had now come out from behind the little building. Overalls grabbed a can of beer from a six-pack resting in the rain barrel.

"Want one?" the guy asked, holding out a cold Budweiser.

Beer drinking against the *Golden Rules*. But Ondragon did not think for long and accepted it with thanks. To hell with them!

"I'm Frank the gardener, by the way, and this is Rumsfeld." He pointed to a large, woolly dog lying as if dead on the grass in front of the small landing stage. Ondragon hadn't noticed him either, which was fortunately mutual.

"Not exactly a guard dog, is he?" He pointed at the woolly bundle. "My name is Paul Ondragon. Pete's already told me about you."

"Pete, that windbag. Has he been driveling on again?"

"No, not really." Ondragon spat out his gum and opened the can. The hiss was music to his ears. He took a big gulp of the foamy liquid. "Ah, wonderful!"

"You know, sometimes the little idiot tells bullshit scary stories. Nothing wild, but Dr. Arthur thinks it scares the guests."

"Oh, you mean the story about that mountain monster." Ondragon looked for the split peak of the mountain, thinking, but the tall trees obscured the view.

"Pah, monster! Such baloney. Only this bunch of Indians that hangs around here from time to time believes any of it. For my part, I think it's a fantasy. Total nonsense! But Pete can't help it. He's not the brightest, you see. Lives with his great-uncle in a log cabin out there in the woods, a real hillbilly. None of his family are quite right. But his father and mother are long dead. He's got a brother who's completely soft in the head." Frank put a grubby index finger to his temple and twisted it back and forth.

Ondragon wondered what he thought of the guests at the lodge.

"Dr. Arthur only employs Pete out of charity," Frank explained. "You see, the doc is a philosopher."

"More likely philanthropist."

"Huh?"

"A philanthropist, a humanitarian." Obviously, Cranky Frank was the opposite of a humanitarian, the way he was going on about Pete. Ondragon reluctantly recalled that he had judged the boy a little differently yesterday.

"Whatever. In any case, you shouldn't believe everything that little weirdo babbles on about the whole time." The ornery gardener poured the rest of his beer down his throat and belched. With the flawless poise of a construction worker, he crushed the can and tossed it into a bucket that already contained several empty tins. It clanged loudly in the summer silence. Ondragon decided to end the conversation. He finished his can, thanked Frank, and set off again. As he was walking away, he turned back to the gardener.

"Oh, hey, Frank, how far is it once around the lake?"

"Just under six miles. But after the turnoff to Mount Witiko, it gets a little rougher."

"Okay, thanks."

"Don't break any bones. Because I don't want to have to rescue you by boat! And, Mr. Ondragon, if you meet a bear, don't run away—it only provokes them!"

Ondragon waved a hand and continued walking.

Frank was right; after about five hundred yards the well-maintained trail branched off. A brown sign with the yellow lettering typical of the state park administration indicated that Mount Witiko was *12 miles* away, and the trailhead in the other direction was *5 miles*. Ondragon had seen no sign for the trailhead on his drive yesterday. It was probably hidden somewhere along the Forest Route. A third sign was nailed under the other two signposts, with the words *bear's den* painted on it in spidery letters.

Undeterred, Ondragon took the trail that hugged the shore of the lake. Bears were nothing unusual here; this was, after all, one of the largest national parks in the United States.

Gradually, he found his rhythm; although he kept on having to jump over roots or stones, his sporting ambition had been awakened. Normally, Ondragon ran his six-mile loop on the paved boardwalk between Santa Monica and Venice Beach. The course there was even with no inclines or surprises, quite different from the bumpy path that lay ahead. Forest runs were a rarity for him, because where in Los Angeles did you ever see forest? Besides, forest was nature, and nature represented an almost hostile environment for Ondragon. He had only ended up here in this remote lodge *because* it was remote, and he had a reputation to protect. The life he led meant he needed the city's garish, hard, concrete embrace, its frantic breath and its flickering, colorful lights at night. Only in the city was he invincible. Nature was nice to look at. But nice was, after all, the little brother of crappy. Although, if he remembered correctly, that was a positive thing. Now and then, he made good use of nature. It helped him dispose of certain problems—certain easily compostable problems.

Ondragon decided to engage with the unfamiliar surroundings, and after a while he even began to enjoy them a little. He felt himself breathing in harmony with his movements. The sound of the air flowing in and out of his lungs mingled with the steady trot of his steps and the melodic songs of the birds. For a while he ran along without thinking about anything in particular. That didn't happen often.

A little farther on he found the next sign marked *bear's den*. It was hanging on a dead tree. Ondragon stopped for a moment, looking in the direction it pointed. A barely discernible path led into a very dark part of the forest, disappearing between rough spruce trunks. A few roundish, mossy rocks loomed on the hillside like the stone marbles of a giant. He would explore this fork another time and would do well to ask someone about it beforehand. He wouldn't want to startle an actual bear living there in its lair.

Ondragon looked back across the lake. The lodge was no longer visible. Too many small tree-covered islands obscured the section of shore where the buildings were located. He set off again and soon reached the northern apex of the lake. The spot was marshy, and a small stream flowed quietly into the lake. Ondragon found a fallen log and in three leaps he was on the other side, where the forest welcomed him into much denser undergrowth. He could just about make out the path, a narrow passage that led between the leaves. More of a deer trail than a hiking route. Ondragon had to knock branches out of the way several times as he ran, to ensure they didn't hit him in the face. He wasn't used to these kinds of obstacles and he lost his rhythm. He stumbled and almost fell, but managed to catch himself, suppressing a curse and slowing his pace as a precaution. Just in time, because he almost tripped over the next obstacle.

Ondragon came to a stop and tilted his head to the side, frowning.

In front of him hung a huge spider's web, with a half-decayed bird of prey entangled in its threads.

Ondragon looked around questioningly. Did they have spiders that size here? Unlikely. Carefully, he reached out a finger and plucked at the threads. Spiderwebs never felt like this. It had to be yarn. But who the hell stretched twine across a path in the middle of nowhere?

Ondragon looked at the branches to which the net was attached. This was a bad joke. Like *The Blair Witch Project* or something.

But what was the bird all about, then? It certainly hadn't gotten caught in the net by itself and died there. Ondragon wrinkled his nose.

White maggots were crawling out of the half-rotten skull. Quickly, he withdrew his finger, the carcass bobbing gently in the carefully woven yarn. Sensing rather than seeing it, Ondragon suddenly felt a cloud move across the sun. The forest suddenly turned dark, even the chirping of birds fell silent. It was like a bad horror movie.

The cracking of twigs behind his back made him prick up his ears. He turned around, but could see nothing except the overgrown bushes and the narrow path.

Another crack sounded, followed by a strangely hollow knocking. As if someone was beating a tree trunk with a stick.

Someone *was* there!

"Hello!" he shouted, determined not to be taken for a ride. Whoever was playing this crude joke on him would realize they had chosen the wrong victim. Paul Ondragon was not to be messed with. "Very funny, you're a real comedian. Come on out!"

Instead of an answer, there was another crunching sound. Closer this time.

Something was coming toward him down the path. Ondragon looked around. He wouldn't be able to evade it, because of the net. Of course, he could cut across the bushes, but he had little desire to do so.

"Go on, show yourself, you joker!" he shouted threateningly.

Again, he heard a crunching sound and a furtive rustling in reply. Barely ten steps away. He glimpsed a movement between the branches. Then the hollow knocking started up again, and against his will, goose bumps spread up his back. Ondragon cursed softly. Why was he getting so flustered by this obvious prank?

Because you're having to run around in this fucking forest instead of sticking to familiar terrain. That's why!

He clenched his fists angrily. "Mark my words, I'll smash your face in if I catch you!" He was about to take a determined step toward the sound when a pungent stench of animal piss wafted toward him. Disgusted, Ondragon blew out, but noticed something else besides the acrid stench.

Something indefinably wild.

The smell became stronger, almost unbearable.

Maybe it's a bear, he thought in alarm, and the anger he had felt a moment ago at the supposed prankster abruptly disappeared.

In any event, I have to get out of here before the beast crosses my path. Ondragon didn't dither for long. He ignored the tingle on the back of his neck, saying, "Don't turn your back on that critter!" and threw himself into the brush next to the net. If he had had a machete, it would have been easy to slash his way through, but as it was, he had to flail his arms against the elastic branches that struck at his eyes and scratched his face. The absurd thought occurred to him that he must look like an out-of-control string trimmer, but now was no time for grace and style. He had to get through!

The tingle at the back of his neck had now spread to the whole of his body, and still he didn't dare turn around. He was only two arm's lengths from the path when his hoodie caught on a branch. Ondragon tugged at it like a madman until he finally freed it. Then he continued his panicked scramble. Leaves flew and branches cracked. He was behaving like a fool!

Like a frightened deer, he finally burst out onto the path; leaves in his hair and welts on his face, but only one thought burned in his brain: He had to know! Was that really a bear behind him, or was it just someone from the lodge who would later make him a laughing-stock in front of everyone? He whirled around and threw a wild look back. Something big was rumbling in the bushes from which he had just come, vibrating the braided twine net. The dead bird bobbed grotesquely back and forth—as if it had come back to life. Ondragon blinked, straining to peer through the dense foliage.

Could he see gray fur? Shaggy hair? A paw?

He blinked again . . . then turned and ran. He no longer cared about his tired limbs, rushing onward at an almost superhuman pace. The disgusting smell followed him for what seemed like an eternity. A half mile, a mile. Ondragon tore through the forest like a bolting nag, his lungs protesting and the muscles in his legs burning as if it were acid flowing through his veins instead of blood. He looked hastily around over and over again, but saw nothing.

Gradually, the path widened, and the undergrowth gave way to calf-high blueberry bushes growing on the light-dappled forest floor.

The lake to his left shone idyllically in the sunshine as if nothing had happened, and a handful of wild ducks were chattering away peacefully. Everything seemed summery and calm.

At record speed and with screeching lungs, Ondragon reached the lodge grounds. He stopped at the edge of the trimmed meadow, leaning on his thighs and struggling for breath. His sweaty joggers and T-shirt stuck to his body, and his beautiful white shoes were completely filthy.

What the hell had that been?

Ondragon couldn't believe it. He had lost his nerve. A reaction he had thought impossible. He had been in far more life-threatening situations: under fire from the Mafia, for example, or in the crosshairs of a professional killer. But that had all been in the city, on his turf. Not out in the woods! Ondragon spat. At least there were no witnesses. What would his clients say if they knew he'd run from a flea-infested North American black bear—which, mind you, he hadn't even really seen—like Forrest Gump.

Bullshit forest!

The dizziness gradually subsided, and every aching inch of his body craved water, but Ondragon was unable to move.

"Well, well, did we overdo it a bit?" a woman's voice next to him asked suddenly.

He had mud on his face, and the rest of him doubtless presented a pitiful sight, but he forced himself to look up.

It was the enigmatic woman from breakfast. She was now wearing a tight, light blue T-shirt and white linen pants. Both highlighted her dark complexion and her sensational figure. Her black eyes were looking directly at him. So directly that he felt quite different.

"Whew, yeah. It was a little tiring. Ran all around the lake." Although he had tried to strike an unconcerned tone, his voice still sounded strained.

She eyed him. "More like once through hell and back?" A dry smile appeared on her attractive face.

"If by hell you mean the forest"—he wiped his face and fingered a leaf from his forehead—"then you're right!"

"Nature lover?"

"Let me think about that for a second. Uh, no." He ventured his first smile; buddy-level. *Don't get ahead of yourself.* Slowly, he felt better and was able to sit up fully. Groaning, he stretched. "Time for a shower and a mineral water!"

The woman continued to look at him with a strangely veiled look. Her face did not betray an iota of what she was thinking.

Ondragon felt embarrassment rising inside him and was surprised. It had been a long time since he had felt embarrassed in front of a woman. He was normally a pretty smooth operator.

"I'm Paul Ondragon," he said, nipping the hint of uncertainty in the bud and holding out his hand to her.

Her hand felt surprisingly cool, probably because he was totally overheated.

"Kateri Wolfe," she said, baring flawless white teeth.

CHAPTER 6

The hoarse, almost disembodied sigh sounded again. Two-Elk had jumped up to check the bolts of the door. Now he stood in the middle of the room, blade drawn, listening. A faint grinding sound caused him to turn his gaze from the rafters back to the door. Everyone could hear snow falling from the roof to the ground outside. The rumbling above their heads came again, this time closer to the edge, and immediately after it, a dull thud right outside the door. Something heavy had fallen from the roof . . . or jumped.

The creature?

Motionless in his blankets, Parker moved only his eyes, glancing anxiously from the Chippewa man to Lacroix. The French Canadian also stood ready to spring, the barrels of both his pistols pointed at the door. He appeared calm and focused. But for a tiny moment, as fleeting as the blink of an eye, Parker saw something flare in his friend's dark eyes. And that shook him more than the ghostly sounds outside the door.

Vincent Lacroix was afraid.

Creeping horror gripped Parker and mingled with the painful pulsing in his feet, forming an ominous rhythm. The heat in the room became unbearable, and his heartbeat pounded so loudly in his ears that he barely noticed the light footsteps moving away from the log cabin outside in the snow.

Then he lost consciousness.

CHAPTER 7

2009, Moose Lake,
Cedar Creek Lodge

Kateri Wolfe's smile was difficult to interpret. Like everything else about this woman. Her inscrutable aura aroused Ondragon's curiosity. He glanced quickly at her hands, checking she wasn't wearing a wedding ring.

"How long have you been here, Mrs. Wolfe?"

"*Miss* Wolfe," she corrected him. "I've been under Dr. Arthur's care for three weeks."

Care. How that sounded.

"And I just got here last night," Ondragon bragged. It wasn't anything to be embarrassed about, after all.

"I know." She tilted her head, her jet-black hair falling over her shoulder. She looked adorable. "You're the one with the Mustang." No judgment.

"I am." Ondragon grinned.

"I'm the one with the Prius."

Oh dear.

"Are you afraid of flying?" Her voice sounded a shade softer.

"Me? Why?"

"Well, we're a long way from LA by car. It's got to be around two thousand miles."

"Oh, I see. Nah, I just felt like a bit of a road trip, wanted to let the Mustang stretch her legs. But how did you know I was from LA?"

Another inscrutable smile. "Word gets around. Fast, here."

Shamgood, Ondragon guessed. Or Sheila?

"Anyhow, I took it easy," he said. "The four days it took to get up here were kind of a little vacation." He wondered why Miss Wolfe was at Cedar Creek Lodge. She was quite clearly not one of the elite. He was sure of that. And that was what set her apart from all the other guests, why she seemed so out of place. She was neither *hip* nor *it*; she was a civilian, an outsider. But how was she paying for her stay here, then? He glanced at the silver pendant on her necklace. It was in the shape of a feather. Native American jewelry? The name Wolfe would fit with that.

"And you? Where are you from?" he tried to keep the conversation going.

"Minneapolis," she replied after a moment's hesitation.

"So almost a local?"

A nod. Shy or deliberately distant? Ondragon couldn't figure her out. Not yet. He clicked his tongue softly.

"I really need a drink. What do you say we continue our conversation over dinner tonight?" It wasn't usually his style to get to the point so quickly, but he liked this woman, and what else was there to do around here? You had to pass the time somehow. And a date was always better than trying to outrun a bear.

"Sorry, tonight I'm taking part in the horseback ride they run every second week. We ride to Mount Witiko, have a barbecue there, and we don't get back until nightfall."

An involuntary shiver ran down Ondragon's spine. Out there in the dark? He glanced briefly back at the path, which was lost among the trees.

"But there are bears in the forest. Isn't that dangerous?" he asked, half joking.

A melodious laugh was the reply. "Mr. Ondragon, you're not any kind of nature lover!"

What had been so funny about his question?

"Bears tend to avoid people. They are rather shy animals."

That's what he'd thought until a moment or two ago.

"Why don't you come with us? I'm sure there'll be a place."

Ondragon was flattered but raised his hands in refusal. "No thanks. It's not my kind of thing." It wasn't that he couldn't ride.

He could do a lot of things, but that didn't mean he liked doing them. His skills were his life insurance. But the mere thought of sitting on the back of a horse brought back unpleasant memories: Libya, at the gateway to the Sahara, fleeing a horde of murderous Bedouins who were anything but kind to Gaddafi sympathizers. Two weeks of dust and pain. An experience that almost cost him his life. That had been five years ago, and it had convinced him to hire his first field officer.

"Too bad."

Did she sound disappointed? Or was she just being polite?

"Maybe some other time," he relented. "Have fun on your ride, Miss Wolfe. Take care!" He wasn't happy about it, but he didn't want to embarrass himself after her obvious amusement, so he kept his creepy encounter across the lake to himself. Hopefully, someone from the lodge would bring a shooting iron with them on the ride into the woods.

Kateri Wolfe smiled shyly, said goodbye, and walked over to the terrace. Ondragon watched her for a moment, admiring her lithe gait, and went into the lodge through the main entrance.

Sheila was hovering low over the counter, studying a document as if she were nearsighted.

"You have your appointment with Dr. Zeo in half an hour, Mr. Ondragon!" she reminded him without looking up.

Shoot, he had forgotten all about it! Grateful for the reminder, which might even have been well-intentioned, he hurried to his room. Two minutes later, he had gotten rid of his sweaty clothes and was standing under a jet of hot water in the shower, sighing with pleasure.

As he made his way to the floor below shortly before three o'clock, he happened to glance out the stairwell window and saw Pete standing next to his Mustang. Almost tenderly, he stroked the hood, which was covered with matte film. Ondragon grinned. He had looked something like that when he and his car had first met. He resolved to talk to the bellboy again later. He might know what was going on in the forest.

The personality disorder specialist's treatment room was located at the end of the corridor on the second floor of the west wing. Ondragon entered it right on time.

Dr. Zeo was a slender woman in her forties, and her Chinese heritage gave her an alabaster attractiveness; however, she left her face deliberately unmade-up and tried to disguise her beauty with businesslike clothing. She greeted her new patient and led him to two comfortable armchairs with their backs to the window. Afternoon sunlight was falling unhindered into the phobia-friendly room, which was kept pleasantly cool by the air-conditioning system. They sat down, and unceremoniously, Dr. Zeo began going through a list of questions, ticking them off neatly. It was a test that gave Ondragon no trouble. The questions were nowhere near as abstract as Dr. Arthur's.

After they had worked through the list, the discussion became more personal, with Dr. Zeo mentioning that she had studied the CV that Ondragon had provided in advance and raising some more far-reaching questions. Ondragon readily answered those as well, although they were very intimate and he felt kind of caught out. What did his sex life have to do with therapy? And why was it important to know whether he had ever killed anyone?

"Don't worry, Mr. Ondragon." Dr. Zeo had clearly noticed his discomfort. "All this remains between us, of course. We treat all our patients' data with the utmost discretion."

"Where do you store this data, if you don't mind me asking?" He wanted to take advantage of the opportunity to find out where to get information about the inmates. When Dr. Zeo didn't answer right away, he added, "I just want to make sure that my stay here is subject to a certain level of security. My clients can't know the first thing about it, and my enemies need to know even less, if you know what I mean."

"Of course, Mr. Ondragon. But I can assure you the data is in good hands."

"Are they encrypted? Are the hard drives stored in a safe?"

Dr. Zeo nodded at both questions.

"Is the safe here in the lodge?"

"Yes, in a room with surveillance and an alarm system!"

"Good. Then I can sleep peacefully again." Ondragon leaned back.

Dr. Zeo smiled. "You're not the only security fanatic here. We have a reputation to uphold as well. Our employees are regularly checked for reliability. If something leaks out, we follow up immediately and investigate the case. If there's a security leak, it's fixed immediately."

"And by 'fixed' you mean the employee is fired?"

"Right."

"And how do you prevent this employee from potentially venting their frustration and revealing more details after the fact?"

"You don't let up, Mr. Ondragon."

"That's my job." An innocent expression on his face, he shrugged his shoulders. "I always have to keep all eventualities in mind."

"Your attention to detail is very similar to my field of activity. You should have been a psychoanalyst."

Ondragon smiled. Essentially, he was like a psychoanalyst . . . and much more besides: He was an economist, an exceptional athlete, an international-understanding expert, a waste disposal specialist, and a jack-of-all-trades rolled into one.

Dr. Zeo returned to the subject of security. "Every employee contract includes a legally binding clause that requires them not to speak about any matters concerning the lodge, even after they leave. Should they nonetheless try to monetize the insider information they have, they are reminded of their obligation by a company specially commissioned by us. In the most severe cases, we pursue criminal prosecution."

"Oh, right. What about the guests? How do you prevent them from blabbing about random events they might have come across?"

"That's why we advise you in advance to keep your most private issues to yourself and not talk about them with other guests. You've read the *Golden Rules*."

"Yep."

"Well then, you know the drill. The session is now over!" Dr. Zeo rose and pushed Ondragon toward the door.

"And when will I find out about my other personalities?" he asked with a charming smile.

"Dr. Arthur will contact you tomorrow."

Before he knew it, he was standing in the hallway, and the door was closing behind him with a friendly "Have a nice day."

Holy moly! But she hadn't exactly been pleased by his questions about security. Obviously, a sensitive topic.

Since it was only a few minutes until dinner, Ondragon decided to go directly to the dining room. He was curious to see where they had moved his table. In addition, he was ravenous.

Carlos, the headwaiter, led him to his table, which had been moved a few feet and which was now screened by a column and a wooden sculpture. Delighted, Ondragon settled into his chair and ordered a starter of clear tomato soup, an entrée of tender chicken breast in a lemon au jus with wild rice, and a small salad.

The soup arrived at the same time as Mr. Shamgood. Seeing that his table was no longer next to Ondragon's, the fashion designer frowned. He sat down primly and threw Ondragon a mortally offended look.

Ondragon rejoiced quietly, eating his soup and watching the six other guests. The Republican politician was dining in the company of the aging movie diva, the broker guy was eating his noodles in a genteel manner, and the blond preppy from Europe was hacking at a poor trout with his fish knife as if it were to blame for something. New arrivals included a distinguished-looking gentleman with reddened hands, whom Ondragon assumed was a surgeon, and a toned guy in tennis shoes with red sand stuck to them. Ondragon knew him: Thomasz Viktory, number eleven in the world rankings. He was a Czech tennis star who lived in Florida, and Ondragon wondered every time he heard the name if it was real or just a figment of his imagination.

As Ondragon was served the entrée, another exceedingly well-groomed man in his mid-forties appeared, outshining even him in matters of fashionable elegance. His dark hair was cut as precisely as if the barber had used a stencil, and his Italian suit was an absolutely perfect fit. When the man raised his glass to take a sip of mineral water through pursed lips, a gold Rolex flashed from under his left cuff. Clearly a banker.

In a calmer frame of mind than he had been in that morning, Ondragon pushed a forkful of chicken into his mouth. The guy looked like a big shot, a manager or CEO or something. Someone who could have potentially been one of his clients or known one of his clients. After all, it was entirely possible that clients of his might also frequent this facility. Being a banker, however, the guy presented no risk; as a matter of principle, Ondragon did not work for financial institutions. There was something strange about the banker though. Ondragon took a closer look. His clothes weren't quite right. But what was wrong with them?

Then it hit him. The man's suit and shirt had no buttons. What was that all about? Did he have a button phobia?

Ondragon shrugged and treated himself to a small selection of handmade petits fours for dessert, which Carlos brought to him on a silver plate. He hardly ever ate sweet things, but that was why he had skipped lunch today. While he was enjoying the delicacies, a surprisingly good-humored Charlie Bloom entered the dining room, flanked by the three models. They were engaged in an obviously amusing conversation and all sat down together at Charlie's table. It was impossible to miss how much the three young women adored the actor.

Ondragon dabbed his lips with his napkin and rose. Unfortunately, the sinister guest number twenty remained elusive. Maybe he took all his meals in his room? Or perhaps he suffered from extreme paranoia or was merely incredibly shy. Ondragon smiled. Nodding toward the headwaiter, he left the Lakeview Salon.

He glanced at his wristwatch. Eight o'clock in the evening.

He walked past the deserted reception counter and went outside. It was still pleasantly warm, and the landscape was bathed in the warm evening light. After taking a critical look at his Mustang, he strolled around the building to the terrace, where he took a seat at one of the teak tables. He wanted to enjoy the ambiance a little longer while planning his nighttime expedition to explore his surroundings.

Someone cleared their throat and he turned his gaze from the magnificent view of the lake.

"*Hej hej*, I hear you're Swedish too." The young European was standing next to him, looking at him through his Ray-Bans. He spoke in Swedish.

Ondragon briefly considered whether to answer or pretend not to have understood him. He sighed inwardly. It was turning out to be harder than he thought to keep his personal concerns to himself.

"Why Swedish *too*?" he finally replied, in English.

The little fellow held out a confident hand. "I am Johan Norrfoss, from Stockholm."

Ondragon reluctantly shook his hand. "Paul Ondragon—and no, I'm *not* Swedish."

"But Tommy, um, I mean Mr. Shamgood, said you come from Sweden."

"I guess you misunderstood, then."

Norrfoss frowned in confusion. Ondragon decided to tell him a false but plausible story; maybe that would get rid of him.

"I'm American." In fact, his US passport was fake, and he mostly used it outside of the States. "But my mother is Swedish; she emigrated in '72." He turned the tables. "Norrfoss? As in the energy empire that has nuclear power plants all over Europe?" he now asked in Swedish.

"Yes, but we're also investing in hydropower and other alternative-energy plants. My grandfather started the company in 1937, and my father took it over in '79, and since the nineties we've been a public company, expanding from Scandinavia to the rest of Europe." Norrfoss rattled off the company's history as if it had been beaten into him.

Ondragon nodded. Norrfoss AB was known for running outdated reactors throughout Europe and calling that environmentally friendly. The reactors were a license to print money though, no matter what safety risk they posed. The Norrfoss family must be incredibly rich. Ondragon hoped the nuclear lobby would never ask him for help.

"It's pretty boring here, isn't it?" Norrfoss yawned as if to emphasize his point. "I'd much rather have gone to Cirque Lodge in Utah;

it's a nicer area and the guests are hipper. This is just like home, isn't it? Forest, nothing but fucking forest." He huffed disparagingly. "I told my old man I'd rather go to Utah, but he stuck me in here anyway. He told me to get my problem under control or he'd disinherit me. The old fart's always interfering; it sucks!"

Just as he had suspected: the rich, spoiled son of a magnate. And suddenly things weren't working out the way he wanted. Ondragon stifled a snide grin.

"And you're here of your own free will?"

"Depends on how you look at it," Ondragon countered, not yet willing to deepen the conversation.

Norrfoss nodded as if he understood, pulled a silver cigarette case with a diamond monogram out of his pants pocket with two fingers, and lit up a Lucky Strike—every movement studiedly casual.

"Want one?" He held out the open case, but Ondragon shook his head.

"No, thanks, I don't smoke. And I'd appreciate it if you didn't smoke around me. After all, I'm sitting out here to enjoy the fresh air. Plus, you're blocking the sun."

"Oh, I beg your pardon, I didn't mean to bother you. I just wanted to say hello to a fellow countryman. I wish you a pleasant stay, Mr. Ondragon. *Hej då.*"

The ironic undertone in his voice was not lost on Ondragon. When the snooty-nosed upstart was out of sight, he leaned back irritably and closed his eyes. He was accustomed to not being liked by everyone, but if he went on being that rude, he would soon have more enemies than friends among the guests.

CHAPTER 8

2009, Moose Lake,
Cedar Creek Lodge

With a mini diode flashlight and a special tool that he always carried in his pocket, Ondragon set out. It was shortly before four in the morning. At this time, the last night owls were usually asleep and the early risers were still in their beds.

The hallways and staircase were dark and quiet. Ondragon wore a dark T-shirt and his black cotton pajama pants. He walked barefoot. That was quietest, and if he was caught, he could claim he was sleepwalking.

He reached the lobby and listened for a moment. The moon shone through the glass of the front door, casting a square of silver light onto the green carpet. From its lofty perch above the fireplace, the empty eye sockets of the moose skull gawked at him.

"Don't tell anyone, buddy," he whispered to the skeletal ungulate, and slid silently behind the counter. Sheila had left everything neat and tidy. The card index was nowhere to be seen and the drawers were locked.

Ondragon pulled out his lockpick collection and opened drawer after drawer. He found a calendar that contained only abbreviations, a small cashbox, writing materials, blank forms, a flashlight, paper clips, hole punches, and a couple of low-carb bars. The usual office stuff, nothing of any use. He locked the drawers again and turned toward the office door. It took him less than half a minute to open the lock, and he entered the room. He left the door behind him ajar, listened again, and then went over to the safe. He looked at the combination lock. The last digit of the combination had been seven, so all he had to do was figure out the first three. He fished a tiny stethoscope-like device out of his pants pocket, stuck one end of the cord in his ear, and placed the other on the cold metal of the safe door. He began turning the combination lock. Fifteen minutes later, the door opened.

"Sentry, my friend, I knew we'd get along!" Ondragon shone a light inside the safe. He found the card index, a bunch of keys, a small aluminum case containing all the guest cell phones, and the box with the car keys. "Bingo!"

First, he took a look at the card index. The cards were arranged alphabetically and had letter codes as titles. At first glance, they meant nothing to him. Ondragon set the box down, took the set of keys from the safe, and slipped out of the room to the reception counter. Carefully, he opened one of the drawers again, grabbed the calendar, and went back to the office. The flashlight between his teeth, he took photos of the calendar and index cards on his smartphone. He would match the abbreviations and time periods later. ON-1, he saw right away, was undoubtedly the abbreviation for him, WO-18 for Miss Wolfe, and SH-2 for Mr. Shamgood. Unfortunately, nothing was noted on the cards about the reasons for their stays. So Dr. Zeo was right; the more sensitive data was kept under lock and key somewhere else. But for now, he had the most important things: the names and addresses of all the guests. He could already do a lot with that.

He put the card index back in the safe, hesitated, and then took out the box of car keys. The lid opened with a soft scraping sound. Four sets of keys gleamed in the white light: the one for the Mustang, the one for Miss Wolfe's Prius, one for a Chrysler, and one for a Ford. Those were almost certainly the two state-of-the-art SUVs parked in the lot. Who they belonged to would be easy to figure out.

A noise caught Ondragon's attention. He quickly turned off the light. Had he heard footsteps? Not inside the building, outside.

He remained motionless but heard nothing else. Quietly, he slid the box back into the safe and reset the combination, leaving everything as he had found it. After all, he didn't want Sheila to suspect anything.

Just as he was putting the calendar back in the drawer, another sound reached his ears. A scraping sound. And it was definitely coming from outside. Someone was at the front door. Ondragon quickly closed the drawer, crouched down, and crept around the counter. For a few moments he watched the glass square in the upper half of the door. Nothing stirred. The *centrifuge* was running.

The excursion group and their horses had long since returned, Ondragon had seen them. So it couldn't be one of them. Maybe it was a branch that had been blown against the wall by the wind. But were there even trees on this side of the building? Ondragon tried to remember. The scraping sounded again. This time right by the door.

Huddled in the shadow of the counter, he fixed his gaze on the square illuminated by the moonlight. In spite of himself, he broke out in a sweat. How many times was that today? He couldn't believe how this place was putting him off his stride. Maybe he should rethink the whole thing.

A shadow appeared in the square, as fast as lightning. A groan rang out, and the door shook once, briefly and violently. Adrenaline shot through Ondragon's veins, and he ducked deeper behind the counter. What the hell was going on here?

Then everything went quiet again. Controlling his breathing, Ondragon waited. Was it a bear? Or a wounded man who needed help?

Slowly, he edged out of his hiding place and felt his way along the wall toward the entrance. He stopped by the door and listened. He thought he could hear faint breathing. A shiver began to creep down his spine, but Ondragon focused on keeping cool. What kind of threat could there be out there? A bear was just an animal, and a wounded man was hardly dangerous. He stepped over to the glass square and looked out.

Of course, there was nothing to see there except the usual shadows of the night. The steps up to the entrance were empty, as was the path down to the parking lot. In the moonlight, Ondragon could make out the individual cars. Nothing was stirring among the trees around the parking lot. He pushed the door. It was locked. The adrenaline in his bloodstream abated. He realized his breath was misting up the cold window and wiped the spot. He didn't want to leave a mark. He took one last look out into the darkness and turned away, shrugging his shoulders. It had probably just been his overstretched nerves. The afternoon's incident had not exactly helped him to achieve inner calm.

Paul Eckbert, you're getting old. You're acting more and more paranoid!

With the door behind him, he left the lobby. In the hallway leading to the recreation rooms, he stopped abruptly. There was a light! Earlier, everything had been dark. Ondragon crept toward the reddish glow emanating from the lounge and lighting the hallway. Reaching the door, he peered through the crack.

In the cozy seating area next to the bar, Hatchet sat in the light of a Tiffany lamp, gleefully devouring a huge plate of cheese-topped fries. Ondragon's mouth watered at the smell. French fries were one of his few vices. He had no idea why, but they triggered all the receptors in his body. As if by magic, the smell drew him into the lounge. He opened the door, trying to look sleepy.

Hatchet lifted his head from his food. He was wearing sunglasses, so Ondragon couldn't tell what the guy was thinking.

"Hey, man! Can't you sleep either? Come on in!" the death metal musician said with his mouth full. "Want some fries too?" Hatchet held out his plate to Ondragon, who sat down opposite him in one of the armchairs.

Ondragon dug in. "Hmm, delicious!"

"I'm always starving hungry at night. The guys in the kitchen know about it and they always leave something for me. Into the microwave and it's done!" He grabbed a french fry off the plate and put it in his mouth. Strings of cheese stuck to his carefully styled goatee. "Hatchet." He held out a greasy hand to Ondragon.

"Paul." Ondragon shook it.

"Cool car."

"Thanks." If he'd known the car would attract so much attention, he would have come in his company car, a slightly less conspicuous Dodge Magnum. He took another fry.

Thanks to his internet research, he already knew quite a bit about Hatchet. He came from Detroit, the son of a working-class family with many children, and had formed a garage band with his buddies in his youth. The usual. In 2002, they had arrived on the death metal scene with a song about 9/11 and got their first record deal. In 2003, the first million trickled in. Hatchet was the lead singer of the pack of unwashed men, playing electric guitar, grunting his incomprehensible lyrics into the mic, and getting up to antics on stage—splashing fake blood around or throwing himself into the audience. A year ago, however, he had injured himself badly in the process. Broken his jaw. Since then, he had not given a concert. "Health problems" was what it said on the band's official website.

"In showbiz too?" asked Hatchet between bites.

"Management consulting."

A grunt came in response.

When the plate was empty, Mr. Evil took a can of beer out of a threadbare pocket and leaned back. Ondragon looked at the can.

"I know, we're not supposed to, but I do it anyway. Pete's a little rocker, always brings me a six-pack from the village. I drink it on the sly; fuck the *Golden Rules!*" He popped the can, drank it down in one go, and sighed loudly. "It's no fun around here without beer. It's a total drag. There's not even a TV. Except for eating, sleeping, and . . . well, fucking's not allowed either. There aren't enough chicks with tits worth looking at here anyhow. Either they don't have any or they're over sixty." He twisted his mouth into a you-know-what-I-mean grin. He kind of reminded Ondragon of the guitarist from Faith No More. No sooner had he thought of that than Jim Martin was singing in his ear: *I'm easyyyy, I'm easy like a Sunday moooorning!*

"And I still have all my time to do. Gee, it's gonna be great," he groaned. The idea really wasn't all that appealing.

"Well, I'll be out of here in a little over a week. Doc fixed me up." Hatchet grinned.

"Congratulations!"

"Was afraid of crowds. Since my accident, I've hardly dared go on stage."

Ondragon was amazed at the musician's openness and let him continue talking.

"It took a real bad toll on me. Not only the pain. The fear too. You know, man," he said, raising both hands and clenching them into claws, "the fear gets to you. Couldn't even go out on the street in the end."

"I see. That's bad."

"CC Lodge was my last resort."

Mine too, Ondragon thought, feeling uneasy.

"But Dr. Arthur is cool. He's got some serious skills."

Ondragon gave an exaggerated yawn and stretched. "No offense, buddy, but I think I'm going back to bed. Need to get some sleep." He stood up swiftly; there was no way he was going to answer questions about what he was doing here. He thanked Hatchet for the midnight snack and left the lounge. A short time later, lying in bed, he switched off the *centrifuge*.

CHAPTER 9

1835, Kabetogama,
fur trappers' lonely log cabin

When Parker regained consciousness, he was looking into the face of Two-Elk. The man had a hand on his forehead.

"Cold," he stated with an enigmatic look.

Parker rolled his aching eyes toward the window. The shutters were open, and sunlight was streaming in. Had he slept that long? In any case, he had had a frightening dream. He had been standing in the Walcotts' cabin amid their mangled bodies, but strangely enough, it had not made him nauseous. On the contrary, his stomach had growled yearningly.

"Is the fever gone?" he heard Lacroix ask. His eyes wandered over to the French Canadian. He was sitting at the table, eating pemmican with rusks.

"Want to eat too," came leadenly from Parker's lips.

Two-Elk picked up a serving of pemmican from the table. "The fever is still in him. It won't stop until—"

"Hungry!" Parker tugged at his blankets indignantly. He was still terribly hot, as if he were sitting in hell drinking firewater with the devil himself, but the hunger was even stronger than the thirst.

Two-Elk put the pemmican to his mouth, but Parker shook his head.

"Don't want." *Why am I talking like a little kid?* he thought, croaking, "Fresh. Any fresh meat?" *Hungry! I am so hungry!*

Two-Elk shook his head, and Parker caught the look he gave Lacroix. His discomfort awoke anew, growing with each painful throb in his shoulder and his feet. Damnation, if only it weren't so hot, he could concentrate!

"What happened last night?"

Lacroix put down his knife and stroked his beard with his hand.

"He was there," Two-Elk said, "I saw his trail. It leads far into the forest."

"He's coming for me," Parker whispered, looking at Lacroix, who avoided his gaze. Despite his pain-clouded mind, he could sense that his friends were uneasy. "You must go! Leave me here and go to Fort Frances. Preferably today! I am a danger to you. If you stay with me, then . . . I . . . he wants only me. Not you. Leave me here. I am lost in any event."

"*Merde!* What nonsense. We won't let you down!" Lacroix glowered at him. "What do you think of us? Of course we will help you."

"How, damn it?" The heat and the hunger were driving Parker almost crazy.

"Two-Elk is going to fetch help," Lacroix said calmly. "He has already packed his things. He will ride out to find the people of his tribe. There will be someone who knows what to do."

"Really? If you think magic will save me, then . . ."

"Stay strong, my brother, fight the ice in your heart until I return. I will find help, I promise. Wendigo is powerful, but not invincible." Two-Elk put a hand on his shoulder for a moment. Then he packed his saddlebags and weapons, said a silent goodbye, and left the log cabin. In the doorway, he glanced briefly at the tuft of white down he had pinned to the doorframe before stepping out into the cold.

Parker groaned as the door closed behind the Chippewa. The pain was threatening to overwhelm him again, and it took him a while to regain his senses.

"Do I get something to eat now?" he asked Lacroix in a weak voice.

The French Canadian nodded and handed him some pemmican. Only with difficulty did Parker manage to choke down the mash. Oddly, it tasted like dusty moss, as everything else did. When he had finished, he leaned back, exhausted, and closed his burning eyes.

Lacroix, meanwhile, unwrapped him from the blankets to change the bandage on his shoulder, but stopped abruptly.

Parker heard Lacroix draw in air sharply and raised his heavy eyelids.

"What's wrong?" He followed his friend's gaze, which was fixed on his feet, and . . .

Oh God! No. It couldn't be!

CHAPTER 10

2009, Moose Lake,
Cedar Creek Lodge

Before breakfast, Ondragon started up the *centrifuge* again, pulled out his cell phone, looked at the pictures from last night, and entered the names of all the guests and all the other information into his notepad, arranged by room number. He was pleased to see that all of his estimates had been correct.

The slimy broker guy was in fact a real estate agent for luxury apartments. Harvey Lyme, 44, from NYC. He was in room 18.

The elderly Republican gentleman was not only a politician, he even had a term as governor of Oregon to his credit; Wilbur Crane, 75, who lived in Portland and was now occupying room 3.

The fat movie diva's name was Lydia Burlwood, 65, and she still had an address in Beverly Hills. She was residing in room 11, one of the four suites available at the CC Lodge.

The Latino's name was Enrique Souza, and finally the penny dropped for Ondragon. It was that singer from LA who had stormed the charts in recent years, scoring a few hits. Every teenage girl's wet dream. He was in room 13.

The man with the red hands was indeed a surgeon. Mikhail Petrovsk, 51, Russian, worked at the Saint Francis Memorial Hospital in downtown San Francisco. He owned one of the SUVs whose keys Ondragon had found in the safe.

He read on, and paused for a moment. Mr. Terry M. Stuart, ACB consultant, 42, from London. Room 6. Was this guy in his line of work after all? But a few turns of the *centrifuge* fed him the missing information. ACB was, of course, an abbreviation for All Credit Bank and the guy was a British investment banker. One of those unscrupulous sharks who were to blame for the economic crisis. That was probably why he called himself a *consultant,* to avoid hostility from any citizens who might have been cheated out of their fortunes by the speculation of the banks.

Ondragon left some space after the names and room numbers of all the guests to allow him to add the particular medical reason the individuals were staying at Cedar Creek Lodge.

The cryptic abbreviations SH-2, LY-3, PE-3, BL-1, NO-1, BU-4, ON-1, HA-1, VI-2, WO-18, etc. were easy to interpret: The letters were the first two letters of the last names and the numbers indicated the number of visits to the CC Lodge. A ridiculously simple code. According to this, the three models and Mrs. Burlwood, with four stays, were regulars. Mr. Shamgood was here for the second time, as was Mr. Viktory. Lyme and Petrovsk had three stays to their credit. All of the rest, including Hatchet, Norrfoss, Crane, Charlie Bloom, Souza, and himself, were making use of the facility for the first time. The phantom with the abbreviation zero zero-6, or OO-6, who had no name or place of residence and was aptly placed in room 20, had the high score, with six visits . . .

. . . if it weren't for Miss Kateri Meoquanee Wolfe. 31 years old, biologist. Room 17.

Ondragon was surprised by her unusual middle name. But the number made him swallow involuntarily.

WO-18!

That would mean she had been here eighteen times.

He had to get to the bottom of it. And he had to do it immediately!

In the hallway to the Lakeview Salon, he met Pete, the bellboy. He was carrying a wicker basket and smirking a little suspiciously.

"Good morning, Mr. *On Draegen*! Settled in?"

Ondragon had to grin at the boy's good-natured manner. He couldn't help it; somehow he liked him. So he forgave him for mispronouncing his name, replying, "Hi, Pete, where are you going?" He pointed to the basket, which made Pete look like an oversized Little Red Riding Hood.

"I'm going to the woods to pick mushrooms. Porcini and chanterelles and stuff, you know. The chef sent me. He wants to make something special with them tonight. Steak with porcini, I think."

"Hmm, sounds good. Good luck with the search." Hopefully, the little weirdo knew what he was doing with fungi—the nearest hospital was over sixty miles away! Besides, there was that bear running around. He wondered if he should warn Pete. Never mind, a real hillbilly never left home without a gun anyway.

"Hey, Pete," he called after the boy, "it'd be nice if you'd check on my car and make sure everything's okay there, yeah?"

"Of course, Mr. *On Draegen,* you can count on me. See ya." Pete tapped his red baseball cap and waddled away.

A short while later, Ondragon reached the breakfast room and saw Miss Wolfe sitting at her table by the window. She was reading the *Star Tribune.* He approached her.

"Good morning, Miss Wolfe."

She lowered the newspaper. "Oh, good morning, Mr. Ondragon." The enigmatic smile appeared on her lips.

"How was the horseback ride and barbecue?"

"Good." She looked at him for a moment, then pointed to the vacant chair. "Would you like to join me?"

"Gladly." He had hoped she would ask and took a seat opposite her.

Carlos brought him his espresso and porridge and winked conspiratorially at him as Miss Wolfe folded up her newspaper. Then the headwaiter went back to his position next to the entrance, from where he kept a hawklike eye on everything.

Kateri Wolfe leaned forward and looked at the oatmeal with amusement. "Diet?"

"No, I eat it every morning."

"Ugh. Really?"

Ondragon told her about his Swedish heritage. That seemed to convince her.

"What about you? What are your hidden roots, Miss Wolfe?"

"Please, do call me Kateri; everything else is so awkward."

"All right. Then the same goes for you. I'm Paul."

Again, she smiled. "To return to my roots, Paul. As you can easily see, I have Indigenous blood in my veins. More specifically, Ojibwe blood. My parents were both members of this tribe, which was also known as Chippewa in the past."

"Why do you say your parents *were* members of the tribe? Did they leave?"

"No. They died in an accident when I was thirteen."

"Oh, I'm sorry." Silently, Ondragon cursed his talent for always putting his finger on the most sensitive points. "So you're a bona fide Native American?" Actually, he didn't give a damn about political correctness, but he didn't want to put his foot in his mouth again; besides, as the son of a diplomat, the art of civilized conversation had been drilled into him from an early age. And it was like riding a bike; you never forgot.

"You're welcome to call me Indian if you like." Mischievously, Kateri's black eyes flashed. "I don't have the slightest problem with that."

"And do you have an Indian name too?" he asked, even though he already knew.

"Yes: Meoquanee. It means, 'wears red.' My parents gave me the name because when I was a little girl, I cut a rabbit's throat and got covered in blood from top to bottom."

Ondragon raised his eyebrows. Rabbit? Cut its throat? This woman was in no way a meek little lamb. It was a subliminal reminder that he wasn't on vacation here; he was in a psychiatric hospital.

"Sorry, I didn't mean to spoil your appetite, Paul."

Ondragon shook off his unease and went on eating his porridge. The next step now would have been to inquire about the reason for her stay, but he refrained and dodged to another question.

"What do you actually do for a living?"

"I'm a biologist at the University of Minnesota in Minneapolis. Together with some colleagues, I'm researching a drug to counter the deadly consequences of oxygen deprivation in cases of high blood loss—that is, when people are bleeding to death. We're studying the hibernation of the chipmunk, which is native to this area. Its blood oxygen level is extremely low during the long sleep, and yet it survives. We want to find out how this effect could be applied to human medicine. You know, most patients don't necessarily die from blood loss itself, but from the lack of oxygen that results from the loss. If you could compensate for that, it would save the lives of a lot of people who would otherwise have died in surgery, in accidents, or from being shot. "

"That sounds interesting. Do you like doing research?"

"Yes, it's kind of my heritage. My parents were both scientists. The apple just doesn't fall far from the tree." She smiled self-consciously. "And what do you do, if you don't mind me asking?"

"I have a consulting firm, Ondragon Consulting. We, my staff and I, advise business people and companies around the world."

"Ah, like the management consultants at McKinsey."

Ondragon hesitated. Should he now play the "program" of his false identity for Miss Wolfe? Or did he dare tell her more about himself? He decided in favor of the "program"; he didn't really know the woman well enough yet.

"Sort of. I started at McKinsey. After I graduated from Harvard, I got a job in Düsseldorf and moved to Germany." The Germany part was true, at least; at the time, he had wanted to know what life was like in the country his father had represented as an ambassador. He didn't tell Kateri he had completed a degree in politics while working on his MBA at Harvard. That would just have been showing off.

Miss Wolfe tilted her head. "Why didn't you go back to Sweden? You grew up there, didn't you?"

Ondragon hesitated. Now he had moved a little too fast. He had been speaking to her all this time with a Swedish accent, as he had with Norrfoss and Shamgood. But that had been a cover. He looked into Kateri's fine and handsome face. She didn't give the impression that she was going to gossip about everything at the first opportunity. There seemed to be an invisible line dividing her from the other lunatics here. He had sensed it the first moment he had seen her.

It was totally dumb, but that was exactly why he trusted her. So he continued to tell about himself, moving closer to the truth than he had originally intended.

"My father was a German diplomat. He met my mother when he worked at the embassy in Stockholm. I was born there, but my father wanted me to be German, so I got a German passport. After Stockholm, my father was posted to other missions. My mother and I went with him—a new place every three years. So I'm a diplomat's child—I grew up in many different countries and cities: Tehran, Nairobi, Cairo, Bangkok, Tokyo."

"It all sounds very exciting."

Yes, Ondragon thought, *it did*, but it had also left him without a real home. He was a man without roots. But for once, he didn't blame his father for that. He had turned him into a freak, but that wasn't his fault! Ondragon forced his surging feelings aside. Miss Wolfe didn't need to know about all that.

Meanwhile, Kateri was pushing a strand of hair behind her ear. She looked interested. "My parents used to take me on their research trips too. That was exciting. I saw many countries and had some great adventures . . . until the accident." She lowered her eyes and a shadow as dark as a raven passed over her face. After a while, she looked up again. "Which is your favorite country?"

"Definitely Japan. It's my second home after the USA. I tried Germany, but it didn't work out. The people there are too . . . how do I put it, not crazy enough."

"And the Japanese are better at being crazy?"

"Oh yes! The Japanese are the craziest people I know."

"Then why don't you live in Japan?"

"The USA is a better fit for my company. Japan and Germany have too many constraints. But I visit Japan every now and then to see my friends there. I don't often go to Germany." In fact, the last time he had seen his parents was sixteen years ago. That was when his father officially left the service and moved to Berlin permanently with his mother.

"Don't you miss your parents?"

"No." Ondragon tilted his head pensively, listening to his thoughts. He hadn't talked about his parents in a long time. Perhaps it would do him good to get off the beaten track for a moment. Of course, he would keep it innocuous. You couldn't be too careful, and his habits had kept him safe.

"You should know that I don't have the best relationship with my father," he relented. "It's your typical father-and-son kind of thing. But my mother—now, she was pretty cool for a member of her generation. She was a soldier in the Swedish army and a passionate cross-country skier. I often went to Sweden with her—more often than I went to Germany with my father—mostly in the winter, so she could train there. In 1976, she won the gold medal at the Innsbruck Olympic Games. I was nine at the time and was allowed to be there with my grandparents. That was a great moment. I was very proud of her."

"I'm sure you were." All of a sudden, Kateri Wolfe seemed miles away and deeply sad. Only after a few minutes did she come back to herself.

"I'd very much like to hear more of your story, Paul. But I'm afraid I have to go to my session with Dr. Arthur now." She glanced at her watch and rose. "Will I see you for lunch?"

Ondragon nodded and stood up too, looking thoughtfully after Kateri Wolfe. The feeling that this woman carried a dark abyss within her was stronger than ever.

Out of nowhere, Carlos appeared by the table. "Bravo," he said softly. "No one has ever done that before."

"What?"

"Sat at the table with Miss Wolfe."

Ondragon looked at the headwaiter, amazed.

"She's special, you should know that."

"What do you mean?"

"I'm not really supposed to talk about the guests, but I think Miss Wolfe is an exception." Carlos lowered his voice yet further and glanced around briefly. No one seemed interested in their conversation, except Mr. Shamgood, who was staring over at them, but sitting too far away to hear anything.

Carlos turned back to Ondragon. "Miss Wolfe comes here twice a year. She's kind of part of the place. Dr. Arthur is sort of her mentor. He's been taking care of her since she was an orphan. He was close friends with her parents."

"What happened to them?"

Carlos looked around again.

"A plane crash over the Canadian wilderness, in the middle of winter. And little Kateri was there, she was the only one to survive. Her parents were piloting the Cessna. The plane belonged to the family. They were on their way to a research station in the Arctic. After the crash, they weren't found for five weeks."

Ondragon whistled through his teeth. "How did she survive, alone in the ice?"

Carlos raised his shoulders. "Maybe a miracle? I don't know. They don't talk about it here at the lodge. But it must all have been very traumatic for Miss Wolfe. That's why she's here so often. Dr. Arthur treats her at his own expense. Anyway, she is usually very reserved and never really has any contact with the guests. Sure, one or two have tried to get their knees under the table. She is very good-looking. But no one has ever succeeded. Except you!" He looked at Ondragon approvingly. "Make the most of it!" With these words, Carlos straightened up and walked over to Mr. Shamgood, who had been waving at him determinedly for several minutes.

Ondragon left the dining room, went upstairs to his room, lay down on the bed, put his earphones in, and thought about the strange Kateri Wolfe while the relaxed voice of Ziggy Marley sang about "Tomorrow People."

Just before eleven o'clock, he set off up the "tower." He waited a few moments outside Dr. Arthur's room, until the big hand of his watch was exactly at twelve. But just as he was about to knock, the door opened and Kateri stepped out. She looked at him inscrutably, stepped back to let him pass, and closed the door behind him before he could say anything.

Dr. Arthur was typing on his laptop, which was on the desk in front of him, and soon looked up to greet his next patient.

Ondragon once more took a seat in the phobic-friendly chair.

"Before we get started," he said, beating the doctor to the punch, "might I be able to see a list of the employees here?"

Dr. Arthur flipped the laptop shut and regarded him with amusement.

"Why are you laughing?" asked Ondragon. There was something about the psychotherapist that unsettled him. And it wasn't just those yellow eyes.

"I'm not laughing. I was just expecting you to ask yesterday, Paul."

"You were?"

Dr. Arthur nodded. "You forget that I am already acquainted with your pathological compulsion to examine everything down to the last detail."

"I'm not a control freak, if that's what you mean."

"No, I don't mean that. On the contrary, it's an outstanding skill of yours, and in this case I'm going to make an exception and give you the list."

Ondragon said nothing, surprised.

"Provided, of course, that you keep the information to yourself. But I think I can count on you for that, can't I?"

"Of course."

"That would be best. Here's the list." Dr. Arthur pulled a sheet of paper from the drawer and handed it to him. "After all, I want your therapy to be successful. Part of that is making sure you feel comfortable here. Will this list help with that?"

"Absolutely. Thank you very much." Ondragon folded up the sheet and put it in the inside pocket of his jacket.

"Then we can begin our first therapeutic conversation." Dr. Arthur pulled out his silver ballpoint pen. "Dr. Zeo examined you yesterday and concluded that you have no personality disorders whatsoever. Congratulations, Paul, you are yourself! Not many of my patients can say that about themselves."

Dr. Arthur's humor really took some getting used to, but it made Ondragon smile.

"At the outset, I would like to mention that I find it admirable that you are able to manage and live with this particular fear. It's truly amazing how far you've come with it. I imagine it was especially difficult in college."

"Well, I've always had someone to help me. And these days, my assistant prepares everything for me and tells my clients what form they need to send information in." *Charlize Tanaka is worth her weight in gold in that regard too*, Ondragon thought. He raised both his hands. "It's all just a matter of organization."

"The life of a neurotic is one hundred and ten percent organization! But woe betide you if something doesn't go as planned. Are you spontaneous, Paul? Can you handle unexpected deviations from your daily routine?"

"I think so. At least I don't immediately go berserk if something in my plan changes—and often enough, it does. I actually consider myself to be quite flexible. If I wasn't, I couldn't do my job."

"You don't have to defend yourself, Paul. You are here so that I can help you, and to do that I have to ask you questions. They are solely for the purpose of assessment and are not intended as a reproach. Your defensive reaction is understandable. You need to protect yourself in your world, but not here with me. You have to be honest with me, otherwise we'll go around in circles and not get to the core of your fear."

"I see. I'll make an effort."

"All right, Paul. I want you to close your eyes now and think of the color of your fear."

Ondragon relaxed, put his hands in his lap, and closed his eyes. Pine green arose in his mind. Magical, destructive, revolting! Immediately, he felt the familiar mixture of fear, hatred, and nausea.

"Now tell me—off the top of your head—who is to blame for your anxiety?"

"My father!" Ondragon didn't have to think long.

"Hmm-hm. And why do you think that?"

While he was telling Dr. Arthur how his father had been a closet sadist, something strange happened to Paul Eckbert Ondragon: He began to shed his initial distrust and, for the first time in his life, talked openly with another person about his relationship with his father.

When the session came to an end, Ondragon felt that he had found the right place at last.

Dr. Arthur seemed to sense this and smiled his jovial Buffalo Bill smile. "I think we've made a good start." He rose, and Ondragon did likewise.

"You are a very rational person, Paul, no-nonsense and firmly anchored in this world. That's good; you're not buzzing around in an imaginary universe you've constructed for yourself. We've already been able to extract one of the root causes of your phobia, the problematic relationship with your father, and we will bring the others to light with the help of hypnosis. I am confident we will resolve your problem quite quickly. Until then"—Dr. Arthur spread his arms—"enjoy your stay! And if there's anything else you need, let me or the staff know. We'll take care of it."

"Yes, thank you, I—"

Ondragon was interrupted by a knock at the door.

Dr. Arthur grimaced. "Well, that's . . . I'm sorry, Paul. I—" Before he could say anything else, the door flew open and an excited Sheila rushed into the room.

"Sheila. You know you're not to interrupt a session under any circumstances. Did you forget?" Dr. Arthur looked seriously annoyed, and Ondragon too felt disturbed by the receptionist. Until he saw that something was wrong. Sheila was as white as a sheet.

"Dr. Arthur. I'm sorry, but . . ." She took a breath. "It's about Pete."

"What has he done now?" Impatience was written all over Dr. Arthur's face.

"He found a body in the woods!"

CHAPTER 11

1835, Kabetogama,
fur trappers' lonely log cabin

Merde!"

Lacroix had gone pale, his voice a mere whisper. *"Merde, merde!"*

He stared down at Parker's feet. They were swollen into a misshapen gray mass and were as big as pumpkins. The skin around his ankles was bulging and translucent, as if it was about to burst open.

Parker groaned and tried to move his feet, but the pain was too much. How would he ever be able to walk again with those monstrous feet? Horrified, he howled and bit his fist.

Lacroix was the first to regain his composure. He bent down and quickly wrapped soft skins around the toeless stumps. Both men were thinking the same thing: the tracks in the snow outside the cabin! They had looked just like Parker's feet.

"I should stick them in the ice outside and maybe the swelling will go down," the old trapper said.

"No, Two-Elk said, no matter what, no cold! You absolutely have to stay in the warmth."

Resignedly, Parker lowered his chin to his chest. He would probably perish in here anyway . . . *or else he'll come back and get me!*

"Right, now I'll take a look at your wound." Lacroix carefully loosened the crusted bandage, and Parker braced himself for the next outcry from his friend. But nothing of the sort happened. Instead, Lacroix cleaned the wound and applied the ointment with practiced movements.

Parker turned his head and risked a glance. The bite did not look so bad. No bloody, festering crater. Even the edges were less swollen and were healing astonishingly cleanly. And the wound no longer smelled of pus. But Parker could not allow himself to feel relief. He knew it was inside of him, and nothing in the world could drive it out of his body. He tried not to think about what would happen once it really set in.

He could tell from Lacroix's somber expression that the same thought was going through his mind, and he put out a shaky hand and clasped his friend's arm.

"When the time comes, you'll go, right?"

Lacroix avoided his eye and instead busied himself applying a fresh bandage. When he was finished, he finally looked up and said, "I'm not leaving until you're well again."

You stubborn, pigheaded fellow, Parker thought, giving a weak smile. It did him good to know that his friend would stay with him.

Toward evening, Lacroix went outside, checked on the adjacent stable, and barricaded the windows. There was a hint of spring in the air, and fleeting wisps of clouds were drifting across the sky. During the day, the sun had thawed the snow, and it would now freeze again during the night. Lacroix glanced into the forest behind the cabin. He had made out some movement between the tree trunks. He squinted. If he lived in the city, he would have procured what people called eyeglasses, for his eyesight was gradually declining. He was getting old.

He spotted a dark silhouette crouching in the snow and reached instinctively for his pistol. But it was only a single wolf, standing there looking at it. Nothing more.

Lacroix waited.

Are you a messenger? A good spirit who wants to warn us, or an evil omen?

The wolf seemed undecided, but then turned away and trotted off. Lacroix relaxed. A single wolf was not dangerous. Besides, they rarely dared approach human dwellings. He had probably just been curious.

Lacroix went back into the cabin, where Parker had dozed off in his chair, and locked the door. As a precaution, he pushed the table in front of it. That should hold. Exhausted, he sat down by the fire and added fresh logs.

Parker stirred under his blankets, muttering to himself. He was probably dreaming.

Lacroix looked at his friend. They had known each other for over twenty years. They had met as young *coureurs de bois*, rangers. Back then, they had worked as scouts for the English in the British-American War of 1812. After the war, they had gone west to work in the woods as trappers. There they had been joined by Two-Elk, who was wandering around lost, in search of his people, scattered to the four winds by the Americans—one of many Indigenous people without a home or a future, driven from the land of his forefathers.

Together, far from the noise of the world and human vanities, they had built this log cabin and lived off what the forest provided. And that was more than enough. Lacroix loved this life and would not for the whole world have traded it for a supposedly more comfortable existence in a town. He knew Parker felt the same way.

Lacroix gazed pensively into the warm flames of the fire. Then a groan from Parker's direction made him sit up and look over at him. His old friend looked at him with gleaming eyes. There was a strange reddish glow in his pupils.

"How are you doing?" asked Lacroix.

But Parker didn't answer; he just went on staring at him unblinkingly. An involuntary shiver ran down Lacroix's neck, and he was ashamed of it. He couldn't help but be frightened by those glowing red eyes. He was about to look away when an eerie howl sounded from outside. Lacroix leaped out of the chair, his trembling hands wrapped around the grips of his pistols.

"He . . . is . . . back," he heard Parker slur, as if his tongue were a piece of dead meat.

Motionless, Lacroix stood behind the door.

He's out there. The Wendigo.

Both men listened. Their nerves were stretched to the breaking point.

At first, there was nothing but silence. But then they heard muffled footsteps and a scraping against the wall of the house. The almost disembodied, hoarse sighing began again. Cold as ice water, it trickled through the cracks of the log cabin.

Lacroix tasted metallic fear on his tongue.

"Get out of here, you goddamn beast!" he yelled at the door, not knowing what else to do. Two-Elk, who might have known a defensive spell, was not with them. "There's nothing for you here! Get the hell out. Go back to your spirit world."

"He wants me. I know he does," Parker gasped. "He wants me. Meeeee!" His voice rose to a shrill howl. He was completely out of his mind, jerking back and forth in his chair with his head thrown back. His face was flushed and covered with a shiny layer of sweat. "Meeee," he screamed over and over. "Meeee!"

"Keep quiet, Alan! You'll only attract him with that." Lacroix gave Parker a resounding slap, and the old trapper closed his mouth in fright. He dropped his chin to his chest and moved only his lips, whimpering softly to himself. It sounded as if he was praying.

Parker was right, Lacroix thought. *Now only God could help them.*

Then something heavy slammed into the door.

CHAPTER 12

2009, Moose Lake,
Cedar Creek Lodge

A body?" Ondragon and Dr. Arthur said together.

"Yes, at the lake." Sheila still sounded as if she had found the dead man, not Pete.

"And who is it?" asked Dr. Arthur anxiously.

"I don't know, but it certainly couldn't be anyone from the lodge. Pete says the body is too old for that, and besides, we haven't had a patient go missing lately. And, oh . . . excuse me." Sheila seemed to realize she had been about to blurt out more details in front of a patient, and cleared her throat sheepishly. "Um, there's one more thing, Doctor. The police are on their way."

"The police?" The frown lines on Dr. Arthur's forehead deepened.

Sheila nodded. "I notified them when Pete arrived here distraught and told me about the body."

"Where is he?" inquired Dr. Arthur anxiously. But Ondragon had the feeling the doctor was using his concern for the bellboy to cover his displeasure that Sheila had called the police.

"Pete's down in the office at the front desk. He's still in a real mess. I think it would be good if you talked to him, Dr. Arthur."

"Who else knows about the body?"

"So far, it's just Pete and me."

"All right, I'll go with you." Dr. Arthur turned to Ondragon. "Please excuse this abrupt end to our session. It will not happen again. I hope you understand that I must now attend to this matter."

Addressing Sheila, he said. "Please ask Nurse Marsha to tell the patients that all sessions for this afternoon will be rescheduled."

Sheila nodded assiduously, and the three of them left the room. They went down to the reception desk. Ondragon would have liked to go into the office and hear what Pete had to say, but it was clear that his presence was not wanted. So he went to his room, but first of all took the opportunity to listen briefly at the door of number 20.

Nothing.

Ondragon shrugged. The mysterious guest would show themself sometime. He would catch Pete and shake him down later. Right now, Dr. Arthur's list of employees awaited his attention.

While the clinic head was on the first floor taking care of the "little matter" of the body, Ondragon was making the indirect acquaintance of all the therapy center employees. To his immense satisfaction, Dr. Arthur had been so generous with the information: For each person there was an entry with date of birth, occupation, marital status, insurance number, and how long they had been employed at Cedar Creek Lodge. In all, including the doctors, there were forty-five permanent members of staff and four seasonal workers who probably saw to the yard and the garden during the summer. What was striking was the equal numbers of men and women, which was probably deliberate, in order to ensure a positive working environment. After all, it wasn't easy to persuade people to live and work in isolation here all year round. It required good salary prospects and a certain amount of leisure activities. In addition, the entire workforce was relatively young, averaging thirty-five years of age. Dr. Arthur was the exception, at fifty-three, as was Frank, the gardener, at fifty-five. In addition to the medical staff, Ondragon identified an administrative assistant, an IT guy who probably kept the doctors' computer network running, cleaning staff, kitchen help, a yoga instructor, a tennis and fitness coach, a riding instructor, and four laundry workers. Nothing out of the ordinary; a structure that most resembled a spa hotel.

After a while, Ondragon was no longer able to concentrate. His mind kept wandering to the body in the woods and to what was going on downstairs at the reception desk. He wondered how long it would take the police to get here. Just for fun, he googled the nearest police station on his smartphone. It was in Nett Lake, about fifty miles away. With an SUV, you could cover that distance in an hour and a half. He glanced at his watch. So it wouldn't be long before the relevant deputy showed up. Quickly, he got up from the leather chair by the window, put the notepad in his pocket, locked everything else in the safe, and went down to the first floor. He peeked discreetly into the entryway. The door to the office was still closed. From behind it came the sound of muffled voices.

Suddenly, the front door opened and the gardener came in. He looked worried.

"Where is everyone?" he asked, looking around.

Ondragon pointed to the office door. "There. And Dr. Arthur is in there too."

Frank raised his eyebrows in amazement and put a hand on the door handle.

"I wouldn't," Ondragon said.

"Why?"

"I think they're discussing something important in there right now, and I overheard that they don't want to be disturbed."

"Aha." Frank eyed him up and down and only now seemed to recognize him. "You're the jogger from yesterday—Mr. Ondragon."

"Yes."

"So?"

"So what?" retorted Ondragon, somewhat irritated.

"How was it?"

"The forest is pretty dense, especially at the top of the lake."

"You were at the top of the lake?"

Ondragon thought he detected a slight change in Frank's voice. "Yes, I ran once all around the lake."

Frank looked at him for a moment and then said indifferently, "Okay, then. I actually just wanted to ask if anyone here had seen my dog."

"Is he gone? He was with you yesterday, wasn't he? Rumsfeld, right?"

"He's always outside in his kennel at night, but this morning he was gone. He likes to do his own thing sometimes, but he always comes to the door in the morning. That's when he gets his food."

"Maybe he found something tasty in the forest and filled his belly." Ondragon's joke stuck in his throat as he thought of the corpse, and quickly added, "I'm sure he'll be back soon."

"If you say so." Frank went back outside with a sullen expression. His boots had left damp traces of soil on the green carpet. Before Ondragon's eyes Sheila appeared, brandishing a vacuum cleaner and looking angry. He quickly left the entryway before he could be suspected of leaving them.

At lunch, it was the usual picture: the governor with the fat movie diva; Charlie Bloom with the models; Hatchet and his burger; Norrfoss, Shamgood, and Viktory. Apparently, no one else had heard about the body; everyone was calmly shoveling their food down. Since Miss Wolfe was not at her table, Ondragon sat down at his own, catching a suggestive grin from Mr. Shamgood. Apparently, the fashion designer had been watching him and had seen him looking for Miss Wolfe. Somewhat annoyed, Ondragon turned away and tried to ignore the guy. He ordered one of the set menus from Carlos: cauliflower soup with Parmesan and pine nuts and a veggie wrap, no dessert.

A little later, Miss Wolfe entered the dining room. She caught sight of Ondragon, came over to his table, and sat down, smiling.

"Oh, that looks good. Is it the vegetarian menu?" She pointed to his wrap.

Ondragon nodded.

"Well, I'll have one too. I'm a vegetarian."

"By conviction, or is there a particular reason?"

"I can't stand the taste of meat."

"Oh. Since you were a little girl and saw the rabbit . . ."

"No, that came later." Her smile disappeared as if someone had switched it off. Avoiding his gaze, she unfolded her napkin. She didn't speak again until she had ordered her food from Carlos.

"Do you know why the police are here?" she asked.

"Police?" Feigning surprise, Ondragon raised his eyebrows.

"Yes, I saw the car arrive and the deputies go upstairs with Dr. Arthur, Pete, and Sheila."

Ondragon wondered if he should tell her about Pete's discovery. Why not? Everyone would know soon anyway. That kind of thing could not be concealed for long.

"The police are here because Pete found a body while he was out picking mushrooms. But please keep it to yourself for now. I'm the only one who knows so far, because I happened to be there when Sheila notified Dr. Arthur."

"Oh my God! A dead body? Do they know who it is yet? Not someone from here?" She glanced around the room.

"No. At least that's what Sheila says. She says it couldn't be one of us, since no patients have gone missing lately." *None of us*—how that sounded!

"That's not quite true," Kateri replied thoughtfully. "A guest disappeared in March. I had just arrived at the time."

"Really? That sounds interesting. Do tell." Suddenly, Ondragon found the whole thing more than entertaining. His instinct for puzzles and inconsistencies was aroused.

"Well, the guest from number twenty wasn't there one morning, but his things were all still in his room. At first, Dr. Arthur just raised the alarm internally, as a precaution. You know how it is, a patient overreacts and takes off, and immediately there's talk. Dr. Arthur sent Pete and a few others out to search the entire area. Unfortunately, it had snowed during the night and there were no footprints to be seen anywhere. Dr. Arthur remained calm the entire time; the guest was probably not considered suicidal. Why he was here though, I don't know, I only spoke to him a couple of times. He looked unremarkable, middle-aged, medium height, blond hair. A totally average guy. His name was Oliver Orchid and he came from Toronto, I think."

OO-6! That explained the abbreviation, at any rate. But why was the guy still listed as being in room 20 when he hadn't lived there for five months? Was something being covered up?

"So it's possible that the guy ran into the woods and froze to death out there?" Ondragon asked, digging deeper.

"No, the whole thing was cleared up a little later. Fresh tire prints were found about a mile away, in the parking lot where the hiking trail to Mount Witiko begins. Mr. Orchid must have been hiding his pickup there all along. No one knew anything about it; Orchid never handed in a key."

"But then how did he get here?"

"He was picked up by the shuttle service at Orr. Later it came out that one of the employees had brought his car here in return for two hundred dollars, and Mr. Orchid must have driven secretly to Orr many times. Interviews with the people there indicated he had been seen there. Whereupon, of course, Dr. Arthur immediately discharged the employee."

"So he assumed that Mr. Orchid had a tantrum, grabbed his car, and took off before his time here was up?"

"Well, everyone gets to decide for themselves when their time is up here," Kateri said with an ambiguous smile.

"And you're sure it was Oliver Orchid you spoke to back then?" Ondragon persisted. The story had set the *centrifuge* spinning wildly.

"Yes, he gave that name when he introduced himself."

"And his car—the pickup—did you see that too, or at least the tire tracks?"

"No, but I understand it was a black Dodge Ram."

"Has there been any police investigation into the case?"

"As far as I know, no. It was all cleared up, after all."

Ondragon pursed his lips. "And how did Dr. Arthur reassure the other guests? Surely all this must have created quite a commotion."

"He made inquiries, of course. And sure enough, three days later, Mr. Orchid showed up at his home in Toronto. Dr. Arthur spoke to him on the phone. He said Orchid had stopped treatment at his own request."

"I see, and Dr. Arthur didn't say any more?"

"Why should he?" Kateri Wolfe glared at him.

Ondragon leaned back and sipped his mineral water. He could go no further. After all, Miss Wolfe didn't know what all he knew. Among other things, the number of times she had been a guest here at CC Lodge and that Dr. Arthur was her mentor—whatever that meant. So before Ondragon ventured any further, he would need to find out more about the relationship between Kateri Wolfe and the psychotherapist.

"And who was the employee who was fired?" he asked.

"A man named Jeremy Bates. He was a masseur and had only been working for the lodge a few months; he was one of the few who lived in Orr rather than here."

"Well, I'm curious to know who's lying out there in the woods."

"Maybe a hiker who was traveling alone." Kateri finished the last bite of her wrap.

"Maybe. Maybe not. We'll find out, I hope." Ondragon drained his glass. There was something fishy about this, he could sense it. His inner watchdog was wide awake and yelping like a madman.

The police entourage, Dr. Arthur, and Pete were in the woods until the afternoon. In the meantime, all the lodge guests had noticed the patrol car parked in the parking lot and that it had been joined by the cars of the medical examiner and the forensic team. There were agitated discussions about what might have happened, and the sofas in the entrance area were filled to capacity, because everyone was hoping to get the sought-after information there. Even Dr. Pollux and Dr. Zeo were standing in a corner, looking worried. Ondragon took the opportunity to talk to some of the staff and at least found out where Pete's uncle's house was, where the man lived. If necessary, he would go there to question him.

When Dr. Arthur finally walked in the door with one of the police officers, all conversation fell silent, and all eyes turned to the two men.

Ondragon leaned in the doorway, waiting eagerly to see what might come next. Given the circumstances, Dr. Arthur looked surprisingly relaxed. He raised a hand, forestalling the onslaught of questions.

"Ladies and gentlemen, yes, it is true that a body has been found out in the woods. But I can reassure you, it's not someone from the lodge. Probably a hiker who had an accident. The police are here to investigate the case. So there is no cause for alarm."

"Where?" asked a voice—it was an extremely concerned Mr. Shamgood. "Where exactly was the dead man discovered?"

Dr. Arthur glanced at the police officer, who gave his permission with a curt nod. "Far away from here," the doctor said. "On the other side of the lake, at the northern tip."

At the top? Ondragon felt himself getting hot. He had been there too!

"Since this . . . incident has nothing to do with the lodge," Dr. Arthur explained, "you may continue your stay here undisturbed. Sheila will see to it that . . ."

"Have you identified the dead man?"

"No."

"Then how can you be sure it's not someone from here?" insisted Shamgood.

Ondragon directed his gaze to the fashion designer, whose line of questioning was surprisingly coherent.

Dr. Arthur sighed audibly. "Well, this may sound a bit macabre, but we're all still here, aren't we?" He made a sweeping gesture that included everyone present, and gave a charming laugh. Several of the guests joined in.

"But that's means there could actually be a murderer running around here," someone interjected again. The merriment fizzled out abruptly.

Ondragon noticed impatience creeping into Dr. Arthur's demeanor. Again, the psychotherapist glanced at the police officer. From a purely visual point of view, the deputy was a typical representative of the "young deputy sheriff from the countryside" genus. A khaki uniform, a broad face reddened by shaving, a flickering gaze, and an anxiously authoritarian posture. Broad-legged and with his thumbs hooked into his belt, he took the floor.

"Ladies and gentlemen, my name is Deputy Hase and I am in charge of this investigation. I couldn't agree more with what Dr. Arthur said earlier. So far, there is no cause for alarm. The dead person, or persons, has been out there for a while, and so it's difficult to determine identity and exact cause of death."

Out there for a while? An uneasy feeling spread through Ondragon's stomach. Then why hadn't he seen the body? Suddenly, the stench near the mysterious net came to his mind. Maybe it was the smell of decay that had so badly polluted the air, and the bear had been attracted by it. But what about the net? Had the police found that too?

"At this time the medical examiner is still investigating," Deputy Hase continued his explanation, "but everything seems to indicate that it was a tragic accident. So there's *no* murderer running around out there, you can be assured of that. However, I would still ask you not to leave the house today. It is only a precaution to ensure that the police work is not disturbed. We will inform you as soon as we have any news." The deputy turned to Dr. Arthur, who looked first at his antique pocket watch and then around the room.

"Unfortunately, sessions are canceled for the rest of today. I sincerely apologize for that, but the police have to do their job, and I still have some issues to discuss with the deputy. Tomorrow's schedule will be adjusted to take into account people who have been disadvantaged today. Sheila will let you know when your appointments are." With that, Dr. Arthur nodded to Deputy Hase and made his way upstairs to his office.

Ondragon's thoughts were racing as he tried to go over what he had witnessed yesterday at the top of the lake. Should he tell the police what he had seen? It was possible that he had unknowingly left traces at the site where the body had been found; they might be attributed to him at some point. Besides, Frank, the gardener, knew he had been there yesterday. He had told him so himself this morning. It couldn't be too long before he became the focus of the investigation, and then he would be in the shit. And he had nothing to do with it.

Outwardly calm, he watched as the other guests dispersed, grumbling. For them, the show was over. They would have to wait for new sensationalist fodder. Ondragon, however, had to do something to get his head out of the noose. Quickly, he pushed himself off the doorframe and headed for the stairwell. He wasn't going to sit around here and wait for information to be thrown at him in bits and pieces. After all, he couldn't be forced to stay in the building, even if that was what the police had ordered. Before that, however, he had something else to do and went to his room, where he took his cell phone out of the safe and turned it on. Once he had a network, he looked briefly at the clock and dialed a number in Thailand.

"*Sawadee khrap*, Paul!" a male voice said, picking up after the fourth ring.

"Hello, Rudee. *Sabai dee mai*—how are you?"

"*Sabai dee*—very good. Not heard from you looong time."

Ondragon smiled as he heard Rudee's accent dragging out the vowels. And all of a sudden, he felt a longing for the smog-blue streets of Bangkok, the honking of the *tuktuk* drivers, and an ice-cold Singha beer in a roadside pub on Sukumvit Road.

He had spent four years of his youth, from the ages of twelve to fifteen to be exact, in the bustling capital of Thailand when his father had worked there in the embassy—and it had probably been the happiest time of his life before he had finally fallen out with his father. But he had always felt at home amid the Asian hospitality, even though he had been a *farang* and a giant, as he grew rapidly taller and taller. He had made one or two really good friends back then, and he still kept in touch with them today. Rudee was one of them. Ondragon had met the clever Thai in a computer club and had immediately hired him as a freelancer when he founded Ondragon Consulting. Even back then, Rudee could do things Paul could not: He was a cyber pirate of the highest order and could hack into absolutely any computer. Even those of the American government!

Rudee was based in Bangkok and could always be relied on to see a job through. His approach was highly idiosyncratic, but nevertheless amazingly effective. Ondragon thought it was high time he paid his friend another visit. Maybe he could take a week off and fly to Bangkok after all this was done.

"I have something for you, Rudee, and it's urgent as usual," he said with an apologetic laugh.

"Wooow, fire away, I'm ready." In the background, Ondragon heard the clatter of a keyboard. It was now four in the morning in Bangkok, but Rudee was one of those people who slept during the day and worked at night. Because of the heat, he claimed. But Ondragon suspected that it was more likely because Rudee preferred to operate out of hijacked computers in the United States. Usually several at the same time, because he always wanted to be there "live" when something significant went down on the net.

"I need information from a computer located here at Cedar Creek Lodge," Ondragon said. "It belongs to a Dr. Jonathan Aaron Arthur, a doctor of medicine and a psychologist. He has a Toshiba Satellite Pro, but there's also a local area network that the staff here uses. And the data is supposed to be encrypted. Internet access is only via satellite, and the administrator's name is Kenny White, at least that's the computer freak here."

"Are you saying I'm a freak?"

"No, Rudee, *you're* a genius—even though you're only three and a half feet." Involuntarily, he had to think of Nick Nack, the henchman from the James Bond film *The Man with the Golden Gun*, who had lived with Christopher Lee on a small tropical rock island.

Rudee laughed. "That's why I prefer 'Napol_e.on' as a nickname; he was a little genius too."

Ondragon grinned and gave Rudee more names of people who might have accessed the network, so that the Thai could find out IP addresses and passwords.

"And what kind of information are you looking for exactly, Paul?"

"There should be data on all Cedar Creek Lodge patients on the laptop's hard drive or internal server."

"Patients? Say, where are you right now?"

"Like I said, at CC Lodge in Minnesota."

"Is this a job or are you on vacation?" Rudee chuckled.

"A little of both," Ondragon admitted. Why was he lying to Rudee? The Thai would find out anyway when he hacked into the patient data. After all, his file was there too. "Specifically, I need the patient files of the following people. Kateri Meoquanee Wolfe and Oliver Orchid, those are the most important. Then I could do with information on an employee named Jeremy Bates, who was fired in March of this year. See if you can find anything on him, most likely in HR. After we've finished, I'll send you an email with the rest of the patient names."

"Fine, I'll encrypt the files and mail them to your phone then."

"*Kap khun khrap*—thank you very much, Rudee. I'll get back to you tomorrow."

"*Laa gon*, Paul. See you."

After Ondragon had sent the email to Rudee, he put the cell phone away. Now he would find out how securely CC Lodge really stored sensitive data!

He got up from the bed, went to the large cabinet, and looked at the clothes he had brought with him. He needed more inconspicuous clothes if he was going to walk around outside in the woods. So he swapped his shirt, jacket, and pants for a T-shirt, jeans, and cowboy boots, and after a glance out the window, grabbed another gray cotton jacket. He was about to close the safe when his eyes fell on the SIG Sauer. Should he take it with him?

He shook his head. He was not paranoid enough to be walking around here with a gun yet. In the city it was a different matter, there it was his life insurance. But here? He thought briefly of the bear. If it had been a bear and not just a bad joke born of his own overexcitement, which had been haunting him more and more lately. Ondragon sighed. He desperately needed a break. But instead of relaxing here in the charmless silence of nature, he was already maneuvering himself back into the obsessive solving of a dubious mystery.

"You're a lost cause, Paul Eckbert," he said aloud. "Just admit it, you just can't help yourself. You're a fucking freak!"

He slammed the safe door shut, fumbled in his jeans pocket for his talisman, and left the room. The first thing he would do was question Pete. Assuming he could find him.

CHAPTER 13

1835, Kabetogama,
fur trappers' lonely log cabin

The trappers were awoken by a loud knocking.

Hastily, Lacroix unwrapped himself from his fur blanket and felt his way through the darkness to the door. He put his ear to the wood . . . and recoiled as another loud thump came.

"Who's there?" he called out.

"Lieutenant Stafford of His Majesty King William IV's Army!"

Astonished, Lacroix put his pistols away and pushed the table aside. When he opened the door, bright daylight streamed in, blinding him.

"Lieutenant, what are you doing here? Do you have the killer?" he asked the dark silhouette in the snow outside, shielding his eyes with one hand.

"No, I am afraid not. May I come in?"

Lacroix had noticed the dozen or so mounted soldiers standing waiting at a distance behind Stafford. He glanced over his shoulder into the hut and saw Parker shaking his head weakly. But what was he to do? He could not refuse the English lieutenant entry. Against Parker's will, he took a step back and opened the door fully.

Stafford entered, took off his hat, and looked around the stuffy interior. Lacroix saw the lieutenant wrinkling his nose, but still made an effort to be friendly. "Would you like some hot coffee?"

"Gladly." Stafford took off his leather gloves and jammed them into his belt while the French Canadian went to work on the fire. The flames were soon blazing under the battered enamel pot.

"What ails him?" asked Stafford, pointing to Parker, who had yet to make a sound.

"He's sick," Lacroix replied curtly, tipping ground coffee into two beakers.

"Sick?"

"Fever."

"I see." The lieutenant kept his distance and continued to look around suspiciously. "Where is the Indian?"

"Gone."

"I can see that too. Where did he go?"

"Why do you want to know?" The water in the pot boiled, and Lacroix poured it into the two beakers. Immediately, a pleasant aroma of coffee filled the cabin. He handed Stafford a cup.

The lieutenant sipped the strong, hot liquid. Then he said, "I have orders to take you all to Fort Frances. You are to be subjected to another interrogation there."

"Why go to Fort Frances? You can do that here. Do you intend to arrest us?"

"Let us say rather that you are invited to attend at the Crown's expense! Besides, the colonel and the governor would like to meet you."

Lacroix was silent. Of course they were under arrest. Why else would the soldiers be there? He looked at the door. There was nothing he could do against twelve men. And what about Parker? He couldn't just leave him here alone.

"My friend is too sick to travel. He can't go out in the cold."

"But he looks quite merry. He'll be able to sit on a horse, won't he? And fresh air sometimes works wonders." The lieutenant sounded friendly, but his words concealed an explicit order.

"It will be on your shoulders if he doesn't make it." Lacroix hoped Two-Elk did not fall into the clutches of the English. The Chippewa would figure out what had happened to them when he got back to the cabin.

Stafford gestured with his hand. "Now, gentlemen, pack your things and come with me."

Lacroix suddenly remembered Parker's feet. How was he supposed to explain what was going on with them? It would not exactly be easy to hide them. And the tracks from last night out in the snow? There were bound to be some. Had the lieutenant noticed them? He put his cup down on the table and cursed softly to himself for failing to cover the tracks in time. He really needed to distract Stafford.

And the Wendigo?

Would it come after them?

In the forest, they would be defenseless and at his mercy.

"I have to get Parker dressed properly first. It'll take a moment. Otherwise he'll catch his death outside." Lacroix bit his lip as the literal truth of his words dawned on him.

"Very well," said the lieutenant, "I'll wait outside. But I don't want to see any weapons in your luggage!" Stafford placed his cup on the table and left the cabin. He had not said so, but his tone left no doubt that any attempt to escape would be futile.

Lacroix began to unwrap Parker from the blankets.

"Leave me here. We'll be lost out there. Save yourself, at least," Alan whispered.

"I can't and you know it. We have no other choice. It is better to go willingly than have them put us in chains. Two-Elk will find us and help us." He took the skins from Parker's feet, ignoring the doughy swollen mass with the barely visible toes, and cut the skins into strips. He wrapped these around the feet and pulled tight. Parker groaned, his face distorted in pain.

"Hold fast, my friend," Lacroix coaxed him, helping him slip into several layers of shirts. Over those he put a leather jacket and two greatcoats. Then he took a sack made of oilcloth and hastily packed a few things: clothes, a small kettle, two blankets, tobacco, pemmican, and coffee. He hid the two small knives in the shanks of his boots.

Finally, he carved the symbol of a saber into the tabletop—to let Two-Elk know that they had been taken by soldiers. Then he doused the fire, shouldered the luggage, grabbed the thickly wrapped Parker under the armpits, and dragged him outside into the blinding sunlight.

CHAPTER 14

2009, Moose Lake,
Cedar Creek Lodge

Getting out of the lodge unseen was not difficult. A little after half past three in the afternoon, Ondragon opened the fire door and quietly descended the steel spiral staircase on the west side of the building. He was aware that he could be seen from the rear windows, so he forced himself to walk quietly, at an almost leisurely pace, across the lawn. Only when he had put a few bushes and trees between him and the lodge did he quicken his step.

He immediately found the path to the log cabin belonging to Peter Parker's uncle. It forked off to the right about two hundred yards before the staff block and led past the stables into the woods.

Ondragon crept in a wide arc around the flat buildings, in front of which was the paddock where the horses were grazing. There was no sign of the riding instructor. Good. Suddenly, he felt a drop on his cheek and glanced at the sky. Rain-heavy gray clouds had built up. Ondragon frowned. He hoped it wouldn't start to bucket down. Quickly, he followed the path deeper into the forest. Under the dense canopy of conifers, the twilight was far less inviting than yesterday's bright sunshine. Shadowy holes opened up on the right and left of the path, breathing wet and cold from their mossy mouths. Instinctively, Ondragon craned his neck, listening intently to his surroundings. But everything was silent; there was no crunching sound and no bear roar. All he could hear was the hollow rustling of the wind above the treetops.

After a quarter of an hour, he reached a clearing with several buildings. Instantly, a dog attacked. The beast hurtled toward him, and Ondragon raised a hand to ward it off, but an unexpected jolt went through its shaggy black hide and it was yanked back with a yelp.

The line had reached its maximum stretch just a few inches in front of him.

Ondragon smiled happily at the raging dog.

"Misjudged it?"

He turned away from the animal and looked at the cluster of buildings: a main house of rough-hewn logs, old but in good repair; a thin cloud of blue smoke curling from the chimney. Next to it, a sort of stable or shed, already somewhat rotten. Rusty animal traps and nondescript animal carcasses hung on the wall under the protruding roof. In front of it was a muddy square and, about twenty paces away, an outhouse boarded up with new battens. And instead of a heart, the outline of Mickey Mouse was cut into the door!

Ondragon looked at the baying dog, which kept jumping at the leash, risking strangulation every time. Drool was dripping from its retracted lips onto the black coat of its chest. Stupid mutt!

But why was no one responding to the barking?

Ondragon let his eye travel back to the main house and almost let out a loud yell.

Standing in front of him, as if he had grown out of the ground, was a wizened little man with a big, white, bushy beard and a pipe in his mouth. He looked like the perfect mountain man from an advertisement for vacations in Switzerland. The only thing disturbing the image was the antique shotgun he was casually carrying in the crook of his arm.

"Can I help you?" croaked Mountain Man, blinking at him with watery eyes.

"Whoa, you scared me, mister." Ondragon ran a hand through his wet hair and was glad the guy hadn't shot first and asked questions afterward. It had been negligent to snoop around here so clumsily. Anyone with half a brain knew that it was generally best not to tangle with hermits living far from civilization.

Keeping his eye on the shotgun, Ondragon apologized to the man and then asked if he was Pete's great-uncle.

The old man grinned, revealing that it had been decades since he had visited the dentist. "Ah, so you're from the asylum," he said dryly.

Charming. Ondragon kept his face straight.

"Pete's . . ." The old man suddenly turned his head, took the pipe—which was already cold—out of his mouth, and yelled at the dog. "Shut it, Bugs!" Then he spat noisily.

Ondragon suppressed a disgusted expression and watched the flea-ridden mutt trudge off with its tail between his legs. Bugs! This family had a truly bizarre penchant for cartoon characters.

"Well, Pete ain't here." The old man put his pipe between his lips and gave the ghost of an unfriendly smile.

"Oh." Ondragon raised his hands apologetically. "Then I'm sorry to have disturbed you." He was about to retreat when the door of the log cabin opened and a balloon-shaped head with a broad face and shaggy gray hair peered out. Ondragon was puzzled. Such a young fellow and already going gray?

"Hellooo, Uncle Joeeel. Where you at?" The boy's voice was nasal and sounded a little sluggish.

Backward, Ondragon guessed. *Why am I not surprised*, he thought.

He let his gaze wander over the dingy, isolated farm. What could you expect from life when you grew up out here in the sticks?

The old man turned to the moonfaced brat and said, "I'll be right there, Momo; go back inside, it's raining!" His tone was affectionate but firm—quite different from the one he then used to chase Ondragon off his land: "You wan' anything else?"

No, Ondragon thought, and turned around. *Better I leave this haven of merriment.*

"Have a nice day, Mr. Parker." He tapped a finger to his forehead and walked bad-temperedly back down the path into the woods. The rain was getting heavier. Of course it was! It clattered loudly on the leaves of the ferns and trees all around him. The first gusts of a storm swept over the treetops. Concerned, Ondragon looked up. He could vaguely make out black clouds through the branches. Something was brewing. He had better make sure he got back to the lodge, where it was nice and warm and dry.

His head down, Ondragon took off at a run . . . and almost collided with the bellboy, who was also making his way along the path, his baseball cap pulled low over his face. Surprised, they both looked at each other.

"Oh. Hi, Mr. *On Draegen*. What are you doing out here? It's raining." Pete sounded glum, and Ondragon could see that he had been crying. Quickly, the boy wiped his reddened eyes.

"Pete. I'm glad I ran into you. I've been meaning to talk to you. Is everything okay?"

The young man nodded but continued to look sad.

"I'm going home. Dr. Arthur gave me the rest of the day off. Because of the thing, you know."

Ondragon nodded sympathetically and crossed his arms. He was cold and his jacket was already completely soaked. The rain was also dripping from Pete's cap. Still, he had to talk to the boy.

"Yeah, it was bad, that thing with the body." Ondragon stepped into the shelter of a tree. "Do they know who it is yet?"

Pete shook his head, his teeth chattering loudly. Probably more from shock than cold.

"And how did the person come to die?" Ondragon asked.

"The medical examiner doesn't know for sure, but it may have been a bear. Oh, man . . . That . . . I'm not supposed to tell anyone." Pete looked up. "You'll keep this to yourself, won't you?"

"Sure thing, Pete. My lips are sealed. A bear, you say?" The back of Ondragon's neck had begun to tingle again. He glanced quickly over his shoulder into the woods. Sure enough, there was nothing there.

"The ME found a lot of bite marks on the body," Pete said wearily.

"But they could have been made postmortem."

"Post *what?*"

"I mean, an animal, a bear, may have chewed at the body after the person died."

Pete shook his head again. "The ME says there are other tracks there too, older ones. But he has to investigate first and he wants to bring in a bear specialist. He can't say anything for definite until then."

"But he thinks the person was killed by a bear?"

Pete nodded and wiped his eyes. It was obvious he was beat.

Ondragon took a step toward him. "I have a confession to make, Pete. But I'm only doing it because you trusted me with a secret too. And you must swear that you'll keep it to yourself!"

The bellboy looked up at him and a glow came into his silvery eyes. "Sure. I swear, Mr. *On Draegen*!" He raised two fingers in the air.

"Good, because the thing is that yesterday I was at the place where you found the body today. At the top of the lake. I left tracks there while I was jogging. Do you know if the police have found them?"

"Yes, if you were wearing Nike running shoes yesterday, size 43 . . ."

What a drag, Ondragon thought, now he definitely had to talk to the deputy.

"Well, I guess they'll be mine," he admitted. "But I didn't see any body. Where was it?"

"In the tall bushes behind the log that crosses the swamp. Right next to the trail. Some brush was trampled flat."

"Hmm, I was probably there too." Ondragon frowned. "That's really strange, isn't it? That I didn't see anything. But I heard something. Maybe it was a bear, maybe not. I don't know. After all, I've never come face-to-face with a bear. But there was something else too."

Pete looked at him watchfully.

"There was a net stretched across the path, where the thicket forms a tunnel. And hanging in the net was a mummified bird of prey. Some Indian thing, I guess. Did you see that too?"

Pete didn't move right away. Then he nodded.

"And the police?" urged Ondragon further.

The boy hesitated again. Then he shook his head.

"Did you take the net down and hide it from the cops?"

Head nod.

"Why? What does it mean? Does it have to do with the body?"

Pete bit his lower lip. At first, he looked like he was going to be as cantankerous as his great-uncle, but then he exhaled with a sigh. "Frank says I'm a whacko, but I believe in it!"

"Believe in what?"

"The forest monster, the Wendigo. It was him, he killed and ate that person out there!"

"The Wendigo?" Ondragon was inclined to agree with Frank. Pete was well out of his depth.

"Yes, the Wendigo lives here in the woods and eats people. He's always hungry and always on the lookout for new victims. The Indians 'round here know it. They have a medicine, or a spell, or whatever it's called, against him. They know what to do to make him leave you in peace too. I didn't know about the body and the net before. Honestly!"

"So it's not yours?"

"No."

"So whose could it be? Why did you take it down?"

Pete looked at the ground and shrugged. Either he didn't know, or he didn't want to say. Suddenly, he began to cry again. "Why does Frank always have to make fun of me? He's always laughing at me and calling me a thickheaded hillbilly. But that's not true! I'm not stupid, and I'm not crazy, Mr. *On Draegen*." Pete looked at him pleadingly.

Ondragon reflected. There had to be a reasonable explanation for all this. The forest monster Pete was talking about existed only in his imagination, that was clear. It must have been something else that had killed the unknown person. And there were only three possibilities: a human being, an animal, or an accident. Nothing else. No monster and also no Indian forest spirit.

Ondragon put a hand on the sobbing boy's shoulder. "No, you're not crazy, Pete. Forget what Frank said. He's off his head himself. Do you hear? By the way, I was just with your great-uncle and your brother. What's his name?"

"Momo. Mortimer, actually. But that's too square, Uncle Joel says."

"He's absolutely right about that. Good old Joel. He's on the ball, isn't he?"

"Did he threaten you with the shotgun?" Pete sniffed.

"It was my fault. I was running around on your property without asking. Please tell your great-uncle I'm sorry."

"Okay. But Uncle Joel isn't as evil as he looks. He's been taking care of us since Mom and Dad died. We were just kids then. I was eleven and Momo was nine."

"Frank told me about your parents." Ondragon saw a shadow flit across the bellboy's pale features at the gardener's name. "What happened to them?"

"Oh, they . . ." Pete cleared his throat. He was obviously uncomfortable talking about it. But then he pulled himself together. "We lived near Orr then. In a cabin in the woods, just like the one we live in now. And . . .when I came home from school one day . . . Mom and Dad were dead."

"How so? Just dead? Were they killed? Shot or something?" Ondragon's mental watchdog, always on the lookout for mysteries, butted in for the second time that day.

"No . . . I'm sorry, Mr. *On Draegen,* but I have to go now. You'd better go too or you'll get soaked. See you tomorrow." Pete turned and walked away without another word, his hands buried deep in his jacket pockets.

Ondragon looked after him, cold water running down his collar. What had happened to the Parker family? Another murder? Another mystery? Did the body have anything to do with it? He felt an expectant tingle rise within him and grimaced. His stay here was turning out to be completely different from what he had imagined.

At dinner, the agitation of the day could still be felt among the guests. Ondragon sat down at his table and ordered the steak, unfortunately without porcini mushrooms.

Mr. Shamgood was suddenly standing next to him, appearing as if out of thin air and fixing him with a meaningful smile. Ondragon ignored him and turned his attention to the steak, which lay, delicious and fragrant, on the plate before him. But the fashion designer showed no sign of leaving and eventually—much to Ondragon's horror—sat down opposite him at the table.

"Don't mind if I do." Shamgood pointed at the chair under his ass and grinned his polished, pearly white grin.

Ondragon overcame the desire to jam his fork into the guy's tanned visage and put down his knife and fork emphatically slowly. The smile he adopted said everything you needed to know. Category: "Wolf"—or rather: "Get too close to me and I'll tear out your throat!"

But Shamgood didn't seem to understand the subliminal threat. At any rate, he babbled on unperturbed. "Guess why I came to join you."

"I don't know. Enlighten me," Ondragon growled, deliberately emphasizing his Swedish accent. He wanted to distance himself from Shamgood's artificial Upper East Side accent, to avoid any chance of familiarity between them. He was fed up with the guy and his intrusive aftershave. Scowling, he regarded the thin figure with the chemical spill on his head.

Shamgood's grin got even wider and he leaned forward, inhaling with relish. "Hmm, that steak smells good . . . so do you, by the way. What shampoo do you use?" He winked at him, but then abruptly became serious. "I saw you, Mr. Ondragon. Outside!"

"So?"

"Well, didn't the police forbid us to leave the building? What were you doing out there? You looked like you were on the trail of a conspiracy. Or did you have something to do with the body in the woods?"

Ondragon had no intention of answering any of these questions. He picked up his cutlery and continued eating.

"Suit yourself." Shamgood waved a manicured hand. "Anyway, I find your behavior highly suspicious. No sooner do you show up here than they find a dead body. That's peculiar, isn't it? And you can say whatever you like, but you're not a management consultant! I could report you to Dr. Arthur. He doesn't like it when people disrespect his orders. He's already thrown out other patients ahead of schedule for disobedience."

Good grief, Mr. Shamgood is a tattletale, Ondragon thought. He felt as if he were about to explode, but tried to keep himself under control. Erupting in rage in front of all the guests would only encourage what gossip there already was. It was no use, he had to get out of there. That wasn't how he liked to do things, but right now it was the most sensible tactic. He would return to Mr. Shamgood in a quiet minute when there were no witnesses. He wondered if Amnesty International's remit extended to gay fashion designers.

"You're not following the *Golden Rules*." Shamgood clearly wasn't done with him yet. He waved an accusing index finger in Ondragon's face.

Ondragon took a deep breath. *Stay calm*, he told himself, *think of something nice!* He put the last bite of steak in his mouth and reached for his napkin.

"You sneak around this building at night and drink beer with that"—Shamgood cast a disgusted glance at Hatchet, who was emptying half a bottle of ketchup over his burger—"with that uncivilized Neanderthal there, and you hit on the female guests completely shamelessly. That's not in the *Golden Rules*."

That was enough! The guy dared to poke his nose into his business? Ondragon threw the napkin down on the table and stood up. He didn't know why Shamgood was Dr. Arthur's patient, but hopefully he would find out soon. In any case, none of them were here for a course in good manners.

"Mr. Shamgood," he said, making an effort to be polite, "you seem to be unaware that you are very pushy. Pushy *and* rude. Those are two very bad characteristics, and I would like to point them out to you. And I think it would better for you to stay away from me in the future, or . . ."

"Or what?" Shamgood grinned offensively. "Are you threatening me? You can't do anything to me; I have much better lawyers than you."

Ondragon leaned down to Mr. Shamgood and spoke the next few sentences into his ear so softly that only he could hear them. "That's nice for you. But with the people I know, I don't need lawyers."

He heard the fashion designer gasp indignantly and left the table without further comment. In the dining room doorway, he met Miss Wolfe, who stopped, puzzled.

"You're leaving already?" she asked.

Ondragon had no desire to speak to Miss Wolfe under Shamgood's burning gaze, and pulled her out into the hallway with him.

"Whoops!" she said in surprise. "What's wrong?"

"Nothing. But I had to finish my dinner earlier than I wanted to." Ondragon glanced involuntarily over his shoulder, as if Shamgood could see right through the wall. "I had a very unattractive dinner companion."

Miss Wolfe still didn't seem to understand what he meant. So he enlightened her, "Mr. Tommy-I'm-a-Big-Noise-in-Fashion was a little too pushy for me, so I made my escape."

"Was he hitting on you?"

Ondragon sighed. "I guess it was love at first sight."

A grin appeared on Kateri's face. "Well, Mr. Shamgood's charms are hard to resist." She laughed and Ondragon let himself be infected by it. Only now did he realize how agitated he had been about the situation, which was in fact funny. But it still worried him that he had allowed himself to be so provoked by an amateur like Shamgood.

"Dr. Arthur has already warned Tommy several times to spare the male guests his crude come-ons," Kateri explained. "If it bothers you, Paul, tell Sheila and she'll pass on the complaint."

Sheila, of all people! Ondragon waved a hand. "No, no, it's all right, I can handle him." He glanced at Miss Wolfe. The open smile on her lips pleased him. And she once again looked quite adorable in her green angora sweater and belt with silver clasps around her hips. "How about it? Meet me in the lounge later? Then we can chat about this exciting day over a drink in complete compliance with the *Golden Rules*."

"I'd like that."

"Great." Ondragon said goodbye with a charming wink and headed for the stairs. Up in his room, he cursed once, loudly, to get rid of his tension, and dialed Deputy Hase's number, which he had looked up on the internet earlier. After just a few seconds, he had the lead investigator on the "bear food" case on the line.

"Deputy Hase. Who's this?"

Ondragon explained to him who he was and why he was calling.

"And you're just telling me this now?" Hase's tone betrayed both surprise and irritation.

"Well, I didn't immediately think of it when you were here earlier."

"Okay, your information is correct, Mr. Ondragon. We did indeed find fresh footprints, size 43. Very fresh, right in the middle of the body's stoved-in ribcage."

Ondragon stared in horror at his running shoes, which were sitting innocently on the carpet next to the cupboard. For a brief moment, he was speechless.

"And can you also explain to me how your shoe prints got there, Mr. Ondragon?"

"Um, sorry?"

"Can you tell me why you didn't realize you had stepped on a dead body?"

"To be honest . . . no."

"I think we should discuss this in more detail tomorrow morning. We will be back at the lodge from eight o'clock. We plan to interview all guests and staff. I suggest we meet right after you've had breakfast?"

"All right."

"And bring your shoes." The deputy rang off.

Ondragon turned off the cell phone and stared at his shoes in disgust. His stomach grumbled. He'd trodden on the corpse! How on earth had he not noticed it? There could only be one explanation: It must have happened during his stupid stampede through the bushes, when the bear was after him.

He ran his hand through his hair. Oh, man, his nerves were more raw than he had thought.

He rose heavily from the bed, retrieved a plastic bag from his travel bag, and stuffed the running shoes into it. Only when he had tied the bag in an airtight knot and bundled it into the bathtub did he expel the breath he had been holding. He didn't particularly want to be reminded of the corpse smell that was undoubtedly clinging to the shoes. When his gaze happened to fall on the mirror, he sighed aloud. He looked exactly the way he felt.

Rotten.

* * *

The rendezvous with Miss Wolfe was the only bright spot in the day, which was just his second at CC Lodge. They met in the lounge around nine, and when Miss Wolfe explained that she liked to sit at the bar, they settled on the barstools. Ondragon found this very pleasant and said hello in passing to Hatchet, who was lounging in the corner of the sofa, listening to music on his iPod. Ondragon ordered a Virgin Caipirinha from the bartender and Kateri a non-alcoholic beer, which she drank straight from the bottle. Even more pleasant.

At first, they chatted about trivial stuff, until finally they got to the second drink and "the world out there." Ondragon told Kateri what he had learned from Pete: that the medical examiner thought a bear might have killed the man.

"That's possible, bears sometimes get into a feeding frenzy. Then they attack everything that gets in their way," Kateri replied calmly.

"Yesterday you said those critters were harmless."

"I didn't mean to scare you; you looked harassed enough already."

"Harassed?"

She smiled enigmatically.

"Well, I guess I got lucky, then," Ondragon said, sipping nervously at his second glass of Caipi. "Because something did actually chase me right where Pete found the body."

"Maybe the bear thought you were going to take the stash he'd put by for a rainy day."

"You mean the body?"

"It's possible."

"But it sounds like there's something to Deputy Hase's bear theory. Pete thinks it was some kind of woodland monster running around." Ondragon shook his head, laughing. "If you ask me, that little hillbilly's got too much imagination. That's what you get for living in the woods too long. I think he called the creature Wendigo. Yeah, that's it: Wendigo . . ." He paused. Kateri had frozen in midmotion. The bottle of beer was hanging in the air in front of her lips. Condensation dripped onto her lap.

"What is it?" he asked.

She blinked and looked at him. Cool detachment and something else had entered her dark eyes. Was it unease?

"The forest monster is not to be trifled with," she finally said. "And it is better not to speak his name aloud."

Ondragon set his glass on the counter. "You're not telling me you believe in it too?"

"I'm Native American, my tribe is based here in the north, and I grew up with the legend. My grandparents passed it on to my parents and my parents passed it on to me. And like them, I will eventually pass it on to my children."

"The Legend of the Wendigo?"

"Shh! I told you, never speak his name!"

"Oh, right. Sorry. Please, tell me about the legend."

She glared at him for a while. "But only if you promise me to show more respect for this being."

Ondragon nodded.

"All right." She brushed a strand of hair behind her ear, leaned forward farther, and continued speaking softly. "The word *Wendigo*, Paul, comes from the language of the Anishinabe tribes, which include us Ojibwe, and it's very old. Older than your ancient Europe. The Anishinabe tribes here in the northern United States and Canada are different from the Iroquois in one particular respect. The Anishinabe have never eaten human flesh!"

"Human flesh?"

"Yes, the Iroquois certainly resorted to this in bitter winters and devastating droughts to save themselves from starvation. They usually consumed members of other tribes or whites who happened to pass through their territory, especially missionaries." Kateri flashed a wolfish grin. "The Iroquois were considered particularly cruel even among the tribes. The Anishinabe, on the other hand, have always condemned the practice of cannibalism and distanced themselves from it. Among us, it is said: If someone eats human flesh, he becomes a monster. A creature that dwells in the forest and is always hungry and has to keep on eating. This cruel creature represents gluttony and greed. Anishinabe would rather die than eat another human being. But the Wendigo is part of our mythology. We fear him like a god and show respect to him. Of course, we try to avoid him, because anyone who crosses the path of a Wendigo runs the risk of becoming one themself. It can happen to anyone who walks alone through the forest."

"And what does that thing look like? Like a bear?"

"No, more like a giant cat on long legs. He is big, bigger than all the creatures of the forest, and his emaciated body is covered with shaggy fur. Emaciated he is because no matter what he eats, he will never be full. He has sharp, yellow teeth and an unnaturally long tongue. But he can also take other forms, such as that of a giant ice skeleton."

"You mean he's a shape-shifter, like a werewolf?"

"No, a werewolf is a human who transforms. The Wendigo is no longer a human. He was one before he became a spirit, and he is still able to slip into human form to deceive his victims. But I think he is closest to a werewolf, except that he can transform whenever he wants. Not only at full moon. In his human form he can be recognized by his bright red eyes and his heart of ice. Not to mention his feet, which are thick and misshapen and toeless. And they burn all the time, so he always has to wander about restlessly. On windy nights you have to be especially on your guard, because then he travels with the cold north wind, and violent movement in the treetops does not mean that the wind is passing through them!" Kateri paused and gave Ondragon an intense look. At that moment she seemed irresistibly attractive. Her lips were shining, and there was an energized flush in her cheeks.

"What is it?" she asked, registering his gaze.

"Hmm. What was that again? How do people turn into the monster?"

She leaned forward until her lips were not far from his ear.

"By eating human flesh or being bitten by a Wendigo. Sometimes just dreaming about it is enough."

Ondragon caught the scent of her perfume, felt the warmth of her skin. He turned his head slightly, so close to her that he could see the fine hairs on her neck. Then he gave in to temptation and kissed her on the soft crook of her neck.

Kateri didn't seem surprised, because she didn't back away. "I have to warn you, Paul," she whispered, "I am a madwoman."

"No problem, you're not the only one here. Besides, we still have Dr. Arthur."

"Yes, and it was he who advised me to be careful of men like you." She moved away and looked at him. Her eyes said something quite different.

Too bad we aren't alone now, Ondragon thought. Unfortunately, the *Golden Rules* were also clear in this regard: no sexual contact with staff or other patients.

Kateri slid off her barstool. "Goodbye, Paul. See you tomorrow, and don't dream about the forest monster." She winked at him and left the lounge.

Sighing, Ondragon looked after her, then glanced at his empty glass. If it had only contained alcohol. He looked back at the door.

To hell with the *Golden Rules*!

He stood up and followed Miss Wolfe.

Behind him, Hatchet sat in the corner of the sofa, grinning broadly.

CHAPTER 15

1835, Kabetogama,
37 miles southeast of Fort Frances

Where am I? Parker opened his eyes. He was appallingly hungry. His stomach felt as if a pit of rats were eating their way through it. Racked by pain, he turned over in his berth. Although it was dark, he could see very clearly. Every living thing had taken on luminous outlines—the trees, the soldiers, the horses. Even Lacroix, who lay beside him, was surrounded by a reddish-yellow corona. Parker noted that all but one of the guards were asleep.

His stomach rumbled once more, and water shot into his mouth.

Meat, he thought, looking at his friend. *Hungry! I am so hungry! What am I going to do? I want meat!* Parker swallowed, but saliva ran from his mouth as if he were a senile old man. His tongue was swollen like a potato and prevented him from speaking.

With all his might, he averted his burning gaze from his friend and sat up carefully. His bones bit into his muscles like frozen iron. He hardly felt that he was lying on snow. On the contrary, it felt like a bed of warm, absorbent cotton. Slowly he rose, every movement punished with a thousand pinpricks, his misshapen feet a glowing mass of pain. But even worse was the feeling in his stomach! Dizziness seized him and he paused. Parker had suffered hunger many times before, but it had been nothing compared to what he felt now. It was consuming him from the inside, as if his stomach were feeding on his own entrails. Parker doubled over. It was excruciating, and the urge to throw himself on his sleeping friend and sink his teeth into his juicy, warm flesh was overpowering.

"Eaaaat! Eaaat yoooour fill!"

Parker turned around, startled. Who had spoken?

"Eat, and come to me! My sssssson. I wait for you!"

Were the words coming from his fevered brain? He shook his head. Or had they come from over there, in the forest? Parker looked into the glowing web of trees and then across to the night camp. The soldiers were asleep; the horses were dozing, standing, huddled closely together. Parker once again examined the glowing contours of the forest. The tree trunks created a vertical pattern of black and orange-red streaks. Firs and brush glowed like a variegated bouquet of colors, as if they were on fire. In between them squatted dark patches where there was no life. But what was that? Back there, something was glowing, bright and white as a star. At first it was motionless, then it moved, dancing from branch to branch like a will-o'-the-wisp, high up in the trees. Parker felt a breeze on his cheeks, but its chill did not trouble him.

"Eat! And then come to me. Come."

Parker felt the strange power emanating from this light. It grew larger and larger and gradually took shape. Magically, it drew him in.

"Yes, I'm coming," he replied, and before he could do anything about it, his clumsy feet walked into the woods as if of their own volition, straight toward the voice. He felt no more pain. The figure before him grew taller, its forelegs longer than its hind legs. Its face was hidden in shadow, only its eyes glowed red. A hellish stench stabbed sharply into his nose. The creature was as tall and thin as a tree and wrapped in a bright wreath of light, cold energy. It stood before him, swaying. Evil!

Parker felt fear rising inside him. He wanted to scream, but his tongue clogged his throat.

No, I don't want to, his mind screamed instead. *Leave me!*

But the creature knew no pity, only loneliness and hunger. Never-ending hunger. Slowly, it bent its massive head down to Parker. The stench became unbearable and almost robbed him of his senses. This was what death must smell like. Death, blowing its foul breath at him. Hopefully, he would be quick. For Parker did not wish to endure his agony for another heartbeat. He was ready to die, just as he had been when they first met.

"Kill me if it pleases you, but I will never be a child of the Evil One!" Parker spread his arms wide and waited for the emptiness to take him.

CHAPTER 16

2009, Moose Lake,
Cedar Creek Lodge

Ondragon woke up from the dream even before his alarm clock rang. It was strange. Why was he dreaming of a snowy forest and a bunch of dirty men in antiquated uniforms in the middle of summer?

He sat up. The pale gray light of early morning was infiltrating the room, and through the gap in the curtains he could see low-hanging clouds in the sky. It still seemed to be raining. Great!

By seven thirty a.m. he was sitting alone at his table, eating breakfast, and at eight o'clock he was about to rise when Sheila entered the room and headed toward him.

"Mr. Ondragon, Deputy Hase is waiting for you upstairs on the second floor in consultation room three." Without waiting for his response, she turned and left the dining room again.

"Thank you very much, Sheila," Ondragon murmured, tossing his napkin onto the table. On his way to the door, he sensed another intense stare weighing on him and turned his head. Norrfoss had joined Shamgood, and they were both gawking at him openly. Then they put their heads together and began to whisper. Well, they were two of a kind.

Without paying any further attention to either blond head, Ondragon left the dining room and went upstairs. First to his room, to get the bag with the running shoes, and then to the second floor, where he entered the makeshift interrogation room.

To his surprise, Deputy Hase had not yet arrived, but a man with a bald patch and rimless glasses was standing in front of the window, next to a woman of around sixty in outdoor clothing. He could tell from the expressions on both of their faces that they had been engaged in a heated debate before he entered. The man broke free of his stiffness first and approached Ondragon with his hand outstretched. "Good morning, I'm Dr. Peter Schuyler, the medical examiner from Hibbing."

Ondragon introduced himself and shook hands, then turned to the lady, who was scowling.

"Dr. Jill Layton," she said in a low voice. "I work as a behaviorist for the American Bear Association in Orr and was called in as a bear expert on this case. I've been asked to clarify whether this was indeed a bear attack."

"And?" asked Ondragon curiously.

Dr. Layton and Dr. Schuyler both opened their mouths at the same time, but the scientist finally gave a resigned hand gesture and let the medical examiner go first.

"I have examined the bite marks and am firmly convinced that these are injuries that could only have been caused by a large set of teeth with four long canines, either postmortem or premortem. And since the saber-toothed tiger has been extinct since the Pleistocene epoch, at this latitude it can only be the work of a bear." Dr. Schuyler cast a sidelong glance at Dr. Layton, who wrinkled her nose dismissively. "Whether it's a black bear or a grizzly though is for Jane Goodall here to determine. I'm only in charge of forensic facts, not zoology."

"*Behavioral science*, Dr. Schuyler! And I'm not going to make a statement until I've examined the site. This is an extremely brutal attack for a bear."

Dr. Schuyler let out a laugh. "Well, I would always call being eaten by a bear brutal!"

"Your prejudices don't help us. Just because you found bite marks doesn't mean it was a bear. The animals in this region are extremely shy. At least it's different here from other national parks, where the bears are fed by ignorant tourists. So they become conditioned and are not shy of humans, approaching them because they expect to get something to eat. *And* they behave aggressively if they don't get it, or if humans disturb them in their territory. Bears don't invade our habitat, we invade theirs. Bears have been on this planet much longer than humans. We should show more consideration for these creatures. And I would bet my life that it was not a bear from this region that attacked the dead man. If indeed it was an attack."

Dr. Schuyler exhaled in amusement, but Dr. Layton was not to be deterred. "After all, we do extensive research here in the Minnesota woods, and we always find that most bears avoid humans, even flee from them."

"You said it: *most*, but obviously not *all*." The medical examiner raised a finger. "For me, the bite marks speak for themselves. And let's face it, what else could it have been? Some crazy redneck who puts on iron claws and murders lone hikers in order to devour them?"

"For instance . . ." Dr. Layton folded her amazingly muscular arms across her chest.

Dr. Schuyler let out an amused laugh. "You know what I think— you don't want to face the truth, Dr. Layton. Because then you would have to admit that your cuddly bears are not so cuddly, they're beasts that could rip you apart!"

"Give me a break. If anyone's going to become a beast around here, it's me, because I can't listen to your unobjective drivel any longer!" The behavioral scientist bared her powerful teeth at her opponent, but before the pathologist could return the insult, the door opened and Deputy Hase walked in. The discussion ceased.

"Good morning," the deputy muttered, drawing himself up in front of them. Today his face was even redder from shaving. Ondragon guessed he was twenty-five, no older. A redneck in uniform.

"So, let's hear what our . . . *witness* here has to say." Hase looked at him with barely concealed contempt.

Reluctantly, Ondragon began to recount his jog, carefully watching the reactions on the faces of all present. Dr. Schuyler seemed increasingly satisfied, while Dr. Layton's expression changed from amusement to disbelief.

"You see, *that's* the proof!" the behaviorist exclaimed after Ondragon had finished his report. "That was no bear."

"Oh yes? Why not?" teased Dr. Schuyler.

"Because a bear would never chase a human who made lots of noise. It doesn't fit with their natural behavior."

"So?" The medical examiner turned to Ondragon, the light from the overhead lamps reflecting off his lenses. "So, what *do you* say?"

"Me?" Ondragon pointed to himself. "Well, I don't know anything about bears or forensics." The first statement was true, the second wasn't, but these two brawlers didn't need to know that any more than they needed to know that there had been a net strung across the trail at the scene. "I didn't see the animal that was chasing me, so I don't want to comment on that. I hope you can understand."

"How diplomatic of you, Mr. Ondragon," Deputy Hase said with a snide smile. "But Dr. Schuyler and I noticed something else when we examined the crime scene yesterday. The brush where we found the body and through which you said you ran is quite high, like a dense wall of branches on either side of the trail."

Ondragon nodded.

"So we're wondering why you didn't just stay on the trail when you were running from the bear? Why did you go right through the impassable undergrowth when you could have easily escaped via the path?"

The provincial cop might not have been born yesterday after all. Ondragon cleared his throat and feigned embarrassment. "You see, the thing is, I'm from the big city, and I don't usually have much to do with the countryside. Before I jogged around the lake, I met Frank, the gardener, and he told me there were bears here and to be careful. Also, there was a sign that said *bear's den*. So when I heard the noises behind me, I thought it was a bear and I panicked. I ducked into the brush hoping the bear wouldn't find me there. That was naive of me, of course, I know, but it was my first encounter with the local wildlife." He gave an awkward laugh.

Dr. Layton nodded seriously, seeming to forgive his unqualified suspicion of her beloved teddy bears. "The *bear's den*," she explained, "is a cave three miles east of Moose Lake. I know it. It's used by the Indians as a place of worship. But bears haven't lived there for a long time." She brushed back her white-blonde hair and smiled in a grandmotherly fashion. "Would you like to know what I think, Mr. Ondragon?"

"I'd love to." Out of the corner of his eye, he saw Dr. Schuyler roll his eyes.

"I think someone set you up. Someone tried to scare you, hiding there and making strange noises when you ran by. It's pure coincidence that the body was also there. The person who played the trick on you might even have been the young guy who found the body . . ."

"Pete? I find that hard to imagine."

Dr. Layton shrugged her shoulders. "Whatever. Anyway, the evidence at the scene will prove it wasn't a bear." She gave Dr. Schuyler a look.

He was about to retort, but Deputy Hase beat him to it: "Don't worry, Dr. Schuyler, we'll solve the case, bear or no bear. But first, take Dr. Layton to the site and give her the chance to examine it, while I arrange for the other lodge guests and staff to be questioned." Ondragon heard Hase clearly struggling with the word *guests*. Dr. Arthur had probably briefed him in detail on the clientele at CC Lodge.

"Okay, that's it," the deputy said. "We'll keep your shoes, Mr. Ondragon, until the forensics investigation is complete. Then you'll get them back."

"Oh, please, keep those things, I don't want them." The idea of having stuck them into the ribcage of a decomposing corpse didn't exactly make him want to ever use them again, even if they were as good as new. He would try to persuade Sheila to order new running shoes for him from Amazon, provided it delivered to this wasteland.

"Your call." Deputy Hase adjusted his khaki hat and pointed to the door. "Please stand by, Mr. Ondragon, in case we have any further questions. Have a good day." With that, he shooed him out of the room.

Since there was no point in checking for a message from Rudee yet, Ondragon went to the spa area first, to work out on the gym machines—the ones you could use without shoes, at least—and then to relax a little. Unfortunately, the bad weather meant he was not the only one with this idea, but luckily most of the guests were perched in the Turkish steam bath next door and there was no one in the good old sauna. All the better; then at least no one would complain about his scorching-hot Swedish infusions!

Lying on the upper wooden bench, Ondragon enjoyed the hiss of the stones and the sweat beading over his skin. It put him in mind of his childhood, of the few weeks he had spent with his mother each winter in Sweden to allow her to train for her cross-country skiing. After all, Tehran, Nairobi, Cairo, Bangkok, Tokyo, all the cities where he had lived with his parents, were not exactly known for being winter sports meccas. But his father had never denied Ava Birgitta Ondragon anything she desired. He had always indulged her; her sport, her success, and also her wish to take her son with her to her homeland for four weeks over Christmas. Why hadn't his father been like that with him?

After the third round in the sauna, Ondragon lay down to rest on a comfortable couch in the anteroom and dozed off. He was awakened only by the slamming of a wooden door; someone going into the sauna. Sluggishly, he rose and tried his luck with the masseurs. One of them was actually free and invited him to lie down on the table.

"Hello, my name is Vernon; d'you feel a twinge anywhere?"

Ondragon shook hands with the Black hunk who looked like a double of Shaquille O'Neal. "I'm Paul, and I think my back could use a little loosening up, and maybe my legs too."

"No problem, man. Cool tattoo, by the way." Vernon pointed with fingers that could crush a pumpkin at Ondragon's chest, where a Japanese-style dragon snaked from his left collarbone to his nipple. In its right claw were the Japanese characters for the word *enigma* and in the other an *O*.

Ondragon looked down at himself for a moment and nodded. "Thank you; it was a little folly of my youth. I had it done when I was eighteen, in Japan, the traditional way with bamboo needles. I really can't recommend it to anyone, it hurt like hell! But it always reminds me of a certain phase in my life."

Vernon contorted his baby face into a smile. He rolled up his left sleeve, proudly exposing an anchor and two swallows on his enormous biceps. A classic.

"From the Reeperbahn in Hamburg! Used to go to sea before I retrained."

"Well, you've seen the world, then." Ondragon lay down on his stomach on the table, and Vernon expertly began his work.

"Don't you find it a little boring here, in the middle of nowhere, then?" he asked the masseur, sensing more than seeing Vernon shrug his massive shoulders.

"I've done, how should I put it, quite a bit of running riot in the past." He laughed, and Ondragon could well imagine what he meant. "But at some point, after you've docked in every port, you realize that the best wharf is at home."

That was wise.

"I'm actually from Minneapolis and the sea taught me that people are hard to uproot. So I came back and, hey, I met a sweet lady and married her. We have two kids."

Enviable. Ondragon wondered where his own roots were. In Sweden? Or Germany? Thailand? Japan? The USA?

"And what about you, Paul? Do you have children?"

Ondragon considered what to say. He didn't even have a steady girlfriend, because what he did was too dangerous to be compatible with a wife and children. For him it was better to be on his own. A family made him vulnerable to blackmail. Sure, even Mafia bosses had a family, usually quite large ones, although they had many enemies. But maybe it was because he didn't feel ready to take on the responsibility yet. He turned his head to bring the giant into his line of sight. The man's hands were rolling and kneading his back as if he were bread dough.

"No, I don't have children. I think I just haven't found the right woman yet."

"That's too bad, man. Kids are the spice of life. There's nothing better than watching them grow up."

"May I ask where your family lives? Surely not here in the lodge grounds, right?"

"They live in Cook, which is twenty-five miles south of Orr. My wife has a job there and the kids can go to school. I do double weeks here. That means two weeks on and two weeks off. It's okay and it's a good living. I don't need much, as long as the family's doing well."

Aha, so Vernon was one of the few who didn't live here all the time. Ondragon decided to view the relaxation of the massage a nice by-product and shifted his focus, asking Vernon more questions to gain more insight into how the lodge operated.

"Of course I know Jeremy Bates," Vernon boomed a little later. Ondragon smiled quietly to himself. How people could talk when you pushed the right buttons. The sailor-masseur even seemed genuinely pleased to be able to recount the story. "Was filling in for Bates at the time," he explained. "That's why I got wind of all the fuss when he was fired."

"Fired?"

"Oh yeah, that was last winter. Bates worked the opposite shift to me, which is why I only ran into him during changeovers. Sometimes not even then. I never saw him after he was laid off. Apparently, he still lives in Orr, but none of us really keep in touch with him."

"Why did he have to leave the lodge?"

"Bates broke the rules. He drove a guest's car into the woods and hid it so the guest could secretly take little joyrides. The whole thing only came to light because the guest Bates was doing the favor for disappeared one day without a trace. We looked for him and discovered the tire tracks from his car."

So far Vernon's story matches Kateri Wolfe's, Ondragon thought. But what the masseur told next was new . . . and extremely implausible.

"Of course, it's just a rumor, but everyone here at the lodge knows the story." Vernon clapped both hands on Ondragon's back. "I heard it from Nurse Marsha. Supposedly, two days before the incident, Jeremy Bates went out back to the spa area in the evening to have a smoke. While he was there, they say, he found strange tracks in the snow and, out of curiosity, followed them into the woods. He heard a noise, and saw a figure creeping through the snowy undergrowth some distance away. Bates hid behind a log and watched. The figure had shaggy fur, apparently, and was twice his size!"

"A bear?"

"No, not a bear." Vernon paused for dramatic effect, and Ondragon wondered if he was pulling his leg.

Then Vernon continued. "Bates noticed the eerie figure drop something in the snow and waited until it had disappeared. Then he went over and dug it up." Vernon laughed. "I expect to this day he wishes he'd left it alone!" His laughter died, and his voice lowered mysteriously, as if he was telling his children a creepy story. In point of fact, he wasn't a bad storyteller. Ondragon listened attentively.

"What Bates found wasn't exactly appetizing, you know. The story goes that he couldn't stop throwing up in his room later." Another pause. "Guess what he found in the snow, Paul."

Ondragon shrugged his shoulders. "I don't know."

"It was a human arm! A bloody woman's hand with painted nails!"

Ondragon wondered again how Vernon knew for sure, if he hadn't been there, and why no one had called the police back then. After all, it was a severed body part. But he let the masseur enjoy his horror story and listened willingly to the conclusion. Of course, the arm had disappeared and the tracks had been unclear when Bates had visited the place with his colleagues a little later. But Bates had repeatedly talked about the figure and had claimed that it had been the Wendigo.

"Honestly, man, the Wendigo!" Vernon's laugh boomed out.

Of course, thought Ondragon. This was now his second encounter with the fabled creature. The forests around here were obviously not good for your health.

"Have you ever heard of it, Paul?"

"Isn't that some kind of Indian forest monster that eats people?"

"Exactly. Pretty *spooky*, huh?" Vernon patted Ondragon on the back again. "There, you can turn around now, and I'll take a look at your legs."

Ondragon lay down on his back. "Nice story. But what did Bates do after he realized the arm was gone?"

Vernon lifted his massive shoulders. "He went nuts. Kept going on and on about the Wendigo. Two days later he was gone."

Ondragon pursed his lips thoughtfully. Was this simply a scary story that the employees here had made up, or was there some truth to it? Long, lonely winter nights were known to make people melancholy . . . but also susceptible to horror stories. Any Scandinavian would immediately agree. There were too many inconsistencies in the Bates case. If what Vernon said was true, why had no one believed the man? At least the story about the arm. Surely, Dr. Arthur or one of the other people in charge would have taken that seriously. After all, Bates was an employee of the lodge and not one of its neurotic inmates.

"Don't worry about it, Paul. There's no such thing as a Wendigo. It's all just made up. Bates was a pain in the ass; there was a lot of talk about him. He was a weirdo and kept pestering everybody about some rocker shoes. I guess he had a sideline in sales. You know the ones I mean? Those stupid, expensive shoes with the rounded soles. They're all the rage now. Bates used to wear them himself. Besides, everybody knew he was never happy here, and he was always afraid of the forest. If you ask me, he just couldn't cope and went crazy. And the missing guest did eventually turn up; he had stopped the treatment at his own request and gone home without telling anyone. It's as simple as that!"

Ondragon nodded, pondering what the missing Oliver Orchid might have to say about his break from therapy.

"Do you exercise much, Paul?" Vernon changed the subject. "Your body is toned; you can tell when you massage it. Little knots here and there, but otherwise your muscles are well developed."

"Thanks. I try to do something every other day, jogging, martial arts, basketball . . ."

"Basketball? Hey, that's a good idea; we can play a game when you feel like it and the weather is better. There's a hoop by the tennis court, and I have a good leather ball. I always have one with me. I even had one back on the ship." Vernon laughed his pleasantly deep laugh.

"Okay, why not? It's a good alternative to jogging. But I won't be able to until I get new sports shoes. Mine were confiscated by the police today."

"Oh no. Then you're the one who stepped on the body! Man, how disgusting!"

Great, Ondragon thought. So word had already spread. It was unbelievable how fast things got around.

Vernon wrinkled his nose. "Revolting. But who's the dead guy? Do you know anything about it?"

Ondragon had heard Deputy Hase say the police were going over all the missing persons cases in Minnesota from the last six months. That could only mean they didn't think the dead man was anyone from the lodge.

"The medical examiner has to examine the body first," he replied, taking the precaution of not mentioning the main suspect, the bear. As he did so, he realized that Kateri, unlike everyone else here, must have kept her mouth shut, because Vernon apparently knew nothing about the supposed bear attack. "Maybe it really was just a hiker who had an accident."

"Well, I hope that's what it was." The masseur's tone was odd, as if he had a nasty hunch. Ondragon would have liked to ask him about it, but he didn't want to come off as too curious. His interest in the matter had to remain unobtrusive. So he thanked Vernon for the excellent massage and rose from the table.

"I hope I didn't scare you off with my scary story."

"No, not at all. On the contrary, you entertained me brilliantly, Vernon. I'll definitely be back. And . . . let me know when you feel like playing a game of basketball."

"Sure, man. See ya."

After Ondragon had been back to his room and dressed for lunch, he headed to the dining room, where he took a seat at Kateri Wolfe's table.

"Did you have a relaxing time at the spa?" she asked.

"How do you know I was at the spa?" he replied, looking at her. Last night he hadn't followed her to her room, which he might well have done, because her signals had been clear. Something had stopped him. He didn't know what. Good sense, his upbringing, decency? Whatever it had been, it was the reason he could now look her openly in the face without being embarrassed. Silently, he thanked his inner chaperone for stopping him. Not that he didn't find Miss Wolfe attractive, but he felt much more comfortable maintaining a certain distance for the time being. Purely for the buzz; he was keen to keep the mystery of this woman alive for a little longer.

"I went to the sauna earlier and saw you taking a nap," Kateri said.

"I see; so you like to sweat too?"

"When I was a kid, I would often go with my parents to a sweat lodge we had built in the backyard. For me, it's more of a spiritual thing. Sweating opens the mind to worlds we wouldn't otherwise be aware of. It connects you to the elements, to life."

Ondragon nodded. For him too the sauna was a kind of retreat, a safe place where he could think in peace. Out of the corner of his eye, he noticed Shamgood and Norrfoss staring steadily at him. The pointer on his distrust scale suddenly jumped into the red zone and gave off a screeching warning signal. Ondragon struggled to regulate it as he watched Kateri spooning up her soup, hungrily but with a certain elegance.

"Tell me more about yourself," she said when she had finished eating.

"Like what?"

"For example, what's this key chain about?" She pointed to the pink talisman lying on the table. He had attached his room key to it, as a placeholder for the car keys. Somewhat bashfully, he put his hand over the little enameled bear on whose belly was written *I love Berlin.*

"Inappropriate, isn't it? But there's a story behind it." And it should really say: *I fucking hate Berlin!*

"Is it classified, or are you allowed to tell me?"

"It's not exactly a secret . . . but . . ." But it revealed the constant risk he lived with. Ondragon decided to tell Kateri the *light* version. "This stupid key chain once saved my life. That's why I always carry it with me. The fact that it's such a cheesy thing is just a coincidence. It was four years ago, when I stopped off in Berlin to visit my parents." One of several failed attempts to meet his parents after everything that had happened. But he had left again without having achieved anything. He couldn't. He simply could not face his parents.

"I went to a shop at the Bahnhof Zoo train station to buy my godchild, Sally, she's eight, a nice souvenir from Berlin—the city of bears. She was mad keen on Berlin and actually thought it was where the bears lived." He laughed softly at the memory of the episode, which had actually happened that way, but had turned into something very threatening shortly after. "I noticed these key chains hanging on a rack by the cash register. I went to pick one up, but it slipped from my fingers and fell to the floor. At the exact moment I was bending down to pick it up, the window of the store shattered, and where I had been standing, a bullet smashed into the newspaper displays."

Kateri's mouth opened in disbelief. "A robbery? Or why was someone shooting at the store?"

Because I *was in there*, Ondragon thought. He looked at Kateri. He couldn't for the life of him tell her that, even if he would have liked to. Deep inside his orphaned mind, he longed to pour his heart out to someone. Instead, he shrugged and said, "I don't know why there was shooting. But Bahnhof Zoo is a nasty place, a transshipment point for drugs and stuff. Maybe two dealers were fighting and a bullet ricocheted through the glass."

"Did they catch the guy who was shooting?"

"No, the police searched for him, but without success. Fortunately, not much damage was done, just a broken shop window." In fact, it had to do with a job he had completed shortly before in India. He had gotten too close to a corrupt businessman, and the latter's widow had immediately hired a hit man to take him out. A somewhat exaggerated reaction, he'd thought. After the assassination attempt, he had fled headlong from the store to avoid being questioned by the police. He had nothing against the police, but the guys were not always the best place to be when it came to the underworld. And luring the hit man to a parking lot near Malibu two weeks after the Berlin incident and killing him there was not the way to impress a lady.

"I didn't realize your consultancy job was so dangerous," Kateri joked.

Ondragon raised his eyebrows. "Highly dangerous! Just think

of all that paper and those tons of files. And then the offices. Nasty places! No, joking aside. When I'm hired by companies or individuals, it's mostly about numbers and balance sheets. Most of them want to optimize their business and restructure it to make it as profitable as possible, and I help them find the right solution. It's that simple." In a sense, his job really was simple: People had problems, and he solved them. But it wasn't about numbers and balance sheets, and the solutions weren't always nice and clean, and were by no means cost-neutral. On the contrary, his intervention was expensive. But he also bore most of the risk. That was the deal.

"If you spend so much time in corporate offices, surely you have access to insider knowledge." Interested, Kateri leaned forward. "Have you never been tempted to profit from it, Paul?"

Before Ondragon could answer, Kateri suddenly raised a hand.

"Stop, don't say anything, so I don't have to lie if someone asks me about it later." She gave him a conspiratorial look. "Instead, tell me what you think we should do on this rainy day?"

"I'm afraid I'm due at Dr. Arthur's Round Table in a few minutes."

Kateri laughed in amusement. "Well, have fun searching for the Holy Grail. I hope the therapy helps you. For me, anyway, it's been a blessing. Dr. Arthur was good friends with my parents and is taking care of me now. He is a great person; he helps me a lot. Without him, I wouldn't know what to do."

Ondragon took his talisman from the table and pocketed it. The stares of Shamgood and Norrfoss were literally burning into the back of his neck. "Well, I hope he can help me too." He stood up.

Kateri cocked her head to one side and asked quietly, "You're afraid of something, aren't you?"

Surprised, Ondragon paused at the table.

"It's something deep inside you, am I right?" Kateri's voice sounded understanding. Too good to be true. Her smile was mild, as if she understood exactly what he was feeling. Their eyes met, and Ondragon didn't know afterward exactly why he had set his principles aside. Perhaps because of the longed-for feeling of familiarity he felt with this woman.

"You're right, Kateri," he said softly. "I'm scared."

She looked at him steadfastly. "Will you also tell me what you're scared of?"

"If you promise not to laugh?"

"I promise."

"Okay." Ondragon glanced over at Shamgood and Norrfoss. They had disappeared. Then he turned back to Kateri, looked her in the eye, and said, "I'm scared of books."

CHAPTER 17

1835, Kabetogama,
37 miles southeast of Fort Frances

Vincent Lacroix awoke with a jolt from a fitful sleep. It was pitch dark and icy cold. The fire that the soldiers had lit for the night camp had gone out. The soldier on guard duty was probably fast asleep and had not noticed.

But that isn't his job, Lacroix thought, trying awkwardly to wrap himself back up in his thick wool blanket. The fir branches that served as his bed crunched softly beneath him. Wet cold moved from the ground up into his bones.

Merde, *we shouldn't be out here*, he cursed silently to himself. A goddamn piece of shit this was! Spending the night in the middle of the forest, in the freezing cold. He hoped Two-Elk would decipher their clue in the cabin and find a way to free them from the soldiers. And hopefully he had gotten something from his tribal brethren for the bite of the beast that had infected Parker with its ominous curse. Lacroix was worried about his old friend.

He rolled over on his bed to see how he was doing. Parker was lying on his side and stared back at him. The whites of his eyes glowed eerily in the darkness.

Lacroix exhaled, startled.

"Eh, *mon ami*, how goes it?" he asked.

Parker did not answer immediately, and Lacroix was worrying he had gone to the eternal hunting grounds, when he heard a slurring sound.

"Alan? What's the matter—can't you speak?"

Another slur, as if the other man was drunk. Lacroix propped himself up on an elbow and nudged Parker. The slurring became a hiss, then he heard a word.

"Wendigo."

Lacroix's blood froze in his veins.

"Where, Alan? Where is he? Is he here?" Frightened, he looked around and felt with his left hand for the knife in his boot. Without his guns, he felt naked and defenseless. If the Wendigo came now, they would all go to hell together!

But he couldn't spot anything unusual in the dark. The snow was reflecting enough light from the sky for him to make out the dark piles of sleeping soldiers around the extinguished campfire. In the background stood the horses, unsaddled and tethered to the light birch trunks. The animals were quiet.

Lacroix relaxed. The horses would be the first to scent a wild creature approaching. So Parker must have seen something else. Perhaps a mirage from his fever dreams. He turned back to his friend. He was now lying there with his eyes closed, breathing heavily. Lacroix felt his forehead. It was cold. Two-Elk had told him that the Wendigo's fever did not burn like a normal fever. It slowly turned a person to ice. But the sufferer endured terrible heat, while his insides gradually froze and became impervious to external cold. Parker, then, was in desperate need of warmth if he was ever to escape this grim damnation. Lacroix hoped the soldiers kept the fort well heated, or his friend would be lost. Carefully, he pulled the blanket over Parker's head and went back to sleep himself.

The next morning Lacroix was roused from sleep by a loud roar. It was the soldier on watch receiving a well-deserved dressing-down from Lieutenant Stafford for falling asleep and letting the fire go out. Lacroix rose with difficulty and went a few steps into the woods to pee.

As he tied his waistband again, his eyes fell on a fresh trail that ran a few steps farther through the snow toward the camp. He froze.

The trail was all too familiar!

Tabernac!

Lacroix turned and followed the trail. It led directly to Parker's sleeping place.

CHAPTER 18

2009, Moose Lake,
Cedar Creek Lodge

Dr. Arthur received him as usual: firm handshake, jovial smile, golden gaze. He did not so much as mention Ondragon's testimony in the case of the dead man in the woods, and after they had chatted a little about the lousy weather, he explained that today would be their first hypnosis session. Ondragon agreed and allowed himself to be escorted to a comfortable couch. Dr. Arthur took a seat in an armchair next to it and took out a pen and notepad.

"So, Paul, we are now going to use hypnosis to travel back into your past to find the moment when your anxiety began. Close your eyes, relax, and think of the color—you know the one."

Ondragon did as he was told, but suddenly felt a growing uneasiness. He had never been hypnotized before. What if Dr. Arthur brought to light not only unpleasant things from his childhood, but also the dark secrets of his job?

"Your concern is completely unfounded, Paul," the therapist said, as if he already had access to his thoughts. "Everything you say will remain in this room. After all, I'm bound by the utmost discretion, just like you."

All right. Ondragon tried hard and relaxed. The color of his fear gradually appeared in front of his inner eye. Pine green.

"That's it," he heard the doctor's sonorous voice. "I'm going to count to three, and on the count of three you'll go to the place where your fear began. It won't hurt. Hypnosis will protect you; it's like a room made of absorbent cotton from which you can safely observe everything. Get ready. One, two . . . three . . ."

Paul looked down at himself in amazement. He was wearing black pleated pants, a white shirt, and a pine-green sweater with a crest on it—his school uniform. He was ten years old again and he hated this garment. He looked like a total nerd!

He glanced out the window. It was noon, and the sun was streaming down from the smog-yellow sky, casting a sharp shadow next to him on the wall. The air conditioner whispered its cold, quiet breath down his neck. He was in his father's library, in the German embassy building, the door was closed and the key was in the lock on the other side—as was so often the case when Mr. Ambassador Siegfried Ondragon was punishing him. Outside the barred window, the noise of the Cairo streets was roaring by, an omnipresent madness of honking, shouting, and rattling engines. Cairo, the city that never slept.

Paul looked calmly at the room that was his prison. All around the walls were ten-foot-high shelves, filled to bursting with books, books, and more books! They eyed him invitingly. Paperbacks, hardbacks, illustrated books, encyclopedias, lexicons, dictionaries; red, green, brown, bound in leather or linen and with embossed letters. Goethe, Schiller, Tolstoy, Kant. Novels here and there, but nothing trivial. His father abhorred that kind of literature, calling it "fast food for the uneducated"!

Paul's throat went dry and he choked down an oppressive, creeping fear. He knew many of these books well, had always passed the time with them when the wait for the door to open became too long. Siegfried Ondragon was all too ready to let him languish there all day; even food was passed to him through a narrow opening in the door, as if he were in prison. His mother often put in a good word for him, but his father mercilessly imposed his punishment. The reason he was sitting here today was clear. He had been hanging around the bazaar again after school and had not come home immediately as his father had ordered. He didn't want Paul to have anything to do with the dirty riffraff there, but the big Khan el-Khalili bazaar had a magical pull for young boys with enough pocket money, and that's why he was always drawn there.

Paul put his hand in his pocket and pulled out the small object he had bought at the bazaar. It was an ancient Egyptian Horus falcon made of turquoise-glazed faience. Paul loved these figures and wanted to be an archaeologist when he grew up. The Egyptian Museum in Cairo was his favorite place. He liked to go there with his mother, who was equally fascinated by the ancient world of the pharaohs.

Paul raised his head. The books loomed and towered over him. The shelves groaned quietly under the tons of dust and paper.

"You're a naughty boy," he heard something whisper. "And you'll never get out of here. Soon you will be ours. Then even your mother won't be able to help you." They laughed quietly. They were insidious creatures, the books. They chewed you up and spat you out if you got too involved with them, and besides, they told him nasty stories. Stories of war, death, jealousy, and greed. And they were all full of bad people. Only a few of the books were kind, like Kipling's *Jungle Book* or Nils Holgersson, perhaps because they were mostly about animals. Paul took a step back from the high wall of books, accompanied by his shadow. He looked up anxiously. His father dragged them everywhere. To every place they moved to. It was always there, the library, like a giant behemoth of millions of words, heavy as stone. A sluggish, apathetic pet that got more attention than Paul. He would be only too happy to get rid of all of them. He wished his father would pay attention to him and not them. But there they were! Always! And they mocked him.

"I hate you!" he hissed at the books. But the response was a multi-voiced laugh.

"We'll get you, Paul, sooner or later. And the other one too!"

"What other one?"

"Your shadow, of course! Hahahaha!" The shrieking laughter sounded ominous, and Paul took another step back.

"My shadow?" He heard the anxious echo of his own small voice reverberating off the books and looked pleadingly at the door. Why didn't his father finally come and free him?

"Hahahaha! Look at little Paul, he's almost pissing his pants! He doesn't know his father has ordered us to punish him." All at once the books shifted, forming themselves into grimaces and faces. They laughed and mocked him. "Paul, don't you know how much your father loves us? He loves us more than he loves you! We are his most precious possession, his treasure!"

Paul felt tears running hot down his cheeks. "Stop it!" he shouted at the laughing wall of books. "I hate you!" He lifted the small falcon figurine he still held in his hand and hurled it with all his might against the spines of the books. In slow motion, it flew toward the hated paper creatures, bouncing headfirst against a wobbly stack of encyclopedias. These rustled indignantly and slid toward the edge of the shelf. They hung there for a moment, but then the force of gravity grabbed them and pulled them from their stronghold. Screeching for help, they fell toward the floor.

Paul, his eyes wide open, followed their trajectory as if fixed to the spot. Just before they hit him, he jumped back . . . and bumped hard against the shelf at his back. It gave a dangerous sigh, and after a terrible second of silence, it toppled forward. Mountains of bound paper came crashing down on him like an avalanche of stones, beating his forehead bloody and suffocating everything that breathed beneath it. Paul opened his mouth to scream, but there was nothing but paper and dust.

Air! I need air!

He swallowed and tasted the disgusting tang of the books.

Then he heard his shadow screaming!

Jerkily, Ondragon came out of the hypnotic trance. He was breathing heavily and his heart was pounding in his throat. Looking around, trying to ground himself, he found the yellow eyes of Dr. Arthur.

"Easy, Paul, you're back here with me. You're safe."

Ondragon sat up and wiped the sweat from his face. His hands were shaking.

Wow! So that was what hypnosis was like. He turned to Dr. Arthur. "So, do you know now why I'm afraid of books?"

The psychotherapist nodded thoughtfully. "I think we've isolated the event that triggered your anxiety. Next, we need to work on eliminating the negative associations you've been linking to it. One thing was a little curious though."

"What thing?" Ondragon rotated his tense shoulders. He felt as if he had been run over by a freight train. Unfortunately, he couldn't remember what had happened during the hypnosis.

"Well, it seems you were not alone in your father's library."

Ondragon looked questioningly at Dr. Arthur.

"There was someone else with you."

"Someone else? Who?"

"I can't tell you that. We'll clarify it at our next meeting." Dr. Arthur rose. "I'll see you again tomorrow. Until then, rest up; hypnosis is taxing on the mind and body, even if you don't realize that right away. If you feel any aftereffects, talk to my staff; they'll know how to help."

Ondragon left the meeting room and went to the lounge. He would have loved a whiskey on the rocks. He desperately needed a strong drink. But the *Golden Rules* didn't offer much scope for that, so he asked the bartender for a double espresso. And indeed, the bitter taste of the coffee brought him back to himself.

"Hey, man, what's up?" Hatchet sat down next to him at the bar, very much the Lord of Darkness with his deathly complexion and goth-black sunglasses.

"Hypnosis," Ondragon replied shortly. Somewhere in the back of his mind was a soft echo:

I'm easyyy . . .

"Oh yeah, that packs a punch." Hatchet ordered himself a Coke.

"You don't say. So how's it going with you?"

Hatchet grinned, his teeth whiter than bone. "Going to be allowed to split in a couple of days. Cool, huh?"

"Absolutely. I'm only on my fourth day and I'm already having a meltdown. I don't understand how anyone can last here for weeks without actually going crazy. When I'm done with this shit, I'm actually going to need a shrink!" Ondragon raised his hand in resignation and lowered it again. He felt downright lousy, though he didn't know why. It must be the weather or something.

"You're right, man," Hatchet agreed. "Some of the sick weirdos around here keep coming back for more. Can you believe it? Nah. But I'll be damned if I'm gonna set foot in here again. Fuck, when

I get out of here, I'm gonna throw a big party with booze, coke, and broads! The whole nine yards. Hey, come by sometime when you get out, Paul. My house is in Malibu; you're welcome any time. Here's my number." He handed him a black business card with a white axe and a blood-soaked phone number on it. Funny, somehow Ondragon had thought the guy lived in Transylvania and not sun-drenched California. He wondered what sun protection factor Hatchet wore when he went to the beach. Well, he probably only went out at night in any case.

"Thanks." He pocketed the card. "Tell me, Hatchet, have you ever heard of a guest named Oliver Orchid?"

"Nope. Why?"

"No reason. I'm just wondering who's in room twenty. Never seen them."

"Neither have I. The room's probably empty."

"In such an expensive clinic?"

Hatchet shrugged his shoulders.

No way, thought Ondragon. They would never leave a room empty here. So who was living in it? A ghost? He looked thoughtfully at his empty espresso cup. The coffee had left dark streaks on the white porcelain. "And Miss Wolfe?" he asked. "Do you know anything about her?"

"That girl is pretty messed up, I tell you, man! But she's also pretty hot. There's something devilish about her. A real Bride of Satan!"

Now Mr. Evil was exaggerating. Bride of Satan! What nonsense!

"But she won't let anyone get near her, which is a shame, really. I'm sure she and I would make a great couple. Hey, Paul, you want to start something with her?" Hatchet nudged him and gave a filthy laugh.

"Maybe . . . But I was actually wondering why she was here."

"I don't know, maybe because of Dr. Arthur's specialty." He grinned.

"What specialty?"

"Cannibalism!"

CHAPTER 19

*1835, Kabetogama,
37 miles southeast of Fort Frances*

Parker was still lying motionless as Lacroix knelt beside him and inconspicuously covered the toeless tracks. Whoever they came from, Parker or the Wendigo, the soldiers must not discover them under any circumstances, or else they would immediately be suspected of having murdered the Walcotts. And the lieutenant would be the very last person to stand by them in this matter. He believed only what he saw with his eyes anyway. He was probably still assuming there was a rational explanation for the family's horrific death. But he was wrong.

Lacroix shook Parker's shoulder. "Hey, Alan, it's time, you have to get up!"

The old trapper opened his bloodshot eyes and groaned.

"We have to go on. You'll be better at the fort; we can help with what ails you there." He thought of Parker's swollen feet and the cold fever raging inside him. Hopefully, he would be able to hold on. With difficulty, he helped him to his feet and dragged him over to the newly lit fire. In the breath of the blazing heat, where the soldiers too were huddled close together, the two prisoners were given hot coffee, dried meat, and rusks. Lacroix drank two large gulps gratefully and took a bite of the dried meat. Then he helped Parker down the brew, but his body was increasingly rejecting anything warm. Again and again he spat the coffee into the snow. Parker looked up apologetically. His head seemed a little clearer again and he felt ashamed of his indisposition.

"It's all right, *mon ami*." Lacroix patted his friend's hunched back.

"Is he getting worse?" Lieutenant Stafford had come up beside them and was looking down with little compassion.

"If he doesn't get into the warmth soon, then . . ." Lacroix left it unspoken. He himself did not know exactly what would come, death or transformation.

"We will reach the fort tomorrow evening. Until then, see that you keep your friend alive so that he can be questioned by the colonel."

"As a witness? And here I was feeling like a convicted criminal." Lacroix smiled smugly, which did not please the lieutenant.

With a grave expression, Stafford continued. "Gentlemen, I appeal to your loyalty and your sense of honor. Help the Army of His Majesty King William IV to solve this crime. I believe it is your duty as—"

Lacroix raised a hand. "Lieutenant, my friend and I have lived here in the forest for half a human lifetime, and the only power we feel a duty to is that of friendship. I would die for my comrade here, but not in order to be interrogated by His Majesty's Army! Besides, I am a Frenchman and have nothing to do with your English laws."

Stafford blinked indignantly. "Watch your mouth. I have many other powers!"

"I don't give two hoots for your powers."

"I just wanted to point out to you, Monsieur Lacroix, that it is in your own interest to help us. A terrible crime has been perpetrated against innocent people. Your friends!"

The dog, Lacroix thought. Stafford knew exactly how much the Walcott thing was getting to him, and was shamelessly taking advantage of it. He rose and looked the lieutenant right in the eye. "If anything should happen to my friend Parker while he is doing his duty as a man of honor, I will do my duty and take my revenge on you, Lieutenant. There is no reason to drag a sick man through the snowy wilderness, no matter how urgently his presence may be required as a witness in any part of this world. That good family out there is dead, and they were *our friends*! So why would we kill them? Of course we want to help find whoever has them on their conscience, but whether we do that today or a month from now, it won't bring them back to life!"

Out of the corner of his eye, Lacroix saw more and more of the soldiers turning toward them with interest. Lieutenant Stafford also noticed that the mood was threatening to tip against him and puffed up his chest in seeming confidence. Unfortunately, he was not in control of his left fist. It was opening and closing incessantly around the hilt of his burnished saber.

Lacroix could clearly read the displeasure in the soldiers' eyes. They too had probably been long wondering why they were running around out here in the miserable cold, risking being slaughtered by a maniacal killer.

"I'll talk to you later, Monsieur Lacroix," the lieutenant hissed, and to get the last word in, he gave Sergeant Hancock an excessively sharp order to break camp and set out.

Lacroix spat disdainfully into the snow and set about packing his things. He took out one of his water bottles and filled it with hot water. He then tied it to Parker's chest, carefully wrapped him in several layers of jackets and blankets, and helped him onto his horse. A short time later, the troop started moving.

Lacroix did not look back, but he sensed the dark presence of the being behind him in the forest. It was like an invisible, unseen pulsation sending cold waves of hatred toward them.

He forced himself to keep his eyes to the front. The fear of the thing that was following them through the cold undergrowth grew with every mile. And soon it seemed to him that he could detect on the wind a hint of the stench that had contaminated the Walcott house. But as quickly as the notion came, it left him, and Lacroix wondered if his overtaxed senses had been playing a trick on him. He breathed in sharply through his nose and sniffed.

Nothing. Just clear, icy cold, underpinned by the subtle scent of wet, mossy wood.

And still his discomfort clung to him like a tacky shadow.

The coming night would be darker than the one that had gone.

CHAPTER 20

2009, Moose Lake,
Cedar Creek Lodge

Cannibalism?" Ondragon looked at Hatchet in disbelief. "How do you know?"

"I heard something about it on the scene one time. You know, the music I make attracts a lot of fucked-up people. Not that I'm like them, but some guys who listen to death metal and stuff like that aren't quite right in the head. One guy at a party told me that Dr. Arthur had supposedly once treated him for cannibalism."

"Like, here at the lodge?"

"No idea. I don't even know if it's true."

"Then why would you say something like that? Cannibalism is a crime."

Hatchet looked at him slyly. "But it would fit nicely with our hell-bride, wouldn't it?"

Ondragon didn't like that at all, and he wondered why Hatchet's reaction to Kateri was so extreme. Well, maybe she had rebuffed him a few times and now he was implying she was more adventurous than she should be. Or maybe he just thought it was cool. Who knew? In any case, it was strange that his advance research on Dr. Arthur hadn't picked up on this. He would have to make up for that urgently. If only to check whether Hatchet was right.

He apologized to the death metal musician and went quickly to his room. He retrieved his iPhone from the safe and spent half an hour unsuccessfully googling cannibalism and Jonathan Aaron Arthur. Nothing. He lowered the phone. So he hadn't missed anything after all. There wasn't anything on the internet on the subject, nor was there in the documents he'd obtained earlier relating to the psychotherapist and CC Lodge. Either Hatchet had been spinning a yarn or Dr. Arthur must have kept his unusual specialty firmly under wraps. But that would make sense; you didn't necessarily want to peddle yourself as an "expert in cannibalism." Especially if you ran a luxurious private clinic. But what if Hatchet's assumption was correct? What if Dr. Arthur *was* treating his special patients here at Cedar Creek Lodge? That would be beyond belief! An unacceptable state of affairs for all garden variety insane guests, to say the least. Ondragon shook his head and turned his thoughts to Kateri. What was wrong with her? Was she really here because she had cannibalistic tendencies? She had told him she was a vegetarian because she couldn't stand the taste of meat. Had that been a lie?

Ondragon shivered. Kateri Wolfe, a cannibal? He had to admit that the idea both excited and frightened him. He glanced at his cell phone. This would also make some sense of Vernon's story about Bates and the severed arm in the woods. And the chatter about the Wendigo, the forest monster that ate human flesh. It all fit together somehow.

Man, what had he got himself into here?

Ondragon quickly dialed the number of his assistant.

"Hello, Chief!" called Charlize from faraway Los Angeles. Hearing her voice made Ondragon long for the big city. His world, where he had the freedom to drive wherever he wanted; all he had to do was get on the freeway and he was away. He missed the smell of hot asphalt, overflowing trash cans, sunscreen, overcrowded bars, cafes, and air-conditioned supermarkets. Wonderful!

"Charlize, could you do something for me?"

"And that would be?"

"It's two things, but they both have to do with one place."

"Yes?"

"Are you writing it down?"

"Hai, Paul-san!"

"Well, it's about Orr, here in Minnesota, a small town, lives off the timber industry. The first thing I want to know is if there was a murder in March 2009 or earlier, if anyone was reported missing or if a body turned up. The second thing is a family named Parker. They lived near Orr and there are two sons, Peter and Mortimer. The father and mother were found dead in their cabin in 1996. I'd like to know what the cause of death was and if the killer was caught. And then I need any medical reports or records from Dr. Jonathan Aaron Arthur relating to cannibalism. Anything you can find on that. Oh, and find out if a man named Jeremy Bates still lives in Orr."

"Chief?"

"Yes?"

"Is everything okay?"

"Why?"

"Sounds like you're sharing a cell with Hannibal Lecter. Let's face it, you're as full of beans as a schoolboy on a ghost train. I've never known you like this."

"I'd like you to get the information as soon as possible, you hear? It's very urgent! And if you need to fly to Orr for a short trip, do it. I don't care. There's no way I can get out of here!"

There was a brief silence on the other end. "Okay, will do." Charlize seemed to be simply ignoring his curtness. It was better that way—his moods weren't always easy, after all. If Paul Eckbert Ondragon classified anything as urgent, it became a law of physics. Distance over time equals speed, or something like that. The first law of Ondragon.

He said goodbye, hung up, and checked his inbox again. Still nothing from Rudee. Instead, there was an inquiry from his colleague Dietmar Hegenbarth in Dubai. He wanted to know whether he would accept a share in an oil well in Abu Dhabi as payment for his consulting services? Dammit, he had redirected these emails to Charlize's account. Annoyed, he sent a reply to his oldest employee, telling him to make up his own mind, and switched off the phone.

A little later, Ondragon left his room and went downstairs. He had to talk to Kateri, wanted to hear from her own mouth the reason she was in treatment with Dr. Arthur. It could be that Hatchet really had just been playing a joke on him, and that the "Bride of Satan" was here because of a problem entirely unrelated to the desire for human flesh.

He found her in the lounge, sitting in an armchair by the terrace window. It was still unpleasantly rainy outside, and it looked like it wasn't going to improve today either. He approached Kateri from behind and was about to speak to her when he saw what she was doing.

She was reading a book!

Like a vampire faced with the cross, he retreated. Silently, his eyes wide open. Cold disgust seeped into his throat. His hands were instantly wet with sweat. He stood there, rooted to the spot, unable to take his eyes off the object that was sheer horror to him. Kateri did not see him and turned a page. The rustling of the printed paper made Ondragon tremble all over. With difficulty, he tore himself away and left the lounge as quickly as possible. Only in the hallway did he regain control. Leaning against the wall, he wiped the sweat from his forehead.

Why was she doing that? She *knew* he had a problem with books.

Ondragon looked at his watch and turned away from the lounge door. He would be able to talk to her in an hour at dinner, so he had to kill time until then. To get rid of the taste of anxiety, he put a stick of gum in his mouth and began to wander through the building. For the second time since he'd arrived, he surveyed the terrain and divided the rooms into two categories: those to which guests had unrestricted access—including almost the entire first floor, with the exception of the office behind the reception desk, the kitchen, refrigeration and storage rooms, and those rooms you had to be authorized to enter or that were completely off-limits to unauthorized persons. These included the consulting rooms, the therapy rooms, the doctors' administration rooms and offices on the top floor, and of course Dr. Arthur's apartment in the tower.

How could anyone stand it here all year round? With all the crazies under one roof? You had to be pretty damn idealistic to do that . . . or crazy yourself.

Ondragon concluded his tour by the door to room 20. He had already listened at it once to no avail, though he had noticed that this door had a different lock than the other guest rooms, an electronic combination lock. He wouldn't be able to open that as easily as he had the office door downstairs. But Rudee had written some useful apps for his iPhone that could even be used to spy on number combinations with multiple layers of security or to hack into certain types of systems. Alarm systems, for example, or electronic locks. All he needed was an uninterrupted moment and his phone, which even Steve Jobs would have been jealous of. But he'd get to that later. First, he had to test the hardware. Ondragon raised a hand and knocked on the door.

No response.

He made sure he was alone in the hallway, then spoke at the door in a hushed voice. "Hello, Mr. Orchid? Are you in there?"

Silence.

"Mr. Orchid, I'm with the police department and I'd like to talk to you about the body in the woods."

Had there been a sound? A soft scuffle, as if someone were getting up from a chair?

"Mr. Orchid? Please give me a sign if you're in there."

It was as silent as a tomb.

Ondragon gave up. He would either have to stake out room 20 for a whole day or break into it at night.

Back in his room, he checked his email again. Annoyed, he noticed that no new messages had come in. There was nothing from either Charlize or Rudee. Dammit, hadn't he said it was urgent?

To cool off, he did a hundred push-ups and then went downstairs for dinner.

The dining room was crowded. The bad weather had driven all the guests to dinner at the same time, probably out of boredom. Ondragon looked around hopefully, but unfortunately there was no Kateri. That was strange; where was she? In her room? For a moment he thought about going back up and knocking on her door, but then he reconsidered and sat down at his table, where Carlos attended to him with a roguish smile.

Not without a certain curiosity, Ondragon looked around at the guests. Was one of them a cannibal? He noticed that Charlie

Bloom was now sitting separately from the models, and that both sides were scowling. Ho ho, had there been a quarrel? Not his problem. But Enrique Souza and the previously unremarkable star attorney Steven Myller had joined forces. An unusual combination. Another odd couple was Thomasz Viktory, the tennis player, and the surgeon, Petrovsk. They were sitting together and having a heated discussion—in Russian, as far as Ondragon could tell. Didn't they say that Russians and Eastern Europeans were more prone to cannibalism? Because of the bitterly cold winters and all that? Ondragon let his gaze wander. Might the film diva be a cannibal? No. The politician? Maybe. Harvey Lyme, the real estate broker? He was sitting stock-still, looking like the epitome of a socially awkward, sexually inhibited bachelor, and eating with little relish. No, he was far too uptight for that kind of extravagant hobby, but as everyone knew, still waters could be deep and marshy. And the British investment banker? Terry Stuart was staring around with a sour expression, as if he were going through all the stock market prices in his head and was annoyed he couldn't do business because he'd had to hand in his cell phone. There was something manic about the guy, but did that make him a cannibal? Ondragon turned back to his food: half a duck, without bones but with red cabbage and orange sauce. If he kept on eating like this, he would be able to work as the Michelin Man advertising car tires once he left.

After dinner—Miss Wolfe hadn't shown up—he strolled over to the lounge, got himself a Virgin Caipirinha, and walked into the sparsely lit entryway. The reception desk was deserted; Sheila had already clocked off. Ondragon went over to the glass door and looked out at his Mustang. It stood among the other cars like a somber veteran of the road, absorbing all the light. The Bolide, which had traveled all types of roads in its forty-plus years, looked almost angry at having to stand next to a red Prius. Ondragon noticed that the cars were positioned differently. An SUV was missing, the Chrysler. He hadn't yet figured out who owned that one. Also, he noted, a new car had arrived, a white Lexus sedan. It probably belonged to one of the employees or doctors. The police cars were long gone. He wondered if Deputy Hase would come back to question more people.

Ondragon sat down on the comfortable leather sofa, sipped his

Caipi, and looked into the gas flames in the fireplace. They weren't as pretty as a real fire, and they didn't crackle, but they helped him think. Tonight he would deal with room 20. Once he had taken a look inside, he might know more. Ondragon drained his glass and sat back. It was amazing how far this unfamiliar environment was throwing him off. It was alien territory, not his home base. He needed the familiar chaos of the city. In the city, people could be as crazy as they liked, there was a place for everyone, but here in the godforsaken wilderness, even the smallest quirk came across as a threat. The lack of alternative types made him vulnerable. He, of all people!

Ondragon got up and went to the lounge to check on Kateri again. There was no sign of her. With a queasy feeling in his stomach, he climbed the stairs. He stopped in front of Miss Wolfe's door, waiting only a few breaths before knocking. No answer. He left it at that. If she wanted to be left in peace, he had to accept that. He returned quietly to his room and spent the rest of the evening doing internet research.

At two in the morning, his alarm clock rang. The air in the room was stuffy. Ondragon got up and opened the balcony door. A fresh breeze was blowing in. The rain clouds had cleared, and the lake was reflecting the waning moon and the black shadows of the trees. He took a deep breath. The spice of damp pine needles and resinous tree bark rose into his nose and thrilled his city-parched sense of smell.

Before Ondragon left his room, he made sure his smartphone had enough juice, then opened the door and peered out into the dark hallway. It was empty. Stealthily, he walked to room 20, listened briefly at the door, and pulled out his phone. He was about to open the app for cracking number codes when he heard a noise in the hallway. He hid quickly behind a sofa and peeked around it. In the dark, he made out movement. But not outside Orchid's or Hatchet's rooms, outside Kateri Wolfe's. Her slender silhouette appeared, paused briefly, and then headed toward the stairs. Even though Kateri was not his target, Ondragon took up pursuit. Quietly, he crept up behind her to the entryway without her noticing him.

At the outer door, Kateri paused, took something out of her pants pocket—she was fully dressed, he now noticed—and busied herself with the door lock. A short while later, the door opened. Ondragon was surprised. Did she actually have a key to the entrance? What a privilege! Perhaps it was because she was a kind of ward of Dr. Arthur; Ondragon could not otherwise imagine why she was the only guest who had a key.

After Kateri slipped out the door, she locked it behind her. Too bad, now he couldn't follow her any farther. Ondragon ran over to the door and peered through the glass. What was Kateri doing out in the forest in the middle of the night?

Less than a minute later, he got his answer, because the Prius rolled silently in reverse out of its parking space. These electric cars really didn't make the slightest noise. As a pedestrian, you had to be careful not to get run over if you relied only on your hearing when crossing the street.

As the Prius pulled out of the parking lot, the side lights came on, Ondragon thought. Hadn't he seen Kateri's car keys in the safe? Then why did she have them now? How had she gotten them? Sheila certainly wouldn't lend them out so you could go for a spin. Or did Kateri have special rights here too? Frowning, he looked out into the night. The woman truly was a mystery.

Shaking his head, Ondragon crept back to the second floor, where he pulled the cell phone out of his pocket again. But no sooner had he switched on the display than another noise reached his ear. It was like Grand Central Terminal in here!

Once again, he took refuge behind the sofa and saw Hatchet coming down the hall. His portion of fries was doubtless awaiting him in the kitchen. Ondragon felt a certain food envy. But that wasn't why he'd gotten up. He looked at the door labeled 20. Should he risk another attempt? Or should he wait and see if anything else happened? Maybe Kateri would come back soon. Or Hatchet. Ondragon felt fatigue gurgle dully into his thoughts, and gave up on Mission Orchid for the night. There was no point. Too much activity in the hallway.

Unusually exhausted, he went to his room. He was greeted by a cool breeze. Had he left the balcony door open earlier?

He was about to close the door when his eyes fell on an object lying on the wooden floorboards of the balcony. It was as big as a soccer ball and looked shaggy in the gloom of the fading night. Had someone thrown a stuffed animal onto his balcony? Who would have done that? There were no children at the lodge. Strange. Ondragon noticed a dark liquid spreading under the hairy ball. He walked slowly toward it. And the closer he got, the clearer it became. Nausea rising in his throat, he hesitantly nudged the dark ball of fur with the toe of his foot. The thing rolled around silently, revealing black lips, bared teeth, and a bloody tongue. The eyes were hidden by the thick tufts of fur, but it was clear: This was Rumsfeld—the dog belonging to Frank, the gardener.

Someone or something had ripped its head off and thrown it onto his balcony.

CHAPTER 21

1835, Kabetogama,
20 miles from Fort Frances

They set up camp on the bank of a small stream that carried ice-clear meltwater. The soldiers lit a big fire, drew a kettleful of water, and cooked some hot soup, which was later distributed to everyone.

Lacroix spooned it up as fast as he could: He was mighty hungry. He let Parker's tin billycan cool down a bit first, to make it more palatable for him. Then he slowly fed his friend while the soldiers prepared their sleeping places. Night came over the camp in great strides, descending like a black cloth. The stars glittered coldly in the moonless sky.

After Lacroix had managed to send most of the soup down into Parker's stomach, he too set about building their sleeping billet. He took several armfuls of fir branches from a gloomy copse nearby and carefully laid them in a pile near the fire. Covered in a blanket, they provided much better protection from the cold ground than the soldiers' woolen coats.

He helped Parker lie down, and after spreading two more blankets over him, he joined the soldiers and drank some of the brandy that was being passed around against the murmur of soft conversation. The brew sloshed warmly into his limbs, but Lacroix could not relax. Silently, he looked at the faces gilded by the glow of the fire. Some of them betrayed tension, coupled with a dull tiredness. Which sensation would win the battle was clear; after a ride of almost twenty miles, everyone felt the pull of sleep in their cold muscles. The fact that there was something out there that could take them to the eternal darkness was beyond their imagination in any case.

Lacroix looked over at the lieutenant and the cowardly sergeant. They were sitting on the other side of the fire's dancing flames, giving the impression that they were already stewing in one of the outer circles of hell. They were engrossed in conversation. What about, he could not tell, but Stafford kept jotting things down in his little notebook.

Lacroix gave a pensive smile. Could the inexplicable be made more explicable by putting it down in words? He thanked the soldiers for the brandy and lay down next to Parker, who seemed to have gone to sleep. After a while he managed to close his eyes. Soon, Lacroix had dozed off too. He did not notice Parker's eyes glowing red in the darkness, watching him as he slept.

CHAPTER 22

2009, Moose Lake,
Cedar Creek Lodge

The next morning it all seemed like a bad dream, but when he stepped out onto the balcony, the thing was still there. Ondragon sighed. Now he would have to talk to Deputy Hase again. This made him uncomfortable; it drew far too much of Hase's attention.

Without touching the grisly relic of Rumsfeld, Ondragon went into the bathroom and took a long shower. He then went down to the front desk and asked Sheila if he could use the lodge phone—he had to keep his cell phone a secret, after all. Sheila reluctantly passed the phone over the counter once he had assured her repeatedly that it was essential he call the police. Sighing, Ondragon dialed the deputy's number.

"Hase." The police officer's voice sounded tired.

"It's me again, Paul Ondragon from Cedar Creek Lodge."

"What do you want?" Irritated.

Ondragon turned away from the prickly receptionist and put a hand over the mouthpiece. "I don't know if this is related to the body in the woods, but Frank, the gardener, lost his dog the day before yesterday and . . ."

"Can you also teach me how to suck eggs?"

Not exactly the friendliest tone, but Ondragon wasn't about to argue with Hase about politeness and good breeding. "Okay, I'll keep it brief: The dog's head is on my balcony, without the rest of the dog, if you know what I mean, and it doesn't exactly look like an accident to me."

"What the hell . . ." He heard the deputy hold the phone away from his ear and cough violently. So young and already he had a smoker's cough? Then Hase was back on the line. "We'll be back at the lodge around ten thirty. Don't touch anything until we get there." He hung up.

But of course, Your Majesty!

When Ondragon arrived at breakfast, Miss Wolfe smiled over at him from her table. He sat down with her. After the nasty surprise during the night, he had little desire to talk to her about her nocturnal trip and certainly didn't want to bring up her potential desire for human flesh. So they talked about the improvement in the weather and other innocuous things. Ondragon didn't mention what he'd found on his balcony at first, because he didn't know if he could really trust Kateri. But then he thought he would test her. After all, she had been out during the night and was thus inevitably a suspect.

"Do you know the gardener's dog? Rumsfeld?"

"That giant ball of wool?" Kateri put her bagel on the plate. "Of course I know him. He's a bit on the big side, maybe, but he's really a little lamb."

Ondragon nodded. "He disappeared the day before yesterday."

"Oh, that's no big deal. He's probably roaming around in the woods again. He does that often."

"Well, if he's doing that without a head, then that would indeed be nothing special."

Kateri didn't respond at first, then she frowned. "What do you mean, Paul?"

"The dog's head landed on my balcony last night." *While you were outside*, he wanted to add, but he only looked at Kateri searchingly.

"His head? I don't understand . . ."

Did she really not understand? Or was she just pretending? Her face, at any rate, did not betray any telltale emotion.

"Well." Ondragon put down the napkin he was holding. "Someone must have ripped poor Rumsfeld's head off and thrown it on my balcony. And I'm wondering if that was a coincidence, or if someone's trying to tell me something."

Kateri had raised a hand in front of her mouth, her eyes full of genuine fear.

"Or could it have been that rogue bear that's running around?" added Ondragon.

"And it happened last night?" Kateri sounded worried, without so much as hinting she'd been out and about at the time. "But that's terrible. Does Frank know yet?"

"No, Deputy Hase wants to look at everything first. I left the head where it was." Ondragon lifted a hand and pointed toward the window. "For my part, I think the deputy should put a hunter on it and just get the son of a bitch shot. That would make me feel a lot better. Actually, it's irresponsible to have people still running around out there while that murderous Mr. Bruin is out there terrorizing the woods. By the way, I was looking for you last night . . ."

Kateri looked up, warily. Was that her first impulse?

". . . and I missed you at dinner."

"I see." Her face relaxed again. "Well, I was very busy yesterday. My session with Dr. Arthur was a little exhausting and afterward, well, I wasn't feeling well. So I had dinner brought to my room. I'm sorry I didn't keep our appointment. Can you forgive me, again?"

Paul actually wanted to be harder on her, but he smiled. "Of course. But you'll keep me company today, I hope?"

Kateri blinked, then nodded.

Ondragon's smile grew a shade wider. No, this woman was definitely not a cannibal. She was far too . . . well, what, exactly? He scrutinized her intently. Kateri Wolfe combined vulnerability with a dignified, almost regal bearing. She seemed confident and yet simultaneously lost, like a gazelle among hyenas. Her distant smile and the brittle coolness in her eyes were her shield. But what was she hiding behind it? What happened when you crossed the invisible border fence that surrounded her? Ondragon was eager to find out. He risked putting his hand on hers. She didn't pull away, but she didn't look at him either. For a few breaths neither of them moved, then Ondragon removed his hand and rose.

"Please excuse me. Before we move on to the pleasant part of the day, I have some business to attend to."

The corners of Kateri's mouth twitched and then a hesitant smile appeared. One he hadn't seen before. It was warm and friendly. "Just come find me when you're done. I won't be leaving the lodge anytime soon."

Ondragon nodded and left the dining room, but before going upstairs, he went back to the front desk again.

"Hello, Sheila sweetie!" he greeted the receptionist in honeyed tones. "I forgot to ask earlier if the package had arrived for me?"

"Hmm-hm." Sheila, barely suppressing a disapproving frown, bent down and came back up with a brown package marked Amazon. She passed it over the counter to him.

"It was really very kind of you to let me place the order through your office computer, Sheila. Thank you so much." He thought of what a struggle that had been. Sheila had only let him onto the computer after he had literally begged. And then she had watched his every click with great suspicion. Ondragon gave her a winning smile, but Sheila didn't change her hard-as-nails expression for a nanosecond.

"You're welcome," she said coolly, returning her attention to the papers in front of her.

No chance! *No open sesame.*

Ondragon left the entrance area. In his room, he opened the package and pulled out a pair of brand-new running shoes. He kissed the package and tossed it into the trash can. Long live ordering online!

Then he took out his cell phone and opened his inbox. Finally! A reply from Rudee and one from Charlize too. First, he opened the email from the Thai.

Sawadee, Paul!
It wasn't easy, but I managed to hack Dr. A's computer and get some data. I am a digital key master :-)

The patient files are attached. Whoa there! What have you gotten yourself into?! I'm also attaching information about the employee Jeremy Bates. I haven't been able to get anything on a Miss Wolfe or a Mr. Orchid, but

I'll give it one more try. I have a feeling that not all the computers are always online. If you need any more help, let me know.

Napol_e.on

PS: If what's in the patient files is true, then I'd get off this ghost train as fast as possible if I were you. And there I was this whole time thinking I was the freak!

"I've heard better jokes from you, Rudee," Ondragon muttered. Although he was dying to know what was in the patient files, he opened the document on Jeremy Bates first. He wanted to keep himself waiting a little longer; he loved the expectant tingling in his limbs. He was an adrenaline junkie.

The file did not contain much.

Jeremy John Bates, born 05/02/1969, single, residing at 33 King Road in Orr, Minnesota. Hired as a physical therapist in the spa on 07/01/2008, discharged on 03/13/2009. Reason: breach of Golden Rules.

Ondragon let out a dry laugh. So the *Golden Rules* applied to the staff as well. That was just like Dr. Arthur!

The file also included a digitized photo of Bates, his application for the CC Lodge position, and a certificate of good conduct from his previous employment at Cook Hospital, but these contained nothing of significance.

Ondragon closed the attachment and, after a moment's hesitation, opened the patient records that had been kept since the lodge opened in 2000. Ondragon was amazed. Rudee was truly a genius.

He flipped curiously through the room occupancy charts and came to a patient register in alphabetical order. He quickly pulled out his notepad, leafed through to the list with the abbreviations of the current guests, and began to match them up. He felt like a kid at Christmas. All this wonderful information. What a gift! He finally had power over his fellow inmates. And the more he noted down about Shamgood and the others, the wider his grin became.

- *Bloom, Charlie:* paranoid personality disorder caused by substance abuse, alcohol and coke, currently clean, patient believes everyone wants to steal his "secret"—Assessment: treatable
- *Bright, Harold aka "Hatchet":* (Bright? No wonder, if I had a name like that I'd have chosen a new one too) suffering from ochlophobia, the fear of crowds, due to a traumatic accident—Assessment: treatment successful!
- *Burlwood, Lydia:* eating disorder, compensates for failure with extremely increased intake of food, strict diet!—Assessment: only partially treatable—likes coming to CC Lodge because it's fancy!
- *Crane, Wilbur:* pedophile (well, well!)—Assessment: partially treatable—but only because patient is willing to change (whoa, controversial!)
- *Norrfoss, Johan:* (now it'll get interesting!) addicted to gambling and sex, bisexual, (well lookee here)—Assessment: almost impossible to treat, patient completely refuses treatment
- *Ondragon, Paul Eckbert:* phobia of books, triggered by a traumatic experience in childhood—Assessment: treatable, if he is willing to open up (well, the doc is optimistic, anyway!)
- *Shamgood, Thomas:* stalker with sadistic tendencies, homosexual, reported for stalking by one of his male models (now doing a happy little dance to "The Power" by Snap! I got you by the balls, scumbag!)—Assessment: partially treatable, because patient is additionally predisposed to narcissism (must keep that in mind too!)
- *Stuart, Terry M.:* phobia of buttons (this is even more stupid than my fear of books)—Assessment: treatable
- *Viktory, Thomasz:* phobia of germs with highly neurotic traits, (ah, a representative of the germ party) resulting from his travels as a tennis professional—Assessment: treatable

. . . to name only the most famous inmates. Unfortunately, not only were Miss Wolfe and Oliver Orchid missing from the register, it also made no mention of Harvey Lyme, Enrique Souza, or Dr.

Mikhail Petrovsk. But why? Did they all have a common factor that was even more secret than the other patient information? Ondragon searched the file but found no other list. Hmm. Rudee had said he wanted to dig a little deeper. So he would have to be patient. Ondragon opened the email from Charlize.

Hey Chief,

1.) There's no one called Jeremy Bates living in Orr, and there has never been.

2.) No murders were reported in Orr between November 2008 and March 2009, nor was a body discovered, but there was a missing person: Dana Straub, 55, lived alone, alcoholic, scatterbrained, reported missing by her neighbors on 03/07/2009, the police searched for her for several days without success. She was declared dead shortly after. The report of the police officer in charge states: Probably got lost in the forest under the influence of alcohol and froze to death, body of Dana Straub could not be found—a series of unfortunate events?

3.) Everything about Dr. Arthur's connection with cannibalism is in the attachment.

So far, that's all I've been able to find out by phone and via the internet. I posed as an employee of the Pasadena Police Department. They didn't notice a thing.

I've not yet been able to find out anything about the Parker family, as the archive in question had already closed yesterday.

I'll get back to you as soon as I have more.

Charlize

PS: Are you sure everything's okay?

Ondragon lined up the new information and set the *centrifuge* to work. That there was no Jeremy Bates in Orr was extremely strange. Perhaps he had been living there under a false name. But the missing woman might fit with Vernon's creepy story—at least the bit about the woman's arm. He really needed to ask Deputy Hase if the body in the woods was male or female. He wrote back to Charlize:

Thanks Charlize, great job!

But I have a few outstanding questions:

On 1.) I discovered that "Jeremy Bates" lived at 33 King Road in Orr. Can you call the house or the neighbors and ask if he stayed there under another name, please. Attached is a photo of Bates and some more information.
On 2.) What was the name of the police officer who signed the report about the missing woman?

Best, Paul

PS: It's a nightmare here: completely bored and any kind of fun is prohibited. To top it all off, there's a crazed bear running around out in the woods, eating people and dogs. So as you can tell, everything's going great.

After he'd sent the email, Ondragon looked at the clock. He still had time before Deputy Hase arrived. So he opened the first file on cannibalism and started reading.

At half past ten, he closed the file, put his cell phone in his pocket, and pondered the shocking reports he had just read. Really heavy stuff. According to the report, cannibalism, also known as anthropophagy, occurred predominantly in men and was regarded by psychiatrists as a mental disorder that was difficult to treat. The definition did not take into account the religious cannibalism of primitive peoples, or the eating of human flesh for medical reasons, a practice that had existed in Europe from the Middle Ages to modern times, whereby body parts were ground into healing powders and ingested to protect against all kinds of diseases and infirmities.

Hmm, delicious, thought Ondragon. Crazy what they believed in back then! But hopefully Dr. Arthur was not involved with that kind of thing here at the CC Lodge. Using cadaver powder to treat mental illness—even that had been tried in the course of human history. Maybe he should check his steak next time . . .

But back to the records Charlize had dug up and according to which Dr. Arthur's specialty was indeed cannibalism! So Hatchet had been right on that point. Time to find out whether he had been right about the rest. With growing unease, Ondragon read through the various gradations of this unsavory practice. Besides the forms that had already been mentioned, there was cannibalism in extreme situations, such as famine in inhospitable regions, and criminal cannibalism, which the science divided into four groups:

1. *Sexual cannibalism: the eating of human flesh to arouse sexual fantasies*
2. *Aggressive cannibalism: the most common form, predominantly about exercising control and power, but also about revenge and hatred*
3. *Spiritual and ritual cannibalism: practiced, for example, by sects and satanic cults*
4. *Epicurean and nutritional cannibalism: the eating of human flesh for its taste or nutritional value*

He had heard it all now! The human being was a true wonder of "versatility". But experts had not yet been able to explain what experiences and factors triggered this severe mental disorder. Some suspected that cannibalism was a symptom of schizophrenia, and thus possibly hereditary, because many perpetrators were simultaneously diagnosed with this type of mental illness. Others, however, claimed that cannibalism was an aspect of sexual perversion that any individual could develop when exposed to certain influences. However, most scientists agreed that the foundations for cannibalism were laid in a person's childhood or adolescence, through experience of violence in the family, for example, asocial relationships, too close an attachment to the mother, or some other kind of trauma.

Tough stuff. Ondragon exhaled. He did not understand why any-one would voluntarily engage with this stinking human swamp. It was an absolute mystery. Nor did he know whether to admire or pity Dr. Arthur for his secret research. But there was one thing about this whole business with cannibalism that he couldn't get off his mind. And that was not the deep psychological abysses that the victims carried within themselves, or the repulsive acts of bloodshed, but how the justice system dealt with such cases. No industrialized countries had laws on the prosecution of criminals who had consumed a human. In Germany, where the most recent cases had occurred only a few years previously, there was still no criminal law specifically against cannibal-ism. As yet, perpetrators could only be convicted with the help of other provisions, for instance on murder, violation of burial laws, necrophilia, or desecration of corpses. In the USA and Great Britain, the situation was even more perfidious. Here, cannibalism was not even deemed to constitute a crime, but was merely an act that was socially outlawed, the ultimate taboo—and yet people ate other people again and again. Inevitably, the image arose in Ondragon's mind of a dilapidated cabin deep in the woods, with a moronic hillbilly inside, shooting and eating people—primarily teenagers on camping trips—instead of deer. The stuff of countless Hollywood horror flicks.

Suddenly, there was a knock at the door, and the image of the hut disappeared abruptly. Ondragon quickly hid his cell phone and opened the door.

"Morning," Deputy Hase said, his face redder than ever, his mood not seeming to have improved since their phone call. Next to him stood Dr. Schuyler, who was probably there to collect Rumsfeld's sad remains for forensic examination.

"Where is the head?" the latter asked immediately, looking around the room curiously.

Ondragon led the two men out onto the balcony and pointed to the fly-covered remains, which were beginning to stink in the warm sunlight. The head was lying on its side, its shaggy fur encrusted with blood.

First, Dr. Schuyler took a few photos, then slipped on a pair of latex gloves and picked up the head. He made a sickening smacking sound as the fur came away from the half-dried pool of blood. Schuyler examined the severed neck. Gristly trachea and shreds of flesh were hanging down from it.

"Hmm, I can't say for sure yet, but it was certainly not a blade that did this." Impassively, he stuffed the dog's head into a plastic bag.

"Could it have been a bear too?" asked Ondragon.

Schuyler regarded him. "Do you think this is connected to the body in the woods?"

"Why not? It at least seems strange that the thing landed on my balcony, of all places. After all, I stepped on the body too."

"Most likely a coincidence," Hase said nasally, disgruntled.

Schuyler held up the plastic bag. "Well, it might have been a bear, the head was literally ripped off." He grinned. "Dr. Layton won't be at all happy about that though. If she had her way, those cute little teddy bears would be lying in the meadow all day picking daisies. Bah!"

"Have you found out who or what killed the man? And was it even a man?" Ondragon looked from the deputy to the medical examiner, who was taking off his gloves and stuffing them into the bag too.

"It was a man, about forty years old, dark-haired, about five feet six. But we still haven't identified him, unfortunately. And his injuries were caused by canines, no doubt about it. Dr. Layton still thinks it wasn't her bears though. And there's actually something very strange about those wounds. I—"

"That's enough, Dr. Schuyler. Mr. Ondragon doesn't need to know everything!" the deputy snapped at the pathologist. "I think we're done here." He turned to leave.

"Bear or man," Ondragon called after him, "wouldn't it perhaps be appropriate to impose a curfew on all guests and employees of the lodge? There's something running around out there ripping the heads off people and dogs!"

"You know what, Mr. Ondragon?" Hase had turned around and hooked his thumbs in his belt. "How about you mind your own business and let us mind ours? I think we've got a pretty good idea of the danger. There's no danger lurking out there."

"Where is Dr. Layton anyway?" asked Ondragon, unfazed by Hase's rebuke.

"At the scene. As Dr. Schuyler said, she still doesn't believe it was a bear and is looking for more clues."

"And what do you think, Deputy Hase?" Ondragon was starting to get mightily fed up with the wannabe sheriff's arrogant behavior.

"I have my suspicions, but I'm certainly not going to discuss them with a layman like you."

Layman—if you only knew!

Hase signaled to Schuyler and the two of them left the room. Ondragon looked at the pool of blood. Great! Someone else would clean it up, wouldn't they?

As he stared at the viscous liquid, a thought occurred to him. Dr. Layton was at the crime scene. Maybe she would be more talkative than the grumpy deputy. He would simply grab his new running shoes, go for a little jog, and just happen to run into the behaviorist.

CHAPTER 23

1835, Kabetogama,
20 miles from Fort Frances

Contrary to his expectations, Lacroix slept through the whole night, even though he had alerted his senses to sound the alarm if anything stirred in the camp. But apparently all had been quiet. His limbs stiff, he rose and checked on Parker. He was lying on his back, staring up at the cold morning sky.

"Are you all right?" he asked, but his friend had already drifted back into the haze of fever. Lacroix checked his pulse. A little fast, but not life-threatening. He looked up and watched the soldiers gradually awakening. One of them struggled to his feet and rekindled the fire, which had gone out once again.

"Confound it, Johnson, you fell asleep again!" The soldier kicked the pile of blankets where he assumed Johnson was sleeping. But the blankets were empty.

"Hey, where is he?" The soldier looked around, but everyone merely shrugged.

"Maybe he went for a pee," one said, and set about heating water.

"What is it?" asked Stafford sharply from the other side of the camp. He rose with difficulty, the fatigue still etched on his face. He put on his belt and saber and trudged over to them.

"Private Johnson has disappeared, Lieutenant," the soldier replied. "He had the last watch."

"Well, go find him, Corporal! What are you waiting for?"

"Yes, sir!" The corporal instructed his comrades to help him in the search. Shortly afterward, they swarmed out, shouting the name of the missing man into the forest. Hollow echoes reverberated through the damp, shiny tree trunks that protruded through the snow like black fingers. A thaw had set in, and water dripped incessantly from the branches into their collars.

Lacroix helped Parker up. The old trapper had grown even weaker and could barely stand without help. Lacroix dragged him closer to the fire and tended to the coffee while the soldiers searched for the missing man. Lieutenant Stafford, meanwhile, straightened his uniform and glowered at him.

Suddenly, loud shouts cut through the silence.

Lacroix and Stafford turned their heads; Parker alone continued to stare indifferently into the flames. But before either of them could speak, two of the soldiers came running out of the forest. Distressed, they flailed their arms, pointing repeatedly into the dense shelter of fir trees.

"Lieutenant. He's over there. Johnson. We found him!" The two men stopped in front of their superior officer, breathing heavily.

"All right, so what's going on? Tell me, damn it!"

"He's dead, Lieutenant!"

"Dead? What in tarnation happened to him?"

"No idea, sir. But he was cut open like a pig. There's blood everywhere!" The soldier swallowed.

"Cut open?" repeated Stafford, drawing his saber. "Lead me to him."

Lacroix followed the lieutenant and the two soldiers into the forest. They were joined by other men, for they too had heard the shouts and called off their search.

When they finally reached the badly mangled body of Private Johnson, a somber silence descended on the group.

While the first soldiers were turning away and vomiting into the bloody snow, Lacroix looked closely at the site. Johnson's body lay on its back, his chest and abdomen ripped open and turned inside out, as if someone, in barbaric greed, had taken a spade and dug into his guts. The dead man's clothes hung in tatters from his body, but his face was an even worse sight. His eyes stared wide open into the gloomy nothingness of death, and his mouth was torn open in a silent scream. The horror had struck while he was fully conscious. What a terrible end!

Lacroix shuddered and noticed that Stafford and the rest were doing the same. With one exception, however: Unlike the gentlemen of His Majesty's Army, he knew who had done this.

"That was no wild animal . . ." said one of the soldiers, looking around frantically. "That was a madman, an insane murderer! And he's going to kill us all, one by one!"

"Hold your tongue!" The lieutenant wiped his mouth. He looked visibly shaken. "Nobody touches anything. I want everything to stay the way it is until I have examined him." He glared at every single person present and then turned fiercely to Lacroix.

The French Canadian knew what his look was saying.

I know you and your friend have something to do with this.

But Lacroix did not allow himself to be cowed by this, and instead rubbed his chin pensively.

"Send your men away, Lieutenant," he said finally, "and I'll tell you what I know about this. Even though it's hard for you, you must trust me now. Only then might we have a chance of reaching the fort alive."

Stafford gave a disparaging snort. "Trust? You joke, sir!"

"Order your men to get ready to march immediately."

"Do not tell me what I should do. I must first examine the body. It could be important."

"Do what you think is right, Lieutenant, but do it quickly. I will help you, although I have to tell you that it is not necessary to examine the dead man."

Stafford was about to protest again, but Lacroix raised his eyes and looked the lieutenant straight in the eye. "I know who did this. He is out there. And he is hungry."

Stafford was silent. Fear shimmered in his eyes, turning them almost black. Finally, he seemed to grasp the gravity of the situation.

Lacroix continued to speak, softly but forcefully. "We will all fall victim to him if you do not listen to me now."

For a moment the lieutenant hesitated, irresolute. Then he turned and ordered his men to break camp and saddle the horses. He then turned back to Lacroix. "I will now examine the body and the site where it was found. You will not dissuade me from that. But I will endeavor to be quick. And afterward, I want an explanation from you."

CHAPTER 24

2009, Moose Lake,
Cedar Creek Lodge

As Ondragon ran along the narrow wooded path on the western shore of Moose Lake, he checked that his SIG Sauer was tucked securely into his waistband. If he came across anything, he would be armed. Nine millimeters wouldn't particularly impress a bear, but it would certainly put him to flight.

The day was gloriously warm, and the soft forest floor was speckled with sunshine. Although everything seemed peaceful, Ondragon kept a close eye on his surroundings. The events of the other day would not repeat themselves, although the boreal wilderness was never likely to be one of his favorite places. Something cracked under his feet and he checked to make sure he hadn't stepped on anything unsavory again. But it was only a rotten branch. When Ondragon looked up, he saw a huge shadow on his left, crouching among the tree trunks. Immediately, an ominous tingling started up at the back of his neck, and Ondragon felt for his weapon. He moved slowly toward the shadow, which still did not move. When he was finally close enough, he let go of the weapon at his waist. The thing that had seemed so threatening was merely the octopus-like roots of a fallen tree.

Ondragon breathed a sigh of relief and continued walking. But his nerves continued to jangle for quite a while and he had to literally force them to quiet down.

It took him longer than he thought it would to reach the spot at the head of the lake. But it looked exactly as he remembered—the dense brush, the tall conifers, and the silence. Ondragon slowed his pace and walked the rest of the way to where the undergrowth narrowed into a tunnel. Uncertainly, he peered into it. The half-light under the matted branches was not exactly inviting. Finally, he gave himself a shake and dove into the undergrowth. He rounded one dark bend after another, trying to take in everything. Had this stretch of the trail really been that long? Suddenly, he noticed a movement to his right. Ondragon stopped and listened. The branches swayed again, only a few steps away. But when that was quickly followed by a torrent of curses, he knew he had reached his destination. For a lady in her sixties, Dr. Layton had an unusually detailed repertoire of swear words that referenced not only the male genitalia, but also other parts of the human anatomy that he would rather not think about. Ondragon cleared his throat loudly to catch her attention. The tirade subsided abruptly.

"Who's there?" a voice asked from the bush beside him.

"Paul Ondragon, ma'am. From Cedar Creek Lodge."

"Come here!"

He obeyed the instruction readily, entering the small clearing that the forensic investigation had created in the dense bushes. It was significantly brighter here. He also noted that the bestial stench that had pervaded the area had disappeared.

"Well, come on, then!" Dr. Layton beckoned him impatiently. She was crouching on all fours in the dirt, holding a branch in her hand. Her white hair fell in a tangle over her face. In her camouflage pants, the green T-shirt with a bear on it and the utility vest with a thousand pockets, she looked like a combination of Rambo and a mad professor, only female.

"Are you out here all alone, without police protection?" asked Ondragon, a little perturbed.

"Pah, those jokers are scared to death anyway! I'm not afraid and I can take care of myself very well. Besides, there's nothing in these woods that poses a threat except man's own stupidity. Look at this." She held out the branch, which was about the width of his thumb.

Ondragon looked at it, but could see nothing unusual. "Forgive me, Dr. Layton, but it looks to me like a perfectly normal branch."

"But it isn't. Normal, I mean. I spotted it over there, on a bush by the side of the trail. Do you see the abrasions? Looks like something was tied to it. There are at least three more marks like it on the branches back there."

They had been made by the net, of course, Ondragon thought, but kept it to himself. He had promised Pete. And he was going to keep his promise for now. "Did you find any other traces?"

"Just some old feathers from a bird of prey and the remains of some moose fur on a tree. I've widened my search again, but there's nothing there. You see, the poor victim's left foot was chewed off, but the police haven't been able to find it yet. It was probably eaten."

"By a bear?"

"No, dammit!" A reproving look burned from Dr. Layton's sun-tanned face. "The bite marks are from a wolf. I'm sure of it. And I'm tired of bears being pilloried around here. Do you know how many people actually die in the United States from bear attacks? Not even one a year!" She held up a grubby finger. "That means you're over sixty times more likely to be killed by a dog, and ninety thousand times more likely to be murdered. Now tell me how dangerous bears really are? Huh?"

Ondragon raised his hands placatingly. "I'm sorry, I don't know anything about bears or wolves. I just want to know who or what killed the man."

"And that's why you're jogging around here?"

"Busted." He gave her his I'm-pretty-stupid-but-I'm-also-very-nice smile. "I must confess that I'm very interested in this case. Something's actually happening here at last. You can't imagine how boring it is, hanging around the lodge all day."

Dr. Layton's gaze lost its edge and she turned back to the branch. "All right, then, I'll tell you something." She drew herself up and brushed her hair out of her face. "This is not bear country. I can't find any evidence within a radius of a mile that a bear has been here in the last few weeks or months. A bear *always* leaves some kind of traces. Footprints, scat, gnawed branches, claw marks on tree trunks, the remains of fur from scratching against bushes and trees, marking its territory. It's ninety-nine percent certain this"—she pointed with the branch to where the body had recently lain—"was not a bear, even if the deputy and Dr. Death would like to believe it was."

"Dr. Death?" Ondragon smirked.

"Dr. Schuyler, that old ghoul."

"You know each other?"

"Yes, and sadly not just from this case. He's a stiff-necked old smart-ass. First, he gets an expert opinion and then he decides he knows better than they do. Thinks he's the only expert in his field."

"Isn't he?"

Dr. Layton exhaled disparagingly. "Would he still be a medical examiner in some crappy St. Louis County district at sixty if he were? God forbid! We'd all be better off if he got himself a job as a funeral director instead of peeling the skin off poor, defenseless dead people." Dr. Layton's opinion of Schuyler was clear.

"Is he incompetent? I mean, with regard to this case. He said there was something odd about the bite marks on the body."

"For once, he's right. The bites were made by big canines, but not a bear's."

"You sure?"

"For sure."

"Then what do you think it was?"

Dr. Layton hesitated, and this aroused Ondragon's uneasiness anew. A dull throbbing began in the back of his head. Did even she, a scientist, believe in this nonsense about the Wendigo?

Since Layton remained silent, he took over. "There's this fairy tale about a forest monster that eats people. The bellboy at the lodge told me about it. He also found the body. He thinks it was the—"

"You mean the Wendigo?" Dr. Layton gave a dismissive grimace. "That's just an Indian legend. The Wendigo doesn't really exist. Up here in the north, people are sometimes a little peculiar. It's the lone-liness and the darkness in winter. Makes people go a little gaga." She looked away jerkily. Probably embarrassed. It had most likely occurred to her that she was talking to an inmate of CC Lodge, and that they were by definition gaga.

"I'm done here," she said when Ondragon didn't reply. "Are you coming back with me, or are you going to keep jogging?"

"Thank you, but I'm going to finish my round of the lake. Take care of yourself, Dr. Layton. Oh, and take a look at what Deputy Hase scraped off my balcony this morning. Might be of interest to you." Ondragon waved and headed off, while the behaviorist left in the other direction.

Once he had cleared the scrub and the sunlight was filtering through the treetops again, the unsettling throbbing in his head dissipated, leaving him free to set the *centrifuge* circling quietly. At an easy trot, Ondragon passed the log bridge over the little stream and reached the turnoff to *bear's den*. Without further ado, he turned down the heavily overgrown path, which rose slightly and led into a dark spruce forest. A gray squirrel shot away, whistling indignantly, as he jumped over a granite boulder and landed back on the forest floor with a thud. The path took several winding turns through the trees, and Ondragon had begun to wonder how long it would take him to reach the cave when he suddenly found himself in front of a pile of huge boulders. There was a dark opening between them. Curious, he walked toward it and felt the coolness flowing from the yawning chasm onto his sweat-damp skin.

Dr. Layton had said that the cave had not housed a bear for a long time and that it now served as a place of worship for the local Indigenous folks. He wondered where they lived. Maybe in Orr or some other backwater? Or in the middle of the woods like old Joel Parker and his two nephews? Ondragon stood in front of the opening, thinking. Would the Indians mind if he took a quick look around their sacred place?

He looked about him, but no one was to be seen or heard. Then he bent down and entered the cave. Musty cold greeted him, and after only a few steps he was swallowed by darkness that hid even the white running shoes on his feet. Since he had no lamp with him, he took out his cell phone and used the display as a light source. It bathed the rough rock face he was feeling his way along in a diffuse, bluish light. Again and again, his path was blocked by outcrops of rock hanging down from above, and he ducked under them. He felt like a submarine diving blindly through an abyss . . . the only thing missing was the monster from the deep.

Another twenty steps later, he paused. His senses told him that the stony ground was leading steadily downhill. He stretched out an arm, shining the light all around. Nothing but blackness.

"Hello!" he called out experimentally.

No echo. Only dull silence. The rock swallowed every sound.

Ondragon had no idea how big the cave was and he couldn't risk getting lost. Climbing around here without a flashlight was suicidal. He would come back later to explore the *bear's den* more extensively, if that felt useful. It seemed just to be an ordinary cave. He hadn't noticed anything unusual so far, at least. So he turned around and felt along the wall with his right hand. After seven steps back up the hill, his fingers suddenly met a soft surface he hadn't noticed before. He stopped and shone his light on the spot. There were dark lines on the wall. Ondragon went closer, and as his fingers continued to explore the object, he realized what he was touching. Hastily, he withdrew his hand.

What the hell?!

Making an effort, he exhaled and looked at the fur. It had been freshly stripped. So the someone must have been here recently. He swung his phone farther to the left and the light fell on an older piece of leather hanging next to the fresh one. It was the hide of a very large animal, with several naive drawings on it.

Ondragon tried to step closer, but his shin hit an object that fell to the ground with a clatter. Startled, he pointed the light at the ground and saw a hearth and what looked like a dented pot. He picked up the object. It was indeed a tin vessel with a handle made of wire. Probably someone had made some soup here. He looked inside. The pot was empty except for a thin, yellowish layer on the bottom. Ondragon stroked a finger across it. It had a strange consistency, hard and yet soft at the same time. He smelled his fingers. Beeswax. Frowning, he put the pot back on the hearth and returned his attention to the drawings on the large piece of leather. They were pictograms arranged in a spiral, telling a picture story.

At the beginning—at least Ondragon thought it was the beginning—there was a picture of an Indigenous village with three campfires, in a forest. Next to it, the creator of the cycle of pictures had painted in red a group of bent and emaciated figures. These thin people were at war in the following picture, at least they were holding weapons in their hands and were striking other people, who were painted in white and bleeding. In the next picture, the white figures had been cut into pieces, and the thin red people were visibly enjoying gnawing the flesh of their victims from their bones.

A beep sounded, and Ondragon looked at the display of his cell phone. The battery was almost dead. He would have to hurry if he wanted to unravel the story.

Next to the scene with the "feast" was a forest with wavy lines above the treetops, probably wind or clouds, and another settlement, this time populated with well-fed red people. Obviously, they had eaten their fill. In the next picture, the reds were in the forest. They were hunting, armed with spears and bows, and were painted with black symbols. They came to a deserted village; the fires at the center were cold. Next came another forest, denser and darker than before. Large round dots represented a trail. It led into the forest, and the hunters followed it. And then suddenly they were standing before him. A shiver ran down Ondragon's spine as he looked at the strange figure. A scrawny torso with long, stilt-like legs, topped by a misshapen, horned head with glowing red eyes and covered with shaggy, gray fur.

That had to be him. The Wendigo.

The chill grew stronger, and goose bumps rose all over his arms. But the spiral of pictures was not over yet. As if mesmerized, Ondragon followed the scraggly figures that surrounded the Wendigo, threatening him with spears and torches. One of the people held a net in his hands and another a clay jug. A third seemed to be blowing something at the forest monster. It looked like snow or down. Suddenly, Ondragon heard a scraping behind him and wheeled around.

"Hello? Is there anyone there?"

Silence. Nervously, he waved the light of the cell phone in the direction from which the noise had come. Something was dangling from the ceiling. He ignored another beep and moved closer. There were several small objects. They were wrapped in skins and attached to the cave ceiling by strings. Without warning, the phone light suddenly went out and he was engulfed in darkness. Ondragon stood listening, not making a sound, until another scrape brought him to the conclusion that he had seen enough. Quickly, he turned and groped his way blindly through the cave until a glimmer of gray light showed him the way out. A short time later, he stumbled outside, squinting in the glare of the sun. After a few steps, he stopped. As he stared back at the cave opening, rubbing the elbow he'd scraped as he made his escape, his latest panic attack seemed utterly ridiculous. But shit, why had people hung dozens of mummified birds from the cave ceiling?

His eyes gradually adjusted to the light and he wiped the sweat from his forehead. At least he now knew with a fair degree of certainty who had strung the net across the path. But he still had no idea why Pete had taken it down and hidden it. Annoyed, Ondragon put the phone in his pocket and headed back to the trail. It was high time he returned to the lodge.

At a leisurely pace, he walked along the bumpy path to the main road. He was about to turn left when he heard a sound. He stopped, listening. What was going on out here in the forest? Some sort of natural landmarks open day? Or were his nerves playing tricks on him?

Ondragon looked around. The bushes where he stood were somewhat denser and tall conifers blocked the sunlight, but there was nothing unusual about them. Or was there some movement back there among the trees? Ondragon ducked behind a shrub and peered into the forest.

There was someone there, no doubt about it. He could hear cautious footsteps in the undergrowth and a male voice calling a name, very softly.

"Momo."

It had to be Pete. He was calling his brother's name.

"Momo?"

Ondragon rose, intending to shout to the young man, but in the same instant there was a cracking sound in the branches above him and something dark fell onto him. There was a hissing sound, and an acrid stench enveloped him. He tried to fight off his attacker, but a heavy weight bore him to the ground. Before he could get up again, a huge blow struck him on the forehead and plunged him into an unconscious blackness.

CHAPTER 25

*1835, Kabetogama,
20 miles from Fort Frances*

Lacroix helped the lieutenant examine the body of the unfortunate Johnson. Meanwhile, the soldiers quickly broke camp and saddled the horses, their fearful shouts echoing across the clearing. Lacroix looked from the soldiers to the lieutenant and found him surprisingly calm in the face of the gruesomely mangled body and the danger lurking out there in the woods. He held a small notebook in his hand and was painstakingly noting down every detail.

The snow around the corpse was trampled and streaked with blood, but in between the boot prints Lacroix could pick out that unmistakable toeless trail that now had him gripped by a dull fear.

"Hmm, strange," he heard the lieutenant next to him say, "exactly the same prints as outside the farmer's family log cabin." Stafford flipped through his book and looked at one of his drawings.

Lacroix raised his head and tried to see where the trail had come from. He breathed a sigh of relief when he saw that this time it did not lead to Parker's billet. Instead, it disappeared into the forest. So it hadn't been his friend who had mangled Private Johnson. Lacroix swallowed dryly and forced his eyes back to the body. Then there was only one other possibility. *He*, the Wendigo, must have done it.

He was lurking out there among the trees and hunting them down because they dared to doubt his existence. And with all his might, *he* was calling to his new companion: Parker!

Lacroix felt his jaws tighten and his teeth sink painfully into his lip. The idea that his friend could become a companion of this diabolical creature and perpetrate a massacre like this one was terrifying.

"We can't follow the trail, we don't have time for that," he advised the lieutenant, who was staring almost longingly at the tracks. "We'd do better to examine the body." He stepped forward, trying to take only shallow breaths because the smell emanating from the dead flesh conjured up memories of the Walcotts' cabin.

Stafford held a handkerchief to his mouth and took a close look at the gaping wounds. "Hmm, the edges of the wound are too irregular for a knife. And there, that looks like a bite mark to me. Good God, the killer bit a chunk out of Johnson." He looked around, but the missing piece was nowhere to be seen. "He clearly ate it. You are right, Mr. Lacroix, there are obvious parallels with the murder at the farm. But what kind of person would do such a thing?"

"Not a person," Lacroix said bleakly.

The lieutenant looked at him, and as he began to listen properly for the first time, he seemed to gradually accept that there was a creature out there committing monstrous deeds, a creature that existed in spite of all rational argument. Lacroix smiled grimly. The time had come at last. The lieutenant was ready to believe in the Wendigo.

"This creature is evil to the core," he explained. "Something out there has roused it from its slumber and caused it to leave the depths of the forest. First, it tried to slake its hunger on the Walcotts, then it grabbed Johnson, and now . . . now it's after us."

"And how . . ." Stafford cleared his throat. "I mean, how do we stop this . . . monster? Can it even be killed?"

"The Wendigo is a powerful spirit. Only the Chippewa know how to defeat it. That is why our friend Two-Elk left, before you and your men took us away, to seek advice from a medicine man of his tribe. We have no choice but to wait for his return. Only with Two-Elk's help can we defy the Wendigo."

At Lacroix's last words, an icy wind blew up like a warning. He looked anxiously into the forest. The Wendigo, it was said, traveled on the north wind. *He* certainly didn't mind the cold.

He drew the collar of his coat around his neck. "We should see that we get out of here. We won't be safe until we reach the fort."

"Very well," Stafford say decidedly, putting the notebook away. "Let us go."

CHAPTER 26

2009, Moose Lake,
Cedar Creek Lodge

Paul, where were you all this time? Oh no, what happened?" Kateri
Wolfe reached out a hand to touch the bloody scrape on Ondragon's
forehead.

"Oh, it's nothing, just a scratch." He brushed it off, but actually
his head was throbbing. He was pissed. Someone had hit him on the
head and then just left him lying in the woods. It was only two hours
later that he'd come around and dragged himself to the lodge on aching limbs. Man, how embarrassing! He'd behaved like such a rookie
and it was all down to this lousy forest!

Now it was past noon and he'd missed lunch and his appointment with Dr. Arthur. He needed a good excuse, because he wasn't
going to tell anyone the truth. But what was the truth? After all, he
didn't know who had hit him. Pete? He'd been too far away. Momo?
The boy was mentally handicapped; could someone like that have
struck such a precise blow? Maybe. Dr. Layton? No. Or there had
been someone else in the forest. But who? Had Kateri known he was
out there running around? He couldn't remember telling her.

"I tripped over a root while I was jogging and hit my head on
a low-hanging branch. It's just not my kind of place out there,"
Ondragon explained, watching her every move. Kateri seemed to be
stifling a laugh.

"You love concrete and level pathways; I get it," she countered.
"But you should still let Sheila take a look at it; she's a trained
nurse."

"We'll see. Sheila and I aren't on the best of terms. I think I'm going to go take a shower and wash this disgusting smell off me." He smelled his T-shirt. In fact, he stank quite horribly. He had probably fallen into a pile of moose shit after being hit and been slumbering in it for two hours.

And then I'll have it out with Pete, he thought. He was about to turn away, but Kateri gave him a strange look. She seemed as if she wanted to accompany him into the shower. Hot excitement shot through his belly. This woman wanted him. And he wanted her! But now? He looked around. The corridor leading to the dining room and the wellness area was empty. Most of the guests were frolicking on the terrace after the bad weather of the previous day. So it would be a good time to break the *Golden Rules*.

Ondragon sensed that Kateri was also glowing inwardly. A meaningful smile stole across her lips. Her short summer outfit flattered her body. Yet he hesitated. If anyone saw him going to his room with Kateri, in no time the whole lodge would know what was going on between them. And it was not clear what the consequences would be. Dr. Arthur might terminate his therapy prematurely. Could he risk that? Could he risk his chance of recovery just for good sex? And even that wasn't certain. On the other hand, he didn't like being told what to do. Suddenly, something his father used to say came into his mind: "Only those who follow the rules are worthy of respect as a member of the community."

Well, thank you, Father! Always around when you're not needed.

Ondragon felt his excitement implode abruptly.

"I'm going out to the terrace," Kateri now said. "The sunshine looks so lovely. I'll see you later." She touched him briefly on the shoulder and then headed outside through the lounge.

The magic moment was over. He had messed up.

Sometimes you give your brain too much airtime, Paul Eckbert! No wonder you're always so edgy! The woman only wanted some fun, and you're such an idiot, you act like you're a monk on a training course!

Ondragon trudged grumpily upstairs to his room, where he got under the shower and turned it to ice-cold. As punishment.

And to cool the bump on his head.

* * *

Later, he apologized to Sheila for missing the appointment and asked her to pass his apology on to Dr. Arthur. The receptionist acknowledged his request with a gracious nod.

"By the way, where might I find Pete?" asked Ondragon, looking at her perfect, green-painted nails.

"I don't know. But I can call him if it's urgent."

"In a way, it is."

"Oh really?"

"Oh yes." Ondragon was about to lose patience with her, but eventually she reached for her rhinestone-studded cell phone and dialed a number most unwillingly. In curt tones she summoned Pete to the front desk, hung up, and looked at Ondragon with a thin smile. "He's on his way." Then she turned and began flipping through a stack of papers.

What had he ever done to this woman? Sighing, Ondragon sat down on the sofa with his back to the counter and stared at the moose antlers above the fake fireplace.

Ten minutes later, the front door opened and Pete came in. He was wearing baggy jeans and a Bugs Bunny T-shirt that read What's up, Doc? When he saw Ondragon, he pulled his baseball cap off his head and saluted. Then he looked over at Sheila, who pointed ostentatiously in his direction. Ondragon smiled apologetically at the bellboy, stood up, and pulled Pete outside. They strolled across the parking lot to the Mustang.

"I saw you in the woods earlier, Pete."

"Yeah, I was out with Frank and Julian; we were searching for the rest of Rumsfeld," the young man replied without taking his eyes off the Mustang. Julian was the riding instructor, as Ondragon knew from the employee records.

"Didn't you see me?" he asked Pete, thinking, *Not even when I was lying there unconscious for a whole two hours?*

"No, sorry, Mr. *On Draegen.*"

"Did you find Rumsfeld?"

"Nah. But I feel sorry for Frank, even though I don't like him much because he's always teasing me about my family, but he loved that dog. We all did. Poor Rumsfeld." Pete rubbed his nose.

"Who do you think could have done it?"

"No idea."

"Maybe the Wendigo?"

Pete cast an anxious glance over his shoulder. "No," he said with obvious discomfort, "I don't think so."

"I heard you calling for your brother, Momo, in the forest. Has he disappeared?"

Pete blinked in surprise. "Yeah, well . . . he took off again. He does that all the time, even though Uncle Joel told him not to go far from the house."

"Has he turned up again now?"

Pete shook his head. "He likes to hide; he thinks it's funny."

"What's wrong with him anyway? I saw that all his hair was gray. But he's not older than you, is he?"

"Frank always says he's like that because our dad is our mom's brother, but that's not true!" The bellboy clenched his fists indignantly. "I've no idea what he has against me!"

"He just wants to tease you. Don't worry about it. Frank isn't the brightest either. Even Rumsfeld was probably smarter than him." For some reason Ondragon liked the young man more and more every day, although he was definitely on the simple side. But his heart was in the right place and he was always ready to help.

Pete looked disconcertedly at the tips of his boots. "Momo wasn't always like that, you know. He only changed when he . . . when he found Mom and Dad."

"*He* found them?"

Pete nodded, still looking down at the floor. "Yeah, I came home and he was already sitting by the bodies. He's talked like a baby ever since, and he hasn't gone to school either. Dr. Arthur treats him sometimes."

The traumatic experience would have rendered me speechless as a child too, Ondragon thought, putting a hand on the bellboy's arm. "I'm sorry, Pete."

"Thank you, Mr. *On Draegen*. But that's life. At least that's what Uncle Joel always says."

"Did they catch your parents' killer back then?"

"No."

"Hmm." There was a pause. Then Ondragon abruptly changed the subject, pointing at his car. "Say, you want to take it for a drive?"

A gleam came into Pete's eyes. "That would be fantastic, Mr. *On Draegen*. Awesome!" He touched the rear of the Mustang reverently.

"You can drive it next time you go to Orr if you do me a favor." He wasn't worried that the man wouldn't handle the car with care, the way he admired it. Pete probably knew the potholes in the dirt road better than he did.

Pete grinned, but suddenly an alarmed expression came over his face. "What kind of favor do you want?" Obviously, he wasn't so naive after all.

"You have to tell me two more things."

"What kinds of things?"

"For one thing, I'm interested in what the story is about two particular gentlemen. Mr. Bates and Mr. Orchid. And for another, I'd really like to know why you removed that Indian net from the scene?"

Peter Parker cast a desperate glance at the matte black vehicle he coveted so much. He chewed hard on his lower lip. Ondragon could literally see the wheels turning in his head. The pros and cons rolling around like stone balls in a hollow gourd.

Later, Ondragon went to Sheila at the front desk and instructed her to give Pete the keys to the Mustang whenever he wanted to drive it. The boy had told him what he wanted to know, and of course he kept his promises.

Sheila stared at him uncomprehendingly, as if he had spoken Japanese, so he repeated the instruction.

"Of course. It's your car," she said with a shrug and made a note.

There you go, Ondragon thought, and headed for the lounge, where he ordered a double espresso. While he drank the coffee, he jotted down his newly acquired information in his notepad. As he did so, he kept glancing through the window at the terrace, where Kateri Wolfe was sunning herself in a deck chair. Her loose hair was shining like liquid tar . . .

When Ondragon emerged from his distracted contemplation of Miss Wolfe, he turned back to his notes. Pete's story of Bates and

Orchid was largely similar to Vernon's and Kateri's. Pete had been the one who had actively taken part in the search for Oliver Orchid back then and who had found the tire tracks from his car. He also knew the part of the story about Bates and the arm in the bag, but thought it was more nonsense that someone had told him to make fun of him. It was interesting that, unlike Kateri, Pete had gotten to know Mr. Orchid a little before he had disappeared. The Canadian guest had told the boy why he kept on having to be treated by Dr. Arthur. He had claimed that he had been in Africa for Doctors Without Borders and could no longer do his job because he had caught an incurable disease there. However, what it was Orchid had suffered from exactly, Pete didn't know; he only reported that the Canadian's hands had shaken constantly. Ondragon suspected that was probably the reason he had given up his profession, since Orchid had also been a surgeon. According to Pete, he had come to CC Lodge twice a year, staying for four weeks each time. He had last been there in March, but had then abruptly discontinued his therapy.

Ondragon snapped the notepad shut. So much for Orchid, who had at least now transformed from a phantom into an actual human being. The second thing had been the net. Pete had squirmed like a spy under torture before finally telling him why he had removed it. Supposedly, it was because he and his brother had felt threatened by it. When asked what that threat was, Pete had shrugged his shoulders and said that Indians were always hanging around their house, watching them, sometimes at night. They would hang these mummified birds of prey everywhere and cast spells against them. Momo was apparently so scared of their shadows that he would crawl under the covers and howl like a wolf with a toothache.

Ondragon grinned. Pete's figures of speech were naive but fitting. He leaned back in his chair, looked out at the terrace, and noticed that a young blond fellow had joined Kateri. Category: athletic outdoorsman with three-day beard and cowboy hat. He was looking at Kateri, smiling.

Ondragon felt jealousy rise inside him and sat forward. Who was that? Now Kateri was laughing with the guy. The two seemed to know each other very well.

Suddenly, Ondragon became aware of a timid movement behind him and turned around in alarm. He raised his eyebrows in surprise when he realized who was standing there. It was Harvey Lyme, the real estate broker.

"I beg your pardon, Mr. Ondragon," he said with an obsequious air. "May I join you for a moment?"

Too stunned to refuse, Ondragon gestured to a chair, and the broker slid eel-like into his seat as if he had no bones. He wore a short-sleeved shirt and over it, despite the warmth, a gray sweater his mother might have picked out. His pale blue eyes squinted uncertainly behind the lenses of his glasses, and his long fingers picked nervously at the tablecloth. An absolutely pitiful creature, with what were very obviously overactive sweat glands. Sadly, Ondragon felt precious little need to engage with Lyme. But now that the guy was sitting at his table, he couldn't just get up and leave either.

"What can I do for you, Mr. Lyme?" asked Ondragon in a businesslike tone.

"I . . . I . . ." The real estate agent cleared his throat, pulled out a plaid handkerchief, and dabbed at his forehead.

Ondragon sighed. How could this nerd sell luxury apartments to Manhattan's rich and famous? He couldn't even get a whole sentence out. He clasped his hands impatiently.

"Well, I'd like to ask you a question, Mr. Ondragon."

He had pronounced the name correctly, at least. One point to Lyme.

"Go ahead," Ondragon encouraged him.

Lyme cleared his throat again. "I understand you've spoken to the police again, and . . . how should I put it, that means you may know more than the rest of us."

"More about what?" Ondragon knew he could make it easier for Lyme by pretending to be understanding, but he didn't feel like it. He found the guy thoroughly unpleasant.

"Well, I was questioned by Deputy Hase yesterday," the broker continued uncertainly, "and I couldn't tell him much about the body in the woods. But word is that there's a man-eating bear running around out there, a beast. Is that true?"

Ondragon hesitated. If he told Lyme what he knew, and Lyme spread the word to all the other guests, it might cause panic, and that was certainly not in Dr. Arthur's best interest. Besides, he hadn't figured out why the broker was at CC Lodge for treatment yet. Sure, Lyme looked harmless, but he was here, and that alone was an indicator that he wasn't quite right in the head.

"Why do you want to know?" Ondragon asked.

Lyme squirmed. His long fingers tightened around the handkerchief like two big pink spiders.

"It . . . it's important to me."

"Important?"

"Yes . . . I won't tell anyone either. I give you my word!" Lyme added with the reptilian smile of a real estate agent. At least he was good at that.

"I'm afraid I can't tell you much though, Mr. Lyme; after all, even the police don't know who or what killed the man in the woods."

"But he was killed *and* eaten, wasn't he? That means . . ." Lyme began to breathe faster, the sweat beading on his forehead. "Th-that means there's something out there eating people!"

The guy really was cracked. He would believe anything.

Ondragon leaned forward and whispered, "And you're sure you won't tell?"

"No, no, definitely not! I promise." Lyme held out a sweaty hand to him.

Ondragon ignored it. "Good. You see, I overheard a conversation between the deputy and the medical examiner. It was about some kind of mountain monster that's supposed to live here in the woods." He paused briefly to see if Lyme was taking the bait. The broker was listening eagerly, mouth half open.

"The Indians worship him. They call him the 'Wendigo'! And he's on a restless search for human flesh, always running hungrily through the forest. If I were you, I wouldn't go out for the time being, as long as the monster is up to his mischief."

Lyme smiled in a strange kind of ecstasy. "So it's true," he murmured. "It is true." He rose and put the handkerchief away. "Thank you very much, Mr. Ondragon. You have been really very helpful.

Have a nice day." With that, he left the table, and Ondragon had no choice but to stare after him, nonplussed. What a freak!

"What did Harvey want, then?"

Taken off guard, Ondragon turned around. Next to him stood Kateri Wolfe, smelling of fresh air and sun-warmed skin. Immediately, he thought of what he might have done on this kind of lazy summer's day by the lake with nothing but this madwoman and a bottle of suntan oil for company. Slightly aroused, he looked at Miss Wolfe. Then he circled his index finger beside his temple. "He's crazy!"

Kateri looked at the door Lyme had gone through and said with a sigh, "Hmm, I kind of feel sorry for the guy."

I don't, Ondragon thought, then asked innocently, "Who was that nice gentleman you were talking to outside just now? I haven't met him yet. Is he a new guest?"

"No, that was Julian Jodie. He's the riding instructor and he takes care of the lodge's horses."

Aha! And he probably takes care of the ladies too, does he?

"We've known each other a long time," Kateri went on dreamily. "Julian has been with us since the beginning. Dr. Arthur hired him back when he first set up here."

So they've known each other for eight years, Ondragon thought. *I wonder if they were ever a thing.* Again, he felt a pang of jealousy, and to distract himself from it, he asked, "How about an early dinner?"

"Good idea." Miss Wolfe hooked her arm through his, and Ondragon led her over to the dining room, hoping she hadn't noticed his little show of emotion.

CHAPTER 27

1835, Fort Frances,
British base and trading post

Tired and drained, the small troop reached the fort. It was already dark, and everyone was glad to finally be safe behind the wooden palisades. Fort Frances was not particularly large, comprising a muddy courtyard of about a hundred and forty square yards. Inside, a long stable, a few more log cabins, and the officers' quarters leaned against the palisades.

Lacroix knew the fort, but he was more familiar with the small village that had formed around the British trading post. They sold their hides and skins here. It consisted of at least two dozen crooked huts and houses, crouched like emaciated street dogs against the Arctic cold. But the run-down look of the settlement was deceiving; behind the doors of the log cabins, the place was full of life and vitality. Here was everything a trapper's heart could desire after a long season in the woods: booze, gin, news, and the warm lap of a whore whose makeup could no longer hide the fact that her best days were behind her. No matter, after six months in the wilderness, even the wrinkliest pussy was a Garden of Eden in full bloom.

Lacroix saw the gate of the fort open and close behind them. Stafford and his men dismounted while Sergeant Hancock yelled out some order or other. An icy breeze swept over them across the gloomy sky. The thought that the Wendigo might have followed them this far worried Lacroix. He glanced up at the palisades. Would they present any obstacle to this creature? His gaze drifted to his friend. Alan Parker was clinging to his horse like a sack of flour. Lacroix went over and helped him dismount. Then he looked around questioningly.

"Hey, Lieutenant!" he finally called out to Stafford, who was talking to two men, one fat and the other a highly decorated officer. "My friend is in sore need of warmth and rest. Where should I take him?"

Stafford and the two men approached. "This is Colonel Richards, the commander-in-chief of the fort," he said, presenting the decorated man. "And this is Governor Simpson. He's very interested in solving the murders."

The fat man eyed the newcomers suspiciously. It seemed beneath his dignity to greet them.

Lacroix nodded to the men. *"Messieurs."* He knew all too well what they thought of him, and had to hold himself back from spitting on the mud at their feet. "Now, what about my friend?"

"Take him to the officers' barracks," Stafford said. "There is a small room where you can set up camp. I reiterate that you are not prisoners, but merely witnesses. Nevertheless, I must ask you not to leave the fort without my permission. And I forbid you to speak to my men about the murders. I don't want to cause any alarm here, do you understand?"

So we're prisoners after all, Lacroix thought.

He moved his sick friend into the small room and settled him down to rest. Parker was still sweating like a bear, and his feet were barely recognizable. Veins as thick as fingers covered his swollen knuckles, which were now a yellowish color and felt as hard as stone. And the whites of Parker's eyes had turned a deep red, with purulent mucus flowing from the corners. Lacroix could only guess at the terrible agony his friend was suffering.

He locked the door from the inside, because he did not want Parker to escape; nor did he want the soldiers to see how the terrible convulsions shook him again and again, making him twitch uncontrollably and wet himself like a little child. Lacroix shoved a stick between his friend's teeth to keep him from biting off his own tongue. But that wasn't the worst of it. He feared Parker might attack him while he slept. Ever since they had found the dead guard and the tracks of the Wendigo next to it, Lacroix was afraid Parker might have had something to do with it. The ravenous beast was inside him and gradually contaminating his blood, that was for sure. And it was only a matter of time before it finally burst out of him. Lacroix had little desire to be the next victim.

He carefully wrapped Parker so tightly in the blankets that he could not move. He then fired up the small stove in the room to keep the Wendigo's cold curse at bay for as long as possible. Keeping his knife to hand, he finally settled down on his own billet and tried to get some sleep. In the snug warmth, Lacroix's eyes quickly closed, in spite of the growling sounds coming from his friend.

A little later, he tore them open again. Next to him, Parker had begun to give a long-drawn-out howl. It did not sound like the clear call of a wolf though, more like a guttural gurgle that seemed to emanate from Parker's entire body. Lacroix kept his gaze fixed on his friend, who had his eyes closed and was baring his teeth.

Like a dead hand, goose bumps settled on the back of his neck as an answering howl came from outside. Piercing and hollow, like the shrieking of the wind. It came from beyond the stockade. And it seemed to be responding to Parker's calls.

Lacroix fumbled for his knife.

He hoped Two-Elk had found their message by now and was making his way to them.

CHAPTER 28

2009, Moose Lake,
Cedar Creek Lodge

The next morning Ondragon awoke at seven o'clock and went straight to breakfast. He calmly reviewed last night's events. He and Kateri had talked late into the night. Yes, talked! That was all. Still, it had been very interesting, because she had told him a lot about herself, about her parents, and her research work at the University of Minnesota. Her father, John Wolfe, had been a renowned biochemist and her mother, Alannah Star Dancer Wolfe, an anthropologist. Both had lived in the Indigenous tradition despite their modern professions and had understood how to combine customs and modernity so that they did not conflict with each other. That was why Kateri knew her way around the equipment in her laboratory as well as she knew her way around the forest. This connection with both the world of her ancestors and the here and now was the legacy of her parents, and Ondragon almost envied her this perfect harmony. But there was something else. At the center of this perfect surface was a fine crack; he could feel it clearly. There was something in Kateri's past that disrupted the harmony over and over, made it crackle and rustle like confused radio waves. Was it the death of her parents? The feelings of guilt at having been the only one who survived?

Kateri hadn't said much about the actual accident in the Canadian tundra, only explained that she'd been rescued by a search and rescue team and what had happened afterward. This drastic event was so painful for her that the memories of it kept robbing her of her ability to see any meaning in life, as she put it. Life as her parents had modeled it for her. This was why she came to see Dr. Arthur. For her, the therapist embodied a kind of Father Earth, a figure who brought all the rivers back into balance. Here with him, the old family friend whom she had known since childhood, she always unearthed renewed courage. This was where she found the helping hand that helped her to cope with her fate.

From Kateri's frank account, Ondragon concluded she was a woman who was not only stunningly beautiful, but also extremely complicated. But that made her all the more interesting to him. He loved complication.

In an outstanding mood, he downed the remains of his triple espresso and then left the dining room, calmly ignoring the stares of Shamgood and Norrfoss. Upstairs in his room, he checked to see if there was any news. Sure enough, the cell phone, which was on silent, notified him that he had an email from Charlize. He opened it and read:

Hey Chief,

First of all hello from Dietmar, you are now a notarized part owner of an oil well in Abu Dhabi! And now to your instructions:

1.) I can't reach any of Jeremy Bates's former neighbors on the phone. The lines are busy all the time. I will keep trying.

2.) The report on the disappearance of Mrs. Dana Straub was signed by a Deputy Hase.

3.) When I called the Orr Municipal Archives, they told me the case of the murdered Parker family was taken over by the FBI. If I wanted to know anything about it, they said I should call the deputy's office. I did, and an extremely bad-tempered Deputy Hase told me to contact the FBI directly, that they had more than enough to do (with your killer bear, perhaps?).

Question: How should I proceed now?

Charlize

PS: Attached are two newspaper articles dealing with the Parker murders. The archive was kind enough to send them to me.
PPS: Hang in there!

Before Ondragon looked at the newspaper articles, he wrote a reply to his resourceful and diligent assistant:

Hi Charlize,
The best thing to do is to get on the next plane to Minneapolis and take a rental car to Orr. On the way to the airport, call a guy named George Hurley. He's an old college friend of mine and works for the FBI. Ask him about the Parker murders. I was told they never caught a killer. And ask Doctors Without Borders about an Oliver Orchid from Toronto who is supposed to have worked for them.
Have a good flight,

Paul

PS: When you're in the vicinity I immediately feel much better!

Ondragon sent the message and opened the newspaper articles. There were two jpg files, each containing a scanned report. The first, dated 5/21/97, showed a grainy black-and-white photo of the Parker family cabin in the middle of the woods—at least you could make out trees and hills in the background. The caption read:

BLOODBATH IN LOGGER'S CABIN
by Steve Boogle
Orr, St. Louis County. A terrible tragedy occurred last Thursday near the quiet logging town of Orr. When 11-year-old P. Parker returned home from school, he found his mother and father dead and gruesomely dismembered in their home, deep in the lonely forests of northern Minnesota. His younger brother M. Parker was apparently sitting completely distraught amid the carnage—which police said was the worst they had seen since the ritual murder of a young woman in 1984—holding his mother's severed arm. The boy himself was unresponsive and covered in blood from head to toe. For now, police do not believe that either of the brothers had anything to do with the double murder. It is hoped that those responsible for this horrific act will be identified through a detailed

FBI examination of the crime scene; the bureau took over the case yester-day afternoon.

Ondragon clicked his tongue and opened the second article, dated 6/5/97. Again, there was a photo. This time it showed three people: a St. Louis County deputy, a fat guy with a mustache, and a man in a black suit and dark sunglasses. The caption read, *Deputy Schoenfield, Dean Coon, Mayor of Orr, and Special Agent Preston, FBI.* The deputy and mayor were looking into the camera, perplexed, while the FBI agent's face was obscured by his sunglasses and betrayed nothing but coolness. A classic, as was the article itself:

MANIACAL KILLER OR KILLER BEAR? PARKER MURDER STILL NOT SOLVED *by Steve Boogle*

Orr, St. Louis County. The FBI is in the dark. Is the summer season at Pelican Lake in jeopardy? It's still unclear who killed a couple found dead two weeks ago. The deceased's two sons said they discovered their parents' mutilated bodies after returning home from school. The boys are currently receiving psychological counseling.

In a press conference at the Orr Community Center, where the FBI has set up a temporary office, Special Agent Preston (photo) said that the investigation was in full swing and that it was hoped a conclusion would be reached before the end of the month. Unfortunately, he could not give more details about the crime, because details of the investigation, along with the list of suspects, needed to remain confidential. However, the two brothers are no longer suspected of murder. The rumor that a wild bear had entered the Parkers' home and killed them was neither confirmed nor denied by Special Agent Preston. In exchange, he asked the citizens of Orr to continue to assist with the inquiry. Witnesses can contact the FBI office at the community center. Any evidence, no matter how insignifi-cant, could be crucial.

Orr Mayor Dean Coon (photo) has also expressed concern about the progress of the murder investigation. Today sees the official start of the vacation season at Pelican Lake and many visitors are expected during the summer. He appealed to all officials to do their best to ensure tour-ists could continue to travel to the area. Likewise, he warned against unnecessary scaremongering. He emphasized that the roads and the area around Orr are safe and people are looking forward to welcoming guests. The small town of Orr is a jumping-off place for the famous Voyageurs National Park on Lake Kabetogama, which is visited by more than 200,000 nature-loving vacationers every year.

This is just like Jaws, Ondragon thought, turning off the cell phone. The articles weren't particularly informative, but at least they gave the names of some additional people whom he could question about this. He would email Charlize later and get her on to it, if she hadn't already learned it all from his friend at the FBI. He glanced out the window. His balcony had been thoroughly cleaned, but the idea of sitting there in the sun held little appeal for him now. So he would have to go to the terrace. Very well. He rose, stowed the cell phone in his pants pocket, and took a magazine to read.

On the terrace, he looked for a sunny spot and settled down on a comfortable deck chair. Just as he was leaning back to enjoy the peace and quiet, a shadow suddenly fell on him.

"There he is, Mr. Fancy-Pants Consultant!"

Ondragon turned and looked into Shamgood's swimming pool–blue eyes. Next to him stood Norrfoss with a superior smile on his lips. What the hell did these two weirdos want from him now? Had they been stalking him? He looked with open hostility at the troublemakers, hoping to put them off. But Shamgood remained where he was, staring down at him impassively. His jaw muscles twitched.

"Just imagine, we know who you are," he said triumphantly.

"Oh yeah?" replied Ondragon coolly.

"Yes. My friend Johan here," Shamgood said, pointing to Norrfoss, "has been making inquiries about you. He has good connections in Sweden, you know."

Here it comes, thought Ondragon.

Shamgood turned to Norrfoss with a smile. "It took a while, but now we have confirmation of your dirty dealings. I suspected from the start that you weren't entirely kosher."

"And what's that supposed to mean?" asked Ondragon indifferently.

Shamgood looked at him, his eyebrows raised. "Well, you work as a spy for enemy governments, that's what!"

Ondragon's jaw almost dropped, but only almost. His years of experience meant he had a good command of himself. His face remained expressionless as he listened to Shamgood's adventurous accusations.

"The fact is that you have extensive contacts with wealthy individuals, including companies and corporations in the Far East and Arabia. You are a thief and a spy, stealing inside information and passing it on to the highest bidder. I don't need to ask you what languages you are fluent in. Japanese, Thai, Arabic, and German, to name but a few."

That was true, at least about the languages. And as for the rest, well, espionage was a strong word. Ondragon was gradually becoming uncomfortable. He wondered what kind of contacts Norrfoss had in Sweden and how he had gotten this information in the first place. One of those two bums must have a secret cell phone just like he did. There was no other way they could have done it.

"After all, you are ideally qualified for a career as an informer," Shamgood continued. "Your father was a German diplomat and your mother was employed by the Swedish military. And as what? As an agent, of course!"

"That's enough!" Ondragon rose indignantly to his feet. "Your impertinence is truly unprecedented, Mr. Shamgood. You are not only a pathological stalker, but also a paranoid conspiracy theorist! Me a spy and my mother an agent? That's laughable. If I were you, I would check your oh-so-secret source thoroughly for credibility. They have me completely wrong." He began to sweat under his shirt. Ava Birgitta Ondragon had been many things, a soldier, a competitive athlete, a loving mother, but never an agent! How dare this guy?

At the word *stalker*, Shamgood made a grimace. "How do you know . . . ?"

"I do my homework too, Mr. Shamgood. And I know a thing or two about my job. And you," Ondragon said, pointing his finger at Norrfoss, "I know a thing or two about you too, sonny."

Now the young Swede piped up in his native language: "Mr. Ondragon, believe me, our source is absolutely reliable. My contacts reach all the way up to parliament and the security services. My evidence against you is in black and white."

"Oh, yeah? Well, show me this alleged *evidence*!" Ondragon was sure that the two psychos had made up this story just to annoy him. After all, the Federal Intelligence Service routinely screened all individuals and their families who worked for the German Foreign Office—that had certainly been the case with his parents. And he didn't believe the service had made any mistake. It was a bluff by Shamgood to draw him out. Ondragon drew himself up and reminded himself to retain the high ground.

"Gentlemen, I think this conversation is over. If you continue to harass me with your unfounded accusations, I will get my lawyer involved and have you charged with slander faster than you can even say 'bail'! Now, if you'll excuse me." He tried to walk past the two men, but Shamgood held him back. Not that the fashion designer touched him, no, he didn't dare, but he blocked his path with his perfumed body.

"Wait a minute, Mr. Ondragon, we're not done yet. There's another thing." The solarium-tanned face was less than half an arm's length from him, giving Ondragon a clear and unwanted view of Shamgood's unnaturally white smile.

He raised his brows and merely repeated, "Lawyer."

Shamgood seemed unimpressed, probably thinking that his overpaid celebrity lawyers would outclass Ondragon, but he was wrong.

The fashion designer grinned. "Look at him, Johan, this guy lies whenever he opens his mouth! I guess that's an occupational hazard, right?"

Norrfoss laughed. It was a shabby and contemptuous sound, coming from the mouth of this pathetic boy. Ondragon would have liked to smash his face in.

"It seems to me that some aspects of your family history have escaped you, Mr. Ondragon. You should really give that some thought, because there's nothing worse than realizing you've been lied to by your own parents, is there? Perhaps you'd better hire your lawyer to investigate the machinations of your sketchy family. A little genealogy never hurt anyone."

Now that was enough! Ondragon wriggled deftly around the obstruction of Norrfoss and Shamgood, having to restrain himself from instinctively deploying a Krav Maga release hold, and looked the two blondies up and down from a safe distance.

"I wouldn't be surprised if I managed to track down that young man you sexually harassed at the fashion show in Milan last year, Mr. Shamgood. Let me see if I can get him to press charges against you. I assume he's only keeping quiet because you're paying him handsomely for his discretion. Maurice Bernard was the name, right?" Ondragon secretly ran his fingers over the phone in his pocket. The modern man's weapon, he would have loved to pull it out right there and threaten Shamgood with a call to Maurice Bernard. But the cell phone was his secret, his little advantage that no one was supposed to know about.

"Let's see if Maurice Bernard is happy with a check that has one more zero ahead of the decimal point. I'm sure he's enjoying his eclairs and champagne right now, but I think he'll have time for me once I explain who I am." He raised a hand to his ear with an outstretched thumb and pinky, mimicking a phonecall. "*Allô, Maurice Bernard, je suis Monsieur Ondragon, avocat aux Etats-Unis. Je voudrais parler à Monsieur Shamgood . . .*" Out of the corner of his eye, he registered Shamgood's complexion change from chocolate to caramel. *Gotcha!*

"I bet it's a number in Paris, right? *Mon Dieu*"—he looked at his watch—"it's 'igh time I spoke to eem. In Paree it is now four o'clock in the afternoon; perhaps the good Sheila will let me place a call from the lodge."

Shamgood's face color turned from caramel to milk. He tugged Norrfoss by the sleeve. "We're done here. But don't think I'm going to admit defeat, Mr. Ondragon!" He rushed away, his hair flying out behind him.

When the two pests were out of sight, Ondragon hurried into the lodge, rushed up the stairs to his room, and only noticed his racing heart when he was leaning against the inside of the closed door. Hastily, he took the cell phone from his pocket and dialed a number in Berlin. A number he had not dialed for many years.

The line buzzed, then it rang. Once, twice, three times . . . Ondragon hung up abruptly. What could he ask his parents? Whether his mother was an agent? That was ridiculous. He slapped his forehead with his cell phone and took a few deep breaths. Shamgood and Norrfoss. Those lousy little sons of bitches! They had actually managed to touch a nerve.

He pushed himself away from the door. Nevertheless, sooner or later he would have to talk to his parents. But not now and not on the phone. He would visit them in Berlin and finally ask them the many questions that had been burning in his brain for so long.

Ondragon looked thoughtfully out the window. Shamgood's accusations, as insane as they might be, had set up a vibration in him. It seemed as if long-buried feelings were making their way out into the light, just as a little boy had once struggled out from under a pile of books weighing tons. Another shadowy memory joined them. Of his mother's frightened face, her red lips parted in a horrified scream. And his father's fit of rage when he beheld the mischief little Paul had wrought. Ondragon saw a shadow as tall as himself, hovering over the books and finally floating up to the ceiling and disappearing. Then there were only his mother's tears, but Paul did not understand why she was crying. Nothing had happened to him. He was alive. Then what was making her so sad?

Stop it! Ondragon shook his head and forced his out-of-control *centrifuge* to stop.

Pull yourself together, Paul Eckbert! What's the matter with you, falling for such garbage? Those two assholes only wanted to mess with you. Sure, they dug up some information about you, but the rest is complete baloney! And the bullshit about the library is only bubbling up now because Dr. Arthur was digging around in it. You'd better think of a new strategy for Shamgood, in case he tries it again.

Ondragon sat down on the bed and ran a hand over his face. He would keep a closer eye on the two blond baboons. They would learn what it meant to mess with the head ape.

CHAPTER 29

1835, at Rainy Lake,
Upper Canada

Two-Elk entered the dome-shaped hut made of tree bark and reverently greeted the man who was huddled in front of a small fire wrapped in bearskins, looking like a graying grizzly. The old man made a sign with his wrinkled hand, and Two-Elk sat down on the spruce-covered floor of the wigwam. Then they were silent for a while.

It was not until the old Chippewa shaman took out his pipe and smoked it that Two-Elk made his request.

The shaman's expression remained unchanged, even when the word *Wendigo* was spoken. After Two-Elk had finished, the old man put the pipe aside, and the younger waited for the medicine man to say something. They both belonged to a tribe that the whites had scattered all through the forest land from here to the Great Lakes. The old shaman who lived here on the birch-lined shore of Rainy Lake with his wife was the pitiful remnant of a once mighty nation. When he died, the last man who could still speak to the spirits would be gone.

"The Wendigo, you say?" The old man cleared his throat.

"Yes, it's him. I saw him with my own eyes when he attacked my friend."

"And this friend now carries the evil spirit within him?"

"Yes, he is suffering from the cold fever." Two-Elk had been on the road for three days to reach Rainy Lake, and hoped Parker would still be alive when he returned to him.

"My son, do you want to save him or kill him?" the old man asked. His voice was as brittle as oak bark.

"I want to save him, if I'm not too late."

"Good, but if you should be too late, then you will have to kill him. We have to maintain the balance. Another Wendigo dwelling here in the woods would not be good, you understand?" His finger, as thin as a dry twig, hovered in the air between them.

"Yes." Two-Elk knew the shaman was right. The balance could not be disturbed. Besides, he had already decided to spare his friend the fate of wandering the woods as an eternally hungry ghost.

"Let me tell you about the Wendigo, my son. It is important you know his story so that you can pass it on to your children. The spirits and *Kitchie Manitou* must always be sanctified. They watch over life and death. They are around us and they protect us. The Wendigo, however, is evil. He is the evil *in* us. He seduces us, makes us do evil things, and reminds us that it is we who do not accept the call of death. He is greed and insatiability. A shape-shifter who can take all forms, including invisible ones, the bad feelings inside us. And you can only escape him if you do not let these feelings into your heart. You can always recognize him by his red eyes. Does your friend have those eyes?"

Two-Elk nodded.

"And is he cold and terribly hungry?"

"Yes."

"Then the Wendigo is in him. Whoever is touched by him, his heart turns to ice and his blood to snow. His feet pain him and so he is doomed to wander forever. He can be as swift as the north wind and as silent as nothingness, as strong as ten bears and as hard as stone."

"Can he be defeated?" asked Two-Elk in a hushed voice.

The old man's lips twisted into an unreadable smile. "The Wendigo is a powerful spirit, it lives forever, but it suffers from loneliness. The only way to defeat it is to capture and burn it. You can only heal a person who has been touched by the Wendigo by thawing his heart, which has been turned to ice. And to do that, you will need this, my son." The shaman held out a pouch.

Two-Elk opened it and looked inside. Then he looked questioningly at the old man. "Beeswax?"

The shaman nodded thoughtfully. "Go to your friend, make the wax hot, and use it to try to rid him of the cold fever. But remember, if you do not succeed, and the spirit of the Wendigo is too strong, do not challenge him. Kill your friend, deprive the Wendigo of the opportunity to create a companion. Push him back into solitude and he will have to go back to the forest. There he will lick his wounds and wait . . . for he will eventually seek a new victim. If not now, then in another time!"

CHAPTER 30

2009, Moose Lake,
Cedar Creek Lodge

After Ondragon had swum in the lake in the morning, talked with Dr. Pollux about an additional therapy session the afternoon, and arranged to play a game of basketball with Vernon in the evening, he relaxed on a lounger in the middle of the freshly mowed lawn behind the main building. A tree provided him with shade, a bottle of mineral water with refreshment, and a copy of *National Geographic* with much-needed distraction. And indeed, the calming atmosphere of the lodge finally seemed to be taking effect, even though the case of the corpse in the woods was still flitting around the back of his mind. Actually, he had to admit, it was not his job to be concerned about it at all. The police were taking care of it, and he had better concentrate on what he was here for: therapy.

The cell phone, hidden under a towel, vibrated. He looked at it inconspicuously, the magazine laid over it as additional camouflage. It was a text message.

Staying in Orr at the Gateway Inn. Had a good trip. Pretty scary here ;-)
The only thing I found out about Orchid is that he hasn't lived in Toronto since April. Apparently, he moved to Europe, probably France.
Will deal with Bates's neighbors right away. Greetings, Charlize.

PS: Check your inbox. Sent you some more material on the Parker murders. Your friend at the FBI, Mr. Hurley, was very helpful.

Charlize was already in Orr? Ondragon grinned. His assistant had always been able to travel at the drop of a hat; she was really good at that. Ondragon looked at his inbox and opened the email. It contained three attachments. The first two were newspaper articles from the Cook City Archives dated July 3, 1997:

HUNTING FOR KILLER BEAR

by Michael Strauss

Orr, St. Louis County. The entire town of Orr is on the go, but its residents aren't taking tourists fishing or hosting barbecues, they're on the hunt. Everyone who can hold a firearm is helping the hunt for the bear said to have killed a family in their lonely cabin in the woods more than a month ago. The FBI is still investigating the murder, but the whole of Orr is certain: It was a bear.

Matthew Coon, the mayor's son, has organized the pursuit, which involves more than a hundred volunteers. Armed to the teeth, the hunters are combing a 1.5-square-mile area north of Orr, where the victims' cabin is located. A hiker had sighted a particularly large bear there three days before the attack.

Only Dr. Jill Layton, director of the Orr-based research division of the American Bear Association, has tried to stop the citizens' illegal action. She said the black bears around the Vince Shute Wildlife Sanctuary are protected and besides, it has not yet been proven that it was in fact a bear that killed the Parker family. The behavioral scientist blames the FBI for unnecessarily throwing fuel on the flames of this discussion. Withholding information about the killing, she says, has brought bears under unwarranted suspicion. She is demanding a clear statement about whether there were indeed bite wounds on the bodies of the Parker couple and which animal made them. The bears at the nature preserve, which was established to the northwest of Pelican Lake in 1995, are part of an extensive study that will tell scientists more about the animals' behaviors. According to Dr. Layton, the bears are also a popular attraction in Orr, drawing countless tourists every year. Orr residents, however, blame the American Bear Association in particular for the Parkers' deaths, as the bear population in the area has increased significantly since the reserve came into being—a conflict that has yet to reach its peak. The first day of the hunt was unsuccessful.

KILLER BEAR DEAD?

by Michael Strauss

Orr, St. Louis County. The hunt for the killer bear, declared by Mayor Dean Coon on Sunday, continues. Once again, more than a hundred hunters are involved on day three of the hunt. Word has now spread that a bear is being hunted in Orr, and this has drawn more hunters from around the state. Spurred on by additional reward money, they are scouring the forest around Pelican Lake.

At the end of the day, there were two shootings to report: a black bear wearing an American Bear Association transmitter around its neck, and a 2,000-pound grizzly bear, which is extremely rare in this region. Dr. Layton of the ABA is clear: This is a premeditated search for a scapegoat. She has announced that she will report this illegal hunt to the highest levels, along with the failure of the police to intervene.

The citizens of Orr, meanwhile, are satisfied. They believe the grizzly killed the Parker family. They are now hoping for a quiet end to the summer season with many enthusiastic tourists.

Well, isn't this a surprise, Ondragon thought. The case bore an unmistakable resemblance to that of the corpse here at CC Lodge. Why hadn't that occurred to anyone before now? Or was Dr. Layton only snapping like a stray dog because she sensed a renewed threat to her bears? And Pete? Why hadn't he spoken up yet? After Dr. Layton, he should be the quickest to see the link between the two cases; after all, he was a direct victim of the Parker murders.

Ondragon took a sip from the water bottle and opened the second attachment. It contained a multipage FBI form in pdf format, like an official report sheet from the sheriff's office, containing all the details of the Parker murders. There was not much new in it, but the list of suspects back then was interesting:

- The sons, Peter and Mortimer Parker: *excluded as suspects following interviews by FBI officials and psychiatrist's expert opinion*
- Unknown regional/transregional killer: *no links to other murders found after nationwide search, potential suspect*
- Friend/relative of Louisa and Herman Parker: *ruled out as*

*suspects after detailed interviews with their circle of acquain-
tances*

- Wild animal (bear/wolf/cougar): *excluded after examination by experts*
- Unknown entity: *potential suspect*
- Accident: *ruled out by forensic investigation*

The subsequent pages of the document contained detailed descriptions of the crime scene, the condition of the bodies when they were found, and the autopsy, which read like a butcher's diary. Ondragon's guts tightened. And this is what Pete and Mortimer had had to witness as children? Horrifying!

At the end of the report was written in red: *Double murder not solved, investigation closed for lack of admissible evidence—reporting agent: Alfred Preston ZR 002. Witness statements, photos, and all documents under file number 200597MPMN.*

Ondragon assumed Charlize would get the rest of the file and let the cell phone slide back under the towel. Through his sunglasses, he observed the tranquil scene on the terrace. The models were sunning themselves, Mrs. Burlwood was attending to her pale, flabby complexion under a large umbrella, and next to her lay Johan Norrfoss on a lounger, wearing swimming trunks, smoking, and listening to music. Charlie Bloom was playing cards with two other guests, and Thomasz Viktory was practicing on the adjacent tennis court—Ondragon could tell by the telltale plop-plop of the balls being hit. And . . . Holy moly, what a pair of stems! He pulled his sunglasses to the tip of his nose.

Kateri Wolfe had stepped through the terrace door out into the sunshine. She was wearing jeans and cowboy boots and looked around, searching. When she spotted him, she came sauntering toward him with a smile, her hair in two thick braids. She was beyond hot.

"Howdy, pardner!" Ondragon greeted her, sitting up. "You look like you came straight from a rodeo."

Kateri briefly studied the tattoo on his bare chest and then replied, "I actually just came from riding. Julian and I did some reining exercises."

Julian and I! He wondered what else they'd been doing.

"You can ride Western style?" Ondragon tried not to let his displeasure with Julian show. After all, he didn't understand it himself.

"Do you think that's unusual for an Indian woman? Well, we've always had horses, and my parents were also enthusiastic riders. I don't get to ride so often now, unfortunately, because of my work. So I like to work with the horses a bit while I'm here. It's relaxing."

Ondragon patted the lounger beside him, and Kateri sat down. He glanced unobtrusively at the terrace, where Norrfoss was sitting, staring over at them. That bum! Ondragon turned to Kateri and consciously inhaled her scent: an exciting mixture of leather, horses, and the sweat on her skin.

"Then next time I'll come and watch you working with the horses," he said.

"What, only watch?" She tossed her braid jauntily over her shoulder. "If I may remind you, the first time we met, you said you might even join us next time."

"I only trust one Mustang, and it has rubber feet and drinks gas!"

Laughing, Kateri poked him in the ribs and they talked for a while, looking out at the lake. Then Ondragon unfortunately had to say goodbye to her and went into the lodge. He couldn't miss another appointment with Dr. Arthur.

At five o'clock sharp, he knocked on the door with the brass sign.

"Ah, Paul, come in!"

"Dr. Arthur, I want to apologize again for missing our meeting yesterday."

The psychotherapist made an understanding gesture. "Apology accepted. But what happened? I heard you fell in the woods and hit your head badly."

"That's right. It's not too bad though." He felt the swollen bump on his forehead.

"Well, then, it's now my turn to ask your forgiveness, Paul. About the unpleasantness you've had . . . I mean the matter of the . . . well, dog's head on your balcony. I can assure you that I have increased security around the lodge. There will soon be an electric fence to keep the bear from entering the premises. And Deputy Hase continues to look into the matter. He is taking it very seriously."

Ondragon waved the apology aside. He was fed up with the subject. "That's okay, we can start the session now."

"Sure."

Ondragon took a seat on the couch, and Dr. Arthur sat in the chair next to it.

"Last time, we returned to the place where your fear began. I would like to repeat that today so that I can gather more details about what happened. As you'll remember, there was still some ambiguity there. It seemed like there was another person in your memory besides your father and mother. I want to get to the bottom of that. Now, just relax, Paul. Later we can talk about what we have brought to light with the help of hypnosis. Think about the color . . ."

Ondragon thought of the pine-green and instantly plunged into the state he might have described as floating in a diffuse in-between world. You were not in the here and now, but also not completely in the then, you were observing from a distance, while being very close to it all. But he was not afraid. He even felt surprisingly relaxed when he saw himself standing in his father's library and felt the pulsating heartbeat of Cairo under his feet, as if he were there in the flesh.

When he awoke from hypnosis, he couldn't remember anything. With sweat on his forehead, he sat up. "What . . . ?"

"Easy, Paul. Look at me."

Confused, Ondragon turned his head and looked into the yellow eyes.

"Look at me! I am your father. What do you want to tell me?"

Ondragon felt himself catch his breath. He saw the ten-year-old boy who had been punished too severely by his father. Anger boiled up inside him and tears burned in his eyes. "It's your fault!" he growled. "It's *your* fault, you old bastard!"

"What's my fault?" asked his father's face.

"The . . . the . . ." Suddenly an indistinct shadow intruded into his field of vision. A human being? If so, who was it? Oliver Orchid? Pete? No, now he had it: The creature kept changing its face. It came creeping up on him through the woods, lunged out with an arm, and hit him on the head . . . no, now it was opening its mouth and . . .

"The murderer, you are the murderer," Ondragon whispered.

"I'm a murderer?" the changing face asked.

"Yes, you killed the man out in the woods and . . . and . . ."

A snap rang out, and Ondragon woke up. Blinking, he looked at Dr. Arthur.

"What's wrong?"

The psychotherapist spread his arms. "We were on the verge of uncovering your secret, but then your subconscious mind pushed in between, protectively. This sometimes happens when the memories are too painful. In this case, the subconscious works like a police officer who immediately locks up unwanted memories in the dungeon. I am now certain that something else happened that day in your father's library. Something that you repress so strongly that even hypnosis can't reach it. We must try another way to get to the key that your thought police officer keeps hidden. We will use this key—it might be a word, a picture, a color, a smell, everything that connects an individual's thoughts—to free your memories. Only then will you be able to process your fear rationally, the first big step in the fight against your phobia. I have one more question though, Paul. Do you ever talk to your reflection in the mirror?"

Ondragon frowned. "Do you mean do I talk to myself?"

"No, I mean, are you talking to your reflection?"

Ondragon pondered. What was the difference? He put his hand up to his forehead. He felt as if he were wrapped in cotton wool. His head was strangely empty, in contrast to the last time when, after hypnosis, thoughts had sprouted like weeds from all the convolutions of his brain. He tried to focus and came to a surprising conclusion.

"Now that you mention it . . . it's true. I actually do talk to my reflection quite often. But what does that have to do with my phobia?"

"Well, I have some suspicions about the incident in the library, but I want to keep them to myself for now. I don't want to influence you, you must understand that." Dr. Arthur tucked the silver ballpoint pen into the breast pocket of his coat. "Now, you're going to get one more homework assignment from me. It would be helpful if you would try to remember your dreams in the morning. Dreams play an important role in psychoanalysis. Focus on your feelings and moods after waking up, be sure to write everything down. Many people immediately forget what they dreamed. I would like to talk to you about it tomorrow, yes?"

Ondragon nodded.

"And if any unfamiliar memories or flashbacks come to you during the day, perhaps from your childhood, make a note of those as well. Hypnosis is like a plow, it breaks up the topsoil of your memories and brings old thoughts back out into the fresh air."

Ondragon admired Dr. Arthur's metaphors. They weren't particularly poetic, but they were easy to understand. He said goodbye to the psychotherapist and left the room.

In the evening, he crawled under his bedsheets and conscientiously laid out his notepad. Then he pulled the covers up to his chin and closed his eyes. He was dog-tired. Vernon had given him quite a beating on the basketball court. The masseur, despite his massive frame, had been a very agile player and pretty accurate, and Ondragon had had to make a big effort to hold his own against the colossus. But basketball was one of the things he was really good at, and in the end, he had recovered with a three-pointer. Vernon was a good loser and had invited him for a drink on the terrace afterward, where they had watched the sunset, sweating. Afterward, Ondragon had gone up to his room and taken a long, hot shower. But sleep would not come despite, or perhaps because of, the exhaustion. Ondragon turned restlessly from side to side and felt the aches from the robust ball game throbbing at various points in his limbs. He wasn't as young as he used to be after all.

After tossing and turning for a while, Ondragon decided that if he couldn't fall asleep he would do a little thinking. He opened his eyes in the dark and stared at the ceiling as he gently circled the day's events in the *centrifuge.* The unwanted intervention of the terrible twins Shamgood and Norrfoss had definitely been the most annoying thing.

His mother, an agent! What were those two nutcases thinking, talking such nonsense? But as absurd as the accusation was, it had unwittingly stirred something deep inside him. Ondragon closed his eyes and tried to remember the hypnosis, but the images remained blurred. Why was Dr. Arthur so sure that there was more to the incident in the library besides the landslide of books? Did it have to do with his mother's tears? Ondragon prowled through his memories like a tiger through the jungle, but all he could see were the tons of books crashing down on him, a young boy, burying him. But wait, there was something else. A shadow. It materialized right next to him. It looked like a dense cloud of black flies. For a moment it hovered silently above Ondragon, then it disappeared into a large mirror that now hung on the wall where previously the bookcase had stood. Ondragon gazed spellbound into the mirror and saw himself in it. His mouth opened as if he wanted to tell himself something. His lips formed the word *you* and *murderer* and his reflection raised a hand and pointed accusingly at him. Before Ondragon could even comprehend what this meant, his self in the mirror transformed into a shaggy monster with red-hot eyes. Startled, he recoiled and fell backward onto the pile of books. Drool ran from the gruesome creature's mouth, and in one claw it held Rumsfeld's bloody head. It moved in staccato jerks, like an undead in a bad zombie movie—somehow ridiculous and yet dangerous at the same time! Then the monster turned its head in his direction and fixed him with a searing gaze. A vicious snarl came from its throat. Horrified, Ondragon stared at the mirror and hoped the Wendigo was securely confined there.

But it was not. The beast took a brief run up and jumped through the mirror as if it were a soft membrane, landing silently next to his bed. Ondragon lay there paralyzed, the creature like a hairy mountain of muscle above him. An acrid stench wafted down toward him and took his breath away.

The pistol flashed through his mind. But the thought evaporated immediately. The gun was in the safe, and the monster was standing directly between him and the safe. It reared up to its full height on its stilt-like hind legs, bumping its head against the ceiling. Red eyes glowed from the hulking mass of its skull, and the stench that emanated from its fur numbed Ondragon's senses. Clawing at the sheet with his fingers, he prepared to roll out of bed if the creature attacked him. But the monster did not move. "What do you want?" flung Ondragon at the eerie visitor.

The beast remained rigid. But then it tilted its head and gave him a piercing look. The tendons on its neck twitched under the mangy fur.

"What do you want from me?" All the fibers in Ondragon's body were taut, rock hard. Would he even stand a chance against this beast?

The Wendigo raised one of his grotesquely long arms and lunged. Ondragon clenched his jaw. He saw the beast's sharp teeth flash in the moonlight, and for a moment the hairy arm trembled in the air. Then it dropped with a growl. At the same instant, Ondragon ducked his head and rolled aside. But it was not the Wendigo's claws that dug into the mattress beside him, it was an object he assumed was Rumsfeld's head. The ghastly ball landed on his bed with a loud smack.

When Ondragon looked up again, the looming shadow of the Wendigo had gone; there were only the curtains, waving gently in front of the open balcony door. Cautiously, he sat up and looked around the room. He was alone. His eyes fell on the head lying on the pillow beside him, and his heart stood still.

Even as he awoke from this terrible dream, Ondragon heard himself screaming—a hoarse, primal sound that slowly faded into the silence of the room. Breathing heavily, he ran his hand over his face. Oh, man, what a fucking nightmare! The image of the severed head still hovered before his eyes. But it had not been the shaggy dog's skull that had looked at him with a dead gaze, but that of a human being. The head of his mirror image. *His* head!

It's sick, what your subconscious does to you, he thought, and was about to turn on the light to look for the notepad when he heard a loud thump outside on the balcony. Ondragon jumped out of the bed. But the rumbling did not come again; instead, he noticed that the balcony door was open, just like in his dream. And the most disturbing thing of all was that he had not opened it.

Without turning on the light, Ondragon crept to the safe and took out his gun. Then, the gun at the ready, he stepped over to the open door, took a deep breath, and leaped out through the curtains into the night. In a flash, his senses registered every single detail on the balcony: the deck chair with the light-colored cushions, the table with an empty bottle of non-alcoholic Budweiser still on it, the wooden railing with the flower boxes, and the lantern on the wall that he could have turned on. Every shadow was in its place, nothing moved, and there was no nasty surprise on the floorboards.

Ondragon glanced down over the railing. Light gusts of wind blew around his nose, and somewhere a few crickets chirped in the grass. Everything seemed peaceful.

Relieved, he lowered the gun. The balcony door had probably not been closed properly and a gust of wind had pushed it open, which would explain the loud bang that had woken him up. He could actually be grateful to the door for pulling him mercifully out of his nightmare.

He went back inside and immediately sensed that something was wrong. Again, he raised his gun and searched the room. His eyes caught a bright square lying on the floor in front of the door. He crouched down and picked it up. It was a piece of paper. He quickly unfolded it and looked at the three sentences written in clumsy block letters on the paper:

I KNOW YOU ARE SNOOPING AROUND HERE
GIVE IT UP
OTHERWISE YOU WILL END UP LIKE THE DOG

Ondragon lowered the note. Clearly, this was a warning. But from whom? Oliver Orchid? Pete? The clumsy handwriting would fit him. Ondragon put the note in the safe; he would send the scrawl for a handwriting test tomorrow. It was only a matter of time before he found out who had written it. The list of suspects was quite limited.

He was about to lie back down on his bed when his eyes fell on another object that was disrupting the usual order of the room. It was on his pillow—where he had been sleeping not five minutes before. And this time Ondragon was sure. He was not alone!

CHAPTER 31

1835, Fort Frances

In the morning, Lacroix stepped out of the officers' barracks. The sun was rising over the bare treetops to the east, and red light bathed the weary figures staggering between the buildings in a bloody glow. Lacroix stretched his limbs, which did him good after his almost sleepless night, and walked over to a group of gray-faced soldiers. They were squatting quietly by the barracks, drinking coffee. Steam rose invitingly from their tin mugs into the cold air, and Lacroix was grateful when they poured him a coffee as well. The first sips were a relief, and he thought of Parker, who could no longer take in anything, neither liquid nor solid food.

"Say, did any of you hear the howling last night? I could hardly sleep with the noise," said one of the younger soldiers with a pimply red face. He looked like a thin matchstick in winter clothes.

Immediately, a general commotion broke out among the men. They talked loudly, speculating about what might have caused the noise. Lacroix saw that the very soldiers who had accompanied them through the forest were keeping their mouths shut. They probably had orders from Stafford not to breathe a word about what had happened on the way to the fort. Nevertheless, their fear was clearly visible.

"Hey, Carl, what are you gawking at? Have you seen a ghost?"

"Oh, leave me alone!" Carl, one of the two men who had found Johnson's body, turned and walked away.

The others looked at each other quizzically. "What's up with him?"

"Carl was out there at the farm too, wasn't he? You know, where that family was slaughtered," someone murmured. "People in the village don't talk about anything else. There's supposed to be a beast running around out there."

"What kind of beast?" asked the scrawny soldier.

"Some kind of Indian forest monster. Windigo or Witiko, or something like that. That's what they said in the tavern."

"And where did this monster come from?"

"Nobody knows, probably out of the forest. Something woke it up and now it's hunting people. Ask the Frenchman, he was there when the family was found. Apparently, he saw the beast. That's why he and his friend were brought here. Maybe the beast is here because of him!"

The scrawny soldier had turned pale. "Then will it kill us all?"

En voilà, une belle merde! thought Lacroix, as everyone stared at him.

"I made it clear yesterday that you are not to talk to the soldiers about the murders. Look what you have done! The soldiers are as scared as a flock of choirboys, just because you couldn't keep your mouth shut." Incensed, Lieutenant Stafford was stomping up and down in front of the big oak table where the colonel and the governor sat. Yet Lacroix had not said a word. The soldiers had picked up the stories of the Wendigo from the villagers.

"Damnation. It's going to take me weeks to get those cowards out there back in line, and it's all your fault!" Stafford continued to rant, but Lacroix was thoroughly indifferent to the lieutenant's troubles. His only concern was to help his friend. And Parker desperately needed food, or he would starve. Although the cold fever had receded somewhat since last night, he seemed very lethargic. His face was sunken and his body was emaciated—except for his feet.

"Just get on and ask me your questions, Lieutenant." He interrupted the lieutenant's lament, ignoring the disapproving looks from the other two stuffed shirts. "Then I'll be done here and I can finally go seek help for my friend."

"Temper your tone, *monsieur!*" the governor admonished him. "You are speaking to one of His Majesty's officers!" His hands were folded over his fat belly, and when he spoke, it was not only his double chin that wobbled, but his whole face, as if the tides were turning on it.

Lacroix glared angrily at him.

"Monsieur Lacroix," Stafford relented. "You are completely help-less out there, are you not? Why not admit it? You do not even know what it is your friend is suffering from."

"*Tabernac!*" Lacroix drew his stocky body up to its full height. "At least out there I'm not sitting around idly, as I am here in your benighted fort."

As he expected, Colonel Richards leaped out of his comfortable chair. "Enough of your insults, monsieur," he said indignantly. His clean-shaven chin gleamed from all the scented lotions that had been applied to it. Absurd fop!

Lacroix gave him a contemptuous look and turned to Stafford. At least he was still a man, if somewhat fastidious. "Lieutenant, I am weary of being treated like a criminal. Either ask me your questions now, or I shall take my friend and go. *Compris?* May I remind you that you told us we are not prisoners, merely witnesses? So—I would like to give my testimony forthwith and then leave this unfortunate place as soon as possible."

Stafford looked at Colonel Richards and the governor. Double chin and polished chin nodded reluctantly. Lacroix began his report. He saw Stafford deftly pull out his notebook and take down what he had not already made a note of. Soon only his own voice and the scratching of the pencil could be heard. Only rarely did any of those present interpose a question; their incredulity was written all too clearly on their faces. *Let them think what they want*, Lacroix thought. He knew what was lurking out there. Something ancient, something very powerful, something that could not be fought with the feudal ignorance of the nobility. Ignoring it would only make it angrier. Lacroix, on the other hand, was determined to face the creature. To fight it. Even if that meant he died in the process.

He was just describing the body of Trooper Johnson when there was a knock at the door and Sergeant Hancock entered the room after a summons from the governor.

"Gentlemen, please excuse the interruption, but the Indian who is with the trappers is out here. He says it's urgent."

CHAPTER 32

2009, Moose Lake,
Cedar Creek Lodge

As if electrified, Ondragon looked at the tuft of feathers lying on his pillow. It had been tied to a leather strap with an elaborate weave of white and red porcupine bristles.

Ondragon felt the back of his neck begin to tingle, and he wheeled around, the gun in his hand. But there was no one there. Cautiously, he checked the inside of the closet and the bathroom. Nothing. Abruptly, he stood still. Was the intruder hiding under the bed?

Like a cat, he dropped to all fours and aimed his pistol into the impenetrable darkness.

But there was no one there either. He gradually began to feel stupid.

As a precaution, he checked the balcony again, and the hallway outside the door to his room. No sign of anything.

Ondragon returned to bed and shifted the feather fetish onto the nightstand with the tips of his fingers. Then he flipped the pillow over and lay back down, the pistol hidden in the gap between the mattress and box spring. Strangely enough, he fell asleep immediately.

The next morning, he carefully examined the room door and the balcony door again and came to the conclusion that the previous night's intruder must have used either a key or a lockpick, because there were no signs of forced entry. The guy had likely hidden in the bathroom when he had woken up, then had positioned the note by the door and then had gone out onto the balcony while Ondragon had stood with his back to the bed and read the note. And they'd been damned silent about it!

Ondragon pondered. Who could be in the frame for such a stunt? The cleverness alone of using the note as a distraction almost certainly ruled out Pete. He seemed too awkward for that kind of thing. Sure, there was no great art in climbing off a balcony here. It could be done without much effort or skill. Ondragon continued to think. It could have been Oliver Orchid. Maybe he was still living in room 20 and had noticed that Ondragon was stalking him. And now he wanted to intimidate him, so that he would leave it alone in the future. Was Orchid afraid they might discover something that would get him in trouble? Something to do with the buried bag and the arm? Ondragon looked at the feather pendant, and a very different thought came into the back of his mind. Kateri?

It was a strange thought, but why not? But what reason could Miss Wolfe have for such an undertaking? She didn't even know he was investigating. Besides, nothing much had come of it so far. On a sudden inspiration, Ondragon reached for his cell phone. Yes! There was an email from Rudee. He opened it.

Sawadee, Paul!
First of all, a piece of advice: If I were you, I would pack my bags imme-diately and go home, or at least always have a gun on my person! And you'd better rub yourself with Tiger Balm—doesn't taste good!

What the hell was Rudee talking about? Ondragon shook his head.

*I'm attaching a document that was hidden **very deep**, I should stress, , in the bowels of the lodge's internal server. I wrote a special program to access it unnoticed through the back door. Read through it and you'll know why the data had more security than Fort Knox. Man, you really are in good company! Just make sure you get through this quickly. Dr. A is the head* *freak. If you ask me, the doc's got more maniacs in there than there are zombies in Resident Evil!*

Greetz
Napol_e.on

PS: Do not forget: Tiger Balm! You'll understand when you read the appendix.

Ondragon opened the file. And as he went through it, cold sweat formed on his skin. It was crazy, but all at once he saw an unpleasant connection between Dr. Schuyler's joking allusion to a cannibalistic and iron-clawed backwoodsman and Dr. Arthur's secret research. What was written here in black and white in the patient files that were so carefully secured would have impressed even good old Fritz Haarmann, the German serial killer!

With trembling fingers, Ondragon scrolled further. Might Kateri also be on this illustrious list? For some obscure reason he suspected it would not surprise him if this was indeed the case. He quickly skimmed the contents and finally reached the end of the file. Some familiar names were on the list, but Miss Wolfe's was not. Good. Not good. Ondragon scrolled back through the file to the beginning and worked through it again, to make sure he hadn't missed anything. Then he turned off the phone and stared at the wall for a while. It was unbelievable, but somehow he should have figured it out sooner.

Later, at breakfast, he looked at his fellow inmates through completely new eyes and added to the entries in his notepad. He felt the triple espresso racing through his veins and bringing the *centrifuge* up to top speed. The pieces of the puzzle, which he had been unware of until just now, fell into place almost by themselves, gradually forming a coherent picture. A picture that still sent a shiver of fascination and disgust down Ondragon's spine. Rudee's words came to his mind. Tiger Balm—a great idea! Involuntarily, he smiled. Rudee was a pragmatist. The Thai thought that human flesh in a marinade of essential oils might not be quite so tasty. Human flesh. What perverted madness!

Shaking his head, Ondragon looked from his notes over to the surgeon, Mikhail Petrovsk, who for once was sitting at his table without the tennis star, Viktory. The Russian was calmly eating his omelet. Ondragon felt sick. Petrovsk's secret patient file noted, among other things, the following:

Strong cannibalistic tendencies, but has his urges largely under control. C not sexually driven, i.e., MP has no sexual fantasies before, during, or after eating human flesh. Compensates for his cravings by eating organs and body parts discarded after transplants or surgery. Prepares them at home like regular food. MP says he does this because he loves the thrill of stealing the organs and considers human flesh a delicacy. Belongs to a small ring of cannibals in California that he supplies with organs. Lives with his wife and two children, who are, unknowingly, fellow consumers.

Ondragon grimaced, disgusted. That was really ghoulish! And also punishable by law. At least the secret siphoning off of organs from the hospital. But where did the removed organs actually go after an operation, and who controlled the disposal chain? Somewhere there had to be someone in on it. At least Dr. Petrovsk, as a surgeon, was positioned right at the source for indulging his unusual predilection. Ondragon's stomach did a dangerous somersault, as if he were on a roller coaster. He raised his hand and beckoned Carlos over. He needed more coffee!

Having received a new cup of steaming espresso, his attention was magically drawn back to his notepad. Petrovsk was still the most harmless among all the full-blown. There was the Latino crooner Enrique Souza, among others. He liked to bite his girlfriends in the neck because he felt an unbridled desire to drink their blood. Naturally, his relationships did not last very long. One of his former partners even reported him for assault in 2008. He had bitten her so hard that he had actually drawn blood. Clear case of vampirism, which was a variant of cannibalism. In addition, Souza's inclination was highly sexualized. He had a tendency to violence and liked to shower himself and his partners with buckets of fake blood during sexual intercourse. This was probably one of the reasons for the brevity of his relationships. Sexually, however, this also meant that Souza was a ticking time bomb. No one knew what would happen if he didn't get what he was craving. At least it seemed to have occurred to the singing boy that he wasn't quite normal, because otherwise he wouldn't have sought therapy. In the CC Lodge, Dr. Arthur, it occurred to Ondragon, had created an asylum like no other in the world for people with the abnormal craving for human flesh. He'd apparently had to promise his patients not to report their criminal activities to the police. Dr. Arthur's address was probably only available on the relevant internet sites, or it would have gotten around. In any case, the doctor maintained a respectable image to the outside world, disguised as a neurologist for the rich. A brilliant move.

Ondragon counted seventy names on the secret list. Seventy cannibals out there running free! A disturbing thought, but apparently also a fascinating field of research. Not that it meant Dr. Arthur was a bad psychotherapist. On the contrary, his brilliant skills were corroborated by an above-average rate of recovery. But was that also true of the cannibals?

Ondragon took a sip of coffee. What would the police and the press say if they found out that there were potential and actual criminals staying here at the CC Lodge? Discreetly. No wonder all the records on C patients were so well secured.

He flipped to two other names of inmates he knew: Harvey Lyme and Oliver Orchid. Finally, he had shed a little more light on the mystery surrounding the patient in room 20. The extensive file noted that Orchid had encountered a cannibal cult while working for Doctors Without Borders in a remote village in Darfur rebel territory in western Sudan. He had first attended out of sheer curiosity, but had gradually become addicted to cannibalism because of its archaic magic. His colleagues had initially warned him about the village, because women and men kept disappearing there under mysterious circumstances. But Orchid's curiosity had been greater than his fear, and so he had traveled to the village. The inhabitants had been reluctant at first, but after some persuasion had inducted the foreigner into their cult, which sacrificed its enemies and ate them to gain their strength. Orchid had told Dr. Arthur that he had been fascinated by the custom and had begun writing a book about it. But then the situation had gotten out of hand, and he had found himself in a blood frenzy one day, machete in hand and his victim's liver between his teeth. Orchid could not explain how this had happened, but he had been deeply shocked by his transformation. He had fled the village in a mad rush and later could not say exactly where it was located. Back at Doctors Without Borders, he had been unable to continue his work after only a few weeks. The curse of the village had never left him, and the desire to kill and eat human flesh had become overwhelming. After that, his hands would begin to tremble at the mere touch of a patient's skin. Before he completely lost control of himself, he had quit his job and traveled back to Canada by the fastest route, hoping the African nightmare would subside in the cool winter of his homeland. But that had been a false hope. Time and again, Orchid had found himself looking at the people around him, wondering if they tasted good and what kind of strength they might give him. And then, one day, it happened . . .

To Ondragon's regret, Dr. Arthur's report on Oliver Orchid broke off at this point; the rest of the file was blank. It seemed that everything else was subject to an even higher level of confidentiality. Strange. Was there yet more explosive information? If so, where was it? In Dr. Arthur's old-fashioned filing cabinet? Perhaps the documents had not yet been digitized and were slumbering peacefully on paper in the shrink's office. Ondragon thought. The office was guaranteed to be better secured than Sheila's office. Still, he could try. He flipped through the notepad and turned his attention to the last C patient currently in residence: Harvey Lyme.

As he read, Ondragon whistled through his teeth. The real estate agent eclipsed everything he had ever learned about cannibalism. Lyme was not a cannibal in the true sense of the word. Rather the opposite. The guy was, well, how should he put it, on the other side of the food chain. And that seemed far more deviant than the other sick shit. In all his pitiful desperation, Lyme did seek out cannibals, but not because he was looking for like-minded people. No, he lusted after a particularly freaky abnormality. It was as simple as it was hair-raising: Harvey Lyme wanted to be eaten!

Ondragon quickly poured the rest of the coffee into his rumbling stomach and leaned back with a sigh. He felt somewhat less happy than a clam, more like Alice in Freakyland. It was already moderately to extremely disconcerting that he was in a drop-in center for people who liked to eat people or be eaten by them without the public knowing. The beautifully situated CC Lodge was, you might say, part of a dark network that existed under the surface of society and played host to the deepest and most repugnant abysses of humanity. The remoteness of the facility, the exclusivity of the community, and the extreme control of the staff, it all fit. It was all part of a secrecy strategy that could only be found in the Pentagon or the CIA. Even the murders, well, maybe the case of the body in the woods could be connected with it. What if one of the C patients had snapped and followed their instincts? What if they had prepared themself a little feast?

That was quite conceivable and would also explain why Dr. Arthur acted as if he knew nothing. His—presumably illegal—research could not be exposed under any circumstances. Ondragon considered how to proceed. Actually, it would be better if he went directly to Deputy Hase with his newly gained knowledge. It put the murder investigation, which had not made much progress so far, into a completely different light. Maybe he could make sure the police didn't go off in the completely wrong direction and that Dr. Layton's bears were cleared of being killers. The lady would certainly be happy about that. But would they believe him? The thing with the cannibals . . . Probably not. After all, he was an inmate of CC Lodge.

Ondragon noticed Kateri entering the dining room and quickly removed the notepad from the table. He didn't want her to know anything about it. He welcomed her with a smile and waved Carlos over so she could order her breakfast.

As he watched her eat, he felt a subliminal relief that Miss Wolfe was not on Dr. Arthur's C list. According to this, she was not a cannibal, and he could confidently get involved with her without fear of being eaten. He suppressed a grin and inquired about her schedule for the day.

"Oh, I don't have much scheduled," she replied. "Dr. Arthur is expecting me at eleven, and I have an appointment with the masseuse at the spa at noon. Need to loosen up my muscles a bit after yesterday's riding practice. How about you? What are you up to?"

"An appointment at ten with Dr. Pollux. Dr. Arthur recommended that I try family constellation, which Pollux is a specialist in. Hypnosis alone doesn't seem to be enough to allow me to plumb the deepest trenches of my subconscious. I'm curious to see what family constellation will do."

"What is there to plumb so deeply with you?" Kateri had lowered her voice and looked at him teasingly. Ondragon's stomach grew warm.

"Well, *that's* what I hope Dr. Pollux will find out—or do you want to get into depth psychology? In that case, might we have our first session this afternoon? Shall we say four o'clock by the lake?"

Kateri Wolfe turned her face away in embarrassment and rubbed her cheek against her shoulder. Then she looked at him again, a coy smile stealing over her lips. "Could be an exciting experiment. I mean, with me as the therapist."

"Then it's a deal?" Ondragon wanted to rise.

"Yeah, but maybe I should play nurse and fix that scratch on your forehead first. It doesn't look good. Could be infected. Don't you feel anything?"

Ondragon ran his fingers over the scabbed wound. He did in fact feel a slight pain in the bump.

"It won't be anything major," he said. "But if it makes you feel better, I'll go see Sister Savage and ask her for some iodine."

"Sister Savage?"

"Well, Sheila."

Kateri laughed. "She's actually okay."

"Actually?"

"Yes."

"And what button do you have to push?"

Kateri looked at him uncomprehendingly.

"It's all right." Ondragon shook his head. "I'll see you at the lake." Before leaving the table, he stroked Kateri's forearm unobtrusively. Inwardly, he was looking forward to getting to know this woman more closely, and perhaps the opportunity would present itself soon. Then he would certainly not say no.

CHAPTER 33

1835, Fort Frances

They prepared the exorcism thoroughly. Two-Elk explained the procedure and Lacroix laid out all the items they would need. Colonel Richards and Governor Simpson had long since left the room. If they had known what pagan cultic practices the man intended to indulge in here, they would have disapproved in any case. They had left Lieutenant Stafford behind to observe what was happening and to intervene if necessary. He sat in a chair and diligently took notes, writing down every word and every hand gesture. Lacroix looked over at him, amused. He thought it was all just a waste of time. Who the hell would read this scribble? Nobody!

He felt Two-Elk's hand on his arm. The Chippewa's dark eyes spoke clearly. He too was afraid of what they might unleash in the exorcism of spirits.

"Spirit of Wendigo is powerful, he is part of Great Universe. But we must drive him out of Alan! *Kitchie Manitou*, the Great Spirit, will help us," he said in a muffled voice.

"Good, then let us begin the ritual." Lacroix turned to Parker, who was lying on the floor between them. A wide variety of paraphernalia was arranged around him, including amulets made of feathers and bones, a mummified hawk, a dreamcatcher, several small pouches of powders and incense, a wampum belt, a charcoal brazier with a copper pot on it, a white-enameled ladle, and the rounded bars of beeswax.

"Is there anything I can do too?" asked Stafford. His face was shining with excitement.

"No, palefaces may not participate in the ceremony," Two-Elk replied firmly.

"But he is also a paleface." Stafford pointed at Lacroix.

"Vincent is my brother." With that, the Chippewa turned back to Parker.

Lacroix saw the lieutenant purse his lips, offended. Then he seemed to come to his senses and, pencil at the ready, waited for whatever would happen next.

"All right, let us begin." Two-Elk took a small bag and poured the contents onto the glowing charcoal. Immediately, a strong smoke smelling of jimsonweed arose, filling the room. Then the man dipped his moistened finger into one of the other sachets. Using a red powder, he drew a horizontal line on Parker's, Lacroix's, and his own forehead and then laid out leather cords to form a net around Parker.

"This will draw out the evil spirit of the Wendigo, and this"—Two-Elk pointed to the dreamcatcher—"will catch it and hold it until we burn it." He placed the hawk mummy on Parker's chest and draped the feathers and bones in his hair. On his belly he placed the wampum belt of black and white shell beads.

Lacroix watched the Chippewa as he executed each movement with deliberation, muttering incantations to himself. Gradually, he felt the mind-expanding effects of the Wysoccan smoke and saw that Stafford did too. The lieutenant was writing sluggishly in his book, staring every now and then into the embers of the charcoal basin, his eyelids heavy.

Meanwhile, Two-Elk took the copper pot, placed it on the hot coals, and put in the beeswax bars. They melted quickly, and the scent joined the dense clouds of nightshade.

As Two-Elk intoned a dark, ritual chant and began rocking his torso back and forth, Lacroix knew his Native American friend was entering into a trance to purify his spirit and make his actions sacred.

The air in the room grew heavier and heavier from the various smells, and colorful mirages appeared before Lacroix's eyes. First, distorted faces and masks floated over their heads, then shadows of trees shot up from the floor and bluish flashes of light twitched from the ceiling.

Parker did not move. His mouth wide open, he stared fearfully into the clouds of smoke. His tongue was black and swollen and his breath was whistling.

In the pot next to Lacroix, the wax began to boil. Fine bubbles rose in the liquid. The flashes of light before Lacroix's eyes turned to red dots, and the dots to glowing pupils. A long, gaunt shadow appeared. The Wendigo. He had come.

The creature bent down toward them and opened its jaws as if it wanted to swallow everything. Lacroix could hardly tell the difference between reality and illusion, so deceptively real did the creature manifesting itself before his very eyes seem. The evil forest spirit was so close that you could have touched its shaggy, stinking fur if you had only stretched out your hand. Like an emissary from hell, he stood over them, ready to take Parker, his new companion.

Involuntarily, Lacroix ducked his head and, hearing Stafford let out a horrified groan, Two-Elk suddenly paused his chanting. Undeterred by the Wendigo's looming shadow, the Chippewa bent over Parker and murmured *"Kitchie Manitou"* into the latter's mouth, then reached for the ladle and dipped it into the liquid wax.

As previously discussed, Lacroix held Parker's head firmly with both hands and the dream catcher between his own teeth. His watched the ladle and its bubbling contents as it approached Parker's open mouth.

With a swift movement, Two-Elk tipped the hot wax into Parker's throat. It steamed and hissed, and an acrid smell arose, of boiling saliva and burnt skin.

The old trapper gave a strange, high scream. He tried to rise and lash out, but strong hands held him pinned to the ground. Two-Elk poured a second ladle into Parker's mouth until his scream ended in a gurgle.

The great shadow above their heads raged and screamed too. He brought his claws down on them, but the sharp pincers passed through them as if they were air. Again, the Wendigo struck at Lacroix, then at Two-Elk, and finally even at Stafford, who flinched fearfully. But they all remained unharmed, for a powerful spell protected them. A spell more powerful than that of the forest spirit.

Enraged, the Wendigo howled and stomped its tree-trunk-like legs until the earth shook. Cold as its icy curse, it blew its fury into the men's faces. It reached for Parker, to drag him into the depths of the forest, but the medicine held him in place like an invisible net. The Wendigo roared in disappointment, viscous drool dripping from its mouth and hissing as it evaporated into the pot of liquid wax. It straightened up and let out a shrill scream toward the ceiling before dissolving into a cloud of vapor.

Quickly, Two-Elk plucked the dreamcatcher from Lacroix's teeth and tossed it into the embers of the brazier, where it burned in a small jet of flame. All that remained was the stuffy silence, settling over the four people and what Stafford later described in his notebook as the iridescent aura of the Great Spirit.

Kitchie Manitou.

CHAPTER 34

2009, Moose Lake,
Cedar Creek Lodge

Before Ondragon went to see Dr. Pollux, he made a plan for the day. Now that he knew about the secret C files, he could see a whole host of new connections. He turned away from the large mirror next to his bed, which he had used to get an idea of the injury to his forehead. It really didn't look good and had begun to throb dully. He would probably have to ask Sheila for medical assistance after all.

A sour expression on his face, he walked around the room, thinking. He would not inform Deputy Hase about the cannibalism until he had excluded any possibility that he might have made a mistake. There was no way he was going to make a fool of himself in front of the young sheriff. But that also meant that he had to wait for more information from Charlize. And he wouldn't get it until this afternoon. He looked at his watch. Ten to eleven. He had to be on his way. After the appointment with Pollux, he would try to find out who had put that nice Indian souvenir on his pillow and written the letter. He was assuming for the time being, of course, that it was one and the same person.

Deep in thought, Ondragon left his room and locked the door, his Berlin talisman jingling softly. A moment later, as he climbed the stairs to the upper floor, a question crossed his mind. Did Dr. Pollux know about the C patients? If so, he was covering up the crimes of these people just like his boss. Perhaps he could sound out the Swiss doctor a little while he was with him.

Punctually as ever, he entered his treatment room, which he had already inspected the day before. It differed from Dr. Arthur's office in one essential way. Dr. Pollux's room was completely phobic-friendly. Cool, smooth surfaces of stainless steel and plastic, rather than antique furniture and artwork. Surfaces of white and gray, microscopically dust free, with no hint of coziness. Even the rustic log walls that characterized the lodge's interior everywhere were covered with Sheetrock and wallpaper here. No pictures hung on the wall, there were no personal items anywhere. Ondragon felt as if he had entered a sterile laboratory—all that was missing was for Dr. Pollux to be waiting for him in a yellow protective suit like in *Outbreak*. He sat down on the chair that was standing in front of the glass desk. It was the same neurotic model as Dr. Arthur had, except that Ondragon had felt much more comfortable in the latter's office.

"How are you doing, Paul?" asked Pollux with a slight Swiss accent. He too had insisted on an informal atmosphere and addressed Ondragon by his first name.

"Good, so far." Ondragon shrugged his shoulders. "Except I'm a little concerned by the talk of the cannibal killer running around in the forest."

"Cannibal killer? Who said that? I thought it was a bear." Dr. Pollux frowned, his high forehead ringed by dark brown hair. His rapidly receding hairline added to the impression that the Swiss man's head consisted only of forehead and a great deal of gray matter behind it. *Brainbug!* That was the first thing that came to mind when you looked at him. Otherwise, Dr. Pollux's face was deeply average, as featureless as his furniture.

"Well, there are whispers going around about the cannibal thing," Ondragon replied. "I don't know who first said it either, but what is certain is that there was a dead man in the woods."

"And he'd probably been there for a while." Pollux smiled placatingly. "A whole four months, I heard. So don't worry, the police will find out what happened." He clasped his hands on top of the table.

Ondragon was disappointed; Dr. Pollux had shown no emotion at the mention of the word *cannibal*. Either he was a good actor, or he really knew nothing about Dr. Arthur's unusual charges.

"We should prepare for your family constellation now, Paul," Pollux continued. "For the moment you should forget any horror stories that are circulating here. Or do you believe we have a cannibal murder on our hands?"

"No, not really."

"See. It's nonsense." Pollux pulled out a questionnaire and began to take his history for the therapy. Ondragon listened and patiently answered each question. He had been suspicious of the practice of family constellation from the beginning, because the method sounded very much like hocus-pocus. *A fortune teller with a crystal ball would be much more likely to deliver a credible result than this*, he thought.

"Are you ready, Paul?" asked Pollux at the end of the conversation.

Ondragon nodded, and the Swiss rose with a satisfied expression. "Then I'll ask the representatives to come in now. Don't worry, they are all employees of the lodge. None of them know anything about your problem, and nothing said in here will leave this room." He pointed to a sliding frosted-glass door behind his desk and pressed a button. The door opened and five women and five men entered the room with their heads bowed. Without greeting him, they sat down on a row of chairs against the wall. It looked like a police lineup. To Ondragon's relief, he didn't really know any of the employees.

"So, we will begin now, Paul. Please choose a representative for your father from among these people. Go to him, tell him what his name is and how old he is, and then take him to a spot in this room that you think is appropriate to your father."

Ondragon looked doubtfully at the people. And that was supposed to achieve what? Finally, he got himself together and went up to one of the men, took him by the hand, and put him behind the desk. Yes, that suited his father—always busy. Then he repeated the whole thing with his mother and positioned her in front of the desk, but with her back to his father, looking at the group.

"Good, now choose another representative for yourself, Paul." Dr. Pollux stood relaxed, watching his patient select a young man in nurse's attire and place him an arm's length from his mother. When he was finished, Dr. Pollux gently pushed Ondragon aside.

He clapped his hands once and said, "Right." What happened next, Ondragon could only describe in retrospect as a kind of puppet show with living people, with an invisible power moving the figures. Dr. Pollux served only as a moderator, gently guiding the representatives. He moved Ondragon's father next to the mother, who then looked down at the floor in dismay. The father also looked at the same spot on the floor. An eerie silence reigned in the room while Dr. Pollux positioned Ondragon's representative on the floor in front of the parents. Seemingly unmoved, they raised their eyes. Pollux nodded. Ondragon did not understand a thing.

Then Pollux had the Ondragon representative stand up again and stand next to the father and mother. All three now looked toward the other participants. Pollux nodded again. He walked over to Ondragon and asked quietly, "I asked you this earlier, and you denied it. But see, it sure looks like someone is missing from your family."

Ondragon stared at the doctor. "I really have no idea what you're talking about. I'm sorry."

"I see. Very well, let's try one more thing." Pollux went over to the group and selected another man to lie down on the ground in front of the other three representatives. Instantly, a jolt went through the father and mother; they moved, went to the prone man, and raised their folded hands to their mouths as if in prayer. The son continued to stand as if frozen, his hands buried deep in his pockets.

Ondragon watched skeptically. Was this serious psychotherapy?

Pollux went to Ondragon's deputy and led him to stand next to his parents. All three now looked down at the prone man and after a while they breathed a sigh of relief. It was a faint sound, you could feel it more than hear it, but still it hung in the room, a clear presence. One by one, Pollux placed a hand on their shoulders; as he did so, mother and father quietly murmured a word Ondragon could not understand. Again, Pollux nodded empathetically and looked seriously at his patient.

"Here's the deal, Paul," he finally said. "There was definitely another member of your family. And as far as I can tell, they were ripped from your midst by an unexpected death. You must have blocked it out, because you and your parents have never talked about it since. Your parents know the person who perished and continue to honor their memory. The rejection comes from you alone; it is only you who have excluded the person and driven them out of your family. I say to you, Paul: Bring that person back into your heart, back into your thoughts! Then you will be able to work through your problem. Bring back the dead person. Give him what he deserves: a place in your memory."

Ondragon's head was spinning. There had certainly been no such death. Dr. Pollux had to be mistaken. He looked at the Swiss doctor, deeply unsettled. All of this was just lazy magic. Why was Pollux ascribing a death to him? And how could these strangers know what had happened in his family? That was impossible. It was all just for show. He hesitated.

Pollux looked at him gently. "I can see you're still resisting this, Paul. Listen, I'm going to tell you the name and position of the deceased person, and then you can tell me if I'm wrong, okay?"

Ondragon pressed his lips together. His eyes burned, and his skull felt as if someone were rummaging around in it with a blender. This was worse than any hypnosis. How was he going to get out of this? Stressed, he exhaled and looked around. When he saw no one who could help him with his predicament, he nodded slowly.

Dr. Pollux smiled sympathetically. He put a hand on his shoulder and whispered, "The person's name is *Per Gustav* and he is your *brother*. I would even dare say he is your twin brother!"

It felt like an uppercut. Ondragon staggered and went down. Tons of books crashed down from the shelves and buried him.

Silence. And then a scream. It was his mother!

"Per! Oh my God, Per!"

CHAPTER 35

1835, Fort Frances

Two-Elk was the first to regain consciousness. After the ritual, the four men had fallen into a strangely exhausted sleep. The man got up and opened the shutters. The fresh air flowed in over them like a cool waterfall, chasing away the last reverberations of the nightshade and the memories of the screaming shadow.

Lacroix rubbed his eyes. He wanted to be sure to wipe away the last mirage. Then he bent over Parker. The old trapper lay there with a peaceful expression on his face, as if he were sleeping. Red welts around his lips testified to the ordeal with the liquid wax. His skin was almost white, as was his hair. Otherwise, he appeared unchanged. Lacroix touched him on the cheek; it felt cool, but no longer unnaturally cold. He breathed a sigh of relief.

Meanwhile, Stafford awoke and rubbed his forehead, groaning. "By all the saints in heaven, what was that?" Cursing, he stood up. But he seemed to feel dizzy, for he immediately slumped back into the chair. "What kind of devil's work was that?"

"No devil's work, Chippewa medicine," Lacroix said with a smile, pointing at Parker. Surprised, Stafford inhaled sharply as he saw the old trapper straighten up amid the mess and look at him clear-eyed. Apparently, the exorcism had succeeded.

"It can't be! Is he healed?" Stafford looked from Parker to Two-Elk.

"I think so." Lacroix turned to his friend. "How are you, Alan?"

"G-good." Parker looked down at himself and contemplated his feet, which had regained their normal size and shape. He scratched his head. "But what actually happened?"

That was him, good old Parker! He was back. Laughing, Lacroix embraced his friend. "Alan, blessed be the day we met Two-Elk. Without him, we would have lost you. Come, let's celebrate your recovery with a bottle of gin in the village. And then let's get out of here. I grow weary of the redcoats." Lacroix wanted to help Parker up, but Stafford stopped him.

"You can't leave just yet; first I have to investigate this . . . this thing."

"Oh, you and your investigations. When will you finally understand that not everything can be investigated and researched?" Lacroix tried to remain calm. They had done nothing and had been locked up in this fort for far too long. Not for one day longer would they allow themselves to be held here. They were men who loved freedom. The freedom of the unfathomable vastness of the forest.

"But, *messieurs* . . ." The lieutenant went to reach for Lacroix's arm, but Two-Elk came up behind him. He spoke very softly, yet Stafford flinched as if someone were shouting in his ear.

"If Paleface shouts too loudly, the spirit of the forest comes back. *Kitchie Manitou* is strong, he has defeated the Wendigo. He is a powerful spirit. But White Man must be silent, or he will bring the Wendigo back to him. Or does he too wish to suffer the cold fate of eternal hunger? This land is cruel, and the Wendigo is always watchful! You can call him if you like. But there is one thing Paleface should know: I only had medicine for one spell."

"Very well." Stafford backed away from the Chippewa. "There's the door; you can go."

"*Merci.*" Grinning, Lacroix helped Parker to his feet.

They quickly packed their things and left the small room. It was the middle of the night, and once they had saddled their horses, Lieutenant Stafford ordered the guards at the gate to let the three men pass. He would probably have to answer for this to the colonel and the governor, but Lacroix cared little about that. Happily, he inhaled the cool night air as they rode out into the freedom of the forest.

CHAPTER 36

2009, Moose Lake,
Cedar Creek Lodge

It couldn't be true!

His eyes closed, Ondragon lay on his bed and twisted his hands in the pillow he was holding on his stomach. He was still terribly dizzy. Everything around him was spinning, as if he were sitting on an out-of-control merry-go-round. For the time being, it was better not to look at this world where he was gradually losing all sense of what was real and what was illusion.

Shit! He was on the verge of actually going crazy! No matter whether his eyes were open or closed, his brain played one trick after the next, suggesting memories from his childhood, with him standing shoulder to shoulder with Per in his father's library. Per Gustav Ondragon—his twin brother, his mirror image. The Per who spoke to him from the mirror. And the Per whose voice he heard, his laughter, high and thin. The laughter of a child's spirit.

Groaning, Ondragon touched his burning forehead and recoiled as a sharp pain ran through him. The wound throbbed dully, as if it were a small drum. Frustrated, he pounded his fist on the bed. Dammit! This was pure emotional turmoil. If only he hadn't had the insane idea of coming here. What kind of inner hellhound had he released in his head?

Cautiously, he opened his eyes. The walls in the room were swaying, coming closer and receding again, dancing around as if they were made not of wood but of paper, blown back and forth by the wind. He felt like he was in a David Lynch movie. What a great trip!

Ondragon propped himself up on his elbows. Only, unfortunately, he hadn't taken any drugs.

He thought back to what had happened in the session with Dr. Pollux. He vaguely saw the doctor in front of him, moving the people who represented his family around the room, and relived the indescribable feelings he had experienced. It was a mystery to him how Dr. Pollux had done it, but his fear of books, hatred of his father, and his mother's grief suddenly all seemed absolutely understandable to him. Deep inside, he remembered what had happened in the library back then. He just didn't feel quite ready to let it fully sink in. He had wrestled the key from the memory police officer, that was for sure, now "all" he had to do was put it in the lock!

Maybe I should call my parents? Ondragon fished his cell phone out of the drawer in the nightstand and looked in the directory for the Berlin number he had almost called the day before. He let the phone ring on the other end. Hopefully, his mother would pick up. But a knock on the door jolted him out of his thoughts. He quickly turned off the cell phone and hid it. Staggering, he rose and opened the door.

"Hello, Paul, it . . . good grief! What happened to you?" Kateri stood before him with her eyes wide open. Was she for real? As if in a trance, Ondragon raised a hand and stroked her cheek. Her expression became even more confused. Of course she was real. He lowered his hand and gave her a pained smile.

"I think I'm cured," he slurred, and was immediately annoyed by his stupid answer. He must look as if his brain had been fried with electric shocks. He pursed his lips. Actually, that wasn't a bad comparison, it was exactly how he felt.

"What's up?" he asked, straightening himself a little and adding with a wink, "It's not even four in the afternoon yet." At least the flirt mode was still working.

"Are you sure you're okay?" Kateri braced a hand on her hip. "Are you drunk?"

"Yes, yes. Uh, no, of course not. Where would I get the stuff from?" Ondragon shook his head, and the last of the giddiness evaporated. He grinned. At last, he was master of his senses again. "And if I had, I would have let you in on the fun."

Kateri did not respond to his joke. She was unusually serious. "You're the only one we haven't asked yet. Have you seen Mr. Lyme today?"

"No." What a funny question.

"He didn't show up for breakfast or lunch."

"Maybe he ate in his room."

"Impossible; his room is empty, and the kitchen has not been instructed to bring anything up to him. Besides, he missed his appointment with Dr. Zeo. No one has seen him; he has dropped off the face of the earth."

Why was Kateri so worried about this guy? And there he was, thinking she had come here for him. Ondragon scratched his head and noticed that his hair was a total mess. He quickly smoothed down his parting.

"Well, he must be somewhere," he said sullenly. "Or he's left, like that Oliver Orchid guy did back then. He'd had enough. Same here, by the way! I've a mind to get my car keys and leave today." An invigorating joyride would be just the thing to blow the cobwebs out of his head right now. "Do you think Sheila would give me the keys?"

Kateri frowned irritably. Her mind seemed to be somewhere else entirely. "I hardly think so. Come with me; we have to find Lyme!" She grabbed his arm and tried to pull him with her.

"Hey, hey, wait, Kateri!" Ondragon resisted her. He did not remotely feel like leaving the room, especially not in his deranged state. He might run into that hyena Shamgood. He could do without that. "What's the hurry?" he asked. "Lyme's all grown up, he can go wherever he likes. Maybe he's just taking a walk in the woods and enjoying himself. He—" Suddenly, a sense of foreboding came over Ondragon. He felt queasy. But he couldn't tell Kateri about that, or he would automatically reveal to her that he knew about the C patients. And he wasn't sure if he could really trust her. After all, she was very close friends with Dr. Arthur and she could go right to him and tell him Ondragon was snooping. Ondragon thought about the threatening letter and noticed that his interlocutor was getting impatient.

"What now? Will you help us?"

"Maybe you're right, Kateri," he relented. "We should look for Lyme. If he's gone out into the woods, he may be in mortal danger; after all, there's a killer bear on the loose. Wait a minute, I'll just change, and then we'll go to Dr. Arthur and tell him what we're up to." It was clear to Ondragon that Lyme had gone into the woods to make his most fervent wish come true. He was going to meet the man-eating beast.

Kateri nodded absently and waited outside the door while Ondragon quickly splashed some water on his face in the bathroom, tidied his hair, and put on a clean T-shirt. Then he tied his freshly washed hoodie around his hips and hid the SIG Sauer inside it. Never again would he go into the woods without a gun!

Together they sought out Dr. Arthur in his office and it turned out that he had long since been informed of Lyme's disappearance. The psychotherapist took off his glasses and said relatively calmly, "Mr. Lyme is nowhere to be found in the entire building, nor on the grounds. He must have left the lodge and gone into the woods. That's not like him at all. He never goes outside. But I've sent word to Pete to get some people together and organize a search around the lodge."

"What could Mr. Lyme want in the woods, unless he broke so unexpectedly with his habits?" Ondragon adopted an innocent expression.

"That's what I'm trying to understand. This behavior is extremely disconcerting. The fact is, however, that Mr. Lyme is not the kind of person who likes to be out of doors. He is a purely urban creature, with a certain fear of the primal power of the wilderness. Anything that can't be controlled is a horror to him. Much like you, Paul." The psychotherapist looked at him, a peculiar flicker in his yellow eyes.

Ondragon ignored the look that seemed to shine right down to his bones. He felt anger rising inside him. He felt insulted to be compared to that puny suck-up Lyme. He had nothing, absolutely nothing, in common with him!

"I'll help look for him," he said. While he wasn't keen on having to run through the undergrowth again, he wanted to prove to Dr.

Arthur that he wasn't afraid of what was out there. Him and fear of the forest—an outright miscalculation!

"I'm afraid I can't let you do that, Paul. You're here for therapy. It's not your job to look for missing guests. Like I said, Pete will take care of it."

"Dr. Arthur, the fact is, Lyme is out there, and the more people who look for him, the more likely we are to find him. There's no telling what will happen if he gets into trouble and it comes out that you didn't do everything you could to prevent it. Or should we ask Deputy Hase for help? He can be here in ninety minutes."

Dr. Arthur raised a hand. "I'm afraid that's not such a good idea. Deputy Hase is far too busy with the other investigations. It wouldn't do to have him and his whole crew parade in here. After all, Lyme is really just out for a walk. It would be extremely embarrassing if we caused an unnecessary panic over this."

"Exactly. And for that reason, we should find him as soon as possible."

Dr. Arthur stroked his musketeer beard thoughtfully. Then he said, "I can't prevent you from going into the forest anyway. But please promise me you won't make a big fuss about this mission."

"Discretion is my business! You know that." Ondragon threw Dr. Arthur a mischievous smile.

"Then I'll go too, Jonathan!" retorted Kateri.

"But, my dear . . ." Dr. Arthur leaned back.

"No! I'm going!" She turned to Ondragon. "Come on, Paul, we'll tell Pete."

"Kateri, wait . . ."

But she didn't wait. She left the worried Dr. Arthur standing there and pulled Ondragon from the office with her.

A short time later, they found Pete in the parking lot in front of the lodge. He was standing in the midst of a small group of men, making sweeping gestures. Ondragon recognized Frank, prettyboy Julian, and three of the seasonal employees. Frank carried a hunting rifle over his shoulder and Julian had two revolvers at his belt. It made the young riding instructor look like some kind of ridiculous Billy the Kid.

"Hey, Mr. *On Draegen*." Pete greeted him with a casual handshake, and Ondragon explained why they were there.

"You'd better not go without a gun though, Mr. Ondragon," Julian said, casually placing a hand on a revolver handle. "Too dangerous!"

What the hell? Ondragon gave him a penetrating look. Anything that blond milksop could do, he had done long ago. He calmly pulled his SIG Sauer out of his hoodie and noticed Pete's eyes widen. Kateri, on the other hand, didn't seem all that surprised. Before anyone could say anything, he explained, "I always carry a gun."

The men nodded, as if this was normal for them, and continued their conversation. Only Julian gave him a brief hostile stare.

"We should divide into groups now," Pete began. "Miss Wolfe, you know your way around here, so you go ahead and take Mr. *On Draegen* with you. I'll take Bobby, Julian will go with Carey, and Dave with Frank." They all murmured their agreement, and Ondragon was amazed that the men, especially Frank, accepted Pete as their leader so readily. He watched the bellboy with interest as he unfolded a tattered map of the area on the hood of an all-terrain vehicle. Pete pointed at different areas one by one, assigning them to groups. He then handed them each a bottle of water.

"I hope we find Mr. Lyme," he said seriously, adjusting his baseball cap and leaving the parking lot with Bobby.

Ondragon and Kateri also took the path that would lead them to their search area northeast of the lake. As they passed the boathouse, Miss Wolfe said abruptly: "Wait a minute. Even though you have a shooting iron, I don't want to be completely defenseless." She went into the boathouse and came out a little later with a large knife at her belt, a sports bow in her hand, and a quiver full of arrows.

Ondragon raised his brows in surprise. "Well, if I'm the cowboy, then you're definitely the Indian! Do you know what you're doing with that?"

Kateri looked at him as if he had almost taken leave of his senses. Then it all happened very quickly. In one single fluid motion, she placed an arrow, turned, and shot. The arrow whizzed almost invisibly through the warm summer air and landed with a hollow plop on the State Park Service signpost. But not on one of the signs, halfway up the pole!

Ondragon cleared his throat sheepishly. "All right, I'll take you, Chingachgook."

"You got it, Hawkeye." Kateri grinned—for the first time since she had knocked on his door earlier.

They turned down the path that led alongside the lake, the one Ondragon had already jogged along several times, keeping a careful lookout for tracks or movements in the undergrowth.

"What if we run into the killer bear?" asked Ondragon.

Kateri turned around and brushed a strand of hair that had slipped out of her ponytail behind her ear. "Then you will do as I tell you!"

"Oh. Okay. And that means?"

"It means that *when* you shoot, you only shoot at the bear's head. Hit it in the body with that small caliber and you'll only make it angry. The best thing is not to shoot at first and retreat slowly, without making any abrupt movements. Then you have a chance."

"Reassuring."

They continued their search and soon reached the turnoff to *bear's den*. On the way to the cave, Ondragon noticed some strange forms hanging in the trees all around. Had they been there when he first visited the cave? He couldn't remember. But he hadn't been paying attention then either.

"What are those things?" he asked, pointing at one of the balls of feathers dangling from a branch. It looked an awful lot like the amulet that had been on his pillow.

Kateri looked up. "Oh, that. That's a kind of defensive medicine."

"Defensive medicine against what? Now don't say, like, against the Wend—"

"Shhhh! Don't call him by name!"

"All right. But what's with the spell? And who put it there?"

Kateri looked at him intently. "Bird of prey feathers help to drive away the spirit of the forest monster." She pointed to the cave entrance. "This cavern is a sacred place for the Ojibwe group who live here. They come here regularly and hold rituals. There's even an ancient burial site a few miles away, and you'll find this medicine everywhere there too. It is supposed to protect the dead from . . . *him* and his hunger!" She pointed meaningfully out into the forest.

Ondragon was torn between amusement and creeping horror. On the one hand, he did not want to believe that the Wendigo really existed; on the other hand, there seemed to be people here who really believed in it. So it was quite possible something was going on in this forest that could not be judged by any normal measure. Maybe it was a Sasquatch or a Bigfoot, one of those forest half-men who were supposed to be related to the Yeti. Everywhere in the world there were stories of such creatures. Just as there were people everywhere who claimed they had been abducted by aliens. This here could be a mixture of delusion and superstition. Certainly, the Indigenous folks consumed drugs like peyote or Wysoccan, which they extracted from the datura plant, during their ceremonies. Both had a powerful mind-expanding effect that could make a person see things that were merely his imagination. Last but not least, initiation rites like the Sun Dance ceremony and the Vision Quest drew their supernatural, spiritual character from this. *The ancient rites could be an explanation for the Wendigo cult in this area*, Ondragon thought, but yet another question occurred to him: Had the net with the dead bird been hung at the scene before or after the murder of the stranger? Had the Ojibwe known about the body? Or was it a coincidence that they had put up their net exactly where the dead man had lain?

Kateri bumped her bow against one of the feather amulets. "Do you want to take one with you? It will protect you."

Ondragon looked at her. "Do I need protection?"

Kateri smiled inscrutably. Then she turned and continued on her way. Ondragon pressed his lips together. The woman was an absolute mystery to him. She managed to make him feel like an awkward, stupid boy in her presence. Disgruntled, he hit out at a branch and followed her along the path, past the cave and deeper into the dark fir forest, which he had not gone into before. Silence enveloped them, and it was as if they were entering another world within the forest. Only sporadic rays of sunlight reached the moss-covered ground. The few glaring spots of light looked like green fires blazing between the scaly tree trunks. Insects bustled about in these islands of light, and they constantly had to shoo away the mosquitoes, which seemed to be very pleased two succulent, warm-blooded animals had come by.

Ondragon felt the first pangs of exhaustion. Gradually, the search became a torture, and he cursed himself inwardly for volunteering. He wasn't usually in such bad shape, but today's therapy session had drained him more than he had thought. He glanced at Kateri, who was walking ahead of him, leading him deeper and deeper into this damned boreal jungle. A dark spot of sweat had formed on her plaid shirt between her shoulder blades. She tirelessly kept an eye out for tracks, looking at a snapped branch here and there and calling Lyme's name aloud.

Ondragon sighed and glanced over his shoulder. Worriedly, he noticed that it looked the same behind him as it did in front of him. Everything looked identical; conifers wherever you looked. And no matter where you moved, their dry, sparse branches blocked your path and scratched your skin. Brown brush, withered from lack of light, and treacherous dead-wood trip hazards lay everywhere. What a godforsaken place!

He swatted at a squadron of mosquitoes on his forearm. The insects burst, leaving small bloodstains. Evolution could not have produced anything more superfluous than these flying pests! If only he had kept his mouth shut, he could have been sitting on the terrace of the lodge with a nice cold Coke—his desires had already become more modest. Or better yet, if he hadn't had the glorious idea of coming to Minnesota in the first place, he would now be taking a little dip in the pool at his villa in LA and then chilling into the evening with a real mojito. But no, instead he was here in Mosquito Paradise looking for a full-on weirdo who wanted to be eaten. *This* was really not to be missed at any price!

Annoyed, he turned around and got a huge fright.

Kateri had disappeared.

Unease gripped him, and he spun around several times, but she was nowhere to be seen. Sweat poured into his eyes, and the bump on his head throbbed indignantly.

"Kateri?"

Hell, she couldn't just leave him here all alone!

Even as he tried to locate the path they had come by, he realized his mistake. He had completely relied on his companion and neglected to pay attention to the route himself. How could he have been so careless? He, who *always* had everything under control and thought things through carefully, had run after this woman, whom he hardly knew, like a dachshund. And now he was in a fine mess: The less than exhilarating realization dawned on him that he would not be able to find his way back to the lodge without Kateri's help. Slowly, his lack of attention was beginning to really worry him. This kind of thing could cost him his life on his next job!

A loud rustling sound startled him. Increasingly nervous, Ondragon drew his gun and took aim at the bushes. Something big was moving about in it. Déjà vu about the bear, or whatever it had been, made the hairs on his arms stand up like little antennae.

"Kateri? Is that you?" Anxiously, Ondragon listened to the mosquito-swirling silence. He swallowed dryly and suddenly felt thirsty as hell. "Kateri, leave off with the joke!"

He did not like the situation. If she didn't show up right away, he would fire a shot into the air!

"What joke?" a dark voice beside him asked suddenly, and he wheeled around.

There stood Kateri not three steps away from him, her bow hitched perkily over her shoulder and a mocking smile on her lips. She had a red scratch adorning her cheek, which made her look incredibly sexy. Ondragon quickly put his weapon away.

"Man, you can be scary!"

"Sorry, my Indian blood ran away with me. You are so delightfully clumsy when it comes to the forest, so I allowed myself a little joke. You should have seen yourself; the look on your face was priceless."

"Hilarious," Ondragon grumbled, turning away.

"Now don't pout, Paul. Please, I didn't mean anything by it." She grabbed him by the arm and pulled him toward her until they were face-to-face. She was so close that Ondragon caught her scent.

"You'd better stay near me," Kateri whispered, looking him in the eye.

He would have liked to put her over his knee, he was so angry with her, but her unexpected proximity made him abruptly forget his wounded pride. Blood shot hotly into his groin.

Now don't do anything stupid, he thought, but his lips were already moving toward hers. Kateri did not resist when he kissed her directly on the mouth. On the contrary. Ondragon felt her greedily returning his kiss. Her tongue drove between his lips and made it clear that she too was on fire farther south. Now it was down to him to take the initiative. And by all the spirits this forest had to offer, in this discipline he was anything but a novice!

He pulled her to the ground, laying her gently on a piece of soft moss. Kateri sighed softly and sought his lips again. She ran her hands over every square inch of his body, and before he knew it, she was tugging his T-shirt over his head. In a frenzy, Ondragon fumbled with the buttons of her shirt, exposing her upper body moments later. He was surprised to see she was not wearing a bra. Her small, dark nipples had risen to hard peaks, and Ondragon leaned down and kissed them. Kateri threw her head back, moaning loudly. With both hands she burrowed into his hair and ran her fingernails down his back to his buttocks, where they took hold.

Ondragon let go of Kateri's tempting breasts to undo his pants, which had become much too tight, and without hesitation, she freed herself of her own. When she was finally lying before him completely naked, Ondragon allowed himself a brief look at her. Kateri giggled and squirmed with pleasure under him. His arousal heightened to the point of unbearability and he finally felt that Kateri had also reached the peak of her impatience. She opened her thighs and welcomed him. Effortlessly, he slid into her, and they both heaved sighs of pleasure. Kateri grabbed his ass as if she couldn't get it deep enough inside her, and Ondragon struggled to follow her fast rhythm. He thrust hard into her, again and again, and felt her breathing intensify. A few moments later, she came with a wild scream, embracing him so tightly with her thighs that he almost couldn't breathe. A little later he sank down on top of her, panting. Only when the fireworks in his neural pathways had gone out did Ondragon withdraw from her and get up.

"That was . . . not bad for a start," Kateri said, looking at him with a perky smile.

Ondragon nodded and began to pick up the scattered clothes and dress. *Not bad*, he thought. What a colossal understatement. That had been millennial sex! He whistled silently. It certainly wasn't the first time he'd done it outdoors, and he'd also done the elevator thing, but this was way up there on the scale of the most exciting places to have sex!

Kateri rose and walked unabashedly toward him. Unlike some other American women, she seemed to have no problem being naked in front of a man. Like the queen of her people, she came striding through the forest, her femininity challenging and inviting him. The blush of their rough encounter was still visible on her belly and breasts, and little twigs and pine needles hung in her loose hair. She looked ravishing, and if he hadn't just had her, he would have taken her immediately! Yes, he was satisfied with what he had done.

He approached Kateri, ran his fingertips lightly over her bare shoulders, and whispered in her ear, "How about we have a second therapy session tonight, Dr. Wolfe?"

Kateri gave him a heartfelt kiss in response and set about dressing. Ondragon watched her and couldn't wait to explore her sensational body again that night. Hatchet really hadn't been exaggerating—she was one hell of a hot woman!

CHAPTER 37

*2009, in the forest,
4 miles northeast
of Moose Lake*

We should get going," Kateri said, having tied her hair back into a neat braid. She picked up her bow and quiver—she had fired an arrow into the bushes when things had gotten rough—and slung both over her shoulder.

Ondragon took several sips from his water bottle, which was almost empty, then glanced at his wristwatch. "Four o'clock already."

"Are you going soft on me?"

"No, but I don't have much left to drink and . . ."

"You can fill up the bottle at the next stream. Come, this way."

Ondragon gave a bow. "Your wish is my command, O Diana, Goddess of the Hunt!"

Kateri threw him a wry grin, effortlessly located the invisible path, and marched ahead. Ondragon followed close behind. He definitely did not want to lose Kateri again.

After about an hour of heavy going and constant calling to Lyme, the rough undergrowth finally cleared a little. The trees grew taller and let in more air. Grass and other woodland plants reclaimed the terrain, and the light cast dappled patterns onto it. The ground rose gradually toward Mount Witiko.

"White pines," Kateri said, pointing to the mighty trunks supporting the forest canopy like pillars. Ondragon looked up at the spreading treetops. As he did so, he spotted something.

"There, look," he called Kateri's attention to it.

"Medicine," she replied simply. "We're at the old burial ground I spoke of earlier."

Ondragon ducked his head uncomfortably as he saw more painted animal skulls, tufts of feathers, and whole, mummified animal carcasses hanging in the branches.

"We should give it a wide berth. Our people don't like this place being desecrated. There's a path back there." Kateri pointed to the right with her arm.

Ondragon followed her finger but couldn't see anything that looked like a trail. "Where's the official trail to Mount Witiko anyway?"

"A few miles northwest of here, but don't worry, I didn't want to go that far."

Ondragon was relieved. On the one hand, he had little desire to traipse up to the mountain, and on the other, he finally knew roughly where he was again. But the uneasiness remained. He looked at the thicket ahead and asked, "Are there actually dead bodies laid out there?"

"Yes, but no fresh ones. That is not allowed. This place has been here for several hundred years, and the dead who were buried here long ago have the right, guaranteed by the government, to remain here. Besides, we Ojibwe believe it's bad luck to disturb the peace of the dead and move them from their ancestral home."

Ondragon took one last look at the skulls dangling above him before hurrying after Kateri, who was already moving away in long strides. They walked around the funeral shrine, and Kateri began calling Lyme's name again. But the damned broker remained untraceable. *Sure*, Ondragon thought, *because he didn't want to be found in the first place*. He chewed thoughtfully on his lower lip. Actually, this was all totally pointless, and it was long past time to enlighten Kateri, otherwise they might still be wandering around here until sunset. She had to know the truth about Lyme.

"Um, Kateri, hold on."

The incomparable Miss Wolfe turned and looked at him questioningly.

Ondragon didn't want to destroy the familiarity he had just gained, so he continued with extreme caution, "I just remembered something. Do you still remember? The day before yesterday, Mr. Lyme sat down with me and talked to me. I'm now thinking it might have something to do with his disappearance."

"In what way?"

Ondragon pulled himself together. "It was strange. He wanted me to tell him if it was true that a bear had killed the man in the forest and . . . well, eaten him."

"So?"

Ondragon scratched the back of his head. "Well, it's a little awkward, but I just couldn't help it. Lyme provoked me. His whole manner, his appearance . . ."

"Now come on, out with it! What did you tell him?"

"So . . . I exaggerated a bit and said Deputy Hase thought the forest monster was the killer. The Wend— you know who I mean."

"You did *what*?"

Ondragon could see storm clouds brewing over Kateri's head. He shrugged embarrassedly. "Lyme was getting on my nerves, and I wanted to be rid of him. But at the time, I didn't know what he was up to. I've only just realized now."

"And what was he going to do?"

Ondragon jumped into the deep end, not knowing if he would ever resurface.

"I think he wants to get eaten."

"Excuse me?" Kateri blinked in disbelief. "He wants to be eaten?"

"Yes. And that's why I don't think we'll find him here in the forest. Especially not if we call out loud for him. He doesn't want to be found at all. All he wants is to be eaten by the monster."

Kateri's shoulders slumped. "And why didn't you say so in the first place? Before we went off. That would have been very helpful."

Ondragon raised both hands apologetically. "I'm sorry, but it only just crossed my mind as I went over the conversation with Lyme."

Kateri shook her head. "By the way, it would have helped Dr. Arthur a lot to know that too!"

"He knows. Believe me, Kateri. After all, he's treating Lyme. He can't be that blind."

She looked at him. "Then why didn't he tell us?"

"What do I know about why he sent us into this fucking forest. Why don't you ask him when we get back?"

Kateri's eyes flashed. "First"—she raised a finger—"Jonathan didn't send us, second, it's probably because he was observing his duty of confidentiality, and *third,* this forest isn't even half as fucked up as your stupid big city!" Kateri's facial expression betrayed hurt. Whether it was him or Dr. Arthur wasn't entirely clear. Ondragon, however, was almost certain she was angry with him for daring to criticize her mentor. She would never allow anything negative to be said about her beloved Jonathan and would probably defend him even if she knew about his illegal activities.

"You should be grateful Jonathan is treating you, Paul. He's the best psychotherapist on the planet!"

"I'm sorry, I didn't mean to attack him," Ondragon said placatingly. There was no way Kateri was going to learn the true extent of his clandestine research if she overreacted to a small thing like this. He wanted to add something, but the headache behind his forehead suddenly became so bad that he had to close his eyes for a moment. At the same time, he was overcome by an unusual hot flush that made him sweat profusely. It was as if he were sitting in a room where someone had turned the heating all the way up and then destroyed the thermostat. He wiped his forehead with the back of his hand and took the last sip of water from his bottle. He hadn't felt this miserable since he had been stuck in a rebel camp in Myanmar, plagued by malaria.

"What is it? Are you unwell?" Kateri took a step closer, but Ondragon shook his head.

"It's okay, I'm fine. I'm just thirsty." To add emphasis, he turned his bottle upside down. Kateri's small supply of water had long since run out too. They both needed a refill.

"In about a third of a mile there's a stream. Can you make it there? Then we can take a little break before we search the rest of the area."

Ondragon nodded and swatted at the millionth mosquito on his neck. So Kateri still didn't want to give up. Very well. He pushed himself off the tree trunk he had been leaning against. "But we should stop shouting loudly so Lyme can't avoid us. He might run right into us that way."

They continued silently on their way, and as they walked, Ondragon kept sneaking glances at Kateri. She seemed thoughtful. It was probably now clear to her too that the doc had behaved strangely. Ondragon sighed. If she knew what else he had found out about her fine Jonathan!

CHAPTER 38

2009, in the forest,
6 miles northeast
of Moose Lake

Shh! Did you hear that?" Kateri had stopped and was listening, her head raised.

"Yes," Ondragon whispered, and looked around. The scream that had come out of the forest ahead of them was not repeated. "Was that a human?"

Kateri nodded. She raised an arm and pointed to Mount Witiko. "It came from over there."

"Lyme?" asked Ondragon.

"If it is, we shouldn't waste any time. Something has happened to him. The best thing to do is split up and head in that direction a hundred paces apart, but keeping each other in view. That way we cover a larger area."

There was nothing to object to, except that Ondragon was not very enthusiastic about making his way through the forest alone.

"Hurry!" shouted Kateri, sprinting off.

Ondragon followed a track to her left, keeping to the prescribed distance and, his pistol drawn, checking continually that Kateri was nearby. She maintained their separation in a disciplined manner and began to call out again, "Mr. Lyme? Where are you? Do you need help?"

They ran uphill, hoping the scream had really come from that direction. After a short time, Ondragon slowed down. His legs were heavy as lead. They had been walking for six hours, and he felt exhaustion and thirst pressing down like a weight on his shoulders. He looked around for Kateri, who was running with dogged perseverance. Unfortunately, he took his eye off the ground at that second and his foot caught in a root. Cursing, Ondragon fell on his stomach and bruised his wrist trying not to lose his weapon. At the same time, a rock drilled into his groin and his chin hit the ground hard, causing his teeth to clash loudly.

"Shit! Fucking forest!" he yelled as he tried to quickly get back to his feet. "Kateri, wait, I fell!" As he stood, he looked around. There was no sign of his guide. She had just kept on going. So much for keeping each other in view! Angrily, he wiped the blood off his chin and started moving again. She couldn't have gotten far yet. From somewhere he heard Kateri calling Lyme. He called back, but received no answer. Damn!

Hoping to find Kateri, he swerved to the right. When a familiar stench suddenly rose into his nostrils, he stopped abruptly, pressing himself into the shelter of a tree trunk. Calmly, he scanned the terrain. The stench was not as strong as last time, but nonetheless Ondragon would have been able to pick it out from a hundred others. He ducked and stalked on like a hunter, continually sniffing the air to determine if the stench was intensifying. But it weakened and soon gave way to the earthy aroma of the forest. Instead, a ripple now reached Ondragon's ear. The brook!

Hastily, he followed the sound. And when he reached the watercourse, he fell on all fours into the mud of the bank, dipped his head into the cool water, and drank greedily. Then he filled his bottle and screwed it shut. The water was loamy and reddish-black. No matter.

Ondragon was about to rise when his eyes fell on a fresh track beside him on the damp bank. He bent down and traced the outline with his fingers. At first, he thought he'd found Kateri's shoe prints, but then he noticed that while the shape was elongated like a foot, it was devoid of any texture . . . or toes. It was also deeply indented into the earth in an unusual way, suggesting that the animal that had passed by here had a heavy body weight. But what kind of animal left such tracks? Ondragon was not very familiar with the local fauna, but he was sure that they did not come from a bear or an elk.

A glint in one of the prints aroused his curiosity, and he fished the object out of the soft, black earth. When he cleaned it, he was amazed. It was a signet ring.

Lyme's signet ring!

So he had to be close on the broker's heels. Ondragon put the ring in his pocket. Then he jumped over the creek and followed the strange trail. The distance between the individual prints was unnaturally large, measuring almost four paces. Unfortunately, the trail disappeared after only a few yards on the dry forest floor.

Suddenly, Ondragon heard a sound. It sounded like a faint whimper and came from very close by. Alarmed, Ondragon raised his pistol and peered into the forest. As he did so, he discovered a new, far more disturbing trail.

It was blood.

Grateful for the adrenaline that rushed instantly into his veins, he took off at a run, following the trail of fresh blood shining damply in the grass.

"Lyme?" he called out anxiously. "Where are you?"

As the whimpering came again, Ondragon's fears intensified.

"Lyme, say something!" Ondragon made an effort to keep an eye out in all directions. He wanted to be prepared in case something approached him.

"Kateri? Are you around here somewhere?"

Go to hell! This better not be another one of her jokes!

His foot hit something soft and wet, and Ondragon began to lurch. But he was just able to break his fall on a tree trunk. Hastily, he turned around and looked back at the ground. When he saw what he had slipped on, the sweat froze on his skin. Like a silvery snake, a section of intestine was lying in the grass. In one place, the intestine had been ripped open, revealing its brownish contents. Some of it was stuck to Ondragon's shoe.

With a dangerous lurch in his stomach, he wiped his sole and followed the snaking guts until he came to a clearing and his evil foreboding turned into merciless reality. Involuntarily, he pressed a hand to his mouth as he contemplated the apocalyptic scene.

The entrails led to a tree. Lyme hung there, tied to the trunk with a rope. His clothes were tattered and his body was covered in blood. The intestines dangled from his open abdominal cavity like grotesque barrier tape cordoning off the crime scene.

Ondragon looked into the fly-covered face of the broker. His eyes were wide open, his mouth distorted with pain. Blood, interspersed with yellowish mucus, ran viscously from the corner of his mouth. The stench of fresh offal and excrement was unbearable. Despite the gag reflex that was triggered in Ondragon's throat, he approached the dead man. As he did so, his eyes inevitably fell on a large stone lying in front of the slashed body. Something had been arranged on it like an altar. He looked at it more closely. The dark red lump looked like a liver.

Someone had taken a bite out of it.

Ondragon flinched. But then he conquered his disgust and turned his eyes to Lyme. Suddenly, a whimper came from his throat and his eyelids began to flutter. Immediately, a swarm of flies sprang up and, after an indignant buzz, settled back on the shiny guts. Shocked, Ondragon froze in his stance. Lyme was still alive?

That couldn't be!

"Hello, Mr. Lyme?" Ondragon broke free of his stiffness and nudged the broker with his gun. "Do you hear me?"

And indeed—Lyme moved his head, very weakly; he was clearly not dead yet.

"Mr. Lyme. Harvey. Can you tell me who did this?"

But the broker merely rolled his eyes and closed his eyelids. Ondragon stepped up close to him and shook him a little roughly by the shoulder. Lyme was beyond help anyway, but he had to at least hear who or what had caused this terrible carnage. The broker lifted his eyelids with difficulty, his lips formed words, but apart from a bloody smacking sound, no sound came out of his mouth. His diaphragm was likely destroyed and his lungs could no longer work properly. It was a miracle there was any life left in him at all.

"Tell me who tied you to the tree here. Nod or wink in distress. Was it someone from the lodge?"

Lyme moved his head, but Ondragon couldn't tell if it was a nod. His eyelids lowered heavily. Ondragon shook his shoulder again. "Harvey, stay awake! Was it someone you know?"

Lyme twitched. It was a bizarre spectacle, as if he were being remote-controlled by the long strings of his guts. With the last of his strength, the broker tried to get a word out.

"Endiiighh . . ."

"What, Harvey? Make an effort. Come on!"

"Uendihghhhooo . . . mmmonsthhh . . ."

"Monster?"

Lyme jerked his head, and Ondragon went ice-cold. All at once he knew what the broker was trying to tell him.

"You mean it was . . . the Wendigo?"

The name of the feared beast echoed ominously through the forest. Instead of a nod, a violent twitch went through the man's body, and as a wet gurgle escaped his throat, Ondragon guessed that his heart had stopped pumping blood through his torn veins. Lyme was dead.

Ondragon took his hand from Lyme's shoulder and saw a deep bite mark in the flesh beneath it. He gasped in horror and disgust. What perverted swine had battered this helpless man like this and then left him hanging from a tree like a gutted deer?

With trembling knees, he moved away from the corpse and wiped his hands in the grass. Then he leaned heavily against a tree. In his life he had already seen many terrible things, but this surpassed everything!

Trembling all over from exertion and shock, Ondragon reached into his pants pocket. No cell phone! Crap! He had forgotten to take it with him. It was probably in the nightstand in his room.

He lifted his head and looked up at the clear patch of sky that the clearing revealed. The sun had sunk farther toward the horizon and its reddish light indicated that it was not long until dusk. Ondragon forced himself to think. From *bear's den* they had gone mainly west, so the lodge had to be to the east. Only, where exactly was east? Ondragon looked from the sky to the forest, avoiding Lyme. He estimated it was six to eight miles to the lodge. He could jog that in an hour, assuming he knew the way.

And where the hell was Kateri? Had something happened to her too?

He had to get out of here and get help! Only how?

Jerkily, Ondragon rubbed his burning eyes. It was like being bewitched; here in the forest he simply could not think properly! In the city or in the open country, he knew where he was at all times. He knew the points of the compass, and used them to orient himself even in the middle of LA, Bangkok, or Tokyo. And yes, he also knew where to find the North Star in the night sky. But here in this jungle, without a clear view of the horizon, his sense of direction was as good as useless.

He slammed his fist angrily against the tree trunk. Lichen dust rose and trickled to the ground. Speaking of lichens. He had read something about them once. Didn't lichens grow mainly on the north side of tree trunks? Ondragon checked the trunks around him, but unfortunately the greenish layer of symbiotic plants was growing on all sides of them. So that was another thing that belonged to the realm of legends.

He looked up to see where the shadows were falling from the trees. If the sun was in the west or southwest, then east was to his left. And if he went that way now, hopefully he would soon come upon Moose Lake, which in turn would lead him to the lodge. He checked his gun. There was nothing wrong with it; he still had all twelve rounds. Since it was getting chilly, he put on his hoodie and quickly set off. Where the ground was clear of undergrowth, Ondragon jogged, but always with his head up and peering intently around him. When he had put what felt like a half mile between himself and Lyme's corpse, he stopped short and ventured a first call for help.

"Kateri?" His voice sounded tired and feeble, but he tried again. "KA-TE- RI!"

Nothing but the echo came back. Where was she? She couldn't have been that far away from him. He hoped nothing had happened to her. Ondragon tried again, this time with the other members of the search party: "Pete! Frank! Is there anybody there? Julian?" But it remained eerily silent amid the tall spruce trunks. Ondragon's shoulders slumped. It was like the earth had swallowed them all.

He ran on and after a while stopped again. He was exhausted, hungry, and thirsty, and he had the feeling that he was running in the wrong direction. He checked the position of the sun, whose light had already taken on a touch of orange. Ondragon looked at his watch. Shortly before seven. If he had guessed right, he was still moving east. Good. He kept walking, mile after mile. But the lake did not come into view. Ondragon felt his panic growing. He glanced repeatedly at his watch. What? Nine o'clock already? How had time passed so quickly? Now he had an hour at most until nightfall. The thought of traipsing around here in the woods at night, with a crazed killer nearby, wasn't particularly enticing and caused him to break out in a sweat again. And his headache had surged to the point of unbearability. Ondragon quickly took three small sips from the bottle. The bog water tasted peaty, but it washed the even worse memories of blood and guts from his tongue.

More limping than jogging, Ondragon pushed on. Around him, it was now getting darker faster than he had anticipated, and soon he could only see indistinct shadows in front of him. The pain in his skull almost robbed him of his senses and blurred his vision. He had to slow his pace to avoid falling. One hot shiver after another shook him. Groaning, Ondragon stopped and pressed his hands to his temples. He blinked several times until his vision cleared.

It's all right. It's just a headache and maybe a little fever, but I'll survive, he said to himself and was about to continue when he noticed a shadow. Motionless, it stood among the trees before him. Ondragon raised his weapon. His arm trembled with effort.

The shadow broke free of its rigidity and slid slowly to the left. Ondragon drew his eyebrows together, trying to see something in the poor light. And finally he was certain that the dark silhouette in front of him in the forest clearly belonged to a human. Anger gripped him. He wasn't in the mood for games of hide-and-seek anymore. His gun outstretched, he walked up to the person and shouted, "Hey! Freeze!"

But the shadow did not think to stop and leaped behind a tree.

Who the hell was that? Ondragon frowned. One of the search party?

Determined, he continued toward the tree. But when he was around the thick trunk and aimed his pistol into the darkness behind it, there was no one there. He heard a noise and out of the corner of his eye he could just see the shadow darting into the thicket with great leaps farther back.

Ondragon froze, not only because he had caught a waft of the familiar plague stench, but also because he had seen something else. An exceptionally bright mop of hair.

"Hey! Mortimer!" he yelled after the boy with the white hair. "Hold it right there!" He was certain it had been Pete's brother who had charged into the thicket. Only why was he running away from him?

The crackling of Mortimer's footsteps in the bushes ceased abruptly. Had the boy stopped?

"Hey, Momo! Come on out. I'm a friend of your brother Pete's. Can you give me a hand? I'm lost." He listened, straining, into the ever-thickening darkness. There was a soft crackle, almost indecisive. The stench was gone again; he had likely imagined it anyway. By now he was so through with the subject that he no longer wanted to rely on his senses. "Momo?"

What happened next was the culmination of a day you wouldn't wish on even your worst enemy.

Just as Ondragon was about to follow the boy into the bushes, a black mass crashed into him with full force. He screamed loudly, dropped his weapon, and scraped his back against a tree. With crystal-clear horror, Ondragon felt his skin crack under his hoodie and a rib crunch. Pain raced through his lungs as he slid to the ground. He tried to get up, but a heavy blow struck him in the chest, nearly robbing him of consciousness. Bright stars flashed before his eyes, and with his mouth wide open, he struggled for breath. But the creature did not let go of him. It squatted on him and struck at his face. Thrashing his arms and legs, Ondragon tried to fight it off. The stench emanating from its fur was indescribable, and its weight crushing. Ondragon felt his strength fading. He tried desperately to reach for the jackknife in his pocket with one hand, but it was impossible due to his pain and the leaden mass of the beast. He began to scream for help as he flailed his fists blindly. And then, suddenly, it was over. With a loud howl, the beast reared up and let go of him. Ondragon saw it rise staggeringly onto its stilt-like hind legs and grab its shoulder with an angry growl. A long, thin object was protruding from it.

I've seen that thing before, Ondragon thought, through the fog of his pain.

Roaring, the beast stood over him and tugged at the object in its shoulder. When it realized that it could not be removed, it gave up and sped away with a mighty leap. Only a few seconds later it disappeared into the darkness of the forest, and an eerie silence descended.

Ondragon laid his head back down on the ground. A hysterical laugh rose in him. What fucking freaky insanity this was!

CHAPTER 39

2009, in the forest,
3 miles northeast
of Moose Lake

Wow, Kateri, that was a master shot!" he shouted mutedly into the night, wincing because every breath hurt as if he had been crushed by a steamroller. He heard a soft rustle, and then the light of a flashlight flickered on. Protectively, he raised a hand in front of his eyes. Kateri stood before him with a bow in her hands, ready to shoot. A white-feathered arrow lay on the string. The huntress held the small flashlight between her teeth.

"You hit that bastard in the shoulder. Great! But why did you only turn up now?" In agony, Ondragon stood up. "I've been wandering the woods like fair game for hours, and none of you showed! The killer got Lyme, I found him, and . . ." He paused because Kateri took her fingers off the string and put them over her lips with an eerie gesture. He understood and listened along with her into the darkness, but all was quiet.

Finally, Kateri took the flashlight out of her mouth and asked quietly, "Did he get you?"

Ondragon felt his damaged body. "I've got a cracked rib and a freakish headache, but other than that, I'm downright outstanding." He didn't mean to be sarcastic, but the day had really sucked.

"That's not what I meant," Kateri hissed. "I wanted to know if he bit you."

"No. Why?" He looked suspiciously at the beautiful hunter.

"If he gets you with his teeth, you'll get a fever and become like him!"

"But he didn't!"

Silence. Then, "Okay, let's get out of here."

"Gladly." Ondragon searched for his pistol and found it not six feet away in the foliage. He tucked it into the front of his waistband and followed Kateri, who obviously knew where she was going.

"What the hell was that?"

"Not now!" Kateri marched hurriedly on.

Ignoring her objection, Ondragon said, "That wasn't a person. That was something else. For sure! But what? The Wendigo, perhaps?"

"I told you, not now. He's still around and he could attack again at any time. You'd better keep your mouth shut or he'll hear us."

She pushed him on forcefully, but Ondragon stubbornly stood his ground.

"I just don't believe it," he said, amused, his bruised rib yelping indignantly. He pressed a hand to his side, but couldn't stop the giggle that broke out now that all the tension had gone. It was absurd. The incomparable Miss Wolfe actually believed in her Indian legend! Tears of laughter came to Ondragon's eyes as he said, "I just can't believe you think it was the Wendigo. That's . . . so stupid!"

"Are you saying I'm stupid?"

"Yeah, uh, no, I . . ." Ondragon couldn't stop giggling. The effect of the shock wearing off. "Sorry, I . . . it's like . . . you *actually* seem to believe in it. That's . . . completely insane. The Wendigo! I can't believe it. Phew!" He took several breaths and calmed down again. "Granted, I almost actually believed in that forest monster nonsense . . . but what happened to Lyme doesn't strike me as something out of a legend. That wasn't a monster, Kateri, it was a very real killer! A person who is sick in the head! He hung Lyme from a tree and ripped his guts out while he was still alive. Do you understand? Neither a bear nor a mythical creature could do such a thing. This was a fucking real *freak*!"

"You shouldn't talk about him like that," Kateri said softly. "He doesn't like to be made fun of; it challenges him. I can feel it; he's around here watching us. The only reason he's not attacking us is because I have this." She pulled a feather pendant out of her shirt pocket and held it under Ondragon's nose. "And it would have been a lot easier if you had yours on you too!"

Ondragon realized he was unsurprised. "So you put that thing on my pillow."

She hesitated, then nodded. "I climbed over the balcony into your room. I didn't want you to think the talisman came from me. Unfortunately, you woke up, and I had to run. I hadn't meant to wake you."

"And the threatening letter, was that from you too?"

"What threatening letter?"

Ondragon could see Kateri frowning.

"Well, the letter that said, 'I know you're snooping around here. Give it up. Or you'll end up like the dog.'"

"That wasn't me."

"Oh, so it was just coincidence that it turned up in my room at the same time?"

She raised her hands, then lowered them again. "It wasn't me, Paul! Why would I write something like that?"

"I don't know. But maybe you have an idea who else it could be from."

Kateri seemed to give it serious thought but then shrugged. "Sorry, I don't know."

Silence followed. Then she asked, "Have you been snooping around?"

"What?" Ondragon snapped out of his thoughts.

"You said the letter said you were snooping."

"Yes . . . a little bit."

"And what did you do?"

"I'll tell you about that later. We'd better make sure we get out of here."

"No, I want to know now!"

Ondragon lost his patience. "Kateri, there's a killer running around out there. He took a bite out of Lyme's liver!"

"There you see it. That's the proof. That was the Wendigo! He eats human flesh."

A hot shiver chased over Ondragon's already irritated scalp. Wasn't that what Lyme had tried to say? Wendigo? At least that's what it had sounded like.

Or you imagined it, Paul! How could Lyme, a man from the big city, come to believe in such nonsense as the Wendigo?

Ondragon thought of the creepy critter that had attacked him. What if it had actually been the Wendigo? Why was he so resistant to that idea? Weren't researchers around the globe constantly finding new species? In the South American jungle, in the depths of the sea, and who knows where else. Why shouldn't it be possible here, in the remote forests of the United States? Just because the science studiously ignored something, that didn't mean it didn't exist.

A vicious twinge shot through Ondragon's head, reminding him they were still out in the forest, unprotected. They had to get to the lodge; only there would they be safe, and only then could he calmly ponder whether the Wendigo really existed.

He took Kateri by the arm and pulled her along. "Come on, you know the way, take us to the lodge. I don't want to play at being live bait for some predator, real or imagined, one second longer!"

They reached the lodge barely an hour later and without further incident. The lights of the electric lanterns on the outer facade shone invitingly in the night; Ondragon had never seen anything more beautiful than this man-made bulwark against the dangers of the wilderness.

At Sheila's counter they were met with some excitement; the rest of the search party had long since returned and had been waiting for them anxiously since nightfall. They were immediately led to Dr. Arthur's office.

The psychotherapist had hung his white coat on the chair and was sitting at his desk in the dim light. He seemed like a tired, fatherly friend, and looked up in relief when his lost children entered the room.

"Thank God, there you are! Kateri, what happened? Why were you gone so long?"

"Dr. Arthur, it would be better if we get Deputy Hase in on this before we report," Ondragon said, dropping exhausted into one of the phobic-friendly chairs. "A painkiller and some cold water wouldn't be amiss either."

Someone fetched a packet of painkillers and something to drink, and Ondragon threw down one of the tablets. He gulped the water in a single swig.

"First, please tell us what happened, Paul," Dr. Arthur said after Ondragon had wiped his dirty face. "And then we'll consider getting the deputy involved."

"What's there to consider?" Ondragon exhaled indignantly, feeling his cracked rib. "The body of one of your patients is lying, or rather hanging, out there. And it certainly wasn't an accident. Not to mention that I was attacked too. Miss Wolfe got there just in time and was able to put the attacker to flight. So please call the deputy immediately, or I will!"

But Dr. Arthur made no move to pick up the phone. Instead, he glanced briefly at Kateri and then asked in a calm voice, "Who attacked you?"

Ondragon also looked at Kateri, who was sitting next to him, strangely still. Why wasn't she saying anything? "What do I know." He shrugged his shoulders. "It was dark, and I couldn't make him out."

"*Him?* Was it a human? Or could it have been a bear?"

"Damn it, there's a killer running around out there! Do something! You know, I'm starting to think it's your fault Mr. Lyme is dead. You didn't take any of this seriously."

"Now calm down, Paul." Dr. Arthur's yellow eyes pleaded with him urgently. "I can understand you're upset. But for the moment, get your thoughts together and describe to me exactly where you found Mr. Lyme and what happened to him."

Ondragon took a deep breath, ignoring the exhaustion tugging at his nerves, and began to describe to Dr. Arthur what he had seen, omitting the intimate interlude with Kateri but not the unsavory details of Lyme's corpse. As he described the broker's condition, Dr. Arthur's eyes widened while Kateri continued to sit there, unmoving. Was she really that hard-boiled? Or was she just trying to protect herself with her petrified expression?

When Ondragon reported that Lyme had been alive and had tried to tell him who had done this to him, Kateri began to shift uneasily in her chair. Perhaps she was finally shaken enough by the details of this heinous act to believe him.

"Was Lyme actually trying to say 'Wendigo'?" interjected Dr. Arthur. He looked skeptical.

Ondragon nodded. "Possibly. The sounds he made certainly sounded like it."

Dr. Arthur leaned back and for a moment it looked like he had to stifle a grin.

"You don't believe me, do you?" Ondragon protested indignantly. "Do you think I imagined the whole thing? But then where, pray tell, is Mr. Lyme? I may be your patient, Dr. Arthur, but I'm not crazy! I saw Lyme and there is no doubt about it. The man was cut up like a slaughtered animal and someone had taken a bite out of his liver!" *One of your crazy cannibal patients*, he almost added, but managed to restrain his anger at the last moment.

Dr. Arthur stood up and raised both hands placatingly. The smile on his lips was gone, if it had ever been there. "Paul, listen, I do believe you. And I'm taking this just as hard as you are. But I want you to tell me again who attacked you."

"And then will you call Deputy Hase?"

"Yes, I will notify him. I'm just afraid he won't be able to do much tonight. It's too dark, and you'd only get lost in the woods trying to find Mr. Lyme again."

He's right, unfortunately, Ondragon thought grimly, and began to recount once again the attack of the beast and Kateri's intervention.

"It's really quite simple," he concluded a little later with an ironic tone, "whether it was a bear, a human, or anything else, Miss Wolfe tagged him for us. He's got an injury to his right shoulder. Find an animal or person with that kind of injury and you'll have the culprit. So, if you don't mind, I'm going to go to my room and take a shower and rest after all this crap. Let me know when Deputy Hase arrives, and I'll be happy to tell him all about it again and try to lead him to the body. Good night, Doctor. Miss Wolfe." He glanced at Kateri. She looked pale and exhausted. But could that alone be the reason she was simply perched there like a wax figure? Why had she been silent all this time, making him look like an idiot?

Disappointed, he turned away, strode toward the door, and opened it. But before he left the room, he turned around. "Oh, Dr. Arthur, by the way, I don't want a therapy session tomorrow. I think I need to reconsider my stay here very carefully." Without waiting for a response, he closed the door behind him and walked away down the hall.

A little later, as he lay on his bed, showered and in fresh clothes, sleep just wouldn't come. Again and again the images of Lyme rose before his eyes, again and again he saw himself fighting the beast, and all at once it occurred to him: He had told neither Kateri nor Dr. Arthur about the fact that he had encountered Momo shortly before. Could Pete's younger brother have had something to do with the attack? Or even with Lyme's death?

Ondragon sprang out of bed, sat down at the table, and opened his notepad. The *centrifuge* rotated at the speed of light as Ondragon hastily wrote down his thoughts. His ballpoint pen flew across the pages as if by magic, while the minutes on the digital alarm clock turned to hours.

CHAPTER 40

2009, Moose Lake,
Cedar Creek Lodge

Ondragon started up. Confused, he looked around. His bed was littered with notes. A glance at the clock told him it was already half past eight.

There was a knock on his door.

"Yes?" he called out loudly, gathering up the notes.

"Mr. *On Draegen*? Deputy Hase is here. He wants to talk to you." It was Pete, there was no mistaking that. "Mr. *On Draegen*? The deputy is waiting for you down in reception."

"Yes, I'll be right there!" Ondragon rose, and in the same moment pain shot across his body. His head felt like an overheated tire about to burst, and his rib howled with each breath. Oh great! He'd probably have to have Sheila fix him up before he'd be able to talk to the deputy, let alone go back out there into the woods. He felt the pulsating bump on his forehead. A strange heat emanated from it, making his mind glow like a broken space heater.

Groaning, he stood up and looked in the mirror. What he saw pleased him even less. An ashen face with an unsightly growth of stubble on his chin and wrinkles as deep as the Grand Canyon. The renovation crew had to get working first. Ondragon caught himself thinking what his brother, Per, might look like if he were still alive. *Like me? Or less spent? What kind of person would Per be? Hopefully, a better one!* Ondragon felt sadness rising within him. Per, his brother, was dead. And nothing in the world would bring him back to life, not even therapy with this quack. *So what am I still doing here?* Ondragon wiped away a tear that had stolen into the corner of his eye and set about repairing the worst of the damage to his face.

When he left the room a little later, he already felt a touch more presentable. Even the handful of painkillers was already starting to work wonders. Long live chemistry!

In the entrance, Pete, the deputy, two police aides, Dr. Schuyler, Sheila, and Kateri were sitting on the sofa. The gas fire in the hearth was flickering steadily and the sunshine was falling through the glass door of the main entrance.

"Good morning," Ondragon greeted those present, who immediately turned to look at him.

The deputy clearly had displeasure written all over his face, and his eyes were surrounded by pretty rings the size of truck tires. Probably not had too much sleep, huh?

Dr. Schuyler, on the other hand, seemed as distinguished as ever, as if there was no inappropriate time for him. On his lap he held the steel case containing forensic tools as if it held a million dollars in small bills. He apparently couldn't wait to get down to business. He gave Ondragon a friendly nod, in place of the deputy.

Sheila, meanwhile, was avoiding his gaze and stroking Kateri's hand sympathetically. As Ondragon stepped closer, she quickly rose with an "Excuse me, gentlemen," and took up her post behind the reception counter with a petrified expression. Ondragon had noticed that Lady Iceberg had seemed all too familiar with Kateri. And he wondered why it had never occurred to him before that the two women might be friends.

"Where is Dr. Arthur?" he asked without joining the group on the sofa. He wanted to get the matter over with as quickly as possible.

Pete took up the question, also looking distinctly the worse for wear. "Dr. Arthur has already spoken with Deputy Hase. He won't be coming with us because he has to prepare for his sessions today."

"So none of the people in charge of the lodge will be accompanying us? I mean . . ." Ondragon was flabbergasted. He hadn't expected the clinic management to be so ignorant. "I mean, Mr. Lyme is . . . *was* one of his patients; that alone should be enough reason for Dr.

Arthur to be there. He is, in a sense, responsible for Mr. Lyme. Don't any of you think that's strange?"

"No, on the contrary," Deputy Hase replied, rising. "Dr. Arthur is as concerned about this incident as I am or you are, Mr. Ondragon."

Oh yes, concerned! *What a true do-gooder Dr. Arthur is.*

"Besides, Mr. Parker will be there," the deputy said.

Ondragon looked at the bellboy, who merely shrugged innocently. After all, he couldn't help being saddled with this responsibility.

"Excuse me." Ondragon turned back to the deputy. "But Mr. Lyme was a guest at this lodge and he was murdered. Doesn't it seem to you that it would be appropriate for someone from the upper floor to handle this?"

"Not at all. Mr. Parker has been authorized by Dr. Arthur to accompany us. I would also caution you not to jump to conclusions. Whether Mr. Lyme was actually murdered is something we have yet to determine."

"Are you suggesting I made all this up?" Ondragon was on the verge of seriously freaking out. Were they all as dumb as the cattle around here, or were they just pretending? "Deputy, with all due respect, Mr. Lyme was slaughtered like a porker, I saw him. And it wasn't a pretty sight by any means. There's a cold-blooded killer running around out there. And it's your job, damn it, to catch him!"

"Did you see him, the killer?" Deputy Hase looked at him appraisingly.

"No, of course not," Ondragon replied. "Then I would know who it was!"

"And you didn't find Mr. Lyme until he was already dead?"

"No, he wasn't quite dead yet, and he was trying to tell me something."

"That it was the Wendigo?" Hase chuckled, just as Ondragon had chuckled about it yesterday. "Dr. Arthur told me. But I think it's easy to mistake a bear for such a monster when you're delusional and on the verge of death."

Lyme was not delusional; he wanted to be eaten, Ondragon would have liked to shout in his razor-scraped face. He pointed outside. "*That,* gentlemen, was no bear. That's as sure as I'm standing here."

"We'll judge what's safe and what's not when we've examined the crime scene and found the body. Dr. Schuyler will examine it and then we'll know more."

"Why are you so keen for it to have been a bear, Deputy? Can you tell me?"

"I don't *necessarily* want it to be a bear," Hase replied calmly, "I'm just considering the circumstances and facts we've already established."

"And for you, the fact is that the killer is a bear. How is that an objective view, I ask you?" Ondragon noticed two of the police assistants, probably the two poor wretches who would have to recover the body, giving the deputy a skeptical look.

Hase did not reply, but Ondragon would not let him off so easily. After all, he had only just started playing this game. He turned to the medical examiner. "Dr. Schuyler, I'd like to know something. Did you actually examine the bodies of Louisa and Herman Parker in 1997?" He cast a quick sideways glance at Pete, who wore an astonished expression and looked slightly dumbfounded, while Schuyler, visibly nervous, adjusted his glasses.

"Well, yes," he said slowly. "I was at the scene because Deputy Schoenfield called me in back then. And yes, I saw the Parkers' bodies. It was horrible." Schuyler gave Pete a guilty look. "But I couldn't investigate them because the FBI took over. After that, we were off the case and also only got the information the bureau passed on to us. How do you know about the murders?"

"Oh, Pete told me what happened to his parents." Ondragon saw that Pete was about to say something but didn't let the boy get a word in. "And if you ask me, the similarities between the Parkers' murders and the case of the body in the woods, and now Lyme, are unmistakable."

"But we're not asking you!" Deputy Hase interrupted. "There's no need for you to rack your brains on our behalf. We have carefully reviewed all previous homicide cases. It's standard procedure for where bodies are discovered and the cause of death is unknown. All available evidence is taken into consideration, including, of course, patterns of previous violent crimes. The cases are unrelated."

Ondragon laughed. "Nice try, Deputy. But I know what you're pulling here. You don't want the FBI to take the case away from you. That's what would happen, isn't it? Because then it would be a serial killer, which automatically becomes a case for the bureau. And that's not what you or Dr. Arthur want, is it? I think I'm beginning to understand."

"You don't understand anything, Mr. Ondragon!" Deputy Hase snapped. "You come in here waving your wallet and thinking you know this neighborhood and the people here. It's always that way with your kind. A fat bank account and an expensive car and you think you're better than we are. But we know exactly what we're doing, even if we weren't born with a silver spoon in our mouths and did not benefit from an elite education. I grew up here and I know how to investigate in this area."

Ondragon pursed his lips in amusement. So that's the way the wind was blowing. The good deputy felt underappreciated.

"I advise you one last time to stay out of our investigation, Mr. Ondragon. Otherwise, I will put you in jail for obstruction. Do your duty and take us to the body and then get on with your therapy, or whatever else you came here for. After all, you've paid a lot of money for it!"

Ondragon twisted his face in amusement. "I'm only too happy to leave this sorry mess to you, Deputy. I certainly don't care to do your work, and you're right: I paid a good deal of money to be here, so I'm going to take you to see Mr. Lyme, and after that you can go to hell!"

Deputy Hase took a threatening step toward him. His face was distorted with rage, his eyes were shooting out poison darts.

Ondragon lifted his chin defiantly and returned the gaze, but for some reason he suddenly started to sway and had to brace himself against the sofa.

"Are you all right?" asked Dr. Schuyler, concerned. "You're dripping with sweat!"

"What?" Ondragon looked down at himself and only now noticed that his shirt was completely soaked. Another flush of heat seized him and his whole body began to glow. With the unsettling feeling that everything was spinning around him, he grabbed his forehead.

"Yesterday wasn't exactly a walk in the park, you know," he replied in a clipped voice. "I think I may have a fever."

"Then you'd better stay here and go to bed," Dr. Schuyler said.

"No, I'm going to take you to Mr. Lyme. It's the least I can do for the man." He suppressed the renewed throbbing in his head and staggered toward the exit. As soon as he got through this unpleasant business with Lyme, he would take care of his tireless storm of thoughts from last night. And then he would straighten this place out. What was the saying? A fish always rots from the head down. And something here was rotten big time!

"Gentlemen, please follow me." He opened the door and stepped out into the fresh air. Out of the corner of his eye, he saw everyone rise from the sofa, visibly relieved, and shoulder their backpacks. Even Kateri, who had sat there as mute as a maggot during his argument with Hase, stood up. What was wrong with her? Was she ashamed of the stunt they had pulled in the forest yesterday? Did she regret having given herself to him? What was he saying, given herself! She had pounced on him like a hungry wolf. So why was she suddenly acting as if they were strangers?

Ondragon gave her a searching look, but she avoided him, wordlessly picked up her jacket and walked past him into the open. Hopefully, she would at least help him find the way to Lyme, because she knew her way around this shitty forest better than he did.

Under the critical gaze of Sheila, Ondragon let the door fall shut, and the small party made its way into the forest.

After a two-hour walk, the group reached the stream where Ondragon had found the mysterious tracks the day before. Thoughtfully, he knelt down and searched the dark mire. The tracks were gone.

He quickly stood up, but didn't let anyone notice that everything went black for a moment. Damned dizziness! Surely, that would subside at some point.

Uncertain now, he looked around. Was he in the right place? He wiped dead mosquitoes and sweat from his forehead with his forearm and looked at the stream. Clearly, he had been here before. After all, there were his own footprints in the damp earth. But where was the toeless trail? It was nowhere to be seen. The rest of the creek bank lay untouched, as if nothing had ever been there. Suddenly, he remembered the ring.

"There was a trail here," he told the deputy, pointing to the spot. "Here, right next to my footprints. Oddly enough, it disappeared. But I found something else. A ring." He was about to reach into his pants pocket and pull it out, but then he remembered that he was wearing fresh jeans today because the other pair had been soiled.

"What kind of ring?" Deputy Hase looked at him questioningly.

"It was Lyme's signet ring. It was stuck in the mud here, under the trail."

"But there are no other tracks but yours."

"I don't know why they've disappeared. I don't understand it either."

"And where is the ring?"

"In my room. I left it in my other pants."

Skeptically, the deputy looked at his two colleagues. It was clear he did not believe him. Damn it, why hadn't he shown the ring to Dr. Arthur last night?

"I'll give you the ring when we get back. Now follow me." Angrily, Ondragon set off across the stream. They'd believe him when they finally saw Lyme's body. Screw the trail!

With a brisk step, he trudged ahead, looking for the trail of blood that yesterday had led abundantly clear to the spot where he had slipped on Lyme's intestines. But again, it was like a jinx. He simply could not find it. An unpleasant suspicion came over him, but he didn't let on and kept walking—soon they would see the body; it couldn't be far away.

When he finally found the blood trail, he was more relieved than he wanted to admit. He pointed out the unmistakable trail to Deputy Hase, and they followed it. After about a hundred yards, Ondragon bent a few branches to the side and the small clearing opened up in front of them. There you go! At last he had found it. He wasn't such a bad pathfinder after all. Satisfied, he turned to the others.

"Over there is the tree Lyme is hanging from, just a few steps straight across the clearing and you're in front of him. You can't miss him. I'd better stay here. I don't need to see that again, I'm sure you understand." Ondragon let Deputy Hase, who was looking at him disdainfully, step forward. His men, Dr. Schuyler, and Pete followed him. Kateri, surprisingly, also stayed behind. Ondragon rejoiced. Now he could use the unexpected moment together to find out why she was being so cool with him. He stepped so close to her that she could no longer avoid his gaze, and grabbed her by the arm.

"What's wrong with you?"

"Nothing," she hissed, wriggling out of his grip. She looked as brittle as an old maid, as if their intimate encounter had never taken place. A new suspicion arose in him. After he had gone to his room yesterday, Kateri had stayed with Dr. Arthur. Had they talked? Had she confessed to her mentor about the little affair? And what had Dr. Arthur said about it? Had he spoken badly of him? Had he chided her for flirting with a patient?

He was about to call Kateri on it when he heard Deputy Hase's voice.

"Mr. Ondragon, come over here, please!"

With a questioning gesture, he stepped through the bush into the clearing. Deputy Hase, Schuyler, and his men stood not ten paces from him in front of the tree in question and gazed at him. Ondragon immediately recognized the fibrous trunk, and the low-hanging branches, and the rock in front of it. But the faces of the policemen seemed anything but affected by the sight of the corpse. They were staring at him with grim expressions, as if he himself was the criminal.

"Can you explain this to me?" the deputy asked sternly, stepping aside. When Ondragon saw what was hanging there on the trunk, he was flabbergasted.

CHAPTER 41

2009, in the forest,
5 miles northeast
of Moose Lake

Confused, Ondragon grabbed his overheated forehead. He felt dizzy, and as if he were trapped in a goddamn oven that was also attached to a roller coaster. One thought kept racing through his pounding skull: *I must still be in my bed, dreaming.* Yes, that's what it was. This whole fucking nightmare was just a dream.

"Explain this to me, Mr. Ondragon!" Deputy Hase's annoyed voice brought him back to reality.

Ondragon blinked. Apparently, he wasn't asleep after all. Apparently, he was wide awake. Shit!

"I feel sick," he muttered, and sat down on the rock in front of the tree under the deputy's probing gaze. Everything was spinning, and Ondragon had trouble getting his thoughts straight. He searched in his pocket for the packet of painkillers and popped two. Dryly, he choked down the bitter pills. Only then did he dare to lift his head, which felt about the size of New Jersey, and look into the deputy's reddened face.

"I'm sorry, but I can't explain." He waved an arm across the clearing. Even though the fever was clouding his senses, he was sure this was the right spot. One hundred percent. He had not been mistaken. This was the clearing, the tree, the stone. Only one thing did not match the memories stored in his brain, and his brain was still vehemently refusing to believe what his eyes were seeing.

Lyme. The body of the broker was not there!

Instead, in its place, an animal carcass, split open, hung from the trunk of the white pine tree. A dark puddle of dried blood had collected under the stump of the animal's neck. But it was not only the head that was missing, its claws and genitals had been cut off too. The carcass had been skinned, and a dense cloud of flies was swarming over the raw flesh. The buzzing made Ondragon feel nauseous. He cleared his throat and shoved a piece of gum between his teeth. The peppermint flavor was like ice on his tongue and helped him maintain control of his stomach. Chewing deliberately slowly, he watched as Dr. Schuyler took out his camera and snapped a few shots.

Suddenly, the medical examiner raised his eyebrows and stepped closer to the carcass. He stroked his hand over the smooth tendinous skin in which the muscles were packed, and lifted the carcass by the hind leg, away from the trunk. He looked at the animal's backbone for a while and concluded his examination with a long drawn-out "Hmmmm."

"Well, I'm not sure," he said, turning to Hase, "but it's not a deer or a stag. Likely a predator, a cougar or a wolf. They're protected though, and I don't know who would shoot one of those."

The deputy seemed to care little about this information; he had positioned himself in front of Ondragon with his arms folded across his chest, staring down at him. His police badge shone gold in the sun.

"And that's why we've been crawling through the woods for two hours?" He pointed at the carcass. "Well, if you ask me, this definitely looks like the work of a trophy hunter. He was probably after the fur and teeth. There are people who pay big money for that. Protected animal or not."

"But what about Lyme?" asked Ondragon.

"Well, he's not here, at any rate, as you can see. I think this is something for Dr. Arthur to take care of, not us. I've heard it's common for people to leave Cedar Creek ahead of schedule without telling us. Not everyone can handle that kind of psychotherapy. In your case, I'm afraid you may have overreacted a bit yesterday."

Ondragon looked at the deputy distractedly. That could be it. He still didn't understand at all.

Hase tilted his head and continued speaking with a subliminal sneer in his voice. "But that can happen, can't it? Especially when you . . ."

". . . are crazy? That's what you were going to say, isn't it?" Ondragon got up from the stone.

"No, I was going to say when you have a fever, as you clearly do." He gave an insolent grin.

"Look, Deputy. I saw what I saw, and this is . . . is . . . wrong, somehow." Ondragon ran an agitated hand through his hair. "I've never been wrong before!"

"Well, I guess today is a historic moment. Because you were wrong. Eureka!" Hase threw up his hands in frustration and turned to his men. "Cut the carcass down from the tree, let the scavengers get rid of it. And then let's get the hell out of here. We've already wasted way too much time on Mr. I'm-never-wrong!"

"Watch what you're saying," Ondragon protested.

But Deputy Hase was not to be intimidated this time. He stepped close to him and hissed in his ear, "No, *you* watch yourself. If you bother the police with your fantasies again, I'll have you remanded to Nett Lake for twenty-four hours. And believe me, neither your money nor your oh-so-weighty contacts will be able to protect you from that. Understand?"

Ondragon was silent, his lips pressed together, and avoided looking at Kateri, who was motionless and looking over at them. Now she must think he had gone completely batty. What an ignominious defeat. Against this baby-faced greenhorn of a provincial cop, of all people.

He gave Hase a deadly stare, but the deputy ignored him and said something into his radio that Ondragon could not understand. A short time later, the deputy put the device back in his fanny pack, signaled them all to move out, and took the lead with Pete. Glowing with fever and anger, Ondragon glared after them. When they were a safe distance away, he quickly bent down, tore off a few blades of grass that still had blood on them, and put them in his pants pocket. A laboratory would be able to determine whether the blood was human or animal.

Before anyone realized he had fallen behind, Ondragon joined the column and, for the next hour and a half, walked along thinking up ways to get back at the deputy. Lyme's ring and the blood samples would convince Hase that he, Ondragon, was not crazy at all, and that something had indeed happened to the broker. After all, why would Lyme throw his ring into a creek so far from the lodge?

When they finally reached the CC Lodge, Ondragon went wordlessly to his room. He closed the door and hurried to the chair where his dirty pants were hanging. He felt with his fingers in the pocket, but found nothing. Hastily, he searched the other pocket. Nothing there either. Annoyed, Ondragon looked at the garment. Where the hell was the ring? In some alarm, he searched the whole room. But the ring was nowhere to be found. He looked around again. Everything was in its place; whoever had taken the ring had been very careful. But who could it have been? Nobody knew about the ring. He had shown it to no one.

Kateri.

Maybe she had once again entered his room during the night and had taken the ring. But why?

Ondragon left his room and went to find the deputy, who was standing downstairs in the entrance hall with his men. Contritely, he confessed that he could not find the ring. That someone must have stolen it. The pitying smile that appeared on the deputy's face almost made Ondragon's anger boil over. But before he could go for the deputy's throat, Ondragon turned, leaving him standing there, and hurried back to his room, where he closed the door firmly behind him. He had to think . . . if that was even possible with this infernal headache!

Sighing, he threw himself onto the bed. He felt as if he had been eaten, digested, and thrown up again! And it seemed to him that in his fever, the borders between delusion and reality were finally blurring. In this newly created mental space, which was suddenly all around him, the trees walked through the forest as if they had feet instead of roots; in the midst of them stood his own childlike reflection with the thought police officer's key in his hand, or was it Per?

Ondragon didn't know—he was too distracted by the bare-breasted Kateri, looking like the goddess Diana, luring him from afar with bow and arrow, and by Harvey Lyme, hanging by his entrails from one of the swaying branches above him as if on a swing, laughing uproariously.

Exhausted, Ondragon threw his arms over his face. If he stayed here any longer, he would actually end up going crazy. He probably wouldn't really feel well again until he was back in the city and could feel the hot asphalt under his feet. Oh, how he longed for the heavy traffic on Olympic Boulevard and the pitiful voice of the 90.1 KBPK traffic reporter on the car radio.

With that comforting thought and three painkillers whispering gently through his blood, he nodded off. The exertions of the past twenty-four hours had taken their toll. But he had actually made his decision hours ago. He would do what needed to be done, and then it would be *adios amigos*!

LA was calling to him. Mother of steel and concrete.

CHAPTER 42

2009, Moose Lake,
Cedar Creek Lodge

Ondragon awoke in the afternoon and struggled out of bed with a groan. Maybe he should eat something sensible before he pulled any more stunts. He went down to the deserted dining room and had a late lunch. Then he went to the reception desk to prepare for his departure.

He asked Sheila about Kateri. He wanted to confront Miss Wolfe once more before he moved on to the finale. But Sheila just gave him a hostile look and claimed she didn't know where Kateri was. Ondragon leaned over the counter, very close to the receptionist, and looked at her intently.

"Listen, Sheila, your dislike for me is completely mutual. Because I don't like you either. But I know that you are friends with Kateri and that you know very well where she is now. So forget your jealousy and hatred of men for a moment and tell me where I can find her, because I have something important to tell her. After that, you can go back to thinking whatever you like about me. And you know what? You're in luck, I'm feeling very generous today. I'll also promise not to let your secret affair with the queen of hearts be revealed." He leaned back. "Well, what do you think of that little deal, *sweetheart?*"

He would not let prickly Sheila off the leash until he had the information. The fact that she was probably in a relationship with Kateri interested him only to the extent that he would use it against her if she did not cooperate. He had only just understood the whole thing over dinner, when he had reviewed the events of the morning.

He had remembered how familiar the two women had been with each other, and all at once he put together a number of things: Sheila's hostility toward him and Kateri's brittle behavior inside the lodge. It was only out in the woods, far away from Sheila's gaze, that she had dared to throw herself at him. For whatever reason, but maybe she was into women *and* men, only she didn't want Sheila to know.

"Well, what is it? I'm waiting." Ondragon raised an eyebrow.

But Sheila simply turned away and began busily leafing through the guest index. Clack, clack, clack. Her green fingernails flitted over the cards. A touch too quickly though. A satisfied smile appeared on Ondragon's face. In a moment, she would fold. There was nothing like having a convincing argument.

After Sheila had gone through the card index from front to back for five minutes with Ondragon staring at her, the receptionist finally looked up. Well, was she giving up now?

"Boathouse!" was all she said, and then busied herself again with the card index.

It was only one word, but Ondragon enjoyed his victory all the more. He blew a kiss to Sheila, and she responded with a look that told him she would tear him apart the next time he got too close. Oh well, he wasn't going to anyway.

He said goodbye and left, whistling happily.

At the boathouse he checked out how the land was lying, but no one was to be seen or heard; even Frank the gardener was absent. Ondragon was just about to push against the half-open door when he heard someone call his name.

"Mr. *On Draegen!*"

Annoyed, Ondragon lowered his hand. That was Pete. He could really do without him right now. He thought about ignoring him, but then he turned around. Trotting hilariously, like a pig, the boy came running up to him, raised a hand, and shouted again, "Mr. *On Draegen*, wait!"

As Pete came up to him, he looked around breathlessly and smiled nervously. "I'm glad I found you. I have something to tell you."

Ondragon looked at him inquiringly.

"Well, I . . ." Again Pete looked around. "So, about yesterday, I'm sorry about the way the deputy treated you."

"Why should you be sorry? It wasn't your fault."

Pete hemmed and hawed, scraping at the grass with a boot. "I don't think that's quite right though," he said finally, "Mr. *On Draegen*. There's something else."

Ondragon understood that the bellboy wanted to tell him something important and took a few steps away from the door of the boathouse. If Kateri was in there, she didn't need to overhear what Pete had to tell him.

The lanky boy adjusted his baseball cap and looked at him uncertainly. "Mr. *On Draegen*, promise me you'll keep it to yourself?"

Ondragon raised a hand. "I swear."

"On your mom's life?"

"On my mom's life," he said solemnly, thinking, *Good thing he didn't ask me to swear on my dad's.*

"Okay. Now I'm going to tell you why I took the Indian net from the place they found the body. Then maybe you'll understand." Pete lowered his voice. "The net is from the Ojibwe people who live here. It's one of those protection things."

"A defensive medicine. But I already know that. Who or what is it supposed to help against?"

Pete licked his lips. "Against the Wendigo. And believe me, it's no joke."

"And why did you take it away?"

The man put a hand to his mouth and whispered even more softly, "Because I know the Wendigo and I didn't want suspicion to fall on him."

Ondragon took Pete by the upper arm and led him even farther from the boathouse. Then he looked the boy firmly in the eye. "It was one of Dr. Arthur's patients, wasn't it? And you tried to cover for the doc because he's treating your brother and lets you work here?"

Pete shook his head.

Ondragon was taken aback. "Not a patient?"

More head shaking.

"One of the employees, then?"

"No."

Hell, it was like a quiz show, Ondragon was irritated. But suddenly it dawned on him and he wanted to give himself a smack upside the head. How could he have been so blind? His performance really left a lot to be desired.

"It was Momo, wasn't it?" he said.

Pete nodded unhappily. He passed a furtive hand over his eyes and wiped away a tear. The fact that he had told his secret seemed to be a relief to him, but at the same time he was deeply distressed. No wonder, it was about his beloved brother.

"Are you saying Momo killed that man in the woods?"

Pete shook his head emphatically. "No, that wasn't him. Definitely not."

"Oh boy! First you tell me you know who did it, and now it wasn't him after all? What now? And what about Rumsfeld?"

Pete shrugged his shoulders. "I don't know. But the Rumsfeld thing wasn't Momo either. Momo loves animals. He could never hurt them."

"I see, but what's going on with Momo now? Why did you take the net if he didn't kill the man?"

Pete took a deep breath, as if his guilty conscience had a grip on his throat. Finally, he whispered so softly that Ondragon could barely hear, "Momo . . . is the Wendigo."

"The Wendigo?" Ondragon shook his head. Everyone was going crazy here! He put a hand on the distraught boy's shoulder and asked, "And how do you know he's the Wendigo?"

"Because Momo . . . our . . . well, *he* killed Mom and Dad!"

Ondragon looked up in surprise. "But the FBI investigated the case and even had you interviewed by a psychologist."

"We fooled them all."

"You lied to a psychologist? And that worked?"

"Neither of us was arrested."

Amused, Ondragon exhaled. The FBI wasn't what it used to be either. Letting two kids pull the wool over their eyes. He wanted to show Pete the clippings about the Parker murders and felt in his pants pocket for his cell phone, but his fingers found only his talisman and the pack of gum. The phone must still be in the nightstand, which meant he hadn't looked at it in over forty-eight hours. Suddenly, he remembered Charlize. She was supposed to have been looking for a lead on Jeremy Bates in Orr, after all.

"You've got to help me, Mr. *On Draegen*," Pete said pleadingly. "It's not my brother's fault. The Wendigo took him."

"If your brother killed your parents, then he needs to go to the police, Pete. There's not much I can do."

"Please, don't go to the police! It's not his fault. Please, help us."

"How am I supposed to help you with that?" Ondragon raised his hands helplessly. It was clear: If Momo had murdered his parents, he had to be behind bars. The FBI would be happy to finally put the case to bed after so many years, and there was nothing that could keep Momo out of jail. Besides, after twelve years, this was old news. Ondragon turned away. He had much more urgent things to worry about, Dr. Arthur, for example, who was playing a far more monstrous game than the intellectually disabled Momo, who had killed his parents in the heat of the moment or whatever.

"Wait, Mr. *On Draegen*, I know you don't want to, but only *you* can help us." Pete looked at him, his eyes blurred with tears.

Heartbreaking indeed, Ondragon thought cynically, but all at once he felt a tiny spark of compassion flare up deep in his raddled insides. Surprised by the feeling, his chest contracted, causing his cracked rib to yelp. Ondragon doubled over in pain, trying to comprehend what was happening to him. Because he had actually sworn never to do anything for others. Never! In the fight for survival, he always had to put himself first, or he wouldn't see much of his old age. It was for this reason alone he had turned his soul into a polar ice desert. Into a refrigerator, where nothing could exist except cold professionalism.

"Are you okay, Mr. *On Draegen*?" Pete sounded concerned.

"Yeah, yeah, it's fine. It's just my rib."

Pete nodded sympathetically. Then he pulled a dirty cloth handkerchief out of his pants pocket and blew his nose into it.

Ondragon listened to the freezer of his feelings. He could only guess how lonely and small the boy felt. He thought of his own father and how much he hated him. Maybe Pete was feeling something like that. Finally, Ondragon gave a jerk and raised a placating hand to the bellboy. "All right, I'll help you."

"Really?" asked Pete, aghast.

"Really." Ondragon nodded, and Pete crashed on.

"Great, Mr. *On Draegen*! You're so cool. All I want is to help Momo. Because he can be cured him. With a book. It's very old, you know. Dr. Arthur has it. Actually, it used to belong to our family, but I gave it to the doctor because he takes such good care of us. He's very interested in old writings, and Uncle Joel once told him the book was about the Wendigo. I hope it will also tell us how to cure Momo."

Ondragon listened patiently to the boy, but he already feared where the conversation was leading.

"You have to get me that book, Mr. *On Draegen*!"

Of course. A book, of all things!

"Where is it?" asked Ondragon cautiously. He wanted to at least try. For the boy's sake . . . and because of that damned soft, flushed feeling in his chest. He sighed, knowing he was going to regret this terribly.

"It's in Dr. Arthur's office, in the desk drawer."

Ondragon felt uneasy. He may have wanted to get the doctor for his unsavory dealings, but breaking into his house hadn't been part of the plan. "Hey, Pete, why don't you just ask the doc to give it back to you?" he said, trying the path of least resistance.

"I already have. But he says he's not done reading it yet."

"Pete, I can't just break into his office."

"Yes you can. I saw you, didn't I?"

"When?"

"The very first night, when you broke into Sheila's office."

Damn, how did the little sneak know that?

"I was outside by the door and recognized you as you slipped through the entrance hall. Before that, I saw your flashlight in the office behind the counter."

So it had been Pete who had made the noises outside the lodge door. At least he had cleared that up. "What were you doing out there?"

"I was looking for Momo. He had been running away from me all day."

Ondragon was content with that answer; he didn't think Pete would lie to him. "Okay," he said, "I could break into Dr. Arthur's office and take the thing. And then what am I supposed to do with it?"

"Bring it to my house. I need you to help me read it."

Ondragon looked at Pete.

"Momo can't read either, and Uncle Joel . . . he would just scold."

"I thought you went to school as a kid."

"I did, but the writing in the book is so hard to read."

"All right. Tonight!" Ondragon ran a hand over his upper lip. *I can't believe I'm helping this guy fight a mythical creature!* "I'll come to your house, then. Make sure that mutt stays quiet."

"Sure, Mr. *On Draegen.* And thank you."

"Don't thank me until it's done," he whispered, and sent the bellboy away. After waiting a while, he went back to the door of the boathouse. He listened, then knocked. No answer. He opened the door and stepped into the dark of the wooden building.

"Kateri?"

A little light was shafting through one of the doors on the opposite side, which let the boats directly out onto the lake. But no one was to be seen. Ondragon stepped over to the opening and looked out at the lake. There was an enchanting view over the water and the islands scattered across it. But this deceptive idyll could no longer hide the fact that this place had turned into the set of a horror movie. Somewhere out there, the killer still lurked, waiting for his next victim. He no longer doubted that Lyme had gotten too close to the madman, despite the fact that this morning he had believed his senses had failed him due to the fever. Lyme's body had disappeared, it was true, but Ondragon's instincts told him that the events in the clearing had clearly been staged. Staged with the sole purpose of deceiving him. Dissuading him from his path. But they would not succeed. His course was unshakably fixed: on collision with the top dog of the lodge.

His gaze lingered on an elongated, black speck that was moving across the water a considerable distance away. After a closer look, he realized that it was a canoe with a human sitting in it. Probably Kateri. She had taken refuge on the lake to escape the hustle and bustle—to get away from him.

Ondragon turned away from the deceptively dreamlike setting and set off back to the lodge. He would talk to Kateri later. Before that, he was going to have a triple espresso to counter his fatigue and unobtrusively investigate what was going on in Dr. Arthur's office. And then he would figure out how to get that damn book to Pete.

CHAPTER 43

At three in the morning, his alarm clock rang. Sluggishly, Ondragon rose and checked his cell phone to see if he had any new messages from Charlize or Rudee. But his voicemail was still empty. What was going on with Charlize? Her research was taking an unusually long time. He went to put the cell phone back in the nightstand drawer, but then changed his mind. He would not leave the lodge again without some means of contact with the outside world. He slid the drawer containing the *Golden Rules* shut and snorted disdainfully, suddenly realizing the irony of the whole thing. It did look like Dr. Arthur was really Dr. *Almighty*. Here in his self-made Camelot, there were no Bibles in the rooms; instead, there were the *Golden Rules* he himself had designed!

Ondragon got dressed and took his small burglaries kit. Outside in the corridors everything was quiet, and he reached the psychotherapist's office on the second floor unhindered. It went without saying that he had to be careful. Under no circumstances did he want to risk being kicked out of the clinic before he had thoroughly read the doc the riot act. He couldn't care less what happened afterward. He would then leave of his own accord.

The door's cylinder lock was not much of an obstacle. How fortunate that Dr. Arthur had a penchant for good old-fashioned things. An electronic lock would have cost him much more time. Ondragon opened the door and closed it quietly behind him, flicking on his mini diode lamp and looking around the office. Everything was neatly in its place. He moved quietly toward the desk, knowing that Dr. Arthur's private quarters were directly above him.

The laptop stood closed on the desk, and Ondragon was briefly tempted to turn it on, but he didn't. If Rudee couldn't get into it, he certainly wouldn't be able to. Computer hacking was not his specialty. Before he turned his attention to the desk drawer, he had something else to do. He went to the filing cabinet on which the statue of Diana stood, took out his lockpick, and opened the lock of the second drawer from the top. For a while his eyes slid over the names on the paper folders. When he found ON-1, he reached in and found a small, square object. A smile flitted across his lips as he slid the object into his pants pocket. He then folded up the few sheets in the folder and pocketed them as well. His file had to disappear, because if the lodge was searched by the authorities after his finale, nothing about his true profession could be allowed to come to light. He would get Rudee onto the digital notes.

He closed the filing cabinet again and turned to the desk. Taking several deep breaths, he crouched down to look at the lock on the drawer. It too was an antiquated specimen and popped open a nanosecond later with a soft click. Slowly, Ondragon pulled out the drawer and mentally prepared himself for the sight of the object hidden inside. Inch by inch, the hated thing emerged: a very old, leather-bound book.

Ondragon felt the sweat on his scalp running down his temples like hot oil. He wiped it away, but it was immediately replaced by more sweat. And finally (because he had already been through this a thousand times) the familiar nausea set in. It was located exactly at the place in his throat directly under the larynx, and gradually squeezed shut . . .

In slow motion, Ondragon moved his trembling hands, which he had protected with rubber gloves for this purpose, toward the book, paused, moved them again, stopped again. Shaking his head, he looked up. Why was he doing this?

He closed his eyes and clenched his hands into fists. The rubber squeaked, his heart beat in his throat. In his mind's eye, he saw the fear rolling inexorably toward him, and he almost thought he could feel the tremor of its murderous force beneath his feet. Shortly thereafter, it flooded him like a tsunami ravaging an unprotected stretch of coastline, sweeping him brutally away. He could do nothing against it, could not escape this fear. He had to endure its onslaught and the memories it brought with it. While his body temperature changed from boiling to freezing, his brain projected strobe-like images on the insides of his eyelids. He saw himself in his father's library, saw his father with that expression on his face that he despised so much, and . . . yes . . . also the image of his brother—a little boy in a green school uniform who looked like him. Per turned to him. But he did not smile.

"*Stop! Not now,*" cried Ondragon with his last breath of sanity, which had sunk itself like a lifeline into the embankment, fighting against the relentless tsunami of fear. He forced his eyes open, halting the crushing maelstrom of his memories. He didn't have time for them now. He would deal with them later. And besides, the invincible Mr. O. couldn't cave in over such a simple task as a ridiculous theft to order!

He forced his pupils to focus on the book again. Breathing heavily, he looked down. There it lay in the protective lap of the drawer. A book that couldn't have been more perfect in appearance: solid leather binding, just large enough to fit comfortably in his hand as he read, marbled edges. Ondragon choked down the taste of panic as he felt the greasy binding under his gloved fingertips. His heartbeat picked up another notch, though that hardly seemed possible. Technobeat had nothing on this.

You're almost there! You can do it!

His fingers closed around the book. Thoroughly nauseated, Ondragon turned his head to the side, lifted the horrific item out of the drawer, and stuffed it into a bag with a spirited swing. Without looking at the drawer again, he pushed it shut. If he had looked more closely, he would have seen a second book with the name *Kateri* handwritten on it. But the drawer had long since been closed when Ondragon, salivating copiously and swallowing hard, hurried out the office door into the hallway.

In his room, he threw the bag containing the book onto his bed and got to the toilet just in time to roar up his guts into the porcelain bowl.

* * *

After he had regained some of his composure, Ondragon dared to leave the bathroom and take a look at the thing lying on his bed. Only the vaguely rectangular shape betrayed what was in the bag. He reached for his jacket and stuffed a stick of gum in his mouth. Maybe that would keep him from throwing up again. For a moment, he leaned against the wall to steady his breathing. After all, he had the darn book. Now all he had to do was get out of the lodge and over to Pete's house without being seen. For the last of many times, he made sure his gun was to hand in its holster and, teeth clenched, swiped the bag from the bed. A dangerous gagging sound set his empty stomach swinging again. Holding the bag between just two fingers, he left the room and a little later slipped out through the fire door into the night.

Bluish moonlight was slanting through the trees, and it had become refreshingly cool. Ondragon immediately felt goose bumps forming all over his body. He was still sweating like a pig. That fucking fever! The painkillers alone were obviously no longer helping. Tomorrow at the latest, he would need something stronger. Would he be able to get something from Sheila?

With the almost comforting thought of another duel with the Bengal Tiger at the reception desk, he crept along the narrow path past the stables to the Parkers' cabin.

When he arrived at the log cabin, everything was quiet. The dog was nowhere to be seen. Hopefully, the beast would stay quiet, otherwise he would turn on his heel, throw the book into the lake, and concern himself exclusively with his own problems!

But the mutt remained out of the way, and Ondragon crept toward the only window of the log cabin showing a light. Cautiously, he peered inside. He saw two beds. In one of them, Momo was sleeping peacefully under a thin sheet, and in the other, Pete was crouching stiffly, his face tense. The light from a kerosene lamp illuminated the scene like an old western movie in which two boys were waiting for their father to finally fall asleep so they could get the hell out of there. Ondragon thought he remembered not seeing any power lines running to the house on his first visit. Did the Parkers really still live here like they had a hundred years ago? Without electricity or running water? Unimaginable, but not a rare phenomenon, even in the United States. Many people were so poor that they couldn't even afford a decent roof over their heads.

Ondragon cautiously tapped a knuckle against the window. Pete jumped up as if stung by a tarantula and disappeared from the room. A little later the door to the log cabin opened.

"Psst, Mr. *On Draegen,* here I am. Come on in, but be quiet. Uncle Joel is sleeping."

Ondragon followed him into the house. Inside, he was hit by a beguiling mixture of smells, stale food and rancid smokehouse. In the faint glimmer of light from the boys' room he could make out the large stone fireplace at the far end, a table and chairs, and shelves of dishes on the walls. In the corner next to the fireplace was a crudely built, oblong wooden box in which Uncle Joel lay snoring, his mouth open. His old shotgun was right next to him, his floppy hat hanging on the barrel. This room obviously served as kitchen, living room, and sleeping quarters all in one, and judging by the log cabin's exterior, there couldn't be many other rooms in there.

On tiptoe, Ondragon followed Pete into the small room that barely fit the two beds. Above the sleeping quarters hung shelves filled to the ceiling with all sorts of objects retrieved from the forest: Elk antlers, a boar skull, some gnarled roots, an antediluvian spirit stove, and junk like a broken backpack and an old shoe.

Pete closed the door and whispered, "Uncle Joel wouldn't even hear if a bear farted next to him, but we should still be quiet."

Ondragon looked around the narrow room curiously.

"You can sit here, Mr. *On Draegen.*" The bellboy patted his bed.

Reluctantly, Ondragon settled on the tangle of matted blankets and immediately jumped up again when something grunted at him from the shapeless pile.

"What the hell is that?" he cried, startled.

"That's just Bugs. Our dog. Don't worry, he's harmless."

Harmless? He had looked quite different a few days ago! Back then, just a few inches had saved him from being mauled by Bugs.

He eyed the black ball of fur suspiciously as it lay peacefully snuggled in the blankets, blinking lazily at him. Bugs seemed to be quite relaxed.

"Buuuugs sleeps here with us. He's reeeeeally sweeeet!" Momo had rolled over on his bed and was rubbing his little black eyes.

Ondragon sat on the edge of the bed at a safe distance from the dog and surveyed Momo at close quarters for the first time. Subconsciously, the *centrifuge* lined up everything he knew about the boy. He literally looked like a mooncalf: faithful donut face, balloon-shaped head, round, almost feminine shoulders, chubby arms and legs, and bulbous feet. If he had worn glasses, he would have resembled a Gary Larson kid.

Momo's hair was actually silver-gray—so unusual for a twenty-three-year-old—but Ondragon had heard that a traumatic experience could suddenly cause a person's hair to turn gray.

Momo smiled at him, exposing yellow teeth that were already extremely ground down. He probably suffered from lockjaw at night and ground the stumps of his teeth with uncanny force, which was probably also a consequence of the trauma he suffered in his childhood. Meanwhile, he registered that Momo's right shoulder was intact. So it had not been him who had attacked him yesterday and taken Kateri's arrow.

"Listen, Pete. I know we shot the Wendigo. Your brother here doesn't have an injury though. So I think we can save ourselves the . . . book. Momo can't be the Wendigo." Hoping to get out of there quickly, he got to his feet.

"Do you have the book, then?" asked the bellboy.

Ondragon slid the bag across the bed, and Pete rubbed his hands together.

"Man, that's top class, Mr. *On Draegen*! We might as well get started." He reached for the plastic and began to unpack the book.

Ondragon put a hand on his arm. "Wait just a moment. First, please tell me everything about the murder of your parents, okay?"

Pete looked at him for a moment, his gaze flickering. Whether from excitement or fear, Ondragon couldn't tell.

"But, Mr. *On Draegen,* I told you it was Momo."

Ondragon looked from Pete to his brother, who looked somber. "That's my condition, Pete! I want to know everything first. Even why you think he's the Wendigo. You scratch my back and I'll scratch yours. Then I'll help you, I promise."

Pete clenched his jaws together. He didn't seem to realize this was a give-and-take. And now it was his turn.

"Okay," he finally said, "I'll tell you. But please don't tell the police, okay? After all, we lied to them back then, including the FBI. And that's not good. If this gets out, I'll be in trouble. But this book tells us how to cure Momo. That's the only thing I want. I want to save Momo."

As if a murderer could be cured, Ondragon thought. The deed had been done, both parents were dead and Momo would have to take responsibility for it, in whatever form. He would probably end up in a psychiatric ward, where he would spend the rest of his already sad existence. But for now, he wanted Pete to believe he could help his brother. Ondragon gestured to him to finally get started.

Pete leaned back against the wall with his legs crossed and cuddled the dog's chunky head, lost in thought. When he finally began to talk, the room became imperceptibly warmer, and soon Ondragon had the feeling he was trapped in another horrible nightmare.

Only this time he was absolutely sure he *wasn't* asleep.

CHAPTER 44

2009, Moose Lake,
the Parkers' cabin

Sweating, he felt the fever slowly reaching boiling point. It pulsed through his veins and throbbed against his eardrums. A glowing swarm of sparks tingled under his skin, and his head had turned into a soccer ball filled with nails and shards of glass.

Ondragon desperately needed stronger medicine. But he couldn't go back to the lodge now. The story Pete had just told him was too cruel and too fascinating.

The family tragedy began with the events of summer 1997. Three weeks before Herman and Louisa Parker were killed, Mortimer, then nine years old, had suddenly disappeared. Pete and his parents had searched for his little brother everywhere within a radius of several miles. They were desperate, but they did not go to the police. Not even after three days, because they thought they knew their way around the forest much better than the cops anyway and preferred to search themselves, scouring every bush, cave, and pond, but to no avail.

On the evening of the fourth day, Momo reappeared quite unexpectedly. Confused and covered in dirt from head to toe, he stood at the door of the log cabin. His hair had turned gray and his mind had run wild. Saliva was dripping from his mouth and he groaned as if his tongue were paralyzed. He had a deep bite wound on his left leg, which his parents immediately treated. Again and again they shook him and asked where he had been. But what the boy finally told them in a sluggish voice was a completely implausible story. He insisted with almost eerie seriousness that he had been playing in the forest behind the house, and then suddenly an animal had appeared between the trees. A very large animal on long legs. It had spoken to him and claimed that it was the Wendigo. And it had come to get him.

"At first, my brother didn't want to go because he was scared," Pete told me, glancing at Momo. The younger nodded unhappily. "But then the Wendigo just bit him and dragged him off. He wanted Momo to be his child and keep him company because he was so lonely out there in the woods. After that, they roamed the neighborhood together, hunting for something to eat, because the forest monster was always hungry. Momo says he only obeyed him because he was so terrified."

Again, the balloon head nodded. "We ate deer and aaand other animals, raw! Blaaa. That was eeeeky. The Wendigo killed all the looovely animals, and I was supposed to eat them. At first, I didn't want to." Momo stuck his tongue out in disgust. "But then I was suddenly soooo terribly huuungry."

"What he says is true; his clothes were covered in bloodstains when he got home," Pete explained.

"But then I took off." Momo grinned.

"And how did you manage to do that?" asked Ondragon.

"Don't know."

"You just ran away, and the Wendigo didn't chase you?"

"I don't know." Momo looked to Pete for help.

"He can't remember," he said, apologizing for his brother.

"But he still talks to me." Momo raised his head proudly, as if he had said something very important.

"Who, Pete?"

Both brothers shook their heads.

"No . . . *him*!" Momo nodded meaningfully toward the window. "The Wendigo! He's in my ear. Keeeps talking, I'm his kid and he wants me to do something for him."

"What?" inquired Ondragon, but Pete beat Momo to it.

"He's asking him to do bad things. Really bad things." Pete took a deep breath, as if he was bracing himself against something. "But

Momo didn't want to do what the Wendigo told him to do. He fought back, but the Wendigo punished him with a disease. A nasty fever with delusions and terrible cramps. Momo was sweating so much that his sheets were soaking wet, and he scratched himself incessantly because he was so unbearably hot. I was constantly trying to keep him from digging his fingernails into his own flesh. Our parents couldn't get a doctor, we had no money. Then one day I came home from school . . . I opened the door to our house and inside"— Pete swallowed—"inside were Mom and Dad. They were in pieces and Momo was sitting there with his face covered in blood. He was holding Mom's arm in his hands. Mr. *On Draegen*, what I'm telling you, the police don't know it and neither does the FBI!"

Ondragon made a simple gesture to signal that Pete could trust him, whereupon the man struggled visibly to keep his composure. His face was crisscrossed by deep wrinkles, and he looked at least as old as his Uncle Joel. The words he then spoke did not seem to come out of his mouth, they sounded so serious and sad. "Momo was holding Mom's arm in his hands. But it wasn't because he was crying for her. His eyes were red and he seemed completely out of it . . . and he was making grunting sounds like . . . like a wild boar eating." Pete wiped his nose. "The arm had been torn out of the socket, and Momo was . . . licking the blood off." Now the tears began to flow down his cheeks, hot and infinitely tormented—perhaps due to the fact that he had finally broken his silence, but perhaps also because of the barbarism he'd witnessed. Pete's voice dropped to a whisper as he told of the gruesome sight.

"I tried to stop Momo, but I couldn't. He was so . . . so repulsive!" Now he was sobbing hard. "The Wendigo destroyed our family. He put a curse on Momo and he won't leave us in peace. If you don't help us, we'll never get rid of him, Mr. *On Draegen*. Please. Momo is the only one I have left. He's still my little brother, after all. And big brothers look out for their little brothers, isn't that right? Unfortunately, I didn't look after him well enough. Momo can't help it. It was the Wendigo who told him to do those bad things, and he's still out there calling for him. He wants to take Momo to him."

"And the FBI believed your lies?" asked Ondragon. He felt uncomfortable and glanced at Momo, who looked innocent. How had these two hillbillies managed to fool an experienced psychologist? Perhaps because they had been children at the time, and one of them a bit slow at that. But Ondragon had no intention of covering up Momo's murder. Who knew what was going on in his screwed-up brain? Maybe tomorrow he would kill his brother!

"The FBI would never have believed the truth, which may be why our lie worked so well. But you, Mr. *On Draegen,* you believe us, don't you? You know the truth, and now you know Momo can't help it."

Ondragon ran a hand through his hair. He was tired, and the fever was raging inside him like an out-of-control forest fire. It was a wonder he wasn't breathing out smoke. And to make matters worse, his stomach was growling. He could really go for a nice steak.

"You know, Mr. *On Draegen,* you're the first person I've told since this happened. We need your help."

Did they really? Actually, the case was clear. Mortimer Parker had, for whatever reason, blown his fuses and massacred his parents. And Pete refused to believe it. Basically, Momo was a ticking time bomb, and possibly only Dr. Arthur's efforts with the boy had kept him from committing another murder. Suddenly, Ondragon was as clear as day about the therapist's interest in Momo. The boy was a perfect research subject. Cannibalism in children! What kind of monstrous mess was Dr. Arthur actually running here? It was high time he put a stop to this bastard.

"He speaks to y-you tooo. Am I riiight?"

Ondragon looked at Momo. "What do you mean?"

"The Wendigooooo! I see it. He touched you too. Theeeere!" He pointed at the wound on Ondragon's forehead.

Surprised, he raised his hand and felt the throbbing swelling. Could it really be that the Wendigo had knocked him out?

"Are you hungry?" Momo wanted to know. "I'm always hungry. And I'm hot too, but I've gotten used to that. Don't need a blanket at night anymore, and I can play longer in the snow, even though my feet often hurt."

That was enough! Such nonsense. Mindless chatter from the mouth of a troll child.

"I'm leaving now, Pete," Ondragon said. "I can't help your brother. I'm sorry." He tried to rise, but Pete abruptly grabbed his upper arm and held him back.

"Please, Mr. *On Draegen*. You promised. I told you everything about our family, and now you'll help us. Please, read the book. That was the deal!"

Ondragon felt anger welling up inside him. Whyever had he promised this? His patience with this humbug was at an end. He desperately needed pills for his fever and a bed, nothing else. The last thing he needed now was to read a crappy old . . . book.

Meanwhile, Pete was crying his eyes out, a wretched figure. He begged and pleaded. Ondragon felt cornered by his desperation. And he hated being cornered.

"You promised!"

Yes, he had. Dammit!

Another dizzy spell overcame him, and his protective shield of self-preservation instincts and close combat training finally failed. He struggled with all his might to think clearly and squinted into the dim light of the room. He felt like he was on a bad ghost train. The room swayed and the creepy figures weren't particularly convincing either. But the crushing sandbag of sensations was there, making it hard for him to breathe. Ondragon fought it, but in vain. He had to face it. He had lost. Lost to a howling hillbilly. A truly memorable moment in the life of Paul Eckbert Ondragon; he should mark it in red on his calendar.

As if remote-controlled, he reached for the wrapped book, removed the bag, and finally held it in his hand as if it were perfectly normal. Ondragon wondered at himself. He felt no disgust, only a dull throbbing that filled his entire body. It was hard to compare an official hash rush with this strange floating state. Almost reverently, his fingers ran over the worn leather cover as if his hands no longer belonged to his body, then flipped open the cover in one fluid motion. The crackling sound of the pages promised both horror and salvation.

Automatically, because his muscle memory apparently still knew how to open a book, his index finger slid across the fold in the middle, smoothing the first page. It was as if he could feel all the microscopic irregularities of the paper under his fingertips, where the capillaries pulsed softly. His pupils constricted as he read the thin, squiggly lines of the author's handwriting:

1835
Notes
by
Lieutenant Dorian Edward Stafford
21st Infantry Regiment
His Majesty King William IV's Army
stationed at Fort Frances on Rainy River, Canada

At least it was in English. Ondragon turned the page and found dense writing . At the uppermost point a date and a place had been entered: *20.3.1835—Lake Kabetogama*. It seemed to be a kind of diary that recorded observations chronologically. On some pages there were even small drawings. The author's meticulous approach almost reminded Ondragon of his own secret record keeping. So it was not difficult for him to quickly immerse himself in the material. Soon he was so captivated by the book's contents that he forgot to read it to Pete and Momo. It wasn't until Pete cleared his throat that he slowly looked up from the pages and slipped imperceptibly from one world to the other. Fascinated, he remembered what it had felt like to read books as a child. As if he were a traveler who could move quite effortlessly between worlds and times. He had completely forgotten that reading a book could have such a magical effect on a person.

"Mr. *On Draegen*, now tell me, what does it say?" Pete's voice vibrated excitedly.

"It is the description of a crime. More precisely, the chronology of several terrible murders committed in this area in 1835. And . . ." Ondragon hesitated. He had not yet fully digested what was in this book, but it was remarkable, if not sensational. The things that this Lieutenant Stafford described bore an almost uncanny resemblance to what had happened here at the lodge. And if the book had not undoubtedly been old, he would have believed he was looking at a forgery. The sensational thing about the whole story was that the massacre of the Walcott family on March 20, 1835, followed the same pattern as the murders of Herman and Louisa Parker in 1997. Both families had been slaughtered in their lonely cabins, and someone had eaten their flesh. And in both cases, the Wendigo was blamed. The only problem was that Momo Parker, who Pete said was the murderer of his parents, had not existed at the time of the Walcotts. No human could have lived that long. So who had killed the Walcotts? Except for the similarity of the crime scenes, there was no other connection between the murders. Or was there?

Ondragon let the *centrifuge* spin. Hadn't he read the name Parker somewhere in the book? He flipped back to the page where Lieutenant Stafford described who had found the family's bodies: trappers Vincent Lacroix, Two-Elk, and Alan Parker. Was this a relative of Pete and Momo? An old ancestor who, like Momo, had been bitten and infected by the Wendigo? If so, then only one question remained: Could there be some kind of madness that was passed down in this family?

Ondragon looked at Momo. The only one who could tell him anything about psychic defects was Dr. Arthur, and he couldn't possibly ask him. So all that was left to get him to solve this riddle— a *Magnum*-level puzzle, that was clear—were his own powers of deduction.

Suddenly, Ondragon felt fresh energy rush through his overheated veins. With burning interest, he turned his attention back to the lieutenant's meticulous handwriting and continued reading at the point where Stafford described another crime scene: the bestial murder of one of his soldiers during the trip to Fort Frances.

CHAPTER 45

2009, Moose Lake,
the Parkers' cabin

Ondragon's stomach was growling again, loudly enough for Pete to notice.

"I'll get you something to eat." He jumped up and disappeared through the door to the dark living room/kitchen/bedroom. There was a rustle and a clink, and then he returned. In his hand was a plate holding slices of white bread and a greasy jar of peanut butter. He handed both to Ondragon, who quickly gobbled down two dry slices of bread. That would have to do.

Before turning back to the book, he glanced at the man and his brother. Their pale faces looked very tired, but their eyes were shining with alert attention. Ondragon knew this kind of condition: dead tired, but still pumped full of adrenaline. He had felt the same way for over forty-eight hours—a mixture that would eventually lead to total breakdown.

But by now he also thought he was very close to solving the mystery. Lieutenant Stafford, like himself, had been a rational thinker. The Englishman, who might have been dead for more than 150 years by now, had only believed those things he had seen with his own eyes. And it seemed that in the end he had found a plausible explanation for all these strange events: the "Wendigo psychosis."

That was the cue. Ondragon pulled out his smartphone.

"You have a cell phone?" asked Pete.

"Yes, but it's a secret!" Ondragon searched for the term on the internet. Fortunately, there was good reception even in this remote wasteland. So the media offshoots of civilization had long since conquered even this lonely patch of earth. *God bless America! God save the mobile phone!*

Unfortunately, there was not much about Wendigo psychosis on the web, but what he did find was enough to give him a concrete picture of the disease. The Wendigo psychosis was not hereditary, that much was clear, but it predominantly affected people who lived in the wilderness and were exposed to deprivation and hunger. The loneliness affected their minds and the hunger brought them to the brink of madness, which eventually led to the affected person going crazy. For example, in the winter of 1878, a Cree trapper named Swift Runner had killed and eaten his wife and five children. In another case from 1907, Oji Creek Anishinabe man Jack Fiddler had been arrested for multiple murders. He had been known as a Wendigo hunter and by his own account had killed fourteen of the creatures. The last, he said, was a Cree woman who was on the verge of finally turning into a Wendigo and had killed and eaten her children. And these were only two of the fifty or so historically documented cases in North America in which men and women had slaughtered their families under the influence of Wendigo psychosis. This rare mental illness got its name from the legendary Native American creature feared by the tribes in the area because of its insatiable hunger for human flesh. In all these descriptions, however, Ondragon found another, much simpler name for the phenomenon, in which people who were confined with each other for too long in a small cabin would go berserk without warning: *cabin fever.*

For Ondragon, everything was clear: Momo Parker had succumbed to the Wendigo psychosis. He had developed cabin fever and killed his parents. No one would be able to absolve him of the crime. And even if he seemed peaceful now, the madness could break out again at any time. The boy had to go to a closed institution; as sorry as he was for Pete, it was the only sensible course of action.

Ondragon flipped the book closed. They had reached the end; at least, after the richly disturbing and—for Lieutenant Stafford, astonishingly irrational—description of the expulsion of the Wendigo spirit from the body of trapper Alan Parker, only blank pages followed. However, someone had written a French poem on the last page in a completely different handwriting:

De la glace
De la neige
La forêt
Sois sur tes gardes,
lorsqu'elle arrive.
La peur dévore ton coeur
Tu sens ton corps refroidi.
Il est insatiable, l'esprit de la forêt isolée.
Insatiable comme la peur. Le Wendigo
Affamé,
glacé.
Le Mal éternel.

Really strange, Ondragon thought, and yawned. He turned to the two boys. "I have to get back to the lodge now. It's getting light out." He looked out the window, where the first silhouettes of trees were peeling out of the impenetrable black of night. "I've got to hurry before anyone else notices I've been gone."

"But we haven't cured Momo yet. The book tells us how to do it. We just need the ingredients."

Ondragon put a hand on Pete's bony shoulder. "I'm afraid we won't be able to cure your brother. Especially not with the completely crazy ritual that Stafford describes in the book. It's life-threatening and can't work at all. It is pure superstition, nothing more. People believed in such nonsense in those days."

"But what if it did work? Isn't that what Stafford writes? This Alan Parker was cured!"

Ondragon sighed. How could he make the boy understand that what was considered a reasonable treatment in 1835 was not considered so in 2009? He looked into the man's reddened eyes. "I told you about Wendigo psychosis. Your brother is sick in the mind, and that can't be cured, at least *I* can't cure it. Only an experienced therapist might be able to do something about it."

"But Momo went to Dr. Arthur, and he's a good doctor. If he couldn't help Momo, then other doctors can't either." The bellboy folded his arms defiantly across his chest.

"How can I explain it to you, Pete? Dr. Arthur was just using your brother to gain knowledge for his research."

"What kind of research?"

Ondragon thought about whether he should tell the boy and then decided to do so. What could he lose now?

"Listen, Pete, Dr. Arthur is not the nice uncle you think he is. He's here secretly researching cannibals and covering up their crimes. Your brother is also a cannibal, so to speak, and the doc is burning with interest. Curing Momo, however, is rather beside the point for Dr. Arthur, I'm afraid."

A single tear stole from Pete's silver eyes and ran down his cheek. "But why?" he stammered. "Why won't Dr. Arthur cure him?" Obviously, he didn't seem to grasp the ambition that drove the famous psychotherapist.

"I'm going now, Pete. Try to get some sleep, will you? I'll see you tomorrow." Ondragon stood up and shook out his legs, which were tingling from sitting so long. The droning headache had also reappeared, as if it had just taken a break only to hammer all the harder on some gigantic anvil in some dark basement.

As Ondragon reached for the door handle, he heard Pete behind him say in a somber voice, "If you won't help me, I'll do it myself! I'll figure it out."

Ondragon turned and took a few quick steps toward the man. "Don't! You hear me? What's in that book is bullshit! It's dangerous—it could get your brother killed! And you don't want that, do you?"

"I want to cure him!" Pete avoided his gaze and defiantly folded his arms over his chest.

Ondragon sighed. He felt like he was talking to an unreasonable child. "Pete! I implore you. Don't do it! I'll take care of Momo after I've spoken to Dr. Arthur. Promise me you won't do anything before then."

"Hmm," grumbled the man. It didn't sound much like agreement.

"Come on, give me a punch." Ondragon held out a hand, but only after further encouragement did Pete follow his prompting and box listlessly against his palm.

"That's it. When it's all over, I'll take you both for a ride in my Mustang. We'll go for a little joyride, all right?" Of course, the two of them had no idea that this would most likely be a trip to the Nett Lake police station. And at least Momo responded with "Awesome."

Ondragon wrapped the book up in the bag again, stuffed it under his jacket, and left the cabin. He could only hope that Pete would keep his end of the bargain. At the very least, the little weirdo would have a hard time getting the ingredients for the ritual. And as long as he didn't have them, he couldn't get into any mischief.

A little later, Ondragon was lying in his bed. The dawn light was seeping through the curtains and despite the painkillers he had been given by the night duty nurse, he could hear it whispering menacingly inside his glowing body.

Wendigo! Hunger! Curse!

As if on cue, his stomach growled. Ondragon closed his burning eyes to suppress the rising hunger. He swallowed noisily.

Had the beast infected him? Like this Alan Parker? Would he now also mutate into a mindless eating machine? And how old could a Wendigo actually become?

The *centrifuge*, paralyzed by pills and fever, twitched briefly in its drugged sleep. *What nonsense,* it said ponderously. *Momo is a mentally handicapped boy and he simply made up this horror story. He was playing in the woods back then and lost track of time. Maybe he did something stupid and wanted to avoid punishment by his parents. That's all.*

Ondragon heard his cell phone beep. Surely, at last, this was a message from Charlize. But even as he tried to reach for the device, Morpheus overpowered him with an expertly applied stranglehold and pulled him down into the world of nightmares.

CHAPTER 46

2009, Moose Lake,
Cedar Creek Lodge

When Ondragon looked in the mirror the next morning—or rather at noon, for he had slept late—he groaned in horror. The furrows in the topography of his face had deepened even more, and an unhealthy pallor had settled over his California complexion. Veins had burst in both eyes, turning the whites red. He looked like a zombie! And he was as hungry as one too.

He looked at the red-rimmed wound on his forehead. It was no longer throbbing quite as badly, and the headache had also dissipated, but his feet hurt like he had run the Minnesota Ironman. Yesterday's forced march was likely still in his limbs. Unfortunately, he still seemed to have the fever. At least, the heat was still coming out of all his pores.

The curse of the Wendigo, his subconscious murmured almost maliciously. But Ondragon forced the thought aside. There was no such thing as the Wendigo and that was that!

Since today was his big day, he first took an extensive shower and then shaved properly. Even if the stay here had brought him to the edge of his self-control, he was still a man of style and good manners. And one always faced one's adversary with elegant superiority; anything else would have been in bad taste.

After he had changed into his good gray suit, his pistol of course hidden in its holster under his jacket, he felt much better. The only thing he could do nothing about was the red eyes. They were what they were. His eyes fell on the plastic bag with the book, lying on the chair by the window. Should he give it back to Dr. Arthur? But the mere thought of having to touch it again brought back the old revulsion. He would just leave it here. When he was finished with Dr. Arthur, the book wouldn't matter anymore anyway.

Ondragon picked up his iPhone and looked at the inbox. Sure enough, there was a message from Charlize. He opened it.

When he read it, he dialed her number.

"*Ohayô gozaimasu,* Chief. How are you?"

"Been better, Charlize."

"Sorry it took so long, but it wasn't down to me. The people of Orr are not exactly what you might call open-minded. Damned cranks! I didn't want to write what I found out in an email. It would have been half a novel. Besides, I figured you'd probably like to hear it in person."

"You thought right." Ondragon massaged the root of his nose. "Let's do it, then."

"Well, I tracked down Bates's landlady, Mrs. Perkins, and showed her the photograph of him. I managed to get her to tell me—after lots of to-ing and fro-ing—that the man had been posing as John McLane and had been employed at Cedar Creek Lodge, so he hadn't been allowed to talk about his work, because the lodge had strict rules about that."

"John McLane? And that didn't strike her as kind of odd?"

"Nope. What do you expect from these hillbillies? Anyway, Mrs. Perkins said McLane, alias Bates, had been quiet and unobtrusive. He lived with her for three months and then disappeared overnight."

"When was that?"

"Sometime in March of this year; hold on."

Ondragon heard his assistant flipping through her notebook.

"Okaaay, there you go. On 3/15/2009, a man suddenly showed up at Mrs. Perkins's front door and told her that her tenant had been fired from CC Lodge and was not coming back."

"What did the man look like?"

"Blond, medium height, nothing else that stands out."

"Orchid?"

"Could be," Charlize said. "The man also asked about the stuff McLane aka Bates left in the apartment, but Mrs. Perkins is solid gold, she didn't let anything go. Still has everything in a box in her attic."

"Let me guess—she wouldn't show you the stuff either?"

"*Hai*. But she's a very deep sleeper."

Ondragon had to grin. "You got in?"

"Quietly. Wasn't hard either. The country bumpkins around here don't even lock their doors at night." Now Charlize was laughing on the other end of the phone. Ondragon loved that laugh. And it made him realize how much he missed his job and his office in LA.

"I looked at the stuff in the box. At first, I couldn't see anything special, just clothes and toiletries and stuff. But there were also a dozen shoe boxes with those rocker shoes in them, you know, the ones with the weird rounded sole."

This word rang a bell in Ondragon's head. The blurred image of a worn shoe floated into his mind's eye.

"I rummaged through everything," Charlize continued, "including the boxes, and in one of them I found what I was looking for. Hidden under the insole of one of the shoes was a small USB flash drive. I took it and read it out on my notebook. And guess what I found out?"

"That Bates wasn't a physical therapist?"

"That's right. He was a private investigator, employed by a small detective agency in St. Louis, and his real name was Simon Ricks. But he was probably working on his own account. That is, he was on the trail of the scandal all by himself. He didn't tell anyone about it, not even his boss. Now wait for it! The scandal stretches from London to Rochester, Minnesota, to here in Orr, or rather, to Cedar Creek Lodge. Ricks put a lot of effort into this; his investigation dates back to 2007, which is probably when he started his hunt, even went to England to do research. If the information is true, it's worth a lot of money, assuming Ricks intended to use it to blackmail the person he was targeting."

"Dr. Jonathan Aaron Arthur."

"Right again! You're in pretty good shape, Chief. In any case, it's clear Ricks was digging around in a lot of dirty laundry, and it wouldn't be surprising if that's why someone had got him out of the way. At least that would explain why he disappeared. I spoke with his boss in St. Louis, you see. He told me Ricks had been moonlighting for some time, and that they had been on the verge of kicking him out. But then Ricks himself faxed in his resignation. He didn't even collect his stuff from the office. That was late last year."

"That was probably when he realized he had hit the jackpot."

"Looks like it."

"I'm going to confront Dr. Arthur today. Then it'll all be over with his little research farm here."

"Research farm?"

"Yes, he keeps a few cannibals here and observes their behavior in the wild, so to speak. That is, he happily lets them indulge their cravings without doing anything about it. This is exactly what Bates, aka Ricks, must have found out when he was working undercover here. Dr. Arthur keeps the cannibals as if it's a zoo and covers up their crimes. Just the day before yesterday—"

"Chief, it'd be better for you not to get too close to Dr. Arthur. Better hold fire and come to Orr. We can just as well stop that son of a bitch from here. With the evidence from the flash drive, we'll have him by the balls."

"Oh, Charlize, I can handle the doc, don't worry."

"Chief, please. This guy is even crazier than you!"

"Come on. Just tell me that Ricks's flash drive is safe."

"*Hai*, of course."

"Well, I have to call it a day now. The finale awaits."

"But, Chief . . ."

Ondragon hung up. He had no desire to be lectured by Charlize. He could handle Dr. Arthur. It would be a duel of equals, gentleman to gentleman. Clear rules, clear weapons. But first a good breakfast and then a final talk with Kateri.

As Ondragon was about to leave the room, his cell phone rang. It was Charlize again. She really did worry too much sometimes. He quickly turned off the phone and put it away. He closed the door behind him, separated his talisman from the key, and slid both into the pocket of his pants.

In the hallway outside the restaurant, he bumped into Shamgood and Norrfoss. Of all people! The two poisonous blond terriers blocked his path, smiling at him hypocritically. They looked as if they were joined at the hip like Siamese twins.

"Good afternoon, Mr. Ondragon. It's been a long time. Oh dear, you look like a rabbit after a forest fire! Had a bad night, did you? Or should I say a bad day? Wasn't exactly your best showing yesterday, was it? I heard the deputy giving you a very foul-mouthed talking to. After all, it's not nice to have to run around the woods for hours on end, all for nothing." Shamgood turned to his younger replica. "I think dear Mr. Ondragon is more wrong in the head than we had supposed. Already seeing ghosts where there aren't any."

Anger set Ondragon's insides vibrating. It was like a pendulum of death, beating faster and faster, and once it reached the right speed, it would fairly knock those two monkeys off their feet. Speaking of feet—or more accurately, shoes—he actually had much more important things to do than bother with these puffed-up goons. Ondragon circumnavigated the two of them without a word and left them standing there.

"Mr. Lyme has gone, by the way. No—not in the way you think. He hasn't gone up to the kingdom of heaven, he's home in New York. Just in case you're interested, he wrote an email to Dr. Arthur explaining why he was discontinuing his therapy. Poor guy was homesick for his big, safe city. Pah, he's just as much of an urban neurotic as you!"

Ondragon didn't know why he did it; it ran completely counter to his own commandment to always keep calm. He saw his fist rise and float in slow motion toward the grinning facelifted visage of the Dolph Lundgren lookalike. Then he heard a scream and the sound of a nose breaking. Blood shot from Blondie's face and he doubled over.

"You'll pay for this!" screeched Shamgood, trying to stop the bleeding with a lace handkerchief he had quickly pulled out.

"No problem," Ondragon said coolly. "Here." He flicked one of his business cards at the hyperventilating fashion designer. "You'll find the number of my attorney there; please file your personal injury lawsuit with him. And do me a favor, please get a new nose, the old one was ugly!"

Shamgood stared at him. "I'm going to tell Dr. Arthur about this incident. He'll kick you out today!"

"Save yourself the trouble, Shamgood, I'm as good as gone anyway. *Au revoir*, or perhaps not." With these words, Ondragon left the two stunned peroxided fascists standing and went into the dining room, looking for the face that now interested him the most. But Kateri was nowhere to be seen. Was she still hiding from him?

He sat down at his table and let Carlos serve him his final meal in this place. As he ate his porridge, he tried to forget the unpleasant episode with Shamgood and enjoy the moment, the wonderfully enlightening moment, just before the resolution of a mystery. Despite his indisposition due to the fever, and despite the small fortune he had thrown away on the therapy here, he was extremely satisfied. Full of anticipation, he sipped his triple espresso and looked out the window. Sunlight shimmered on the lake, and a flock of waterfowl bobbed on the glistening surface. It was the calm before the storm. Ondragon felt electrified; like a racehorse sensing the starting gun. An expectant trembling took possession of his limbs. Then he put down the empty cup. The time had come!

CHAPTER 47

2009, Moose Lake,
Cedar Creek Lodge

Ondragon found Kateri only after another bitter battle with Sheila. Firstly, over his car keys and secondly, over the whereabouts of Miss Wolfe.

And again, the winner is . . . Misteeeerrrrr Oooondragooon!

When he entered the stables, Kateri was saddling a horse to ride out.

"Howdy, Kateri!" he greeted her nonchalantly, looking around for Julian. But the riding instructor was nowhere to be seen. Surprised, Kateri turned around.

"Well, your friend Sheila just couldn't resist my charms."

"I don't care. Step aside."

"Ah, we're back to the formalities!"

Energetically, Kateri tightened the girth. The horse resisted, but then exhaled and let Kateri have her way. Then she reached for the bridle. Unbelievable. She was ignoring him!

"What's wrong with you?" Ondragon had written Kateri off long ago, but he wouldn't leave here until he had cracked this riddle too. He grabbed her by the shoulders and forced her to look at him. "Why did you sneak out of the lodge the other night? The very night someone threw the dog's head onto my balcony. It's no use denying it, I saw you drive off in your car. What were you doing? Were you seeing someone? Were you with Sheila? I think I know the reason you won't talk to me anymore: Your lesbian girlfriend is jealous!"

That hit the mark, because Kateri broke away and barked at him, "The thing with Sheila is none of your business!"

Ondragon raised both hands. "Whoa, easy there."

This infuriated Kateri even more; she took a step toward him, raising a hand.

"Go ahead. Let it out." Ondragon grinned. He had to admit it, he enjoyed provoking Kateri. After all, she had allowed him to get to know her hot-blooded character in a particularly exquisite way. A pity, actually. Her body had been stunning. Ondragon saw the slap coming and fended it off effortlessly. He grabbed Kateri's wrist and pulled her toward him with a jerk so that the tips of their noses were almost touching. He felt her excited breathing on his cheek and almost kissed her, but his close-combat instincts warned him against such an irrational counterattack.

"See this?" He raised his other hand, in which his car keys dangled. "In less than two hours I'll be out of here, and then you'll be rid of me forever. But before that, let me tell you about your fine friend, Dr. Arthur. It'll give you the opportunity to distance yourself from him in time. Once I'm done with him, it could be difficult for you too."

She remained silent. Only her eyes shone, full of hatred—the enmity between Indians and whites 2.0.

"Because Dr. Arthur's got a lot of skeletons in his closet," Ondragon continued. "He treats psychopaths illegally and covers up their crimes. Some of them are murderers. You know what I mean? Dr. Arthur may think he's abiding by the Hippocratic Oath when he cures the most extremely mentally ill, but the truth is he's a perverted voyeur who gets off on the heinous acts of violence committed by his patients. And then he calls it *research*. Outwardly, he plays the kind father who cares for his children, but in his soul he is a Satan in white. Think about it, Kateri. Why do people keep disappearing here?"

"I don't care! I know who Jonathan is and what he does. Unlike you."

"Oh, I know very well what a clean-living gentleman your Dr. Arthur is, Kateri. This is about cannibalism, eating human flesh. Dr.

Arthur runs a cannibal farm. A monstrous masquerade in the guise of science."

Ondragon saw something change in Kateri's gaze, a deep crack appearing in her carefully maintained protective shield. And all at once he knew.

She was one of them!

He had to swallow, because he had simply not wanted to admit it. And yet it was so obvious.

"Well?" Kateri looked at him with her chin raised. "You didn't mind screwing with a cannibal either, did you? Isn't that perverted too? Are you really asking me to believe you didn't know? You're nothing more than a fetishist looking for kinky adventures."

There was something in that. Somehow.

"Sex with a cannibal—how high does that rank on your list, huh?" She hissed like a belligerent alligator.

"Now listen, you weren't exactly averse to doing me either! I guess Sheila doesn't bring it like a real guy, huh?"

The next slap caught him, but it only made him more reckless. He grabbed Kateri's hair roughly and bent her head back. She groaned, and Ondragon bared his teeth in arousal. Kateri's neck, so vulnerably exposed, had an exceedingly erotic effect on him, and it would have been easy to take her, right there on the stable floor. Then she would have gotten to know his dark side. But Ondragon controlled himself. Julian could show up at any time. He let go.

"You ate your parents, right? Back then, after the plane crash in the tundra," he said.

Kateri rubbed her scalp, then nodded. Nothing more. Ondragon guessed why. What else could she say? That she was sorry? That she would never do it again? If she hadn't, she would have died like her parents. Should she be condemned for that? For a situation in which anyone would have been faced with the same decision. To live or to die? To eat or be eaten? In such an extreme emergency, ethics and morals were empty words, arbitrary terms that civilization had thought up and filled with meaning, but which nature, wild and merciless, did not know. Nature knew no words; it knew only the raw act of survival.

Ondragon realized that he might not have acted any differently. He could not condemn Kateri. It had been an accident, a tragic chain of events. It was her fate. And he truly did not envy her that. Nevertheless, she had to realize that Dr. Arthur was a criminal. A self-important healer who had overstepped the boundaries of society. A wolf in doctor's clothing. And he had to be stopped.

"Kateri, I still . . . like you. And I wish we had met under different circumstances. But you have to face the truth. You can't stay with Dr. Arthur. I can take you with me to Orr later, if you like; I'm going to inform the police and the FBI. You can still pack your things and leave this place unharmed. You don't have to tell the police that you knew about the machinations of your mentor. You were his patient and you were dependent on him, under his influence."

She didn't nod, but she didn't say no either. Silently, she looked over his shoulder into the void.

"Kateri?"

Her pupils contracted as she returned her gaze to his face. The fire in it had gone out. Replaced by dull resignation. "I'll think about it," she whispered, resting her head against the horse's neck as if it were her only true friend.

"Is everything all right?" Julian had come around the corner and stood up in front of Ondragon. "Did he do something to you, Kateri? If so, I'll smash his face in, the lunatic!"

That little whippersnapper, Ondragon thought, raising a placatory hand. "Nothing happened, tiger. Simmer down." He turned to Kateri. "You know where to find me." He then left the stall, hearing Julian ask behind him, "You got something going on with that one?"

Grimly determined to initiate the finale, Ondragon walked back to the lodge. As he did so, he noticed Pete, who was just turning onto the path to his uncle's cabin. The man was moving even more awkwardly than usual, as if he didn't want to attract attention. He was carrying something on his arm, wrapped in a dishtowel. Ondragon was hard on his heels. It suddenly dawned on him what the boy was up to. He stopped him halfway.

"Pete!"

The man wheeled around and dropped the bundle in shock. Two dozen white candles rolled out of the tea towel.

"What do you want with that? We have an agreement, don't we?"

The bellboy looked sheepishly at the candles in the grass.

"Man, Pete! Don't do anything stupid. I'll take the candles back to the lodge now and tell Carlos to take care of them so you don't steal them again. We'll help your brother later. I promise."

"But you're leaving today, Mr. *On Draegen.*"

"Who told you that?"

"Sheila. She said you picked up your car keys."

Sheila's Silent Post! Gradually, the lady truly was becoming his nemesis. "I'm going to Orr later, Pete, I'm meeting someone from my office there; it's an urgent matter. But I'll be back later."

Pete nodded. Hopefully, the boy had bought the white lie.

"That reminds me, where did that shoe come from, on the shelf in your room?"

"Momo found it in the forest. The hikers sometimes throw things away. He collects them. He's always very proud when he finds something."

"Can you maybe let me borrow that shoe? It might help clear your brother about the body in the woods."

It was better if Pete had something to do for now; then he wouldn't get any ideas. And errands were a good distraction. Besides, he still needed the shoe.

Ondragon let Pete go, picked up the candles, and went back to the lodge. There he handed them to Carlos, apologized on Pete's behalf, and told the headwaiter to keep the candles under lock and key in the future.

A little later, Pete brought the shoe to his room. Ondragon accepted it gratefully and sent the man on another errand: checking the oil on the Mustang. After all, the car had to be in good shape if he was going to make his exit soon.

After Pete had scurried away, Ondragon got ready and headed up to Dr. Arthur's office on the second floor. He was in a brilliant mood, looking forward to the upcoming high-profile duel. Actually, he could have gone straight to Orr and told the police, he had enough evidence, but he wanted to enjoy his victory to the fullest. He wanted to witness the defeat of Dr. Arthur in person and see the pain in his eyes.

The door opened and Ondragon entered. He eyed his adversary like a hunter examining the game he was about to bring down. The doc looked as if he had anticipated this unannounced meeting. He was not wearing his white coat, and his office was tidy. Without saying anything, he offered Ondragon the chair, but he declined. Dr. Arthur nodded as if he had guessed that would happen too. It was clear to Ondragon that this man would not be an easy opponent. Like a Japanese swordsman, he positioned himself at the most favorable point in the room: between the door and the desk, his left leg slightly behind him so that he could quickly leap forward or backward. Dr. Arthur, on the other hand, settled himself in a relaxed posture on the edge of his desk. His yellow gaze was calm but alert.

Be careful, Paul, this guy is up to no good. He's been messing with your head. He could use weapons against you that you don't know about yet. Psychological tricks that only he knows.

Ondragon shifted his weight to his back foot and slid his hands into his pants pockets to signal nonchalance as well. Before he spoke, he jutted out his chin. After all, he was better than his adversary and was allowed to show it.

"Hello, Dr. Arthur."

The psychotherapist nodded imperceptibly. His hands were clasped loosely in his lap. The choice of weapons was still open.

"It's about your lovely facility here," Ondragon said. "I'm in possession of hard evidence that clearly proves you are treating criminal patients. Evidence that shows the nature of the research you are doing here, and for which you certainly have no official authorization from the authorities, neither here in the US nor in the UK nor anywhere else. In short, you are covering up the crimes of your patients and even condoning murders. You may even have ordered the elimination of certain people yourself—the FBI investigation will determine that. But you are certainly complicit and an instigator. Not to mention your failure to render aid, your assault and your fraud against patients."

Dr. Arthur said nothing, listening quietly to his lecture.

"You, Dr. Arthur, have created a network where cannibals can contact each other and, instead of hiding their way of life, cultivate it even further. You threw out a fishhook suggesting that you could help, and the fish bit eagerly. How many cannibals have you treated here? Seventy, a hundred, or more? A good number. But you did not invite all these desperate people here because you intended to prevent them from committing their crimes or possibly to cure them of their suffering. No, you are just on the hunt. On the hunt for victims who willingly let you look inside their heads and have no idea what you use their case files for. The only thing that moves you, Dr. Arthur, is professional recognition. You long for fame and prestige, just as your patients long for human flesh. You can't wait to make your field of research public and thus be instantly proclaimed a luminary. You want to become the Sigmund Freud of cannibal research. Someone who is often quoted, someone who will go down in history and who will be sought out for advice around the world. That's why you tried to get an unassailable lead by starting your cannibal farm. You wanted to be in the unofficial Guinness Book of World Records. You wanted to be the doctor who studied the most cannibals in the world before you made it official. The main thing was that you would end up standing there like the Sun King of science. Radiant and immortal. That's the way it is, isn't it, Dr. Arthur? In truth, you are a victim of your own pitiful ambition." Ondragon looked at Dr. Arthur. He didn't expect the psychotherapist to respond to his accusations. The guy was too smart for that. He watched his counterpart thoughtfully raise a hand and stroke his musketeer beard. The doctor was silent; only his eyes were fixed unwaveringly on Ondragon. They did not blink once.

A shiver gripped him. This man did not behave like other men who were shown their failure. Ondragon summoned his instincts. He would have to be on his guard.

At the same moment, a superior smile appeared on Dr. Arthur's lips. "Your courage is truly admirable, Paul. Or should I say your stupidity?"

Ondragon, for his part, now looked back in silence.

Dr. Arthur laughed softly. "You, of all people, are threatening me with the police? I find that very, how shall we say, droll. You do realize that I know what you do for a living, Paul? Or do I still have to tell you what I found out about you during the hypnosis? I think the skeletons in your closet are exquisitely close to mine."

"Are you offering me some kind of stalemate?"

Dr. Arthur pursed his lips.

Ondragon looked at him intently. Had the psychotherapist actually found out more about him than he should have with the help of hypnosis? Had he learned his deepest, darkest secrets? Or was he just bluffing?

Ondragon shook his head. No matter. It wouldn't change the fact that they now had to cross swords anyway. And which of them held the more effective weapon would be revealed in the end. In any case, he would not be satisfied with a stalemate. There could be no draw in this fight. Dr. Arthur was only too aware of that as well. Ondragon was prepared for the doctor to lure him onto unstable terrain—a footbridge with rotten planks that only he knew, on which his enemy would tumble if he put his foot wrong. But he would not fall for this feint. He had too much experience in psychological hand-to-hand combat for that.

Ondragon smiled. "Dr. Arthur, whatever you think you have on me, you can't prove it anyway. And in the end, you'll be the one on trial, not me. You'll have to explain yourself to the jury, and I don't think anyone will believe you if you point your finger at me."

"I have tape recordings, Paul. Where you talk quite frankly about your shady operations!"

"I know that. I heard the click of the device just before I woke up from hypnosis. You hadn't said anything about recordings beforehand and had carefully tried to hide the device under the couch. At first, I didn't think anything of it, but then I realized why you needed the secret recordings. You wanted to cover yourself. Just in case. Well, I did the same thing. I covered my ass." Ondragon pulled a small old-fashioned tape from his pocket and held it up. It came from his file in Dr. Arthur's office. Trump number one!

"You must mean these recordings here, Dr. Arthur. It's just too bad they won't be of any use to you, because I erased the tape with a magnet. It's blank!" He tossed the tape to the doctor, who deftly caught it with one hand. For a split second, his features darkened. A moment later, however, they were perfectly smooth and hard as marble again.

"And if you should get the idea," Ondragon continued, "of disposing of me somehow, I must expressly advise against it. My assistant already has the evidence and has instructions to turn it over to the FBI immediately if anything happens to me. She has, first, the personal notes that I have made over the past week here and a sample of Mr. Lyme's blood that I found out in the woods and took with me—I put both in your internal mail this morning, which has already been picked up and should be on its way to Orr. In addition, my assistant has access to detailed material on your cannibal patients, which I extracted from your digital database. So your top-secret files are no longer secret. There's also a wealth of information that a certain Simon Ricks, aka Jeremy Bates, compiled over years of research about you and your career." *Voilà*— trumps number two, three, and four! Bam! Ondragon's smile grew wider as Dr. Arthur sat transfixed on the edge of his desk. His foot had stopped bobbing.

"Surely, you remember, Doctor. Jeremy Bates? A private investigator from St. Louis. He was on the trail of your scheme. He had infiltrated Cedar Creek Lodge as a physical therapist in order to get the last piece of evidence he needed to finally convict you. I'm afraid he succeeded in getting it, and that was his death sentence. You fired him and a little later he disappeared without a trace. It's him lying out there in the woods, isn't it? Bates aka Ricks is the unknown corpse!"

Dr. Arthur folded his arms over his striped tie. A first sign of nervousness? But he remained silent, so Ondragon kept talking.

"I found the missing Bates rocker shoe at Mortimer Parker's cabin." Trump number five! "The boy found it by Bates's body and took it home. Could it be that he also saw who killed Bates?" Ondragon looked sharply at Dr. Arthur. The latter's eyes had now turned the color of liquid sulfur. A corrosive mixture of hatred and amazement was being beamed toward him like radioactive waste.

Ondragon set about his final blow. "You must think you're in the clear now. Because it wasn't you who killed Bates, you have your accomplices for that. They won't be able to prove anything against you. The blood's not on your boots. Well, I suppose Deputy Hase is one of the poor dogs working for you. But will he also stick his neck out for you when it all comes to light? Will he want to end his young country bumpkin life in jail so you can continue to do your so-called research scot-free, or will he consider talking instead? And what about the others you have turned into your henchmen? Are you so sure of their loyalty? Or might the prospect of reduced sentences loosen their tongues as well? I'm thinking of Dr. Zeo and Dr. Pollux. I'm sure they're reluctant to give up their licenses to practice." Ondragon raised his eyebrows in victory. Now came the best part: the push over the cliff. "Admit it, Dr. Arthur, you're screwed. You have bungled. Your grand plan has failed. You're only human. Too bad about this excellent clinic; its reputation is ruined. Your private investors will not be too happy when they learn that you have destroyed their money printing machine. Well, what do you say to all this?" Ondragon's lips twisted into a confident smile. That should be enough; he had said it all. Dr. Arthur would have to realize that he no longer had a chance.

But the psychotherapist still did not move; even the sulfurous hatred had disappeared from his gaze. Instead, he was happily bobbing his foot again, and the corner of his mouth was twitching in amusement.

Ondragon watched him suspiciously. What was the doc up to? Had something escaped him? A tiny detail that would now turn against him? Expecting an attack, he took his hands out of his pockets and let his arms hang loosely, ready to use them to defend himself at any moment.

What followed, however, was not a physical attack—brute force would have been an insult to Dr. Arthur's intellect anyway—no, the psychotherapist merely smiled. "Go ahead and leave, Paul," he said calmly. "There may be someone out there who will believe your story. However, these people will also ask you questions. I hope you're prepared for that."

Ondragon furrowed his brow in irritation. Why was the doctor letting him go so easily?

"Please." Dr. Arthur pointed to the exit. "The door is open, Paul. No one is going to stop you. The termination of therapy is at your own request. You don't mind if I make a note of that in your file, do you? Besides, you are welcome to return if you are interested in continuing the treatment. And that is urgently necessary, as I can see. But I forgive your impertinence toward me; I owe you that as your doctor." He raised both shoulders as if to indicate that even a man like him could be wrong sometimes. "Goodbye, Paul, I wish you the best of luck out there."

Ondragon was flabbergasted. Either Dr. Arthur had completely lost touch with reality, or he himself had a major chip on his shoulder. Normally, he was used to encountering fear exclusively in the faces of his enemies, but Dr. Arthur did not give the impression of being afraid. On the contrary, the doc was laughing at him.

This was not going at all as he had imagined. Laboriously, Ondragon exhaled. He felt the fever awaken from its painkillers sleep and begin to pulsate quietly in his veins. Suddenly, his mouth became dry and his palms moist. His armpits followed, and finally the warm, liquid fear ran down his back and collected in his underwear.

My good suit, Ondragon thought, and pulled himself together. Dr. Arthur was just bluffing. All this was nothing but hot air.

But what if it wasn't? What if he had something that would finish him off? Another tape? A video recording of the hypnosis? Then he'd be busted along with the doc, if he pulled this one off. That sucked!

Ondragon shifted his weight onto his back leg. His limbs felt heavy, and an excruciating pain throbbed in both feet. Perhaps Rudee could get him a new passport. In Thailand, there were many small remote islands he could retreat to for a while. Dreadlocks and beachwear, a cover as a surf hippie, a hut on the beach, and a pretty Thai girlfriend. The *centrifuge* went through all the possibilities.

Yes, Thailand sounded good, and Dr. Arthur could kiss his ass. He had far better options for surviving a scandal than the doctor did.

"Dr. Arthur, I hope you don't mind if I take my leave now. I'll see you when I get back with the FBI!" With those words, Ondragon turned and left the office. He didn't care if Dr. Arthur snorted in amusement behind his back.

CHAPTER 48

2009, Moose Lake,
Cedar Creek Lodge

When Ondragon reached his room, he saw Kateri waiting by it. Wordlessly, he unlocked the door and took her inside.

"I'm leaving now," he said, lifting his ready-packed travel bags off the bed. Bates's shoe was in one of them. In Orr he would hand it over to the policemen who were not in cahoots with Dr. Arthur.

"I'm coming!"

Surprised, Ondragon looked at her. He had confidently expected her to stay in the lodge with her mentor.

"Well, what brought about this change of heart?"

Kateri avoided his gaze. "I've been thinking about it again. I don't want to get involved in this; it wouldn't be good because of my past. There's no way anyone can find out what I've done. That would be a disaster, I could forget everything I have built up so far. Because I'm attached to my life as it is now. You have to know, Jonathan has always been like a father to me and he made sure then that as little as possible about my fate leaked out to the public."

"He succeeded too. I found out almost nothing about it."

Kateri nodded. "Jonathan made it possible for me to lead a normal life in the first place. Who else would have gotten involved with a cannibal? All I could have done was change my name and leave the country. It is only because of him that I am still alive at all. If it hadn't been for him, I would likely have killed myself. So you see how much I am in his debt. But if your accusations against him are true, then he has committed a serious crime, and for that he must be held accountable." She looked at him. "You don't look well, Paul." She stroked his glowing forehead with her cool fingers.

Ondragon gladly welcomed her touch. Maybe something would come of them after all. He took her hand and kissed it. Kateri smiled unhappily.

"Now I'm losing another person I love." That she meant Dr. Arthur was clear.

"I'm sorry, Kateri."

"You don't need to be; if anyone should apologize, it's me. I should have believed you sooner." She brushed his lips with a kiss and turned toward the door. "My bags are in my room. I'll tell Pete to take them to my car. I'll drive myself."

"Won't Sheila be mad if you leave the lodge with me?"

Kateri looked at the window. "Sheila has always been a good friend to me. She's kept me grounded. I hope she'll get through this thing okay, because she has nothing to do with it. She doesn't know anything about anything. The night you saw me, I actually had a date with her. We always meet secretly in the shelter at the hikers' parking lot. I didn't want anyone to know we were a couple."

Ondragon raised a hand and nodded. "It's okay." He picked up his bags. He looked around the room one last time, then stepped out into the hallway with Kateri. He left the key in the lock.

Down at the reception desk, Kateri demanded her car keys from Sheila, earning an uncomprehending look. The two women had a brief and cautious discussion, and Ondragon hoped Kateri wouldn't blurt out too much. But the abrupt blush in Sheila's cheeks and her fierce gestures reassured him. They revealed that Sheila felt nothing but raging jealousy. She would cool down again.

Kateri ended the conversation and came over to him. Of course, he couldn't help but give Sheila one last victorious look. The receptionist was fuming and shouted a soft "Fuck off, you straight asshole!" after him as they left the lodge.

Outside by the car, Ondragon stowed his luggage in the trunk, and while they waited for Pete, Kateri looked uneasily into the forest. Did she think the Wendigo would come and stop them from leaving this place at the last second? Even though Ondragon was suffering from the effects of the fever that still threatened to cloud his mind, he guessed why Kateri, Pete, and the others had kept talking about the forest monster. Here in this world, the unfathomable realm of the forest that had its own laws; it wasn't surprising. The Wendigo was a synonym for them, another term for a human being who had committed unimaginably disturbing deeds. Deeds that were far beyond human comprehension. Momo and Kateri were mentally ill. They lived in their own universe. And in this universe, the Wendigo existed.

Ondragon was relieved when Pete finally arrived and hoisted the two suitcases into the trunk of the Prius. Afterward, the man tapped his Bulls cap. "Have a good trip, Mr. *On Draegen*, Miss Wolfe."

"See you soon, Pete. I'll be back." Ondragon winked at the boy.

"Where shall we meet?" asked Kateri. "At the Nett Lake Police Department?"

"No, first I'm stopping off in Orr at the Gateway Inn. I have to do something there. After that, we'll notify the Cook Police Department. We can't trust Deputy Hase from Nett Lake. He's in on this."

"Well then, see you at the Gateway Inn," Kateri said, getting into her car.

The bellboy waved after them as the cars rolled out of the parking lot. First, Kateri in her Prius, then the Mustang.

Ondragon rolled down the window and enjoyed the fresh air. He glanced alternately from Kateri's taillights to the rearview mirror until the lodge disappeared behind him, then focused only on the potholes Kateri was trying to carefully avoid ahead of him. The Prius's shock absorbers seemed even less suited to this kind of road than those of the Mustang. The Toyota jerked roughly back and forth, while the good old Ford bobbed along in a leisurely manner, humming and sucking up the dust, as if it, like its driver, was happy to finally be on the road again.

To the right and left of the car, the trees passed by, and with them Ondragon's thoughts went on a journey. He thought about the future of the lodge; perhaps it would be turned into a luxury hotel or a base for hikers. Or maybe a hunting lodge for rich businessmen who wanted to relax after shooting animals. He thought about how excited he was to see Charlize again. He wondered what his assistant would say to Kateri? Would he and Kateri even see each other again after this?

They passed the hikers' parking lot. Between the trees, Ondragon could see the shelter where Kateri had met with Sheila for a nighttime romantic tryst. A strange feeling gripped him. Did it offend him that she had been with other people besides him? And with a woman too?

Ahead of him, the Toyota braked abruptly, and Ondragon brought the Mustang to a skidding halt. What was going on? Had Kateri forgotten something? He watched her get out and walk toward his car. With a questioning look, he leaned his head out the window.

"What is it?"

He saw her attack coming, but could do nothing about it. Surprised, he cried out as the syringe needle bored deep into his neck. And while Kateri held him almost gently, waiting for the anesthetic to take effect, she whispered in his ear, "You didn't think I was going to betray Jonathan, did you?"

Ondragon wanted to nod, but his limbs would no longer obey him. The last thing he remembered before everything went black was the incomparable Miss Wolfe turning off the Mustang's engine.

CHAPTER 49

2009, Moose Lake,
somewhere in the forest

With a cry, Ondragon awoke from his stupor. Unfortunately, he found he was still surrounded by darkness. But it wasn't the blackness of the chemical substance Kateri had injected into his bloodstream. This blackness was somehow claustrophobic.

Ondragon tried to sit up and hit his head hard against a wall barely three handspans above him. It sounded dull and metallic. His skull thudding, he lay still and checked his position. His hands were tied behind his back, probably with cable ties, because the thin material was cutting painfully into his wrists. The area felt moist. He was probably bleeding. His feet were also bound together, but before that, the bitch of a deceiver had stripped him of his cowboy boots, doubtless finding the one-handed knife in the shaft. The SIG Sauer was also no longer in its holster, and a thick layer of duct tape was stuck over his mouth.

As best he could, Ondragon felt around his dark surroundings with his bound limbs, although he already suspected where he was, for the smell was very familiar. When his feet first bumped against something soft and then something hard, it was clear where he was. He was in the trunk of the Mustang, along with his travel bags and the always-be-prepared case, like forgotten luggage at the airport. Apparently, that had been Kateri's intention: He was to disappear from the scene forever and rot in his own car. Nice work. Like an amateur, he had let her trick him. He really was a chump!

Ondragon felt his left arm begin to fall asleep and shifted his weight. If only he could reach the metal case next to his travel bags.

He squirmed and writhed, but his posture changed little as he did so; instead, the pain in his wrists intensified. Gasping, he paused. He was condemned to immobility. Yet salvation lay not a handsbreadth from his feet. Inside the case was a precision rifle and an exclusive selection of cutting and stabbing weapons. Everything a man in his situation could do with, but unfortunately could not reach.

Exhausted, Ondragon lowered his head and thought. Fortunately, the trunk of the Mustang was big enough. He wouldn't run out of oxygen for a few hours. Again, he was seized by anger. Damn her! She'd taken advantage of his feelings for her! But she was nothing more than a bitch in heat who adored her cannibal guru. It was quite impressive how well Dr. Arthur had his disciples under control. He would never have believed Kateri would do such a thing for him.

Even as he thought this, he heard a noise from outside. Someone had leaned something against the car and was now tinkering with the trunk lock. Ondragon tensed up. As soon as the lid opened, he would leap up and slam his head into Kateri's chin. But then, unfortunately, he didn't get to do that, because the bright light blinded him. To defend himself at least a little, he began to kick aimlessly, but his attack was repelled with ease.

"Knock it off, asshole!" he heard a voice curse.

Blinking, Ondragon looked up into the bright opening. There stood Kateri. The Bride of Satan!

If only Hatchet knew how right he had been to give her that title. Ondragon snorted indignantly under the duct tape.

With a wicked smile, Kateri pointed the SIG Sauer at his head, bent down, and with a jerk, ripped the tape from his lips.

"Shit! What are you doing?" shouted Ondragon.

"Shut up! Or I'll tape your mouth shut again! And don't you dare kick me again. I'm going to untie your feet now and then you'll get out of the trunk very slowly. But I warn you, screaming is useless. We're miles from the lodge. And don't try any other nonsense, or I'll test that gun on you right now."

Ondragon saw that the safety was off and nodded. What was she going to do?

Kateri cut his shackles with the one-handed knife from his boot and backed away from him. "Go!" she ordered, twitching the barrel of the pistol.

After climbing out of the trunk with difficulty, he stood in his socks in the damp grass and looked around. It must have been raining hard, because everything was wet and still dripping steadily from the canopy above their heads. It seemed like it was going to be dark soon, but Ondragon could make out squat silhouettes crouching in the dense undergrowth as if they were hatching something. There were two other vehicles keeping his Ford Mustang company in this idyllic junkyard: a nearly new Dodge Ram pickup with a cracked windshield and an old Nissan that already showed obvious signs of rust. All of the cars had their license plates removed. Ondragon cast a sad look at his car. His baby didn't deserve to end up like this. He bit his lips. He didn't want to end up like this either, in this shitty forest!

"The Dodge is Oliver Orchid's, isn't it?" he asked. "And the Nissan belonged to Bates aka Simon Ricks, the detective. Nice little junkyard where you dump your victims' cars. So? Was it you who killed Bates?" He turned to Kateri and looked directly into the muzzle of his gun.

"I said shut up! Now shift your ass. That way!" She jerked her head in that direction. "You lead the way."

Ondragon did as he was told, walking down the narrow trail that led deeper and deeper into the damp forest. As they walked, the light gradually faded and thin wisps of mist drifted up. Weightless as spider webs, they floated up from the wet grass to the black tree trunks. After a short time, Ondragon had no idea where he was. Nor did he know what time it was, or the direction they were moving in. With aching limbs, he dragged himself along the path, feeling his swollen feet howl every time they hit something sharp. Finally, fed up with his grim captor's silence, he tried to strike up a conversation. Maybe he could still get something out of her.

"Why are you allowing yourself to be exploited by Dr. Arthur? Why are you risking prison? Think about your career at the university, your research. Isn't that the life you wanted to lead?" he asked, but didn't dare turn to Kateri.

"What do you know about my life? Nothing! You're just another affected city slicker with a little pseudo-problem. You don't have the slightest idea what it's like to have real problems! Every night I have nightmares. Every night I see my parents wagging their fingers at me accusingly. Is that a life worth living? This guilt that follows me everywhere and that no one can take away?"

Ondragon shook his head. "So why are you making it worse by committing murders for Dr. Arthur? You are an intelligent and extremely attractive woman, Kateri, think about it. Dr. Arthur's just using you. You could end up in prison for the rest of your life for him, and that fine gentleman would do nothing but laugh up his sleeve that you were so stupid as to listen to him."

"So what? At least this would finally be over!"

Ondragon said nothing. The conversation had worked, but it seemed to be a hopeless undertaking. This woman was cold as ice. She was a madwoman. A cannibal who simply took what she craved, who satisfied her hunger for human flesh in a sexual way. Whether with male or female, she obviously did not care.

"Did you know my mother was still alive after the crash?" continued Kateri in a hushed voice. "Unfortunately, her legs were crushed between the fittings and the seat of the plane, and the broken control stick had drilled into her abdomen." She paused, during which Ondragon thought he heard a sharp intake of breath. "She begged me to kill her. At first, I refused—I was a thirteen-year-old girl! How could anyone ask such a thing? But our tribal rules say that a child must never disobey her parents' wishes. So I held my mother's mouth and nose until she stopped resisting. I fulfilled her wish and I was all alone after that, with no help and no food. Our plane was not loaded with food because we were on our way back from the camp to civilization; you don't take provisions with you. I only found a bag of candy bars. Our tribal rules also say not to eat people. There was no way I was going to become a Wendigo; that was an absolute horror to me. So I did the only thing I could and divided the rest of the candy bars into small rations, but they were finished after three days. After that, I ate nothing but snow, but the hunger was relentless. It felt like it was eating me from the inside out. It took another three days to make the decision. I was already very weak, but I didn't want to die. And my parents offered me that way out, even though they were long dead. After that, I pulled my father out of the plane into the snow and started to cut him up. Later, it was certified that I had been in shock. And this shock would have enabled me to do these horrible things."

Ondragon could feel her cold anger directed at his back. As if he could do anything about this tragic accident. Poor, crazy Kateri; she would never be normal again.

"I don't blame you for that, Kateri," he said placatingly. "Who knows, maybe I would have done the same in your situation. But for you to let Dr. Arthur use you for his dirty games is unforgivable."

"We are not doing anything wrong here. We are just trying to live with our fate. A fate that normal people like you will never understand. Jonathan is a great man; he helps us where others have failed. He created this place here as a refuge, an oasis in the midst of the rejection of the outside world. This is where we feel at ease. This is our home."

"How utterly romantic."

"Everything was fine until Jeremy Bates came along. He was going to destroy everything! He was going to blackmail Jonathan. But Jonathan didn't do anything bad; all he did was take care of us. Is that a crime? Bates is to blame for everything; he brought the disaster."

"Disaster?" asked Ondragon.

But Kateri wasn't listening any more. Her voice sounded as if her thoughts were far away. "This will become a beautiful place again. I'll make sure of that."

"What did you do with Bates?"

"If he had just stayed in his swamp grave, no one would have noticed. But some fucking bear had to dig him up again and nibble on him."

"And what about Oliver Orchid?" echoed Ondragon. He wanted to take advantage of Kateri's communicative mood. As long as she talked, she wouldn't shoot him, and he could consider his escape options.

"Orchid, that fucking asshole! He would have ruined everything too. Luckily, he and Bates were blundering about at the same time. So we cleaned house."

"What happened?" asked Ondragon.

"Orchid was a wanker, arrogant and self-absorbed. He simply wouldn't listen to Jonathan. He thought he was in control, but he couldn't handle what he experienced in Africa."

"The thing with the cannibal village in Sudan?"

"That son of a bitch was one of us!" spat Kateri in disgust.

"One of you," Ondragon repeated somewhat mockingly, daring to turn around. Briefly, he thought about throwing himself at his captor, but the black eye of the pistol's muzzle stared at him from a disturbingly short distance and finally persuaded him to let it go. Frowning, he trudged on through the wet thicket.

"You wanted to know what happened to Oliver Orchid," Kateri continued a little later in a conversational tone. She seemed to be immensely enjoying the fact that she could tell him the whole story, defenseless as he was. It was like a bad gangster movie, where the bad guys always had a heartwarming concluding speech at the end, explaining why they had done what they did, instead of just shooting. That's why the bad guys usually lost.

"Orchid, the bum, drove secretly to Orr in his pickup, which Bates had brought here for him unnoticed. There, for several days, he stalked his prey. A lonely and neglected alcoholic—just a sick and weak member of the herd who wouldn't have made it much longer anyway."

"Dana Straub."

"I don't know what her name was. Anyway, the police have been looking for her for a while and have also been snooping around here at the lodge. Jonathan didn't like that at all and felt compelled to act. Orchid kidnapped the woman and cut her up to eat. He was a psychopath!"

Oh, and you're a French gourmet club.

Didn't Kateri realize the absurdity of what she was saying?

"Where is Orchid's body?" asked Ondragon. "Did you make him disappear too, like Lyme?" Along with the fever, anger was now boiling up inside him again. What did this self-proclaimed charity think it was? Kateri seemed to think cannibals were doing something good for humanity by killing the sick and weak. Like a hunter, Kateri apparently thought she was all-powerful. And if there was one thing Ondragon particularly hated, it was this kind of hubris.

"Lyme was something else," Kateri countered. "He wanted to die. You heard it from him yourself. And Jonathan granted him that wish. The fact that you found him was a stupid coincidence."

"Coincidence, aha! And? Are you telling me that you didn't know about all this until recently? That Dr. Arthur only told you *after* I found Lyme's body, because he had no choice but to tell you. Admit that it scared you to learn about what had happened to Lyme and the others. Admit to being deeply disappointed in your great friend."

Kateri didn't speak. Ondragon could literally feel the cloud of her hatred from behind him, but despite the impending danger, he just couldn't stop taunting her. "Your honorable Jonathan has been lying to you all along. Made a fool of you. But that night after I found the body, he had to confess to you about Lyme, Bates, and the others. He knew I wouldn't rest easy, so he convinced you to help him with his plan. The plan to get rid of me and thus protect the lodge. You obeyed him because you were afraid your little paradise here would be destroyed."

Since she didn't reply, he dared another attempt at appeasement. "Kateri, listen, you haven't done anything serious yet; you can still turn back. Because I don't believe you've murdered anyone yet. You just want to protect Dr. Arthur, and I understand that. But he alone would go to jail for his crimes, not you!"

He was unprepared for the blow with the handle of the gun in the back of the head and he saw stars. He clenched his jaw tightly to keep from groaning. "Kateri, if you think what you did to Rumsfeld is punishable, I can reassure you. It was just a dog."

He was prepared for the second blow, but he still bit his tongue painfully. Damn beast!

"You want me to gag you again?" hissed Kateri. "Rumsfeld wasn't me. That was Julian! The threatening letter was from him too; he was jealous. Why did you also have to stick your nose into things that are none of your business? Couldn't you have just been a normal patient? Then we could have just had fun together." She almost sounded as if she regretted having to get rid of him.

"My assistant will go to the police if I don't show up," Ondragon reminded her of his hedge, which he had fortunately engineered earlier.

"Oh come on, your assistant is long dead! Julian paid her a little visit in Orr; you were only too willing to tell me where to find her. All I'm saying is Gateway Inn!"

Thunderstruck, Ondragon stopped. Charlize dead? The wonderful Charlize, murdered by an amateur? Slowly, he turned to Kateri. "If I ever get my hands on you, bitch, you'll wish you'd never met me!"

"If you say so," Kateri replied unconcernedly. She looked around. "That tree over there looks good. Go on, put your back against it."

Ondragon quickly reviewed his chances. If he threw himself at her with his hands tied, it certainly wouldn't surprise her. Besides, she was too far away to hit cleanly with a Krav Maga kick, and too close for her to miss him with a bullet. It was hopeless. So he stood against the tree trunk as she had ordered, hoping she would look away for a tiny moment.

But Kateri kept a careful eye on him as she retrieved a roll of duct tape from the leather cartridge pouch at her belt and ordered him to hold still. "If you so much as bat an eyelash, I'll puncture your fancy suit!"

I'm a goner anyway, thought Ondragon, and let the woman have her way.

Without saying a word, Kateri bound him to the trunk with the duct tape. She walked in circles around the tree, holding the tape in one hand and the gun in the other. The sound of the tape pulling quickly from the roll was like popcorn popping, underlining this silly cowboy and Indian act. It was completely undignified.

"What's the point, Kateri? You can shoot me just like that, without this whole bondage game. Or does that turn you on?"

"You wait and see, Paul. You'll see what it's good for." Smiling, she stroked his lips with a finger and circled the tree a few more times, her hair blowing behind her as if she were dancing around the *Stangår* at midsummer.

Anger throbbed hotly through Ondragon's fevered bloodstream. He had already had to deal with several female assassins. Sometimes they had been on his side, sometimes not, and he would rather have been done in by any of them than by this amateur bitch!

He saw Kateri stop and cut the tape. She had used up almost the entire roll.

"Like this," she said, tearing off another small piece.

"Are you finally going to kill me?" asked Ondragon before she taped his mouth shut.

"No. Not me. *He'll* take care of that."

"Hmmmmmm?"

A rapturous smile appeared on her lips. She patted his cheek. "Have fun with the Wendigo!" Then she turned around and disappeared into the forest.

CHAPTER 50

2009, Moose Lake,
somewhere in the forest

It got dark, really dark. And the forest around him was frighteningly quiet. So quiet that he could hear his own heart beating. It was a sluggish rhythm. Dull and powerless.

Ondragon raised his head—the only part of his body he could still move; the rest was suffering from blood stasis and waves of sweating fever. Blinking, he looked around. He could feel the tree at his back, hear the back of his head scraping against the brittle bark, but could see nothing in the dark but the tree trunks close around him, surrounding him like silent observers. Again and again, his vision blurred, his eyes burned, and Ondragon closed his eyelids in exhaustion. Darkness was not his greatest enemy. The silence was much more brutal. It acted as an amplifier, turning every sound, no matter how small, into the footfalls of a brontosaur. Ondragon's imagination played vivid tricks on him, making him hear the most impossible things. Once he thought a bear was approaching him. He heard a growl and the scratching of claws on tree trunks. Another time he heard a child's voice, calling for him.

Per?

Ondragon hung his head. He was terribly tired, but his ears were wide open. Almost painfully, they listened to the black void like NASA's parabolic antennas listened to space. Among the five senses with which man was endowed, hearing was the only one with the power to jolt the organism out of sleep, to warn it of possible danger. Silently, Ondragon asked his ears to finally give him a break.

He needed no warning. What was the point? He was tied to a tree here, unable to even wiggle a toe. What could he do if something approached him with the intention of eating him? Panting, he sucked in air through his nose. The tape on his mouth made it difficult for him to breathe. Suddenly, he stopped, gasping again. Had he succumbed to a sensory illusion, or did it really smell like decay here?

Then hot adrenaline surged through his body, and an uncontrolled tremor took hold of his constricted limbs.

He was there!

Out there!

Ondragon's eyes snapped open. Quickly, he turned his head to the side and froze when he saw the shadow. It was completely crazy. He didn't believe in Pete's horror story or Kateri's forest monster, and yet it was standing over there among the tree trunks.

The Wendigo. Made of flesh and blood. Or rather, made of fur and teeth!

The figure detached itself from the dark undergrowth and slid toward him with awkward steps. Twenty yards, ten, five. Two stifled breaths later, it was standing right in front of him.

With a pounding heart, Ondragon looked up into the small, red-hot eyes. This was a bad dream. A fever dream! He blinked to scare away the image. But the Wendigo remained. Its body seemed to be over ten feet tall and was covered with smelly fur. The monster bent down and sniffed at the wound on Ondragon's forehead. Growling, it expelled a gush of foul air. Ondragon held his breath. The stench was infernal. An indescribable mixture of exploded entrails and putrefaction. Growling, the Wendigo stared at him.

It's all over now! The phenomenal Paul Eckbert Ondragon would be torn to pieces by an equally phenomenal being, with nothing but the silent trees as witnesses and the damp forest as grave. Oddly enough, he felt some relief at this thought. After all, it was more dignified to be massacred by a Wendigo than to have a bullet put in you by an amateur. And from your own weapon. The Wendigo, however, would give him an almost epic end.

Calmly, Ondragon closed his eyes and waited for the pain and the warm feeling of blood on his skin.

But nothing happened.

Instead, he heard a hissing voice. Not with his ears though, right inside his feverish head.

You are one of us!

Surprised, he opened his eyes. But the Wendigo had disappeared. Only its terrible stench still hung in the damp night air. Hastily, Ondragon turned his head, looking around. Nothing. Only darkness.

Relieved, he rested his head against the tree trunk and expelled air. What in the name of Bigfoot's balls had that been?

CHAPTER 51

2009, Moose Lake,
somewhere in the forest

Ondragon heard a crackling sound and pulled up. Had he dozed off? He looked around. Nothing had changed about his situation. It was still pitch dark, and he was still stuck to the tree. The Wendigo had come and gone, and every neuron in his body was sending out hellish pain.

To get his thinking machine working again, he wondered what Kateri would do if she found out the beast had spared him? What would she say about it, and why had the Wendigo spared him in the first place?

You are one of us!

One of us? What did he mean by that? That he was a Wendigo? A cannibal?

Another sound made Ondragon prick up his ears. Rustling footsteps were approaching. Was the forest monster coming back? Did he want to send him to the eternal hunting grounds after all? He lifted his nose into the wind and sniffed. No beast smell. But a breath of old sweat and mothballs. Suddenly, a gurgling hiss sounded and a hairy figure leaped into his field of vision. It was much smaller than the previous visitor. Ondragon looked at it in irritation. Was this a Wendigo cub?

The beast slowly approached him. Its eyes shone as red as those of the big monster. Perhaps the Wendigo mother had only spared him so that her young could now use him to practice disemboweling a human being.

The small Wendigo straightened to its full height and raised a clawed paw. The claws gleamed ominously before Ondragon felt them dig into his shoulder. They were ice-cold and razor-sharp, and warm blood immediately shot from the wound. With a satisfied growl, the creature pulled its claw from the trembling flesh and thrust again. Ondragon winced. The injury to his ribcage was not deep, but it sent a mortal fear coursing through his veins. His heart beat wildly against his ribs, and the tendons in his neck stretched into hard cords. Unable to move, he watched as the monster ran its claw across his belly. He smelled his own blood mixing with the dripping drool from the beast's mouth. Finally, it lunged, about to thrust its paw deep into his guts, but another figure appeared out of nowhere. It threw itself against the beast and knocked it down.

Ondragon saw the young Wendigo and its attacker fall to the ground, wrestling with each other. He recognized long black hair, tattooed arms, and a black T-shirt with a white axe on it.

Hatchet! Thank hell! The son of darkness himself had come to his aid.

Craning his neck, Ondragon watched the battle between the two figures: two hairy creatures rolling back and forth on the ground, emitting strained grunts. Hatchet seemed to be gaining the upper hand. With a well-aimed blow to the throat, he knocked the creature down, swung behind it, grasped its neck with one arm, and strangled it. The beast fought back with all its might, flailing its claws wildly, but Hatchet would not be shaken off. It looked as if he was just searching for the right grip; then he jerked the creature's head around and it slumped, lifeless.

Panting, Hatchet sat staring down at the young Wendigo. Its head stuck out from its neck at an unnatural angle. The death metal musician had broken the monster's neck in the best GI fashion!

Finally, Hatchet rose and approached Ondragon like a black avenging angel, his hair falling over his pale face and a diabolical smile on his lips. With a quick movement, he removed the tape from Ondragon's mouth.

"Is the beast dead?" he asked breathlessly.

"I think so. His neck cracked pretty badly. So if he gets up again, I'm gonna eat my entire Iron Maiden record collection!" Hatchet bared his white teeth into a JR grin. With a knife, he cut through the duct tape restraints.

Groaning, Ondragon sank to the ground. Only slowly did the blood begin to circulate through his tingling limbs again, and it was some time before he was able to stand up. Gritting his teeth, he limped over to the creature. He had to make sure. He kicked the head with the tip of his foot, and it rolled to the side as if it had been completely severed from its neck. The beast was dead.

"Told you he wouldn't get back up," Hatchet remarked dryly, kicking the creature's misshapen head away with a flourish. With a hollow plop, the ghastly thing flew into the forest. Ondragon looked after it in amazement. Only then did he understand. Of course! It was a mask! He quickly turned and looked into the true face of the beast. A shriek of surprise escaped him.

CHAPTER 52

Vernon!" In disbelief, Ondragon gawked at the sailor-masseur's face, which looked completely relaxed, as if death were only a temporary meditation.

"Yes, him! I was on my nightly walk to the kitchen when I saw him leave the lodge through the back door. He was wearing this strange costume, and I followed him out of curiosity. Little did I know what that pervert motherfucker was up to. That sick bastard!"

"Thanks for the rescue, Hatchet."

"No biggie, man."

Ondragon patted the death metal musician on the shoulder. He was still wondering how this anemic-looking man had managed to knock out the lights of the colossus. He bent down to Vernon and uncovered his massive shoulder. A bandage appeared under the costume and suddenly he knew how it had all gone down. Vernon was one of Dr. Arthur's personal henchmen. First, he had gotten Bates and Orchid out of the way, and then the doc had hired him to grant Lyme's wish to be eaten alive. For this he had disguised himself as a Wendigo to make the perfect illusion for the broker. He had attacked Ondragon only because he had unfortunately discovered Lyme's corpse. Kateri had not known the first thing about this until that moment. She had actually believed that it was the Wendigo who was trying to kill Ondragon, and had accidentally shot Vernon in the shoulder. Poor, confused Kateri. A little later, Dr. Arthur had enlightened her.

Ondragon picked up one of Vernon's gloves. It was equipped with four-inch blades. Either the guy was a fan of old horror movies or completely nuts. Dr. Schuyler's words came to his mind. *There's something strange about the wounds. This was no bear.*

No wonder—bears don't have knife blades for claws. Vernon's gloves were an almost laughable copy of Freddy Krueger's murder tools, but obviously more effective than those of the scar-faced nightmare from Elm Street. The ravages he had inflicted on Lyme's body with them had been highly believable. Shaking his head, Ondragon rose. The icing on this Black Forest gateau of madness was that Deputy Hase was covering it all up. He had doubtless radioed from the clearing where the animal carcass had later hung in place of Lyme's body, to instruct someone at the lodge to remove Lyme's ring from Ondragon's pants pocket. Vernon, for sure. And Ondragon had actually doubted himself and his sanity, so almost perfectly had everything been staged. But now it was over, the illusion was shattered. It was Paul Eckbert Ondragon's turn. He turned to Hatchet.

"Have you seen Kateri?"

"The Bride of Satan?"

"That's the one!"

"*Nope.* Didn't come across her. Why?"

Ondragon was about to explain that he still had a bone to pick with the cannibal, because she had not only assaulted him, but had also betrayed his wonderful assistant Charlize to this Julian, when he heard a sharp whirring sound. Hatchet snapped open his eyes in disbelief and opened his mouth, but only a wet gasp came out. A white aluminum dart was lodged in his throat.

Before Ondragon realized what was going on, a second projectile whizzed in and narrowly missed his face. He felt the breeze from the feathers against his cheek. With a leap, he dove for the dubious shelter of a bush. Another arrow whirred past him and struck the ground not two paces from him. Leaves rustled nearby. Hastily, Ondragon got to his feet, but his foot caught in the undergrowth and he stumbled. Arms flailing, he stumbled forward, regained his balance, and ran on, barefoot and bleeding, like an animal fleeing its hunter.

Branches whipped at his face and it was so dark he couldn't see more than an arm's length ahead of him. But he ran and ran, ignoring his pain. The slayer was somewhere behind him. He could hear her, but he couldn't see her. Suddenly, a thought came to him. If he couldn't see in the dark, neither could she. She would only be able to locate him by his sounds. Abruptly, he turned a corner, took cover behind a thick tree trunk, and listened to the hostile silence of the forest. Now that he was no longer tied up, he didn't feel quite so exposed, but Kateri certainly had more experience with stalking. He would have to rely on his fever-impaired instincts alone to deal with her.

Quietly, Ondragon crouched down. He dug his fingers into the rain-softened earth and smeared mud onto his face. Then he stripped off his flashy clothes except for his dark underpants and gave the rest of his body a mud pack as well. When he had completed the transformation into a primitive warrior, he turned his thoughts to a possible weapon. He could use stones or thick branches, but against a bow and his SIG Sauer, that seemed very Stone Age. If only he had taken one of Vernon's knife gloves with him.

Ondragon didn't like it, but the only thing left for him to do was to stay undercover and hope he could escape Kateri before the sun came up.

CHAPTER 53

2009, Moose Lake,
somewhere in the forest

Ironically, he suddenly remembered something. About the hide-and-seek games in his childhood. With Per. Back in Sweden, his brother and he had romped through his grandparents' house and large garden, playing cowboys and Indians. In those days, he must have been happy indeed. A happy child who had felt secure. Unfortunately, in the here and now, the child's play of those days had turned deadly serious. And it seemed to him that fate was mocking him; that out there now it was an *Indian* woman, of all people, who was skulking, waiting to put an arrow through his heart, and not Per, with feathers in his hair and shrieking. Per had always been the Indian. Per was long dead.

Suddenly, bright anger flared up in Ondragon. Anger at himself. Damn it, what was he whining about? He was a professional and he would show Kateri that he was up to this deadly game!

Like a predator, he sank down on all fours and sniffed. He smelled, felt, and listened with all his senses. Yes, he could even taste the forest on his tongue. A distant crackling sound reached his sensitized ears. Someone was moving through the undergrowth. Someone who was being very careful not to make a sound. Kateri.

Ondragon felt like Gollum as he crawled on his hands and feet through the moss clad only in his underpants—directly toward his victim. His only weapon was the element of surprise. He would ambush Kateri and attack. If he was lucky, she would have only the bow at the ready, not the pistol.

Silently, like a poisonous snake, he crawled toward her. It was tiring work, and he advanced only very slowly, because Kateri was also moving extremely carefully. Whenever she stopped to listen, he also paused. With difficulty and in slow motion, they moved toward each other. Suddenly, silence fell, and Ondragon stopped crawling. He could no longer hear Kateri, but he suspected her to be not ten steps away, behind a juniper thicket. That was still too far to take her by surprise. He had to get closer to her. Within three or four steps, perhaps, then he would have a chance. But Kateri remained silent and hidden. Had she noticed him? Or was she listening like him? Ondragon tensed his body. He wanted to be prepared in case something happened.

But Kateri eventually walked on, putting one foot carefully in front of the other.

Ondragon inhaled softly and started moving again, reducing the distance between them to a few steps. Then he heard the familiar, deadly whirring sound, and suddenly an arrow hit the ground next to his hand.

Shit! She was shooting on the move!

Ondragon jumped up and ran as fast as he could. He had to escape her! Without looking back, he zigzagged like a rabbit. Another arrow narrowly missed him, and stuck trembling in the bark of a fir tree. It had bloodred feathers. Ondragon swallowed. The fact that he could see what color it was could only mean that it had now grown lighter. The impenetrable blackness of the night had given way, revealing the outlines of the trees more and more clearly. Fuck!

Like a tank at full throttle, he smashed his way through the undergrowth. He didn't care that the soles of his bare feet cried out every time he stepped on something sharp. If he didn't find a hiding place soon, he was screwed! Again, an arrow zipped past him. Cursing, Ondragon changed direction. Why was she hunting him with the bow? Why didn't she just use the pistol? Was she getting a kick out of taking the cowboy down in Indian fashion? That would have unexpected style. But she probably just wanted to avoid making too much noise with one shot. That, in turn, could only mean that they were closer to the lodge than Kateri had claimed.

Hastily, Ondragon turned his head in all directions. If only he knew which way to run. But he saw nothing. No indication of where he was. Neither the lake nor any other waymark that seemed familiar.

There was a whirring sound but no thud. Ondragon ran a few more paces, then looked down at himself. With sober realization, he saw that the arrow was lodged in his side, two fingers' breadth below his bottom rib. The tip was protruding from his front. A barbed hunting tip.

As he continued to run, Ondragon grabbed the aluminum shaft of the arrow, broke it, and pulled both ends out of his body. The adrenaline that flooded generously through him prevented the pain from reducing his speed. He wanted to throw the broken projectile away, but changed his mind and kept the tip with the razor-sharp blades. After all, it was a weapon.

With the bloodied half of the arrow in his fist, he ran on. Behind him in the eerie silence, somewhere the slayer was lurking.

The wound was bleeding, and he realized his blood was leaving tracks that could easily be read by a skilled hunter. He pressed a hand to his side and jumped over a fallen tree. The spot looked vaguely familiar. But there was still no sign of the lodge. He thought feverishly. Should he hide behind the tree trunk? Or keep running? He looked down at himself, a red trickle running down his mud-stained leg. There was no point in hiding. Kateri would track him down!

All at once he noticed that no arrow had been shot at him for a long time. What was Kateri up to? Did she want to cut him off? Was it tactics or was there something in the forest ahead that could save him? He continued to run straight ahead. The dark blue dawn had turned to a diffuse gray. He could see pretty well, up to a certain distance. Kateri was probably calmly taking aim at him that very moment. Ondragon could almost feel the arrowhead in his neck. Instinctively, he pulled back his head and making an abrupt turn, threw himself into a dense bush. The arrow landed exactly where he had been a tenth of a second before. That snake! She was damn good!

Suddenly, he bumped into a large, hard shadow and rebounded, bewildered. He was standing in front of a small hut, just big enough for one person. For a moment, it was not clear to him what that meant, but then realization shot through his adrenaline-infused brain. He had made it! This was the Parkers' outhouse! And not twenty paces away stood the log cabin. Inside were people who could help him. And weapons.

Seized by new energy, he ran to the house and yanked open the door. But what awaited him inside made him freeze on the threshold.

CHAPTER 54

2009, Moose Lake,
in the Parkers' cabin

The pain in his side exploded as violently as if the effect of his body's own drugs had abruptly worn off. Ondragon doubled over, but his gaze was fixed unwaveringly on the scene into which he had burst so unexpectedly.

This can't be true, he thought, slamming the door.

"What did you do?"

"Mr. *On Draegen*?" The man was crouching on the floor and looked up at him with teary eyes. "What's the matter with you?"

Ondragon realized how he must look to the boy, almost naked and covered in mud. He walked toward Peter Parker, who lowered his gaze fearfully.

"It . . . it didn't work, Mr. *On Draegen*." Next to Pete, his brother, Momo, lay on his back. The mentally handicapped boy's eyes were wide open, his face puffy, and his hands had tightened around his neck. His tongue and lips were covered with festering blisters, and a dried yellowish mass stuck to his skin.

"Damn it, Pete! Of course it didn't work." Ondragon knelt down beside the unfortunate Momo and felt for his pulse. The boy was dead. He had choked agonizingly on the hot beeswax Pete had poured down his throat.

Goddamn Wendigo exorcism! I wish he'd never read that book to those two!

"I was just trying to help him," Pete wailed.

"Where did you get the wax from?" Ondragon snapped at him. But when he spotted a dented pot next to Momo, he knew where. Pete had gone to the cave and grabbed the wax from the Indians. The idiot!

"Man, Pete." Ondragon ran a shaking hand over his forehead and looked around the cabin. "Where's Joel?"

"You're bleeding."

"I know that. Where's your uncle?"

"He's gone."

"Gone? Where? Damn it, tell me!" Ondragon shook Pete, but he was sobbing so hard he couldn't get another word out. He let go of the boy and walked over to his uncle's bed. He breathed a sigh of relief. There stood the old shotgun in the corner, an antediluvian muzzle-loader, must be two hundred years old. The initials AJP were carved on the butt. With the ramrod, Ondragon checked to see if there was a bullet in the barrel. Fortunately, the shotgun was loaded. Unfortunately, he would only be able to fire a single shot with this thing, as reloading would take far too long to be able to defend himself permanently with it. "Pete, where's your hunting rifle?"

"In the shed," sobbed the bellboy.

Crap! He would likely not be able to access it for the time being, because Kateri would certainly have reached the log cabin by now and would at this moment be holed up somewhere out there behind a tree. He would have to make do with what he could find here in the hut.

Ondragon slung the old rifle over his shoulder and scoured the Parkers' kitchen for suitable stabbing weapons. With some success: Joel Parker was a trapper, so he owned no less than three good bowie knives hanging from nails above the makeshift sink. That should do the trick. Paying no further attention to the howling bellboy and his dead brother, Ondragon tore up a shirt and used it to dress his wound, noticing that he had left bloody footprints on the wooden floor of the cabin. Fuck it! More urgently now, he needed a plan that would get him to the lodge without being pierced by an arrow. He extinguished the oil lamp and crept to the window beside the door. Cautiously, he peered out into the dawn, but could see no one. Then he checked the views from the other two windows. No sign. If Kateri was out there—and she was!—then she was hiding damn well.

Ondragon thought. Fortunately, Kateri was a lone hunter. She could keep an eye on a maximum of three sides of the cabin at the same time. So he would have to find out which sides they were.

"Pete!"

He did not move. He was crouched in the dark, next to his brother's body.

"Pete! I need your help!" Ondragon walked over to the boy and dragged him to his feet. "Do you hear me? I'm being followed. Miss Wolfe is out there trying to kill me!"

Pete looked at him blankly. Of course, he didn't understand anything.

"I need you to distract her so I can escape undetected. Pete?"

"But . . ."

"Now listen to me for once, at least. Get over to the door there." He pushed the boy toward the entrance. He had to accept that Pete might get hit, whether he liked it or not. He hoped, however, that Kateri would spare him. After all, Pete wasn't her target, he was.

"Open the door!" he ordered.

With a trembling hand, Pete pushed down the latch and pulled the door open.

"Go out now, very slowly, and pretend to go to the outhouse, keeping an inconspicuous lookout for Miss Wolfe. She's hiding somewhere. Give a sign when you see her. Cough into your right or left hand, depending on which side she's on, you understand?"

Pete nodded heavily.

"Well, go!" Ondragon pushed the boy out and immediately closed the door behind him. Tensely, he watched the lean figure. Pete moved as conspicuously as if he had a blue light on his head and a megaphone in his hand into which he was about to shout, "Mr. *On Draegen*, I've found Miss Kateri!"

Ondragon sighed and pressed a hand harder on the throbbing wound.

Pete disappeared around the corner. Unfortunately, Ondragon could not see the outhouse from his observation post, because it was on the side of the log cabin that had no windows, of all places. So he had to wait until Pete reappeared in front of the house after his circuit. If he reappeared. Because otherwise the whole thing would have been of very little use, and he would have to come up with something else as fast as he could.

Ondragon waited and looked through the window, hard. Outside it became brighter and brighter. But nothing moved. And there was no sign of Pete. An eerie silence settled over the forest and the hut. Ondragon became restless. He clenched his teeth because the wound in his side was sending out incessant waves of searing pain. It was clearly taking too long! Had Pete stormed off? Or had Kateri grabbed him? Maybe she hadn't hesitated to eliminate him with a single shot.

While Ondragon was still trying to figure out Kateri's tactics, an acrid smell suddenly rose to his nostrils. He looked around and discovered the reason. Smoke was seeping from the roof through the cracks in the beams. A moment later, the first flames flickered inside the hut.

Kateri, that fucking bitch! She was trying to smoke him out! So she hadn't given up her guerrilla tactics yet. The best way to get rid of white settlers was to set fire to their huts!

Ondragon went over to the kitchen counter, soaked a towel, and wrapped it around his mouth and nose. He would stay in the hut as long as possible and watch the outside. Only at the last moment would he rush out under cover of the clouds of smoke and hope to escape Kateri.

But the flames spread through the wood of the hut faster than he had expected, from the roof beams to the walls and eating their way down to him. Ondragon had to duck to escape the heat of the fire. The flames hung over his head like a burning sky, hot smoke cauterizing his eyes. He would not be able to stand it much longer. Again and again, he looked out, trying to detect a movement somewhere, but the forest lay motionless.

As the first flames licked over his skin and scorched his hair, Ondragon readied himself. He would not run out the door, Kateri had her sights set on that for sure. The window at the back offered the best opportunity of escape. He grabbed a chair that had not yet caught fire, lifted it over his head, and threw it through another side window as a distraction. The glass shattered with a clang, and immediately the flames leaped higher. Quickly, Ondragon turned to the window at the back and ran. Holding his breath, he jumped through the window and out into the open. Outside, he threw himself to the ground and rolled in anticipation of an approaching arrow. But it failed to materialize. Back on his feet, he rushed over to the sheltering trees, rifle in one hand, knife in the other, flying like the wind. Instead of an arrow, he was now followed by a loud curse that drowned out the roar of the fire. Kateri had indeed been deceived.

Ondragon used his head start and ran as fast as he could, deeper into the forest. The narrow path that led directly to the lodge was on his right. Like a primitive ranger, he hunted through the undergrowth, barefoot and covered in mud. Backward evolution: from urban man to Neanderthal!

The longer he ran, the harder it was to breathe. The wound in his side hurt like hell, and he was losing more and more blood. Behind him, he heard the slayer storming furiously through the undergrowth. She was no longer trying to be quiet. The hunt was on.

Kateri screamed, shouting wild profanities at him. She was getting closer and closer. Ondragon knew that she would use his pistol next. So he zigzagged, putting dense undergrowth between himself and his pursuer. Just when he thought the lodge must finally be about to appear ahead of him, he noticed a movement beside him in the woods. Startled, he jerked his head around, but the shadow had already disappeared before he could catch it. If something had been there at all. Ondragon could no longer be completely sure of his senses, for the fever and the blood loss were causing him great discomfort. His steps became slower, and he felt his strength ebbing away. He was well aware of the irony that he was being pursued by someone who had actually wanted to save people from bleeding to death with her research.

A loud crackling sound reached his ear, as if a tree was falling behind him. Ondragon ran on, not looking back. Surely, the lodge would appear any moment. Suddenly, a muffled growl made the forest tremble, and Ondragon paused in mid-run. It was a primal, menacing sound that was followed by absolute silence. Even the birds had fallen silent in fright.

Then Ondragon heard a scream.

His heart pounding, he turned around and stared into the bushes behind him. They were shaking as if being rumpled by a storm. Branches broke and another strangled cry was heard. Then another cracking sound. Was it coming from the wood? Ondragon felt goose bumps all over his body. No, it sounded more soft and moist, like bones and flesh being crushed. Oh my God, Kateri!

When a pleasurable lip-smacking sound began to emanate from the bushes, Ondragon whirled around and ran on, filled with horror. The horror in this forest was simply endless. Something had killed Kateri and was eating her!

Stumbling and using the last of his strength, Ondragon finally reached the trimmed meadow behind the lodge. He had expected the silence of morning, a building where everyone was still asleep, not the bees' nest that greeted him, already bustling with people. The lodge was lit up like a Christmas tree. Dozens of people were going in and out, some wearing state trooper uniforms, and several blue lights were flickering in the parking lot.

Ondragon intended to duck behind a bush to see what it all meant. But one of the state troopers had already turned his head toward him. For a moment it seemed as if he hadn't seen the naked, mud-smeared man in the lush vegetation, but then he pulled his revolver from his holster and took aim at him.

"Put down your weapons and step out of the bushes, slowly!"

Ondragon briefly thought about disobeying the man's order and fleeing, but quickly became aware of his lack of alternatives . . . and his exhaustion. Besides, he definitely did not want to enter that shitty forest again!

He tossed away the shotgun and the long bowie knife and walked with his hands up toward the state trooper, who to his relief turned out to be not a trigger-happy youth but a fully grown man with a thick mustache.

"Who are you?" shouted Mustache.

"My name is Paul Eckbert Ondragon, I am a guest at this lodge." He saw the man speak into his radio and then nod a little later. At last, he lowered the revolver.

"Okay, come with me, Mr. Ondragon, we're expecting you. Here, take this." The state trooper handed him his jacket and Ondragon gratefully put it around his shoulders. Trembling with weakness and relief, he followed the trooper into the brightly lit main building to the entryway. More men in uniform stood there, along with two guys in dark suits and a woman. When the woman turned to him, a weight lifted from Ondragon's heart.

"Charlize! You're alive!"

"Chief!" The Asian Brazilian beauty ran up to him and flung her arms around him.

Ondragon had never been happier to see her.

CHAPTER 55

2009, Moose Lake,
Cedar Creek Lodge

Ondragon ran his hands over the temporary bandage that one of the nurses from the lodge had put on him. The painkiller she had injected him with was also beginning to take effect. The glowing twinge slowly turned to a dull throb. Relieved, Ondragon leaned back on the bed. He could use his old room as long as the police and FBI were turning everything upside down. Charlize sat across from him in the chair, looking at him. The crease of worry between her eyebrows was no longer quite so deep.

"Hopefully, the helicopter will come soon," she said.

Ondragon nodded. It was always good to have money. So he was spared the ordeal of the bumpy road through the forest and another sixty miles on the country road to the hospital. Charlize had bathed him and freed him from the mud, but the wound urgently needed cleaning and stitching. A private air service would get him out of here and Charlize would drive his Mustang to Cook. The poor jalopy was still languishing in the junkyard in the woods.

"The things you get yourself into, Chief!" Reprovingly, his assistant shook her head.

Ondragon shrugged his shoulders innocently. "I kind of stumbled into it. Honest."

"Yeah, sure."

Shortly before, Charlize had told him all that had happened since Kateri had tied him to a tree. She had waited for the agreed time in Orr and, after he had not shown up, had taken the action they had discussed. Then, when that dilettante prettyboy Julian had shown up at the Gateway Inn to kidnap her, it had been clear to her that her boss was in trouble. She had overpowered Julian with almost ridiculous ease and locked him in a closet in her room. She had then immediately notified the police and the FBI, who had arrived in less than an hour and picked her up. With an entire cohort, they had driven up to the CC Lodge and arrested Dr. Arthur and a few others. Charlize, meanwhile, had searched everywhere for Ondragon. To no avail. Finally, she had sent out the state troopers.

Ondragon smiled. Professionals were still his favorite!

"What are you grinning at, Chief?"

"Oh, nothing. I just remembered that I almost fell victim to an amateur."

Charlize's expression hardened. "The state troopers are still in the woods looking for her. I hope they find her and bring her to justice. From all you've told me, she must be quite a beast, that Miss Wolfe. A lunatic." She circled a finger next to her temple.

Oh yes, she was a madwoman, Ondragon thought, pressing his lips together regretfully. *But she was also insanely exciting.* He reached for the glass of water on the nightstand and drank it down thirstily.

Charlize eyed him again.

"What is it?" he asked, exhausted. He felt fatigue reaching for him now that he knew he was safe.

"Did you have a thing with her?"

Ondragon started up. "Me, what are you thinking? She was a Bride of Satan!"

Charlize screwed up her face, amused. "I know you, Chief. You thought she was hot; I saw a picture of her. Just your type."

Ondragon wiggled his head. "Well . . ."

Suddenly, they heard footsteps and loud shouts outside in the hallway. A moment later, a muffled bang sounded. Ondragon jumped out of bed and quickly pulled on his robe, ignoring the accelerated throbbing in his side.

"At last!" he said, yanking open the door. "I was hoping to be there."

"What?" shouted Charlize after him, irritated. "Paul-*san*, would you please enlighten me!" Cursing, she hurried into the hallway, but when she saw what was going on, she stopped next to Ondragon.

Several FBI officers were kicking in one of the doors. The wood was splintered and the door had a hole in it, but the lock held.

"They're opening number twenty," Ondragon murmured meaningfully as one of the FBI men lifted his foot and gave it another kick. With a crunch, the lock gave way and the door popped open. Immediately, Ondragon was with the agents, trying to peer over their shoulders into the darkened room. One of them held him back.

"Sir, please stay away!"

"But I . . ."

"You have no business here. Go to your room."

"Listen . . ."

"Let him in, Richard," a voice suddenly said from behind them. "That's the man we have to thank for all this."

Ondragon turned around and his eyes widened in delight. Standing before him was his friend from the FBI.

"George! What are you doing here? This isn't even your territory."

George Hurley nodded with a smile. "True. But when I heard from your charming assistant that you were in trouble up here, I set out right away."

"Gee, George. This is really a surprise. How long has it been? Five years? How are you?" They shook hands.

"Fine, Paul. But I'd better not ask you how you're doing right now. After all, I don't want to embarrass you by telling fibs. You look pretty battered, my friend. And your eyes are red. Have you been smoking too much hash?" Hurley raised a hand. "Oops. Sorry I asked."

Ondragon laughed and aimed a feigned punch at his friend's upper arm. At that moment, a shout came from inside number 20.

"Special Agent Hurley, could you come over here, please. You've got to see this."

Ondragon and Charlize followed the FBI agent into the room. The curtains were drawn; only the light from the flashlights and an unhealthy bluish glow illuminated the furnishings, which were in fact quite sparse. Ondragon saw a table, a chair, and a large white box, nothing else. The black-clad taskforce officers were standing around the white box, gazing in disbelief at the cold glow emanating from it. Ondragon heard a monotonous buzzing sound and guessed what the box was. Together with Hurley and Charlize, he approached the agents, when suddenly one of them turned around and, his hand pressed to his mouth, rushed past Ondragon out of the room. A short time later, unmistakable gagging sounds reached their ears.

"That's some heavy shit, sir!" one of the agents said, moving to give them a view of the box.

It was a freezer.

Ondragon stepped closer. The cold hit him and made him shiver as he leaned over to look at the chaotic pile inside the chest. It was a considerable accumulation of freezer bags.

Carefully, he nudged one of them with his fingertip; it crackled softly. When Ondragon realized what was inside, he quickly withdrew his hand.

"Oh my goodness," he said, now truly feeling sick to his stomach. "I think that's enough to put the good doc and his henchmen behind bars for another hundred years."

"Looks like it," muttered Hurley, who in turn now stuck a gloved hand into the pile and pulled out the pouch Ondragon had just touched. Ondragon swallowed and heard Charlize inhale sharply behind him.

The bag contained a foot.

"Man, that's disgusting," one of the agents croaked. "Hannibal Lecter's secret stash, or what?"

"More Dr. Frankenstein's spare parts store, I guess," another chuckled.

"Quiet!" shouted Hurley. "Those are dead people in there, and they have dignity, damn it!"

The men sprang automatically to attention. "Yes, sir, sorry, sir."

Hurley growled something and continued to rummage through the freezer of horrors. Ondragon could hardly look, there were so many other body parts. A hand, a thigh, an entire arm. But no heads—fortunately. All the limbs seemed to have been neatly cut off with a saw and then packed away like chops at the meat counter.

Ondragon felt nauseated and put a hand to his mouth. Fortunately, the bags smelled neutral, otherwise he would likely have followed the young man outside.

"Can I see that one again?" he asked.

"What, the arm?"

Ondragon nodded, and Hurley lifted the body part. Reluctantly, Ondragon bent down and looked at it more closely. The arm, unlike some of the others, was all gray, its skin wrinkled, and the nails on the curved fingers painted red. Ondragon straightened up again.

"I think I know who this arm belongs to," he said.

"Oh yeah, and to whom?" Curious, Hurley looked at him.

"Dana Straub. She's a victim of Oliver Orchid, the Canadian. You'll find all that in the documents we gave to the FBI."

"Okay. This one is every investigator's nightmare, but it's a great bust. Thanks, Paul."

"Don't mention it," Ondragon gasped. It was only with difficulty that he was keeping himself under control. The urge to flee the stuffy room was overpowering. But Ondragon did not want to lower his guard. He choked down the metallic taste in his mouth and took a deep breath. As he did so, he saw Charlize's knowing expression, and once again he realized how well she knew him. She had guessed what he was thinking right now. He tried to avoid her half-amused, half-concerned look and pretended to rub his aching side.

At last, Hurley let go of the freezer bags and turned to his men. "All right, now, everybody out. This room belongs to the forensics boys!" The FBI agent grabbed the lid of the chest and closed it noisily.

CHAPTER 56

2009, somewhere over the Atlantic

Ondragon put his talisman back in his pocket, leaned back in his first-class seat, and took a sip of the champagne that a brunette stewardess had just served him with a dazzling American Beauty smile. Her dimples were adorable, and so was her butt. He glanced after her down the aisle. The plane had left the Halifax control area and was now turning its nose in a gentle arc to the east. Soon the rugged shores of Greenland would come into view, then Iceland, and then eventually the flat, green marshes of the Dutch lowlands. After that, it would be just under two hours until he landed in Berlin-Tegel.

He had firmly resolved not to back out this time. His parents were expecting him; he had finally managed to talk to his mother on the phone. He now knew what he wanted to talk to them about: Per Gustav Ondragon, his brother, who had died in the accident in his father's library back then. His grave was in Berlin's Central Cemetery. Ondragon was going to visit it and see what happened then.

He shifted his weight; he could still feel the arrow wound in his side a little. It was healing nicely and made a fine addition to his collection of scars. Who else could say they had escaped the Indians? In any case, since the night of horror in the woods, he was strongly opposed to bowhunting. It was absolutely not worthy of the name. He sighed. Besides, not only was the wound healing, but the strange fever and the resulting nightmare fantasies had finally subsided, and only now and then did Ondragon still hear that strange whispering in his head.

You are one of us!

He blamed this on his subconscious, which had apparently not yet processed the traumatic events. He was also still a little uncomfortable when he thought of Kateri. His beautiful slayer.

Thanks to the scar, he would never forget her. Just as it would be some time before he forgot the events surrounding Dr. Arthur and Cedar Creek Lodge. The bitter taste of this strange case would be on his tongue for a long time to come.

Ondragon closed his eyes and tried to escape the pull of the memory. Unfortunately, without success. With ruthless clarity, the *centrifuge* played back his mental record of what had happened, and before he knew it, he was in the middle of the Minnesota woods. Covered in mud and wearing nothing but a pair of underpants.

Kateri had lied to him more than once. That was clear to him today. Her whole life was a complicated and extremely fragile construct of lies, which is why she had been so determined to kill him. She *had* to protect this construct, or her unsavory past would have come to light, and the life she had painstakingly built would have been irretrievably destroyed. Ondragon could understand her motives. Kateri had been desperate, she had seen no other way out. He forgave her, but only because not one of the beautiful hairs on his assistant Charlize's head had been harmed.

Good old Charlize. Because of the damning evidence she, Ondragon, and Detective Simon Ricks had assembled, the FBI had no trouble bringing Dr. Arthur and his accomplices to justice. The bureau had been able to secure all of the cannibal doctor's files and had also subjected the lodge's guests to extensive questioning. Mr. Shamgood and Mr. Norrfoss had not been particularly pleased about this, he had heard. Ondragon smirked.

But then he thought of room 20, and a cold shiver ran down his spine. He had never seen anything like it. A secret storehouse for human flesh. Meat that had been served up to cannibals as a gourmet meal. To Dr. Arthur, an act of charity. And there had been no safer hiding place than one of the guest rooms. The patients supposedly lodging in it had been faked by the doc, and the loss of earnings for the lodge had been paid from his own princely salary. And all of this, just to be the first, the best, and the greatest in his research field. Utterly sick. Ondragon shook his head. And there was something else that was totally insane about it. The FBI had informed him shortly before leaving Los Angeles that with the help of DNA tests they had also identified Oliver Orchid among the dead in the chest, or at least parts of him. So the cannibals had eaten a cannibal. An almost ingeniously crazy form of recycling. But the arm with the painted fingernails had also been matched. As Ondragon had suspected, it belonged to Mrs. Dana Straub. So Vernon's horror story had actually been true.

And Deputy Hase? He had tried to cover up the death of Dana Straub by falsifying reports for Dr. Arthur. But why Simon Ricks, alias Jeremy Bates, had not been among the disgusting meat supplies in room 20 but had ended up in a marshy grave by the lake, remained a mystery. Ondragon simply chalked it up to "sloppy amateurism." He would never have made such a mistake.

It occurred to him that Dr. Arthur could have easily avoided his downfall by simply hiring him, Ondragon, to solve his problems at the right time. After all, Ondragon Consulting didn't work exclusively for the good guys. But the doc had challenged him, and that had not served him well. The dragon had bitten back!

The FBI had been able to arrest Julian, Dr. Zeo, and Dr. Pollux, Head Nurse Marsha, another nurse and two of the cooks as clear accomplices of Dr. Arthur, in addition to Vernon. Ondragon felt a pang of nausea and quickly finished the glass of champagne. He had the nice brunette refill it for him, but still could not free himself from the viscous fog of his memories. Human flesh had indeed been prepared in the kitchen of the Cedar Creek Lodge; the investigators had found that out as well. But only for very special guests. Of course.

At least that's what Ondragon hoped.

Sheila, Frank, the gardener, and Carlos, the headwaiter, had turned out to be totally ignorant of everything Dr. Arthur had been up to at the lodge. On this point, at least, Kateri had been telling the truth. Mr. Lyme's missing body had been found by the FBI a few days later in the old Indigenous burial grounds. Rumsfeld's carcass had also been kept there on one of the wooden racks until the dog had been skinned and hung as a fake poacher's prey from the same tree where Lyme had died earlier. And all this just to deceive Ondragon.

He heaved a sigh.

Sadly, Hatchet's band would also have to find a new lead singer. The death metal musician had saved his life and been killed in the process. But Hatchet had died such an appropriately early death that his CD sales had soared and he had achieved immortal fame. What more could a rock star ask? Ondragon was grateful to the man and had attended Hatchet's funeral at the Los Angeles National Cemetery. Black roses and a skull and crossbones on the headstone had been just two of the tributes to Hatchet's morbid taste. In his honor, Ondragon had added Faith No More's "I'm Easy" to his Eternal Music List.

His recollection jumped back to the previous track: Kateri.

Her body had still not been found. The forensic experts had recovered gallons of blood, one of Kateri's shoes, her bow, and Ondragon's gun. They had also found countless scraps of skin, hair, and battle scars, and had followed a trail of footprints that had led into the forest, but had been completely lost after less than a mile. The blood, hair, and skin were mostly Kateri's, later tests had shown. For the experts, Miss Wolfe had most probably—and this would not have pleased Dr. Layton at all—been killed by a bear.

Ondragon clicked his tongue disapprovingly, which brought out the fruity bouquet of the champagne. *He* would not have been satisfied with that probability level. Even if something was ninety-nine percent certain, there was still that one percent. One percent improbability. But despite his objections, officials had called off the search for Kateri a week later. As far as they were concerned, Miss Wolfe was dead. Ninety-nine percent probability was enough to convince them of that. Well, Ondragon hoped they weren't wrong.

He felt himself finally relaxing after all the commotion. The hum of the plane and the champagne made him sleepy, and his eyes closed. But his mind did not seem tired at all. It still clung to the images of what had happened. Ondragon suspected that this was part of the coming to terms that was taking place within him. He put his hands in his lap. All right. If he had to, he would not resist and think it all through to the end.

The Parkers' family tragedy seemed no less catastrophic in the whole CC Lodge affair than the unlucky star that had hung over Kateri's life and death. The two seemed to have been fatefully linked. Pete had been found only a few steps from the west side of the log cabin with his skull bashed in. Ondragon was as sorry about him as he was about Hatchet. The hapless man's life had not exactly been a bed of roses, but he had valiantly tried to make the best of it. To numb the quiet sense of guilt within him, Ondragon had arranged Pete's lonely funeral, giving him a grave next to his parents in Orr Cemetery. Of Momo, however, not even a single finger bone remained. His body had been completely burned, along with the log cabin, of which only the brick chimney remained standing like a charred memorial. Ondragon had told the FBI about Momo's past deeds, and the bureau had gratefully shelved the Parker murders case.

That left just Joel Parker—and that was the only inexplicable thing about the whole story: The old man remained untraceable. The forensic scientists had not been able to discover a single trace of him, nor had the sniffer dogs with which they had scoured the forest for several days. It seemed as if Joel Parker, the old trapper, had never existed.

Ondragon opened his eyes and drank the rest of his second glass of champagne. Involuntarily, he thought of Lieutenant Stafford's diary. It was the only tangible thing to remind him of that crazy episode in the Minnesota woods. Of the dark mystery of the Wendigo. Maybe the forest monster really did exist, maybe not. Maybe it was just a legend.

Before they left the lodge for good, Ondragon had asked Charlize to take the book with her. Now it lay in a brand-new special safe from the Sentry company, in the basement of his mansion in LA. It was the only book in his house and, despite its hermetic storage, it caused him a certain uneasiness. Someday he would have it digitized and donate it to a museum. Or maybe one day he would manage to put the book on his first virgin bookshelf. Maybe. Because, as is well known, miracles kept on happening.

EPILOGUE

1835, Kabetogama,
fur trappers' lonely log cabin

They reached the log cabin and entered, frozen through. To dispel the cold and darkness, Parker lit the fire in the fireplace and put on water for coffee. Lieutenant Stafford had grudgingly let them go. After all, there was no evidence against them, and Stafford had not succeeded in further substantiating his suspicions about them. Especially not after Parker had made his statement, at least as far as he could remember what had happened. The fever had affected his memory. But now he felt completely healthy again.

Glad to be back in their humble realm, Lacroix locked the door and the trappers took off their thick fur jackets.

"Two-Elk, what have you got there?" Parker heard the French Canadian ask, and turned to his friends. He saw that the Chippewa had dumped the contents of his leather pouch on the table. On top was a small book.

"This is the book from the lieutenant. I stole it; the ritual must be kept secret."

"Oh, Stafford won't be too happy about that. After all, he took such pains with his investigations." Lacroix laughed gleefully.

"*Kitchie Manitou* does not like White Man writings. I will destroy book." Two-Elk went to throw it into the flames.

"Stop!" Lacroix took the book from his hand and leafed through it for a while. "I'd better keep it, *mon ami*. Who knows, we may need it again. I'm sure the Great Spirit will magnanimously overlook it if I keep it."

Two-Elk nodded, and while Parker poured the freshly brewed coffee into three enamel mugs, Lacroix pulled out the pencil from the spine and wrote something on the last page.

Parker watched him and sipped his brew. Maybe he should read the book sometime too, so he would know what exactly had happened after the fever had taken him. But maybe he should just leave it alone. His friends' tales were enough to send shivers down his spine. Parker left it at that and gazed pensively into the flames. Spring would come soon, and then he would visit his brother and his brother's family at Fort Snelling, not far away. A little care from his family certainly would not hurt. But he would never be able to turn his back on the forest. He loved the harsh beauty and the deserted expanse too much for that. Smiling quietly to himself, he drank the strong, warming coffee.

When Parker woke in the middle of the night, it was as if he had heard a voice. He listened for a while, but all was silent. Shaking his head, he got up and felt his way through the dark room to the fireplace. The fire had burned down and was barely giving off any heat. Parker stoked it, and there was some light in the room again. On the table beside the fireplace, he spotted the lieutenant's book. It was open at the last page. Lacroix's writing glowed darkly on the bone-white paper. The flickering light of the fire made the letters seem almost alive.

Ice.
Snow.
The forest.
Be on guard,
When it comes.
Fear eats your heart.
You feel your cold body.
He is insatiable, the spirit of the lonely forest.
Insatiable as fear.
The Wendigo.
Hungry,

Ice-cold.
The eternal evil.

Strange lines. And by Lacroix, of all people.

Parker poured himself the rest of the cold coffee from the pot and took a thoughtful sip. Slowly, he turned to his sleeping friends.

With a loud clang, the tin cup fell to the floor, and the cold liquid poured out over the wooden floorboards. Parker's hand began to tremble, more and more, so that the tremor soon seized his whole body and shook him like an earthquake. What his eyes saw in the dim light of the embers made him think he was still in a dream.

A bad dream.

Lacroix and Two-Elk lay before him with their throats slit. Their waxy faces stared at the ceiling. Their guts were spilling out of their bellies and their blood was a red sheet on which they rested. Lacroix's right arm had been torn from its joint, and Two-Elk's ears and lips were missing. With horror, Alan Joel Parker recognized the bite marks in his friends' flesh. He felt something dripping from his chin and ran his quivering hand over it. He looked for a long time at the red liquid on his fingers.

ABOUT THE AUTHOR

Anette Strohmeyer is a German crime writer. She began her career illustrating comic books but unfortunately never developed the skills to rival her role model, Jean Giraud aka Moebius, so she decided to focus on the speech bubbles instead.

Now, Strohmeyer is known for her fiction writing and meticulous, often immersive research work. She has participated in a voodoo ceremony in Haiti, eaten termites in the jungle, generated lightning in a high-voltage laboratory, and trekked through Japan's infamous Aokigahara Forest along the edge of Mount Fuji.

Since 2018, Strohmeyer has lived in Denmark, where she splits her time between Copenhagen and the island of Møn. She also writes as Anne Nørdby, author of the bestselling Tom Skagen thriller series.

Podium

www.ingramcontent.com/pod-product-compliance
Lightning Source LLC
Chambersburg PA
CBHW020642120726

47906CB00001B/86